ECHOES OF THE IMPERIUM

TALES OF THE IRON ROSE
BOOK ONE

NICHOLAS ATWATER
OLIVIA ATWATER

STARWATCH
PRESS

Copyright © 2024 by Nicholas Atwater
https://nicholasatwater.com
All rights reserved.

Cover design by James T. Egan of Bookfly Design

No part of this book may be reproduced in any form or by any electronic or mechanical means, including information storage and retrieval systems, without written permission from the author, except for the use of brief quotations in a book review.

This is a work of fiction. Names, places, characters, and stories are the product of the authors' imagination or are used fictitiously. Any resemblance to any actual persons (living or dead), organisations, and events is entirely coincidental.

CONTENT WARNING

Dear Readers,

　We would like you to know that *Echoes of the Imperium* includes themes around war and military violence. There are the ghosts of slain civilians, soldiers committing suicide, and depictions of violence (which includes the loss of limbs). This novel also explores (fantasy) racism, classism, and imperialism. Lastly, the topic of grief and the loss of loved ones is very relevant to the story. Please be kind to yourselves.

PROLOGUE

FALL OF THE IMPERIUM – THE SOVEREIGN MAJESTY – IN DEATH – TREASONOUS HEARTS

I should have died the day the Avalon Imperium fell.

I recall the blast that tossed me from my feet; the dizzying sensation of falling; the sharp slam as the deck rose up to meet me. The sails of our airship snapped angrily in the howling winds above me. In that moment, I thought they looked like the spectre of Death Victorious come to claim me.

"Mr Blair!" My name echoed loudly in my ears. Hands clawed at me frantically. Stress, concussion, and sleep deprivation all conspired to blur familiar faces into frightening shadows. I fought and flailed; more than one of my fellow crewmates found themselves at the unfair end of my lashing fists. Rashid, a tattooed crewman from Aarushi, soundly returned the favour, ringing my head like a bell. The blow cleared my mind, though it left my cheekbone throbbing. My reeling panic receded. I registered my fellows—their faces grim and concerned, their uniforms stained with blood and gunpowder.

Strong hands closed around my arms, hauling me to my feet. It is a testament to the effects of the war that the men of the ship showed any worry for me at all; not a single navy man flinched away from touching my green-tinged skin. Back home, on the streets of Morgause, those same men might have spat at me and called me names... but on the deck of the *HMS Caliban*, even a goblin from the poorest part of town could be called comrade.

The deck shuddered again beneath my feet—but I had caught my mental and physical balance, and this time, I did not fall. Vice-Admiral Wakefield's stern voice continued to drone unhurried orders, anchoring the rest of us through the chaos. It was hard to make out the details of his broad, dark features in the smoke and gloom that surrounded us—but every so often, a stark flash of cannon fire highlighted his proud figure, rooted like a stubborn mountain by the helm of the ship. Briefly, I thought I saw the steely spined man glance my way, as though to note my survival. The vice-admiral inclined his head in my direction. It was a minute gesture—but to a soldier of my lowly rank, it might as well have been a commendation. I straightened in place, forcing myself to echo our officer's rigid posture.

"I think he's beginning to like you, Mr Blair," Rashid joked, with a grim laugh. He tried to wipe the soot from his face, but succeeded only in smearing it among the blood and sweat already there. He smiled helplessly; the sharp white of his teeth stood out against the darkness. "It'd be a pity if you tumbled over the side *now*, eh?"

"Yessir," I replied, still mildly panicked. "I mean, no sir. Won't happen again."

I was by far the lowest-ranked man on that ship. Everyone was 'sir' to me.

"That's the spirit," Rashid said. He clapped a firm hand upon my shoulder.

Wakefield bellowed out another order, and our cannons fired a broadside that shook the deck beneath our feet. The cannon fire ripped into a nearby Coalition frigate, tearing apart its hull. Fire blossomed; the Coalition ship's airmen fell from the sinking wreckage into the city below, and the frigate soon tumbled after them.

The Coalition's boldness had won them early gains—even now, they continued to charge through Imperial battle lines both above and below, heedless of their losses. They vastly outnumbered us, it was true. But the Imperial Navy was better trained than they were, and far more disciplined... and we had begun to turn the battle against them.

A deafening cannonade off the port bow sent shells shrieking over us; the thunderous broadside made even able sailors wince. The deadly barrage tore three Coalition frigates to absolute tatters. One of their ships detonated in a sudden, violent explosion, as the cannon fire struck either its munitions or its aetheric core. Our saviour—an enormous ironclad warship, nearly a city unto herself—soon flew into view.

Cheers went up among the crew, loud enough to break through the din. The *Sovereign Majesty* had arrived.

"Those rebels just lost the last chance they had," Rashid laughed exultantly. He scaled the rigging next to us to get a better view. "Imagine those yellow-bellied traitors, shivering on their little boats!"

I joined in with the cheers, whooping as loudly as I could. I was barely a part of this engagement—but I felt pride in my small role in it, all the same. The rush of battle thrilled in my veins; I sipped on secondhand glory, drunk on the feeling of impending victory.

"That's what you get, you honourless scum!" The yell came from Chamberlain, our captain of the marines; his blue-coated marines soon echoed it.

"Noble Gallant gives no quarter today!" one of them hollered at the distant Coalition ships.

The *Sovereign Majesty* was our Imperial flagship, and the largest warship ever to grace a battlefield. Even at the distance we currently maintained, a broadside from the *Majesty* was deafening. Nothing, it seemed, could withstand her; her great cannons tore apart outflyer and frigate alike, smashing them to pieces like children's toys. We cheered as the *Sovereign Majesty* boomed again, shredding another formation of Coalition ships to ribbons. Already, she moved to charge another enemy line.

"Chamberlain!" Vice-Admiral Wakefield shouted over the din. "I need a boarding party! Get me twenty men; you have five minutes!"

"Aye-aye, Vice-Admiral!" Captain Chamberlain screamed back. He barked orders to his lieutenant in turn, gathering up more men. "No mercy, gentlemen!" he yelled at them. "I don't want to see a single rebel breathing when this is over, do you hear?" He turned upon me quickly. "Blair! Make yourself useful and grab my rifle, will you?"

Captain Chamberlain never had liked me much—but I couldn't help admiring him all the same. He had always cut a heroic, unflappable figure; his fearless mien genuinely soothed me, and his snapping orders gave me something to focus on. I scrambled to obey the order, searching the deck for the rifle he'd lost in the sudden turbulence. I snatched it up just a few feet from the railing, ducking through the sudden chaos to retrieve it. Marines hurried to the main deck, readying themselves for their boarding action.

I handed Chamberlain the rifle.

"Get my drop-line, Blair," Chamberlain ordered me next, as he inspected the rifle.

I rushed to the mainmast, snatching up one of the hooked drop-lines attached to the metal ring around it. The cable spooled out behind me as I hurried back to Chamberlain—but I stopped for a few seconds to watch as the *Majesty* let loose another barrage of rolling thunder. Coalition ships blew apart like fireworks. The marines, ever a rowdy bunch, let loose a whooping volley of cheers as they readied their harnesses.

Chamberlain grinned at me. "Look at that, Mr Blair," he said. "Almost makes you feel bad for the poor bastards—"

The marines were still cheering as the first explosion came from within the *Majesty*.

Her bridge burst outward—outward! No Coalition ship had attacked her with any real menace… and yet, fire blossomed from her innards.

Her cannons ceased their terrible booming, all at once. She lurched in the sky like a drunken sailor. The sight would have been funny, if it weren't so foreboding.

Smaller explosions burst around the *Majesty*. Pustules of fire popped, spitting forth steel and debris. The ship's great aetheric drives flickered and coughed, and a heavy groaning filled the air.

Horror dawned upon Chamberlain's normally fearless features. That, more than anything, made my blood run ice cold.

Heat washed over us as the remains of the Imperial flagship sank off of our port bow. Something had gone badly wrong with her aetheric drive—even as we watched, she lost her float, plummeting many thousands of feet down towards the city she had been meant to protect. Our own cannon fire faltered and died, as the gunnery men stared in shock.

One last blast rocked the falling flagship—followed by a monstrous wail of howling wind and twisting steel.

Even at such a distance—even among that cacophonic dirge—I thought I could hear the wails of the soon-to-be-deceased upon that ship. Of course, those screams could have come from the doomed citizens below, who knew that there was no escaping that plunging behemoth... and the rest of what was to come.

"Brace yourselves for evasive manoeuvres!" Vice-Admiral Wakefield bellowed. The *Caliban*'s warning klaxons blared.

"Hold fast!" Rashid echoed from the rigging. "Hold for your lives!"

I didn't need to be told twice. I clutched desperately at the rigging, with the drop-line's hook still clenched in my fist.

Vice-Admiral Wakefield pointed our ship towards the sky. The *HMS Caliban* tilted sharply, taking as much altitude as she could muster. The other ships around us followed suit, abandoning the battle in favour of more immediate concerns.

The *Majesty* had been a ship like no other. We all knew that its dying blast would be just as unprecedented.

I watched, stunned, as the flagship of the Imperium—our greatest guardian, our fair symbol of might and ingenuity—came crashing down into the capital. Walls of ash, flame, and debris swallowed entire boroughs, full of doomed people. Even over that awful din, however, a telltale whine rose upon the breeze.

The ship's crash was barely the beginning. The *Majesty*'s core had begun to rupture.

The last explosion came as a series of pops. Sections of the hull glowed an angry red from within—and then, gouts of molten steel spewed forth.

Fire belched outward. The aether inside detonated. A blinding white-hot light conquered the entire sky at once. Even at our altitude, the force of the blast struck us like a giant fist.

In all of the excitement, I'd completely forgotten about Chamberlain's drop-line.

As the shockwave struck, the drop-line in my hand wrenched itself from my grip, burning at the skin of my palm. Chamberlain tumbled across the deck of the ship, along with three other marines. I saw him reach out for purchase, scrambling to grasp at the deck, at the railing, at the other soldiers—but gravity was stronger than he was. The captain of the marines plummeted over the side and out of view, before my brain could even fully grasp his danger.

Others fell from the rigging next to me, screaming as they lost their hold. I clutched mindlessly at my rope, holding on for dear life. My feet dangled in the air—I saw the burning city beneath my heels, thousands of feet below me, and though I couldn't hear it, I knew that I was screaming. The rope dug into my palms. My knuckles began to tremble with effort, and I worried that my hands might soon betray me.

Our ship's klaxons whined in my ears. Two ships collided off the starboard bow, smashing themselves apart. Vice-Admiral Wakefield grappled with the helm, veins standing out on his thick neck as he plied every ounce of his strength to keep the vessel aright.

Finally, the *Caliban* levelled itself again.

My feet touched the deck. My bloody palms released the rope next to me, and I collapsed to my knees.

As the ship limped her way to stability, a hush fell upon the crew, broken only by the distant roar of secondary blasts behind us. Even Vice-Admiral Wakefield looked drawn and defeated, behind his steely moustache.

In the space of only a few breaths, the Avalon Imperium had broken.

I knew it with soul-breaking certainty—for every one of us had sworn a sacred Oath upon entering the navy: that we would protect the Avalon Imperium to our very last breath. I'd thought that wording was a formality at the time. But now, I felt the cracks in my Oath, like slowly shattering crystal. I clutched at my chest in horror, grasping at an indescribable pain that had no physical form. Though I yet lived, my honour was dying... and there was nothing I could do about it.

I wasn't alone.

Every single man aboard our vessel wore the same stunned expression. All at once, our Oaths had come undone—every soldier on every ship in the sky that bore an Imperial flag must have felt the same thing. The firm sense of certainty that had buoyed our service now rotted in place, transformed into a sickening sludge of faithless cobwebs. When the last of our Oath died, I knew that we would all be Oathbreakers—hated and reviled by anyone who came near enough to feel the corpse of our broken promise.

I heard the Coalition cheering aboard their vessels—singing songs of victory and liberation. All the while, entire city districts full of people crumbled to ash. Murder kindled in the eyes of my fellow crewmen. Rage and despair broke through their vaunted Imperial discipline; our battle-scarred bosun, Alcazar, held one man down as he screamed deprecations at the distant enemy.

"—surrender, and stand trial for your crimes," a buoyant voice dictated over our longhorn. "*Stand down, and prepare to be boarded.*"

Vice-Admiral Wakefield calmly removed his sidearm from his holster and blasted the longhorn. The squeal of ruined machinery interrupted the exultant Coalition officer and his demands.

No one dared to speak, in the resulting silence. Nor, I think, did any of us know what to say.

Every man on the ship stared at the vice-admiral. He was, after all, our ranking officer. Wakefield must have felt the weight of all those gazes—for eventually, he forced that steel back into his spine and turned his iron gaze upon us.

"On this day of days," the vice-admiral began, "I beseech your forgiveness." His voice trembled. Vice-Admiral Wakefield was made of stone, they said... but even mountains can be moved. "I have done all that I can to lead you to victory—and upon our final stand, we have lost. I pray that you will find it in your hearts to forgive me and my fellow officers. We have led you only to defeat."

A Coalition frigate angled towards our vessel. The Coalition ships raised flags, signalling the remaining Imperial ships to surrender. Shamefully, some of them did. Our broken Oaths meant that the emperor of the Avalon Imperium was dead—and what good were Imperial ships and Imperial crew, without an emperor to lead them?

Guns cracked in the distance, and dread flooded my veins. A heavy hand landed on my shoulder, squeezing there with an iron grip. I looked up to find the ship's physicker towering over me, a friendly and familiar presence.

Physicker Horace Holloway normally prided himself on being the neatest fellow on the ship. Cleanliness, he liked to say, was every bit as important to a physicker as a steady hand. Today, however, Physicker Holloway's black hair looked wild, and his pristine white uniform was sullied with blood and splinters. A fresh bandage covered the hobgoblin's right eye; its colour stood out, stark white against the green skin of his face. The right lens of the spectacles upon his nose had shattered, and only a bit of surgical adhesive now welded the frames together. One of the two short tusks that protruded from his lips had splintered painfully, and I wasn't at all sure whether it would heal.

Worry crept across the physicker's normally pensive face—but he gave my shoulder another gentle, reassuring squeeze, even as he stared ahead at Vice-Admiral Wakefield.

I felt Physicker Holloway's Oath dying around him, just like mine. Surely, we had only a few seconds left before we all became Oathbreakers forevermore.

"There is but one last task I would ask of you," Vice-Admiral Wakefield continued loudly. "Remember your Oaths, men of the Imperium." He held his head high. His voice was clear and proud. "We swore to protect the Avalon Imperium to our very last breath. And so we shall."

He brought up his pistol and rested it against his temple.

An echo of similar motions rippled across the deck—slowly, at first, and then more quickly, as men felt the last dying gasps of their Oath.

I stared ahead blankly, unfeeling. It hadn't occurred to me, somehow, that there was another way to fulfil my Oath. Was this... expected? Had everyone known but me?

I swept my eyes uselessly across the deck. It did seem expected. Only a few feet away from me, Rashid pressed his own pistol to his chin.

I was a good soldier, I thought. I had sworn the Oath. Everyone else seemed so certain of their decision—and besides, the Coalition would surely kill me, even if I acted the coward. I could die now, with my honour intact... or later, as an Oathbreaker.

I raised my bulky pistol with trembling hands. Though pride steadied the weapon beneath my jaw, I still had to close my eyes in fear.

But my treasonous heart kept me from pulling the trigger with the rest of the crew.

Pistols discharged in an echoing thunder. Bodies dropped, each with a sickening thud. I opened my eyes, ashamed, as the last dregs of my Oath became an ugly scar upon my soul.

I was not alone.

Holloway's pistol slipped from his hand. He grimaced in humiliation, clapping his free hand over his mouth. Two cabin boys stood side by side—one with warm copper skin and dark hair, the other one black-skinned and scrawny. Both were shivering, horrified —incapable of performing their final task. And how could anyone blame them? They were only twelve years old, after all.

Then again, so was I.

1

A WORLD GONE SIDEWAYS – ALARM – NO QUESTIONS ASKED

I know this all sounds awfully grim—the end of the war, the suggestion of my final duty, and the scurrilous Coalition lot about to capture me. But you needn't worry; if I hadn't survived, I wouldn't be here to regale you with my later exploits. Suffice to say, I was still alive and kicking near to two decades after the fall of the Imperium.

In the event of their impossible victory, the Coalition had hoped to usher in an age of juvenile democracy. Against all odds, the Imperial Navy's defeat and the capital's destruction had fulfilled that impossible hope… but the Coalition's lofty dreams fractured all too quickly. Imperial order—mostly maintained by harsh discipline and fear—had spiralled into chaos. In the place of an empire, we now had more than a dozen petty states, each worried first and foremost for its own survival. Twenty years later, those dozen states still waged a dozen little wars between them—though the former Coalition forces had at least enough dignity to change who warred with whom, every once in a blue moon.

Everything I'd once known had gone sideways.

As I opened my eyes on this particular day, I discovered that I was no exception to this rule; I was on the floor, still lying a few crucial steps from my bed. My skull throbbed with a dull headache—though that could very well have been the humming of the engine below deck. My cabin was in a state of haphazard disarray, as though some drunken blaggard had taken a hatchet to it.

With a groan, I pushed myself up into a seated position, letting go of the hatchet in my right hand and the empty bottle of fire-rum in my left. My vision bobbed unsteadily, conspiring against my sense of equilibrium. I stared at my coat, still hung up next to the bed. The patchwork garment bore recent injuries. Dimly, I remembered fighting off a shadowy apparition in my quarters the night before. At least, I mollified myself, I had given my opponent what-for—as my ruined coat now testified in the light of day.

The empty coat, of course, had still won the battle.

I saluted the garment hazily. "A valiant effort, sir," I said. "I commend you." I searched around for my hat and let out a sigh of relief as I found it to my right. The battered old tricorne had escaped my drunken wrath unscathed. I shoved the hat onto my head and began the slow, laborious crawl towards my bed.

A keen wailing noise cut me short.

The ship's warning klaxon blared, alerting the crew to man their battle stations. I winced in pain, even as I scrambled to my feet. I wasn't quite sober enough for the endeavour, unfortunately—I pitched forwards, barking my shin against the sideboard of my bunk. For some unknown reason, I had pried off my boots and left them on top of my bedding the night before; one of the two boots now plummeted behind the bed with a depressed sort of *thunk*.

"Captain!" a voice shouted from the main deck. Someone hammered at my door.

"Yes!" I shouted back. "I can bloody well hear you!" I grabbed the one remaining boot, jamming it onto my foot, and then snatched my coat from the hook with a few well-chosen curses. As I stuck my arm through the coat's right-hand sleeve, my hand came out through the elbow mark, where I'd chopped a splendid-sized hole in the fabric the night before. I hopped for the door regardless, stashing the hand-axe in my sash and shoving my way out onto the deck.

I have made many mistakes in my lifetime—and we will no doubt discuss several of those mistakes in due course. But for now, if you heed only one warning, mark this one and mark it well: An entire bottle of fire-rum and a face full of midday sun *will* kill you. Well, rather—you might just *wish* that you were dead.

The light outside drove needles through my eyes and into the back of my skull. *Goggles!* I had forgotten my goggles!

I staggered, and my foot caught a wayward yard line. Gravity betrayed me, and I sprawled across the deck. My precious tricorne went flying once again. I clawed at the railing with a piteous moan, blinking away sunspots. When my temporary blindness finally abated, I found myself surrounded by an entire semi-circle of booted feet.

Dougal MacLeod held out my hat obligingly, just in front of my face.

Dougal was a towering northern man, nearly seven feet tall. He had a few decades on me; his intricately braided beard was more white-blond than rusty red, and his gut had begun to show a comfortable paunch. War had carved harsh lines upon the ageing pilot's face—but defiant good humour still punched dimples into the corners of his mouth. Dougal's leather aviator's coat was about as battered as he was, but he wore it with a rakish air that I had always aspired to imitate. His faded yellow Coalition kerchief dangled from his neck, fraying at the edges.

"Cap'n on deck!" Dougal called out.

The warning klaxons died. The crew around me chuckled and exchanged coins, fulfilling their wagers. I became keenly aware that the ship wasn't moving. We were in port—a fact that I would have recalled, if not for my addled wits.

I'd been had.

I groaned in embarrassment. "Damn it, MacLeod," I mumbled. "Battle stations? Really?"

Dougal grinned. "Been knockin' at yer door fer the last hour," he said. "Should've seen yer face, lad. Bravely blundered." He let the hat fall atop my head. Good-natured laughter trickled in around me. I grimaced and adjusted my hat.

"Bravely blundered," I repeated in a grumble. "Well—I learned from the best, didn't I?"

"Flattery'll get ye places," Dougal said cheerfully. "Like back oan yer feet!" He smiled, and hauled me up by the hand with enviable ease. As I reached standing, Dougal slapped me heartily on the back, and I nearly floundered again. "Speakin' of gettin' places—" he began.

A memory sparked through the haze that shrouded my brain. Right. "We've got a meeting today," I observed. I tried—and failed—to stifle a yawn.

"Aye, we do," Dougal replied. He shot me a wry smile, gauging my dishevelled appearance. "Should probably make sure ye look respectable for it."

"You want me to look respectable?" I repeated sceptically. "In Shackleton. Are you trying to get me killed, MacLeod?"

Now that I had put the murderous midday sun behind me, my vision slowly returned. I took in the sight of the floating skyland to which we'd moored ourselves—a onetime Imperial prison turned lawless haven. Ramshackle buildings teetered along piers that had never been intended for anything more than prisoner transfers. Now, those piers bustled with all sorts of trade, both legitimate and otherwise. Shackleton's people had freed themselves from the empire and broken their literal shackles; very close to our place in port, I could see one of the city's three shattered chains still dangling, each link the size of a small frigate. The ancient prison fortress at the heart of the city rose above the rest, visible even from the outskirts—but we wouldn't need to worry about that criminal haven, as we were destined for the docks.

"Yer right," Dougal muttered. "Can't have ye looking respectable." He dusted off my shoulders, adjusted my coat, and angled my hat. "There we are. Ye cut a fine scoundrel this way."

I grinned despite myself. "Speaking of scoundrels," I said, "fetch Mr Strahl, will you? We might not be looking for trouble—but if it finds us anyway, I'd like him around."

Dougal snapped a sharp salute. "Ah've got yer six, Cap'n," he answered. There was a certain understated irony to the salute that few people on board probably understood. Of all the people on my ship, Dougal MacLeod had never truly answered to me as captain—and probably never would. Over the years, our relationship had prevaricated between warmth and distance, aggravated by our past together.

Because we had seen so many of the same things, Dougal and I understood each other very well—but no amount of familiarity could ever erase the fact that we had seen those things from opposite sides of the war. Stranger by far was the fact that I owed Dougal MacLeod my life... while he owed me nothing at all.

Dougal turned to disappear below decks, and I soon heard his voice bellow upwards: "Oi! Strahl! Where are ye, ye peelly-wally jackboot?"

My head threatened to split from the noise. I squeezed my eyes shut until the pain receded.

A steady hand came down on my shoulder, offering a measure of brotherly comfort.

"I'll be all right, Sam," I mumbled. I cracked my eyes open and looked up.

My first mate, Samuel "Little" Méndez, was a broad fellow. For a man who hadn't a drop of clanfolk blood in him, he took remarkably after Dougal MacLeod—in shoulder width, if not in height. Little had a robust physique and sun-kissed bronze skin, earned from long years among the rigging. Small details made him feel sharp and meticulous; he kept his coal-black hair and his beard both neatly trimmed, and his alert brown eyes often scanned the area around him.

Glad to hear it, Captain, Little signed. His fingers flashed deftly on the words.

So, I signed back. *A MacLeod Wake-up Call?* I tilted my fingers wryly.

Little smirked impishly, moving his hands in reply. *I suggested sending Miss Brighton to wake you instead.*

I baulked at the suggestion. A flutter of panic seized my heart as I imagined my gunnery chief and her trigger-happy knitting circle busting into my cabin to wake me.

Miss Brighton would just as likely blow us all to the Court of the Evernight, I signed back quickly. *If that ever happens, you are putting this airship back together piece by piece.*

Aye-aye, Captain, Little signed back innocently. He turned back to the crew and clapped his hands thunderously. *Back to work, you layabouts!*

Slowly, the crew dispersed, satisfied that the morning's show was over with. Little directed them with the occasional idle gesture, in ways that suggested he was expecting us to leave port.

The deck is yours while we're out, I informed him—though the phrase was really a formality at this point.

Think we'll get the job? Little asked restlessly.

I'll make sure we do, I answered. *Two days here is two days too many.*

Aye-aye, Little signed dutifully. *I'll send out word for people to head back from shore leave.* He saluted me crisply—a lingering echo from our days in the Imperial Navy—and headed off to oversee the crew. I turned back in the opposite direction, opening the door to my jumbled, war-torn quarters.

I squinted. "Now. Where in rot and ruin did I leave my goggles..."

* * *

THE WORLD SEEMS like a more ominous place when everyone in it is taller than you.

It certainly didn't help matters that most of Shackleton's population of ex-convicts were burly, murderous, and heavily tattooed—or at least two of the three. Though the people here were mostly human, there were still plenty of hobgoblins, goat-legged satyrs, snake-haired gorgons, and massive centaurs scattered among the crowd. Many of them hailed originally from different corners of Avalon, judging by their clothing and their mannerisms.

I found myself drowned in a veritable cascade of languages and dialects, only some of which I could identify. A bit of clanfolk brogue leapt out at me, followed by a splash of Rustlands twang. A weathered, brown-skinned woman argued loudly with a muscled tough in lilting

Aarushavi. (Were they discussing blood or fruit? My Aarushavi was terrible, so probably it was neither.) A thread of Castellano trickled through the press of people, utterly incomprehensible to my ears. Above it all, however, Imperial Avelish still maintained its hegemony as a common tongue.

I earned no small number of glares as I navigated the sea of scoundrels; many of the people we passed reached for their coin purses, wary that I might try to sneak my fingers into their pouches. I tried not to take it personally; Shackleton's residents were a generally suspicious sort. Besides, the irony wasn't lost on me. Once, the people here would have been right to suspect me for a thief—but I'd abandoned that career on the day that military service had lifted me out of the gutter. Either way, Dougal and Mr Strahl made an imposing wall of muscle, so that the crowds of Shackleton and I need not meet each other directly.

My bosun, Mr Strahl, was a dangerous man. Everything about him suggested a long history of soldiering. His rigid posture instantly set him apart from Shackleton's undisciplined crowd; he kept his sturdy jaw clean-shaven and his cold white hair shorn close to its roots, where only a faint, snowy stubble remained. A long, faded scar slashed across his face from his cheekbone to his nose—a relic of some previous battle, long before his time on the *Rose*. Whatever colour Strahl's hard eyes had once been, they were now a faded dishwater grey—and bright, unnaturally blue veins threaded visibly beneath his skin. Today, he clattered through the dockside in his patchwork armour with his pistols at his hips, a blunderbuster gripped in both hands, and a stolen aethermancer's sword across his back. He walked through the press of shady ex-convicts as a man perfectly at ease—perhaps even unimpressed.

For their part, the ne'er-do-wells of Shackleton had a healthy wariness of my bosun. Only extreme aether exposure could leave someone's eyes so ashen and their veins so bright. Normally, that sort of pigmentation suggested that the individual in question was either an engineer or—more dangerous by far—an aethermancer. I knew for a fact that Mr Strahl was actually neither of these, but while he'd never discussed with me the incident that had stolen his pigment, the fact remained that his unnatural mien and the stolen sword on his back gave people heavy pause. Only an aethermancer should have been able to use a sword like that—but my engineer Mr Finch had spent long hours tinkering with the weapon so that even Strahl could use its unique properties for brief periods of time.

Strahl's withering glare carved a path as cleanly as Balor One-Eye's stare would have done. As a result, we reached the shipping office that was our destination in excellent time. The wooden stairs outside groaned their displeasure beneath Strahl's weight as he took point, casually shoving his way through the door. I followed in his wake, with Dougal on my heels.

The reception room was a mess of crates and chests. In one corner of the room, a caged bird flapped and squawked. Little rays of daylight filtered in from the holes above, lighting the area to a comfortable dimness. A half-dozen mismatched aromas assaulted me; the sweet, pungent smell of fruit mixed badly with the rusting, metallic stink of the steel slats that served for a roof. From deeper inside the office, I heard the shuffling sound of another living being.

"Hello?" I called out. "Picket?"

"Blair?" a voice called back. The voice's owner shuffled towards us, clattering his way through the mess. "Blair! Oh, aren't you a sight for sore eyes! How are you today, Captain Blair, sir?"

Picket was barely five and a half feet tall—perhaps an inch or two taller than I was. The old fellow boasted a truly impressive beard of wiry white hair and a neatly waxed moustache that reminded me of Vice-Admiral Wakefield's. His watery eyes were wide and bright as he looked at me. A set of magnifying goggles dangled down around his neck.

I reached out to shake his gnarled hand.

"Tuath bless you, Captain Blair," Picket said. "I thought of you the moment I heard you were in port." I was still feeling dull from my hangover, but Picket's anxiety was so keen that even a dead man could have picked up on it. I sneaked a cautious glance at Dougal, who frowned back at me silently. Neither of us commented on the atmosphere just yet.

"How can the *Iron Rose* be of service to you today, Mr Picket?" I asked, as-pleasant-as-you-please.

Picket glanced for the door. I wondered if he was expecting something terrible to come bursting through it. The old man licked his lips nervously and fiddled with one of the rings on his fingers. I was used to him being far calmer and far more composed.

"Let's talk about this in my office," Picket said. "Can I offer you a drink? I've got a fantastic iced cider, all the way from Lyonesse."

At the mention of alcohol, my stomach threatened to rebel. I shook my head quickly. "No, thank you," I answered, as politely as I could. "A little too rich for my taste. The cider *and* the city."

"Ah'll drink to that," Dougal chuckled. Picket forced a high answering laugh.

"I wouldn't turn down a glass of water," I added. I had a particular fondness for water that few of my crew shared. Clear, clean water had been a luxury where I'd grown up. Even decades later, I'd never learned to take it for granted.

"Of course, of course!" Picket assured me, all too eagerly. A bead of sweat hovered on the edge of his lip as he turned to lead us further inside.

Picket's office was crowded with neat piles of ledgers and manifests. Dougal and I had to squeeze to fit into it; adding Strahl to the mix in his piecemeal armour would have been impossible. My bosun remained in the doorway instead, staring suspiciously back towards the entrance. I stood in front of Picket's desk, since the view from both chairs was currently blocked by several towers of documents.

The old fence served us our drinks and helped himself to a glass of the aforementioned cider, fidgeting in his chair.

I let him sweat a little longer. I didn't want to be cruel—but my sense of wariness had steadily grown, ever since I'd walked in the door. I needed the old man to talk.

"So," Picket said finally, with a nervous smile. "The job." He swallowed a healthy mouthful of cider. "One-way trip. Here to New Havenshire. Cargo. No passengers. As soon as you can swing it." The drink went down the wrong way, and he had to cough lightly to clear his throat. "The, uh, clock is ticking."

"What's the cargo?" I asked.

Picket winced. "I... I can't tell you," he admitted.

I turned around to leave.

I liked Picket—unlike many of the humans I'd met outside of my crew, he never let his race go to his head. Common understanding in Avalon had it that the Tuath Dé had bestowed the right to rule upon humanity. Whether that was true or not, humans unsurprisingly enjoyed the thought. But Picket, scoundrel that he was, still treated everyone as though he was their fretting grandfather. In short—I didn't enjoy the idea of leaving the old fellow in the lurch.

But there were some things on which I was no longer willing to negotiate.

"Sorry to be wasting your time, Mr Picket," I said. I imagined I could taste the old man's bitter disappointment through the pungent smell of fruit.

"But—" Picket started urgently.

"The last time I didn't ask questions, a Rustlands cartel tried to load a hundred bricks of ambrosia onto my ship," I told him. "Never again."

I hadn't quite reached the door when Picket stopped me with a strangled cry: "Aether!"

Our small group shared a look.

Aether was the lifeblood of Avalon—the raw essence of Arcadia. It fuelled our ships; it lit our lanterns; it powered our guns. Aether was the great gift of the Tuath Dé to the mortals of this world.

"Long way from Rifton to be carrying aether, aren't we?" I asked. I turned around to face Picket. The old man hunched his shoulders and crossed his thin arms over his chest, as though trying to protect himself from a chill.

"Please, Captain Blair, sir," Picket stuttered. "*William*. I... I could really use your help."

We could all feel the danger heavy in the air... but danger often meant a lucrative reward. Besides which, the Lady of Fools doesn't bless those who idly sit by whilst opportunity calls—and I've always liked to think She has a soft spot for me in particular.

I'd like to say that's what motivated me to stay. But the truth is, I've got an overactive conscience for a sometime-smuggler, and it's not as much of a secret as I'd like it to be. The tremor in the old man's voice bothered me. We needed the job anyway, I consoled myself. What harm was there in hearing him out?

I could *feel* Mr Strahl's gaze burrowing into the back of my skull in silent warning.

"So," I sighed. "Aether. From here to New Havenshire, as soon as possible." I paused. "What has you so rattled, Picket?"

The old fence hesitated. He licked his lips, then reached up to twirl the end of his moustache. "I've already said too much," Picket whispered, "so you didn't hear this from me." He leaned in. "One of my contacts was supposed to lift the goods and make the shipment directly to New Havenshire. But they bungled the job and got caught red-handed. They burned their way here to drop off the cargo, and we *need* to get it moving. We have a client waiting after New Havenshire, and it'll be our heads if they don't get what we've promised them."

There was genuine fear in the old man's voice. I wasn't accustomed to hearing it.

"Who's the client?" I asked warily.

"No," Picket said. He shook his head emphatically. "No, I've already said too much." He reached down into a drawer in his desk. "Blair, listen to me. Here. Look at this—this is what I'm willing to offer. You'll get the other half upon delivery."

He thrust a certified note my way. I checked the number; it made my eyebrows disappear beneath the brim of my tricorne. I whistled. "That's... generous," I observed. "A little *too* generous, just for shipping aether."

"We stole it from some very dangerous people," Picket breathed. "But they're off chasing our original transport. If you leave now, the danger will be minimal." A pleading note now entered the old man's voice. "It's a sweetheart deal, Blair. I just need this done on time."

I frowned. Aether was valuable, of course—but this struck me as an awful lot of trouble for a shipload of stuff that could be acquired through normal channels. "What's so special about this aether, Picket?" I pressed. But the man remained silent.

"It's unrefined aether," Dougal cut in. "Isn't it?"

Picket didn't answer—but he paled significantly. Most aether came from the Dawnspring at Rifton, gathered in accordance with ancient, formalised contracts with the Court of the Everbright. But if you were willing to skirt danger, you could *steal* aether from the faeries' homeland of Arcadia instead.

I had learned—against my will, during one of Mr Finch's impromptu aetheric engineering sermons—that unrefined aether most often manifested as a gas. Though unrefined aether could technically be used as a fuel source in this natural state, it was an extremely temperamental substance, and prone to, in Mr Finch's words, 'abrupt, explosive destabilisation'.

Because of this, most of Avalon ran on aether which the faeries of the Everbright had refined for us into either liquid or crystalline form. And though there were no longer any blanket laws against gathering unrefined aether, most people still understood that there was something wicked and maybe even heretical about stealing from the faeries that had created our world.

That said... desperate people will inevitably do desperate things. I couldn't remember a time when there had ever been enough refined aether to go around. Despite the very real, very explosive drawbacks to using unrefined aether, there had always been a brisk black market trade in the stuff.

The idea of carrying unrefined aether made me uncomfortable... but I decided to move past the unease. I wouldn't have stooped to mining unrefined aether myself—but the stuff was already here. If it was causing Picket this much trouble, he'd owe me a favour for getting it off his doorstep.

"If we leave now and go hard, we can probably get it there by end of week," I said.

Picket shook his head. "We're already behind schedule," he said. "It's got to be tomorrow."

"We *could* get it there by tomorrow," I observed carefully, "but that would involve cutting straight through the Ironspine Pass. If that *thing* wakes up, my ship and your precious cargo won't be making it anywhere."

Picket pulled another note from the desk drawer, as though he'd been expecting the reply. "It's got to be tomorrow," he repeated. "Throw in cost of fuel—they'll top you off when you get to New Havenshire." He handed me the note. I scanned over the document. As I did, I realised that the sizable sum mentioned wasn't the total of the shipment.

It was the price per crate. And there were *many* crates.

I must have been goggling—because Picket didn't wait for my response. Instead, he simply offered out a ledger. "Here's the manifest," he said. "The aether canisters will be at the bottom of the crates, underneath the rest. You can keep the junk. Dump it, sell it—I don't care."

I downed the glass of water and reached out for the ledger. As I was about to take it from Picket's gnarled hands, however, he held on for an extra moment.

"I need your Oath, in return for this note," Picket said. "The cargo gets delivered to New Havenshire by tomorrow. You and your crew don't toy with it." He searched my eyes. "I mean it. It's as much for your safety as it is for mine."

Dougal sucked in a gasp through his teeth. Strahl gave a displeased grunt.

Oaths were more than just serious business; Oaths were *sacred* business. If I took an Oath, the words would rise to the ears of Noble Gallant himself—the god who'd granted us our honour and our sense of duty.

I had been an Oathbreaker once. All of the men who'd served in the Imperial military and lived to tell the tale were Oathbreakers by default—for we'd been meant to take our lives in failure. For more than a decade, I had lived with that unbearable shame, with the heavy awareness of Noble Gallant's all-too-personal loathing. I had borne that invisible mark, tangible to all around me like a rotting stench. Some days, I had been convinced that being an Oathbreaker was indeed a fate far worse than death.

Only a true miracle—forgiveness from a faerie—could remove that red mark from a soul. After many years of divine shame, I had stumbled on just such a miracle. My slate had been wiped clean.

I couldn't bring myself to risk that shame again. Not for money—not even for an *absurd* amount of money.

"Look at me, Picket," I said. I met the old man's gaze. "Friends don't ask friends to swear Oaths. Are we friends, Picket?"

Picket grimaced. "That's not fair, William—" he began.

I held up a hand. "I'll make you a *promise*, Picket," I told him. "You know how much that matters to me. I'll keep it even better than I would an Oath."

Picket worried at his lower lip. Already, it looked much abused from whatever stress he'd been through in the last few days. Finally, he pressed a weathered hand against his eyes. "Anyone else," he muttered reluctantly, "and I'd tell 'em to go kick rocks." He screwed up his features as though he'd bitten into a lemon. "If anyone asks, I made you take the Oath. But William… you *cannot* let me down. Please. I need this to go smoothly."

Giddy relief washed over me. I did my best to hide it with a grim nod. "I'll do everything in my power," I assured him. "The cargo gets to New Havenshire by tomorrow evening. Until we deliver it to its intended recipient, my crew won't tamper with it."

I held out my hand to Picket, as though we were truly sealing an Oath. He reached out to grasp my hand in his, nodding shakily.

"That's a promise, William," he mumbled. "May the Lady of Fools smile on us both, since Noble Gallant won't. Or else we'll both be *very* dead men."

* * *

"This trip tae New Havenshire, Cap'n," Dougal began, as the three of us marched back for the *Rose*. "Yer certain it's a worthwhile risk?"

"I'm sorry," I laughed, "I must have heard that wrong. Was that a MacLeod telling me to be cautious?" Dougal shot me a pointed look, and I patted his thick arm reassuringly. "You're talking about the incident with Barsby," I observed.

"I heard you tried to kill him," Strahl rumbled from behind us. He had joined our crew after the incident—but the story came up so frequently on the *Iron Rose* that he probably knew all of the details, anyway.

"I most certainly did *not* try to kill Barsby," I said. "I was just trying to defend myself."

"Evie was there," Dougal mused. "He said ye *did* draw yer weapon first."

"Barsby sold us out to bounty hunters!" I defended myself. "What was I going to do—politely ask them all to leave at their earliest convenience?"

"Whole incident caused quite the ruckus over in New Havenshire, didn't it?" Strahl asked dryly.

"Suppose the burnin' warehouse might have upset someone," Dougal said with a laugh.

Strahl's face remained stony. "And... Barsby lost an eye?" he said. "I seem to remember that part."

Dougal made a whistling sound, drove a finger towards one eye, and squished it against his eyelid. "Little weasel had it comin'," he said conspiratorially.

"It was a ricochet—and an *accident*," I said emphatically. "I sent Barsby a lovely eyepatch, as an apology. Not that... not that it would matter much now."

Both men fixed me with curious, sideways glances.

"Barsby's been hanged," I informed them. "I've heard it from... several people."

An awkward silence fell between us.

"An' yer... alright with that?" Dougal asked me finally.

I winced. As infuriating and duplicitous as our sometime-ally

Barsby had been, a part of me *did* feel uncomfortable with the knowledge that he was dead. I tried to shrug off Dougal's question, but the gesture came off listless and uncertain.

"Are ye sure?" Dougal pressed, unconvinced. "Because ye dinnae look so sure."

I shot Dougal a pleading sort of look. He lifted his hands, as though to drop the subject.

Strahl continued on, pragmatic. "You think the local constabulary will give us any trouble?" he asked.

"No one in New Havenshire ever posted a warrant for us," I replied. "Besides—the contract is clear." I patted the documents in my coat pocket. "This shipment is meant for the mayor. We're going out of our way to get this shipment to him in record time. You really think he's going to stop to quibble with us over past transgressions, if he's on the same time limit Picket is?"

"For the record," Strahl replied, "I think it's a bad idea."

"You think all of my ideas are bad, Mr Strahl," I pointed out.

Strahl opened his mouth—then paused. He shut his mouth again with a nod.

As we reached the *Rose*'s gangplank, I halted to let Strahl go on ahead. "I understand the risks," I told Dougal, once my bosun had left our hearing. "But be honest—you'd have taken the job too." I quirked an eyebrow at him.

Dougal pursed his lips. "Ye wear yer heart on yer sleeve, lad," he said, instead of answering the implied question.

"Again," I reminded him, "I learned from the best."

Dougal tried not to smile—and failed miserably. "Well then," he said leadingly. "Guess you'd be witty, too. An' handsome, I suppose—"

"I didn't learn any of that from you," I joked.

Dougal chuckled and shook his head. He took to the plank, leaving me behind to stare up at my ship.

My ship. I never got tired of saying those words.

Once, the *Iron Rose* had served the Imperium—but on the day that she became mine, I'd traded in her black square-sails for white ones. The *Rose*'s thick hull was made of solid oak; though it had become chipped and scarred over the years, its unique creaking sound made it feel like home. A series of beautiful carved roses wove their way up the prow of the ship, echoed in etchings upon the railings.

As a third-rate ship of the line, the *Rose* was smaller than the first- and second-rates—but though she packed less of a punch than her betters, she made up for that with her lovely legs. I'd had to save up quite a bit of money to refit the ship's drives, but I'd never had cause to regret the expense. And while she'd certainly never be a dreadnought, we had at least improved her armaments from those of thirty years ago, when she'd first rolled off the line. The gun deck bristled with cannons heavy enough to handle most modern vessels, and our turrets were enough to dissuade any particularly daring outflyers from getting too close to the deck.

Of course, very few outflyers ever actually made it within firing range of the *Rose*. Dougal MacLeod was a madcap veteran pilot of the northern clans—in all of my years with him, I'd never seen him outclassed. Dougal's own vessel remained tucked away against the *Rose*'s hull, suspended over the several-thousand-foot drop of Shackleton's skyland pier. It was a gull-winged outflyer barely older than the *Rose* itself, proudly draped in ageing Coalition colours.

Imperial ships and Coalition colours shouldn't have mixed so well. But somehow, we'd all made it work.

I walked up the steps of my ship to a main deck come alive. Shackleton had not been a friendly place for shore leave, which meant that most of the crew still lingered aboard the *Rose*. There was a mildly oppressive air about the skyland pier, despite its open nature, such that the promise of sailing free had put a Caphean wind in everyone's metaphorical sails.

Riggers scampered across the ropes with alacrity, preparing the sails for cast-off. Aeronauts hauled lines across the deck, while engines warmed beneath my feet in cautious, purring fits. Little conducted the chaotic dance around him with his hands, punctuating signs with the occasional sharp whistle. When that failed to suffice, Mr Strahl repeated his orders in a much more hostile manner.

Even now, Mr Strahl signed furiously with Little. My pale bosun had known Imperial Handsign well before he'd ever come aboard the *Rose*; his vocabulary hinted that he'd learned it in the army, rather than in the navy. Ironically, he'd had to adapt himself to our hodgepodge dialect aboard the *Rose*, which had now diverged so much from any Imperial convention that it might as well have been its own language entirely.

Mr Strahl turned away from that signed conversation to shout my first mate's orders with a will; his deafening voice rang out clearly, carrying to every corner of the ship. I sometimes imagined the man could strip paint with a single blistering word.

"Everyone accounted for?" I asked Little, as I joined him and Dougal on-deck.

Almost, Little answered. *A few stragglers aren't back yet from shore leave, but they should be on their way.*

"Well, they'd best get back here soon," I said, as sternly as I could manage. "If the cargo is onboard before they are, we'll have to leave without them."

Evie's not back yet, Little clarified for me.

I sighed, hanging my head. "Or... I suppose we could wait," I amended myself.

Don't we need fuel? Little asked.

"We'll have it once we reach New Havenshire," I said. I signed a careful follow-up: *We'll be cutting through the Ironspine Pass tonight.*

Little looked warily between me and Dougal.

"We've gone through the pass a'fore," Dougal said nonchalantly.

And New Havenshire? Little signed slowly. I knew he was really talking about our last misadventure. *We did turn a warehouse into a smouldering pile of 'where's the house'?*

"Cap'n said it'd be fine," Dougal declared. He clapped a hand on Little's shoulder. "So long as there ain't no bounty hunters te start up trouble 'gain, right? Just dinnae burn anythin' down, and we'll be grand."

I let out a breath I hadn't realised I'd been holding. Whatever his private misgivings, Dougal had no trouble backing me up in public. It shouldn't have surprised me—once upon a time, my crew had all but shoved me into the position of captain, so they really had only themselves to blame.

My ship. My crew. What a strange thought this all still was.

A sharp whistle from the docks drew our attention, and I looked over the railing. A familiar face waited at the bottom of the gangplank, beaming up at me with a boyish smile. Evie wore his blue halcyon's sash more prominently today, signalling his faith in the Benefactor in such a way that I knew he had been out on holy business.

"Permission to come aboard?" Evie called up.

I grinned down at him. "I'll think about it!" I shouted back.

The halcyon extracted himself from a small group of local toughs, each of them repeating goodbyes in a different language entirely, holding out their index and middle fingers in the holy sign of the Benefactor's mercy. Evie replied to each man in his own language, pressing one hand sincerely over his heart. Finally, he turned to head up the gangplank and onto the main deck. How Evie had managed to make such easy friends in a place like Shackleton, I couldn't imagine—but the company he'd gathered was clearly sorry to see him go.

All four of the Seelie Tuath Dé had mortals dedicated to their service. Noble Gallant's servants, known as "judges" in most parts of Avalon, were unflinching arbiters of justice. Skalds who followed Death Victorious researched glorious histories or wandered Avalon in search of history being made. I'd never met a proper fool in service to the Lady of Fools (though all the goblins back home in Morgause swore up and down that they existed).

Priests of the Benefactor were known by many names in many parts—but I had most often heard them called "halcyons", after soft and sunny days. Their duty was to comfort and console, which meant that they were often the most welcome of the Seelie's servants. Halcyon Everett Seymour lived up to his sunny title, and then some.

You'd never find another living soul as gentle as Evie; he had a gift for languages and a knack for conversation, and he put both talents to use spreading the mercy of the Benefactor, whom many believed to be the most generous of the Seelie Tuath Dé. Evie was a slim man, with a rounded face marred by years of laugh-lines and brown skin as dark as swaying cattails. His kind smile and warm brown eyes made him seem younger than his three decades and change, though I knew he'd taken to shaving his head in order to hide his thinning hair. In all of the years I'd known him, his sprightly attitude had yet to dim; I fully expected that he would still be running circles around me when we were both old men.

"I was beginning to worry we'd have to leave you behind," I joked.

"Ha!" Evie answered. "You wouldn't dare. I have an excellent husband. I'm sure he'd start a mutiny on my behalf." Little threw his arms around Evie, embracing the other man strongly enough to lift him from his toes. Evie held him back with an affection so sweet, my teeth ached just from watching it.

Little shot me a sheepish expression as he disentangled himself from his husband. *Maybe just a small mutiny,* he assured me. *A very polite mutiny.*

I snorted.

"Here," Evie said, fishing in his satchel. "I got you a little something while I was in town." He handed a small package over to me, and I peeled aside the waxy paper. Inside was a small chunk of delicious brown heaven. My mouth watered, and I pressed a hand to my chest.

"How did you even *find* chocolate here?" I asked. "We're a long way from Aarushi."

The halcyon beamed. "Everyone loves the Benefactor, Wil," he said.

"No," I countered, "everyone loves *you*. Especially when you show up bearing chocolate."

Evie's friendship with me, I reflected, was really made up of over twenty years of little acts of kindness. Even back when we'd served together under Vice-Admiral Wakefield, Evie had been a cheerful, overly helpful sort of soul. I had grown to appreciate that more and more over the passing years.

I couldn't remember the last time I'd had to spend a day apart from either Evie or Little. I would say that we were best friends—but sometimes I suspected those words didn't quite describe us well enough. I might call us brothers instead—except that brothers rarely lingered at your side for more than twenty years. I loved them both, but not the way they loved each other.

Whatever we were, we depended on each other greatly, and we'd shared some harrowing experiences. Twenty years ago, we had all broken our Oaths together, taking on that lifelong shame as one. Later, we had all received the same forgiveness for our Oaths, as well. But that was something we were very careful never to mention outside of the *Iron Rose*.

"And where's *my* chocolate, boyo?" Dougal declared from behind us.

"I'm sure Wil would be happy to share," Evie said graciously. He turned his gaze back towards me expectantly.

I swallowed. Three sets of eyes fell upon the empty bit of wax paper in my hands.

Evie rolled his eyes and flicked my nose. "What do we do with the Benefactor's gifts, Wil?" he asked.

"Enjoy them to the last chocolatey morsel?" I offered, with a sheepish smirk.

"We *share* them," Evie sighed. "Though… I suppose I could keep *this* to myself." So saying, he pulled a leather-bound package out from his satchel.

You were able to find the right seals for the forgery? Little inquired.

Evie winked. "Like I said," he repeated sanctimoniously, "everyone loves the Benefactor. I was able to finish on time. Our papers are up-to-date in the Duchy of Mavra—and in Lyonesse, if we need it." His voice turned rueful. "Not that we *will* need it."

"Papers would be the least of our troubles if we went back to Lyonesse," I agreed sheepishly.

Strahl could always give the aethermancer his sword back, Little signed jokingly.

"Oh yes," I said. "Stolen property returned, a few heartfelt apologies all around… I'm sure we could smooth it over, once some very angry aethermancers finally die." I cleared my throat. "Let's focus on our current job, shall we? Best we get ready for departure. As soon as the cargo comes aboard, we're off."

"Aye-aye," Evie confirmed. "Where are we off to?"

"New Havenshire," I said.

Evie narrowed his eyes at me. "Isn't that where the warehouse burned—"

"*Yes*," I sighed.

"And how are we getting—" he started.

"Through the Ironspine Pass," I finished. "We need to be there by tomorrow."

Evie blew out a long breath—but he gave a glum sort of nod. Down along the pier, I heard a driver bellow and saw a small procession of wagons heading towards us. No fewer than four heavily armoured men and women accompanied each of the three cargo-laden vehicles. A longboat trailed some thirty feet above and behind, acting as an extra escort.

"That's for us?" Evie asked. I saw his surprise echoed in the expressions of the rest of my crew. Even Mr Strahl took a moment to appreciate the caravan and its contingent of heavily armed toughs.

"No," I said. "That's for New Havenshire. And I promised I would keep my mouth shut, so I'm afraid that's all I can tell you."

Evie and Little took this in stride. They knew, more than anyone, how much my word meant to me.

"What *can* you tell us?" Evie asked softly.

"I can tell you we're about to make a lot of money," I said. "And we all know how much we need it." I paused. "Let's just avoid talking too much about it. It'll all be sorted by tomorrow evening, anyway."

I knew Evie wanted to say more—but he wrangled down his curiosity into uncomfortable silence instead, chewing over his worries in his mind.

As the crew moved the cargo aboard, I prayed that the Lady of Fools would put her finger on the scales in our favour just one more time.

2

I'VE GOT YOUR SIX - WHISPERING WINDS - WHY CHOOSE - RED REAVER'S REVENGE

Three children and a physicker were the only Imperials left standing on the main deck of the *HMS Caliban*. Slender Evie trembled like a leaf. Little stared into the distance with an empty look in his eyes. Holloway towered above us—a giant in a white, bloodied surgeon's uniform. As the Coalition ship approached, the physicker wiped tears from his face with one bloodied hand. The gesture left scarlet smears across his green skin.

He left his firearm where it was on the blood-soaked deck. There was no point, really, in remaining armed.

"Let's go below deck," Holloway said gently to the three of us.

"Are they going to kill us?" Evie asked. His eyes were bright with tears, and his voice quavered with fear.

"No," Holloway said. "No, I—I'll take care of you." His voice shook on the words, though, and we all knew that he wasn't certain of them. He forced a smile all the same and leaned down to pick up Little with one well-muscled arm. Holloway offered his hand to me—but I recoiled at the blood there. He blinked down at his skin, as though just noticing the stains, and wiped his palm against his sleeve. "Grab on to my coattails, Mr Blair," he offered instead. "Come along, double time. Close your eyes."

Holloway guided us through the ship, helping us over the bodies we chose to ignore. When we next opened our eyes, we found ourselves in his quarters, just next to the sickbay. The cosy room smelled of sawdust and peppermint. Inside, sheltered from all of the horrible sights above deck, I could almost convince myself that everything that had come before was just a terrible dream.

The physicker settled the three of us onto his bunk and tossed a blanket over us. As we huddled beneath it, Holloway excused himself to wash his hands. During his brief absence, the sound of the Coalition ship docking echoed through our vessel. Our ship changed course as the Coalition ship began to drag us away.

Holloway hurried back into the room and closed the door. He hesitated next to it—but I couldn't tell just what was going through his mind as he did. Evie's crying intensified, though, and Holloway's unbandaged eye flickered towards a little book on his desk. His hesitation passed.

The physicker took two steps across the room, snatched up the book, and thumbed through it. When he'd found the spot he wanted, he lowered himself carefully in front of Evie.

"You can read, aye?" Holloway asked. Evie nodded, hiccuping through his tears. "You know what helps me through rough storms? This page, right here—under the Benefactor's section. Can you read it for me? I'm having a bit of trouble." He tapped the broken glasses perched upon his misshapen nose and pointed to his bandaged eye beneath them.

Evie took the book. The pages were bent in corners, and the writing was terribly small. Nonetheless, he wiped his eyes and recited from it resolutely, interrupted only by the occasional hiccup.

"*Noble Gallant has given you honour, and the Lady of Fools has made you courageous,*" Evie choked. "*Death Victorious has offered you glory. But I give you that which is most precious to me, that you may offer it to others in turn; for mercy may be given a hundred times, and never is it any lessened in the giving. Though honour breaks and courage fails and glory is forgotten: Know that you shall always have my love.*"

Distant voices trickled down through the hallway outside. For just a moment, we all stopped breathing, Holloway included. Little clutched at Evie's arm.

"Keep reading," Holloway told Evie. "And whatever you do, stay put. All three of you."

The tall, dignified hobgoblin walked towards the door. He stood there for a long moment—and then, with a steadying breath, he stepped out into the hallway. At the time, I wondered why he hadn't bothered locking the door. Many years later, the answer occurred to me: If the Coalition wanted us dead, there would be no stopping them.

I strained my ears to listen as Holloway's ponderous steps took him down the hall. He called out to someone further away. Voices answered loudly, followed by the rush of booted feet.

I couldn't stand the uncertainty. I shimmied off the bed and cracked open the door to peer down the hallway. I saw them: three men in mismatched uniforms and yellow Coalition kerchiefs, their swords and pistols drawn. Two of them, large and burly men, had grappled Holloway to his knees and slammed his face against the bulkhead.

"I'm a physicker!" he gasped. "Please! We surrender!"

"A physicker?" one rebel spat sceptically.

"What a lying coward," another one laughed.

"This is for Pelaeia, you Imperial scum," the last one said. His voice was cold enough to chill my bones. He lifted his pistol.

"No!" I screamed. I burst out from behind the door. The man with the pistol spun around and pointed the weapon at my face.

Holloway screamed—but one of the men pinning the physicker saw me, and he moved even faster. He relinquished his hold on the sawbones and lunged for the other man's hand. The two of them struggled briefly, before the hand with the pistol twisted with an unnatural *crack,* and the shot went wide.

The man with the pistol shrieked and dropped the firearm. He clutched at his hand, and I saw that his trigger finger was now badly broken.

"Fer goodness' sake, Cauldwell," the other man shouted, "it's a child!" He was an enormous, red-headed man with a neatly kept beard —the very model of a northern man. His beaten leather aviator's coat marked him as a Coalition pilot.

Holloway stumbled my way, hurrying over to wrap his arms protectively around me. "Please!" he begged. "There are two others in the room. For pity's sake, spare them—even if you can't find it in your hearts to spare me." I had never heard such sharp fear in the hobgoblin's voice. The Coalition man who'd tried to kill me frightened me... but seeing my idol brought so low scared me even more.

Cauldwell looked back up at me. In his eyes, I saw a deep and wild hatred. It was a curiously aimless hatred, though. It was directed at me; at Holloway; even at the Coalition pilot that had broken his finger.

I had been hated before, as a goblin on the streets of Morgause. Before I'd ever worn a uniform, I'd been shoved aside, beaten, and spit upon. The people of Morgause had seen me as a gutter-gob nuisance; theirs was a hatred born of disdain.

But this? This was a *new* sort of hatred I had never seen before. It mystified me, even as it terrified me; there was an element of the unknown to it that I didn't yet understand.

"Children, Cauldwell!" the pilot roared. "Bloody children! What's wrong with ye!" He shoved Cauldwell sharply towards the last rebel, who caught the man by the shoulders.

Cauldwell pressed harder against the wrist above his broken finger, as though he could somehow staunch the pain. His face was pale and sweating. "Those aren't children," he hissed. "They're wee Imperial monsters. Look at they proud uniforms they're wearin'. Bet ye they cheered wae the rest when they heard 'bout Pelaeia."

The Coalition pilot reached down to pick up the pistol on the floor, holding it warily at his side. "None ae us is in our right heads, lad," he said softly. "But that decision's not yers or mine. Fer now, mark me—hurt 'em, an' ye'll never have children of yer own."

The hatred in Cauldwell's eyes flared with a strangely painful frustration. His rage overflowed into helpless tears. I stared, dumbstruck by the sight. I had never seen a man cry in hatred before.

The pilot turned his attention back towards Holloway. "Physicker, eh?" he observed. "We're lucky we stumbled 'cross ye. Cauldwell here broke his finger. He'll be needin' someone tae patch him up."

"Ah'd rather cut off ma hand," Cauldwell rasped.

"Suit yerself," the pilot sighed. He shook his head wearily. "Ye're prisoners, physicker. You an' the wee ones. Long as ye come quiet an' do no harm, ye'll get a fair hearin'—we've got a halcyon of the Benefactor with us, an' she'll chew our ears off otherwise."

Holloway nodded silently. He tried to speak again—but all he managed was a few trembling sobs.

The pilot watched Holloway uncomfortably. As he did, I saw in his features a flash of the same aimless hatred that had moved Cauldwell. That hatred was tempered with other things, however; and as the pilot lowered his gaze to me, he forced some softness into his face.

"Thank you," I whispered. I had to work the words past a knot in my throat.

"What's yer name, lad?" the pilot asked me.

"I'm... William Blair, sir," I choked out.

"William," the pilot repeated slowly. "Well, William... I'm Lieutenant Dougal MacLeod." He let out a breath, and I saw the last embers of that curious hatred die—replaced, now, by the expression of a man looking down at a scared child. "Stop worryin' yer head fer now. Ah've got yer six."

* * *

THE *ROSE* WAS PROBABLY the only ship with a crew foolish enough to travel through the Ironspine Pass in the dead of night. To be fair, I had an ace up my sleeve which made the endeavour slightly less perilous than it seemed: My navigator really was an otherworldly talent.

I mean that literally. My navigator was a faerie—one of the strange servants of the Tuath Dé who had created our world.

Faeries were a rare sight within Avalon; the Avalon Imperium had counted a handful of faeries among its allies, but I'd never seen a single one during my time in the Imperial Navy. In theory, I'd fought once or twice alongside the Envoy—the Tuath Dé's handpicked messenger and advisor to the royal house—in battles where the crown prince had been present. But the Envoy had perished alongside the prince before I ever laid eyes on them. As such, Syrene was the first faerie I had ever met face-to-face.

I still wasn't certain whether I was exceptionally lucky or exceptionally *unlucky* to have stumbled across Strahl and Syrene. I'd met them both in Lyonesse several years prior, during a disastrous scuffle with the local Wardens. Somehow, I'd escaped the situation with a bosun and a navigator, and with my broken Imperial Oath miraculously forgiven. To this day, I harboured uncomfortable suspicions that both Strahl and Syrene had once been very important to the Avalon Imperium... but Strahl had assured me that he held no love for the old empire, and his actions so far had supported that claim.

As for Syrene... well. She was frankly terrifying. But she owed me a debt, and faeries take that sort of thing very seriously indeed.

I stifled a yawn as the morning light crept over the lip of the great walls of the canyon, forcing myself to keep my grip on the wheel as I did. I risked a glance at the tall creature at my side.

"Almost through," I mumbled. "Thank you, Syrene. Your skill humbles us all, as always."

"We are most pleased to offer our wisdom, Captain," the faerie beside me intoned. Her voice echoed like wind chimes in the air, strange and melodic.

Syrene was rail thin, with long, delicate limbs like boughs of polished oak. Her waist couldn't have been thicker than one of my thighs, yet she stood taller than most mortals—which meant that she positively *towered* over me. The flowers atop her head changed with the seasons and with our location—and sometimes, simply at her whims. Today, sophisticated braids of real, woven lavender trailed behind her, fluttering in the wind.

Syrene regarded the world with two pairs of spider-like, jet-black eyes. No lips, no nose—her face resembled a carved doll. I sometimes wondered how she managed to speak without a mouth, but I never dwelled too long on the matter. Mortal minds were not meant to fathom faerie magics.

"And what does the wind tell you today, Syrene?" I asked.

The faerie's unblinking eyes alighted upon me. Her mirth emanated from her like the fires of a warm hearth. As always, her emotions were contagious. "The skies greet us as kin, Captain," Syrene answered. "They warn us of harsher winds ahead, but no storms threaten us from here to New Havenshire." She canted her head to the side in an absent-minded pose. "The Old One is restless in his slumber... but he has not noticed us."

"Excellent," I sighed. The reassurance sent a relieved shiver through my body as I steered us around the next bend. The manoeuvre afforded me a stunning view of the Ironspine mountain's slopes, where a canyon wall dipped sharply.

Slate-grey, rocky slopes stabbed the sky with snow-capped peaks. Streaks of rusty-red iron spattered along the mountains, oxidised by prolonged exposure to the winds and rain. A day might come when Ironspine's bones were picked clean—but it would be a long time coming, if so. The mountain still lived... and it did *not* take kindly to scavengers.

Nor did the mountain take kindly to guests—a thought which had kept most of us wary as we floated through the pass.

We still had a decent stretch ahead of us, but I was flagging at the helm. I became aware of Syrene's willingness to help in the same way that I often knew when she was cheerful, contemplative, or displeased. I traded places with her, allowing her the wheel.

Not too far from the helm was the longhorn—a brass contraption of levers, knobs, and dials, with an ear and a mouthpiece set in the centre. I used it to call down to the engine room. It was early yet, but I knew that my chief engineer would be awake; Mr Finch was an early riser.

"Engineering," answered a posh, lightly nasal baritone. I could all but hear his raised eyebrow.

"Ah, Mr Finch!" I said, with more cheer than I felt. "How are the repairs to the engine holding?"

"Perfectly, Captain," Finch replied. *"Though I would like to make some final adjustments at New Havenshire if time permits. Our departure was a bit... hasty."* My engineer's tone held a prideful tinge, but it was well merited. The last time my venerable vessel had been fully up to snuff had probably been the day it first went skyward. Mr Finch had taken advantage of our time in Shackleton to strike the last items from his sacred checklist—a meticulous record of necessary repairs which he had started on the day that he first came aboard, so many years ago.

"I'm just taking out my cup for a spot of tea before I return to my duties," Finch added. *"Will that be all, Captain?"*

"Yes, Mr Finch," I assured him. "That will be all." I paused, contemplating my next line of conversational attack. "Have I told you of late how much I respect your genius—"

The other end of the longhorn clicked shut. The droning tone of the empty line filled my ear. I sighed, hanging up the device. Curses.

"Mr Finch has not yet forgiven you for breaking his tea set," Syrene observed. Her pent-up laughter danced inside of me as though it were my own.

"I'll win him back yet," I grumbled. "He's about to settle down with some tea as we speak. The *new* tea set cost me a small fortune. He'll have my apology right under his nose, every day around teatime."

"One must pay an expensive price to court human genius," Syrene observed laughingly.

The morning crew had started filtering out onto the deck as we spoke. I paused to confer with Little, confirming our heading and conveying Syrene's observations on the weather. I promised to get some rest before the hour was up—though inwardly, I found the idea dubious.

Rest. Ha. I'd be a bundle of nerves, sitting awake in my bed until we were through the pass.

The longhorn bleated, and I answered. Dougal's boisterous cheer crackled through.

"Mornin', sunshine!" my outflyer chuckled. *"Nobody had tae scrape ye off the deck today?"*

I grinned despite myself. "No indeed," I rejoined. "No idiots blaring the alarm."

Dougal *ooh*'d and laughed uproariously. *"Get some rest soon, lad,"* he advised. *"Ye been up all night. The others'll have it under control."*

"Did *you* sleep well last night, flying past a grumpy mountain?" I muttered. I said it quietly enough that only he could hear it.

"Hah!" Dougal answered blithely. *"Ah slept like a log."*

I sighed. *Northerners.*

"Get that rear into gear, MacLeod," I told him. "You're cleared for flight."

"Roger that, Cap'n," Dougal replied. *"Firin' 'er up."*

I stayed on the line, listening to Dougal run through his pre-flight checklist. His outflyer's engine coughed and sputtered to life.

"Chimaera One, ready tae cause a little trouble!" he declared.

"Please don't," I begged.

The northerner laughed. *"Who do ye take me for?"* he asked.

"Dougal MacLeod," I answered with a grumble.

Dougal's laughter redoubled. The *Rose*'s clamps released the outflyer, and he revved the small ship's engine just enough to drop into our wake. I turned to look directly at him in his cockpit, fishing out my pocket watch. I dangled it in front of me and pointed emphatically at the time.

"I want you reporting on the hour and every half hour after that," I ordered. "Understood?"

"Roger that, *Iron Rose*," Dougal said. *"Ah've got yer six."* The plane saluted me with a little wobble of its wings before it angled upwards, out of the canyon.

I headed into my cabin and tried to manage a few winks.

* * *

The Lady of Fools had smiled on our midnight voyage, but She must have turned her attention away from us that morning. Maybe She'd gone to sleep around the same time I did.

Five minutes after the first mark, Little sent someone inside to shake me awake. Dougal had yet to report in.

I headed directly for the quarterdeck, searching the rocky valley and the skies above for any sign of that old Coalition outflyer—but I saw no signs of it anywhere. I moved for the longhorn with a frown, snatching it up and double-checking the outbound frequency.

"MacLeod, you bloody twit!" I called into it. "Where are you?"

Static was my only response. I tried a few more times, adjusting the settings minutely in between each shout.

Long minutes went by. I was nearly ready to give up when the longhorn finally crackled. Distant, garbled words mumbled through the static—but they were utterly unintelligible. At least, I thought, it *sounded* like Dougal. His tone sounded distinctly urgent.

A deep rumble came over the longhorn. An instant later, I heard it in the distance behind us. I looked skyward; the skies were clear and blue, with lazy wisps of white cloud. Not a single storm cloud in sight.

I glanced towards our navigator, still standing at the wheel. Her wooden face remained serene. The winds had suggested no storms on the horizon, and that didn't seem to have changed. A deep dread clenched at my stomach. That meant there were only two possibilities behind that sound... and neither of them was pleasant.

I deeply hoped we were under attack. I rarely have occasion to feel that way—but we were more likely to survive an attack than we were to survive an angry mountain.

"All hands on alert!" I called out.

Little caught my order and followed it up with a sharp whistle of his own. He started out onto the deck, smacking heads and urging people on with his hands. *High alert!* he signed. *You heard the captain!*

I changed frequencies on the longhorn, calling down to my gunnery chief.

"*Brighton here,*" Lenore answered, almost immediately. "*What's the fuss up there?*"

"Trouble," I said. "Not sure what kind just yet. If you're lucky, maybe you and the ladies will have a chance to shoot something today." I took a deep breath, forcing my tired mind to work quickly. "I want your best people armed and on the main deck, sharpish. And for the love of the Benefactor, *no one* takes a shot with the bloody cannons —if we hit the mountain, we won't need to worry about the rest of our troubles ever again."

Lenore laughed a bit too gleefully at that. I heard her step away from the longhorn to start barking orders to her fellow gunners. I closed the longhorn and hurried to help prepare the ship for battle.

A few minutes later, however, the longhorn made its telltale clattering ring. In my current mood, I likened it to the sound of a bleating sheep trapped in a piano. I rushed to pick up the receiver.

"Oi, Cap'n!" Dougal's voice filtered over. *"MacLeod 'ere! Listen, we—"*

"Damn it all, MacLeod!" I interjected. "Tell me you didn't give Ironspine a MacLeod Wake-Up Call!"

"Ah did not!" the northerner replied cheerfully. *"The rotters on ma arse did that when they fired oan me!"*

The Lady of Fools, I decided, was awake and in a fickle mood. "Of course," I groaned. "Two troubles at once. Why choose?"

Dougal *laughed*. The maniac.

I reached over to the longhorn and pulled the headset onto my ears. The warbling static on the line slowly cleared, and I knew that Dougal had started coming back into range.

Syrene glided smoothly aside as I took back the wheel; her long wooden legs melded with the deck as though it were made of water. Dougal's laboured breathing sounded in my ears as I gripped the familiar brass spokes of the helm. I noticed a strained quality in the noises that came through the longhorn, now that I could hear them better. The outflyer's aether engine was whining a bit too loudly. I thought I heard something hissing—maybe escaped steam.

"Status report," I ordered Dougal.

"Wing's damaged," Dougal hissed between manoeuvres. *"Ah've got it. Dinnae worry 'bout me. Ye've yerselves tae worry about more. S'a right nasty ship headed yer way. Countin' more'n a score of cannons—"*

"You can count?" I interjected.

Dougal's laugh was a bit less boisterous this time. *"Sure,"* he said. *"Ah count ye still owe me three drinks, lad. Maybe another one, after this."*

I scowled. "How far are the brigands?" I asked. "And I want a name."

"Red Reaver's Revenge is all carved 'pon her bow," Dougal replied. *"On ye soon, since I disengaged. In fae yer sou'west, in maybe a few minutes."*

I leaned my head back and let out a brief, hysterical laugh.

Red Reaver. *Red Reaver.*

No wonder Picket had been so loath to give me details. He'd stolen aether off the bloodiest, most ruthless pirate this side of Lyonesse. And now, one of her ships had come looking for our cargo… along with its weight in blood, if the stories were anything to go by.

"Ye want me t'buy ye more time?" Dougal asked.

"No," I replied. I forced myself back to the moment. "You're damaged. Hang back. I'll call you in when we need you. Let them think you've cut and run."

"If ye're sure," Dougal confirmed reluctantly. *"Ah'll be here."*

I glanced behind us. The distant form of a large ship had come into view, its hull spattered with telltale red. Its sails were a black affair, each one smeared with a scarlet-painted skull. The *Red Reaver's Revenge* was a stout ship, utterly devoid of grace and finesse. It was clumsy as it lumbered over the crest of the canyon, but that hardly mattered—the ship flew with a frankly unnatural speed, gaining on us like an Unseelie monster.

A high-pitched, keening scream sounded over the air between us, sending chills down my spine. It took me a long moment to realise that it wasn't a scream at all; the sound originated from the *Revenge*'s aetheric engine, as it picked up pace to gain on us. In my entire life, I'd never heard an engine like that.

We weren't going to outrun that ship.

My head swam with nervousness. I tried to work my way through it, searching for options. Normally, we could have outmanoeuvred the clumsy *Revenge*—but in our current environs, boxed in by the canyon, even that slight advantage was useless.

The *Revenge* was bigger, faster, and more heavily armed than the *Rose*. We were doomed.

Evie bounded up the steps to join me on the quarterdeck. He stared out towards the scarlet-spattered ship that currently hounded us; his dark eyes were wide with genuine fear. "What in the name of the Everbright is that?" he whispered hoarsely.

"One of Red Reaver's fleet," I answered bleakly.

Evie muttered a horrified prayer. Red Reaver was not known to be a religious woman—in fact, the most nightmarish stories about her involved her treatment of captured clergy. Her flagship, the *Malefactor*, had been named to evoke a sense of vicious, gleeful blasphemy.

The expression on Evie's face steeled my resolve and galvanised my courage. Those pirates would have him over my dead body, I decided.

I hurried over towards the railing that overlooked the main deck. "Mr Strahl!" I bellowed.

"Aye, Cap'n?" Strahl called back. He was lashing on the last straps of his armour. A nearby crewman held his helmet for him as he geared up.

"The *Red Reaver's Revenge* will be upon us soon!" I informed him. "Time to earn your keep again. *Iron Rose*, prepare to repel boarders!"

A grin slipped across Strahl's face, nearly as wild as Dougal's. My bosun was no airman, but he knew battle well. Strahl plucked his helmet from the man next to him and pulled it down over his head. He turned to address the crew loudly.

"You heard the cap'n!" he bellowed. "Time to dance with Death Victorious!"

I became aware of Evie standing next to me, staring down at the gathering below. "You think we can outfight them?" he asked softly. The fear had yet to leave his voice, but I could hear him trying to wrangle it down.

I turned to face him. "So long as we stay in the canyon, the *Revenge* won't risk firing its guns on us," I explained. "They want this cargo back. That means their best bet is to overpower the *Rose* and pilot it out of here safely. They'll board; I'm sure of it."

"Oh no," a woman's voice observed behind us, without an ounce of actual fear. "What shall we poor ladies do, Captain Blair?"

My gunnery chief, Miss Lenore Brighton, had finished gathering up her gunnery ladies. They were a ragtag group of marines, scarred and battle-tested—many of them wives and daughters to men who'd fought on both sides of the civil war. The Sundering War had not been kind to those left behind, and neither had the many little Coalition wars after it; the women on my crew had long since taken their lives into their own hands, rather than meekly accepting the lot in life they'd been offered. The sole young man of the group, Mr Billings, had learned much of what he knew of a rifle from the older women.

Lenore didn't *look* like an expert sharpshooter—but her appearance never seemed to bother the trajectory of her bullets. An ex-schoolmarm from the Rustlands, she kept her grey-streaked black hair tied back into a no-nonsense bun. Her high-necked blouse was crisp and clean, and her sturdy-heeled boots made a satisfying stomp beneath her plum-coloured skirt as she stormed about the deck. There was a dainty white ribbon tied about her throat, but her other accoutrements were a bit less prim; she had multiple bandoliers draped across her torso, a munitions belt at her waist, a multitude of holstered pistols, and a large rifle across her back. Truly, Miss Brighton knew how to accessorise.

Lenore had a cold, hard face, dark walnut skin, and a narrow nose, once broken—but many people still said that my gunnery chief might be a great beauty if only she would smile. Such remarks had got more than one man shot.

I flashed a vulpine grin at my deadly gunnery chief. "I happen to have an idea of what you could do," I told her.

3

CAPTAIN GRIEVER - ACTING CAPTAIN - DAMN IT, MACLEOD

The *Revenge* hungrily ate up the air between us. It came within striking distance much sooner than I would have preferred. The sound of Red Reaver's pirates hooting and hollering cut dimly through the screaming of their engine. As their ship manoeuvred above us, the pirates began to rappel down on tethered lines, swinging off their main deck towards the *Rose*'s quarterdeck.

I swerved the *Rose* out of their immediate path, giving them a miss. Some of the hanging miscreants fired at us with their pistols anyway as they swung through the air, though none of the shots seemed to connect. Reaver's people were mostly northerners, like Dougal, with the same cultural relish for great thrills. They were a scarred and motley bunch, beneath the frightful red dye they'd smeared across their faces. Many of them wore their clan braids prominently; a few had dyed their braids crimson too, and had wound them about their heads in an obvious attempt to evoke the image of an Unseelie redcap.

My crew opened fire at the suspended pirates, picking a few of them out of the sky. One brigand's line snapped, and I heard him shout as he plummeted to his doom below. The *Revenge* adjusted its course again, however, and the hanging pirates swung back towards us for another attempt at the quarterdeck.

I had to give their helmsman credit—whoever they were, they knew their trade well. That lumbering vessel shouldn't have had a Fool's chance of matching our smaller ship's manoeuvrability in this canyon. I greatly suspected some zealous northern pilot was behind the wheel, torturing the ship into complying with their erratic desires.

I barely urged us out of the way this time, leaving another wide gap between us and the boarders. The crew defending the *Rose*'s quarterdeck took another few shots, taking advantage of the airborne pirates' lack of cover. Once the boarders landed, they would be far more difficult targets.

My best bet was to maintain our speed while we searched for a branch off the canyon through which the larger *Revenge* couldn't follow us. For the time being, that meant playing cat and mouse with the ship above us. I had some backup plans in place, of course—but they were risky enough that I wanted to *keep* them as backup plans, if at all possible.

As we came around the next bend, I decided to test the *Revenge*'s daring helmsman. I slipped the *Rose* as near as I could to the canyon wall—this time, as the *Revenge* swerved to follow suit, it clipped the edge of the rock face. Sparks flew from its hull, and chunks of stone showered down into the canyon. A few of the suspended raiders lost their lines, but most held fast.

The mountain, however, gave a dreadful growl.

The sound was so loud and deep, it made my bones tremble. Stone shifted and clattered into the surrounding canyon. Far behind us, a section of mountainside began to shake off loose dirt and snow. Were I not terrified of being crushed like a bug, I might have felt a pang of sympathy for the mountain that merely wanted to catch a few more winks.

The *Revenge* ignored the warning sound and gave another burst of speed. It was focused on our cargo, and nothing would dissuade it.

"Incoming!" someone shouted.

Pirates descended upon us, and the first ones began to land on the main deck and the rigging. I counted quickly, spotting a dozen that had managed the initial charge. Gunshots cracked, steel clashed, and the battle on the *Rose* began in earnest. Each of the pirates arrived with a belt of small canisters, which they tossed out blindly onto the deck. The flash bombs erupted one by one with harsh claps of thunder, deafening the crew and sending them off balance where they landed.

More boarders had swung in my direction, intent on taking the quarterdeck—and the helm, with it. I knew I had to free up my hands if I was going to help my crew defend it.

"Syrene!" I shouted. "Take the wheel!"

I stepped away and yanked my sawed-off blunderbuss from the sling along my leg, trusting that Syrene would seize the helm and fly us straight in my absence. Out of the corner of my eye, I saw the wheel correct itself as the faerie that had melded with my ship took control of it.

My crew fired at the *Revenge*'s boarders as they swung in to land. Two of them thudded down onto the deck, only a short distance away from me. I leapt for cover behind the mast, just before the pair of advancing Reavers got off shots at me with their pistols. Bullets chewed the wood behind me and nipped at the hem of my poor, much-abused coat. I hauled my triple-barrelled blunderbuss up and leaned out of cover, pulling the trigger.

The sawed-off gun bucked in my hands with a peal of thunder, jarring my arms. My shot caught the first invader—a tall, broad-shouldered northern man—somewhere between his neck and his chest. The discharge spattered a bloody cravat across his front, and his body went limp. The pirate behind him, a fierce-looking woman with one of those crimson fighting braids, snatched up his body before it could hit the deck, using it for cover as she rushed me. I hefted my gun to hazard another shot—but something small and heavy knocked against my boot, and I glanced down at it instinctively.

An active flash bomb had rolled against my foot.

I heard it *tick-tick-tick* at my feet with a strange mechanical loudness. I scrambled backwards in a panic—but an instant later, my mind caught up with the situation, and I kicked the flash bomb desperately towards the advancing Reaver.

I threw an arm over my eyes just as the bright, thunderous detonation went off. The gesture did little to help me. My ears rang; black spots danced across my vision.

In between the floating blotches, I saw Little's imposing figure rushing past me, with his telescopic staff in hand. Little hammered the female pirate across the back of the head with a vicious slam. She reeled on her feet, dropping her comrade's body. Little hauled her unceremoniously towards the edge of the deck, shoving her against the railing—and then, with one ferocious boot to the chest, he sent her over the side.

Another of the pirates on the quarterdeck rushed Little from behind. The balding, red-splashed northerner raised a boarding axe, aiming for my first mate's back. I tried to shout a warning—but with my ears still ringing and the general din of the battle still raging, I couldn't tell whether Little had heard it.

Little hadn't waded in alone, however. Evie rocketed past me next, deflecting the boarding axe with a deft unarmed manoeuvre. The halcyon slammed his other fist into the pirate's solar plexus, driving the breath from his lungs. As the other man staggered back, Evie brought his heel down onto his enemy's knee from the side. The resulting snap of bone and the man's rasping scream earned an instinctive wince from me. Evie grabbed the pirate's head and drove it into his knee with enough force that the scoundrel flopped backward, with his eyes rolled up into his head.

Halcyons of the Benefactor were forbidden from killing... but some of them could still make a man regret his life choices in a hurry.

Little turned, belatedly noticing the neutralised threat. The three of us shared a moment of mutual gratitude—but with the fighting still going on below, it had to be brief.

"You two!" I yelled at them, uncertain of my own volume. "Main deck!" I pointed emphatically down the stairs, since I couldn't hear myself. "We're fine here, help *there!*"

Evie nodded at me, yelling back something which I couldn't quite hear. He and Little whirled down the stairs to join the larger battle that still raged.

Thankfully, my bosun was earning his keep. Even half-deaf, I could hear his booming voice as it cut through the noise of battle. Strahl had long since spent his pistols; he'd now switched to using the bayonet on the end of his heavy blunderbuster, slashing viciously through the growing number of pirates on deck. Somewhere during the fighting, Strahl had lost his helmet. Splashes of crimson blood now clashed against his blue-veined, ghastly white mien, making him look like a vengeful faerie spirit born from the depths of Arcadia itself. Unlike Evie, Strahl had no compunctions about sending others to tell their tales to Death Victorious.

One of the Reavers dropped from the rigging, slamming into my bosun. By sheer brutal accident, Strahl's bayonet struck the surprised-looking brigand in the chest, even as the two of them went down in a heap. Strahl fumbled for the blood-slicked grip, trying to dislodge his blunderbuss's bayonet from the dying man's body—but another Reaver took advantage of the pause to tackle my bosun, shoving him away from his weapon. Strahl was a bit more solid than the pirate was expecting; he stumbled back a few steps, rather than hitting the deck, then slammed one gauntlet into the Reaver's face.

The two men stumbled apart, desperate to regain their bearings. The pirate recovered first, rushing in to swing at Strahl with a rusty-looking sabre—but Strahl turned to take the blow upon one of his mismatched bits of armour. My bosun then surged forward like a tidal wave, drawing the large blade he carried over his shoulder and bringing it down in a double-handed swing.

The pirate tried to slap the sword aside with his sabre—but Strahl's stolen aethermancer's blade tore through the sabre with uncanny momentum, and I saw that he had activated its aetheric battery. Strahl's sword glowed red hot, as though pulled from a forge. It caught the Reaver just under the chin. Blood hissed and steamed as it burned along the hot blade. Another splash of red caught Strahl across his ashen face, and he grimaced, reaching up instinctively to wipe it from his eyes.

Strahl had now become an object of terrifying interest to the pirates; though he was undoubtedly dangerous, he was also wearing heavy armour, and they hadn't given him much time to catch his breath. Another pirate turned to close the distance between them, and I cursed my position on the quarterdeck. There was no way I could assist with my blunderbuss, given its spread—it was meant for short-range stopping power.

The dead man closest to me still had a gun, though. I turned to snatch the weapon from him, quickly checking the chamber. The two-shot heavy pistol had one bullet left. I returned my attention to the main deck and took careful aim.

The pirate closing in on Strahl jerked as my shot clipped him. The opportunistic jab of his cutlass went wide. Though Strahl was undoubtedly still recovering his breath, he took advantage of the opening with a heavy swing of that burning sword, which connected hard enough to put the Reaver down. Strahl jerked a brief nod in my direction, and I saw that the fight on the main deck had finally turned in our favour. My crew had taken back control.

Unfortunately—as we very soon realised—the Reavers had just been distracting us with cannon fodder.

A hum slowly grew upon the air, setting my teeth on edge. Shadows flickered across the deck, and I glanced up warily at their source. While we were busy, the *Revenge* had sent out longboats manned by ruthless, armoured veterans. Three of those vessels now descended for the *Rose* like falling bricks. There were ashen-grey northern hobgoblins among the new boarding parties, and a few Reavers who sported deadly mechanical limbs—no doubt properly earned in place of those they'd lost in battle.

Of course, I'd planned a few surprises of my own.

One of those imposing longboats was destined never to reach us. Another smaller craft crossed above it, casting a brief shadow across the pirates there. I'd sent out Lenore and her marines before the pirates closed in on us, instructing my gunnery chief to choose her moment. Several distant cracks broke the air, as the marines started taking shots at the pirates below with their rifles. Lenore's slim figure leaned over the side of that relatively tiny longboat, tossing something overboard.

That *something* turned out to be an entire satchel of grenades.

The pirates realised their danger an instant too late. The resulting explosion tore apart the armoured longboat. The vehicle careened drunkenly for a moment, scraping painfully across the side of the canyon—before plummeting down to its ultimate doom.

The mountain growled again. It sounded *very* displeased. The canyon was beginning to feel decidedly unfriendly.

I wanted to worry more about that—but the two remaining pirate longboats felt slightly more pressing. One surged towards the *Rose*. The other noted Lenore and the marines and changed course to angle towards them, opening fire with a heavy repeater to drive them off. The *Revenge* chuffed and roared above us, belching horrendous clouds of smoke from its howling aether drive.

Briefly, I wished for Dougal's nimble outflyer—but I'd told him to hang back for good reason. Even an ace pilot could only do so much with a damaged vessel. The *Rose* was just going to have to fend for itself.

The pirate longboat headed for the *Rose* passed over our stern, just next to me. I shoved my stolen pistol hurriedly into my coat, intent on retrieving my blunderbuster—but a heavy repeater mounted on top of the longboat swung in the direction of the quarterdeck then, and the bottom fell out of my stomach.

"Gunner!" I screamed—but the weapon's monstrous roar drowned out the word. I dived behind the only cover available on the quarterdeck; the mast nearest to me. The *Revenge*'s gunner opened fire with indiscriminate glee. Rigging snapped; woodchips sprayed into the air. Bullets tore through members of my crew and the first wave of Reavers alike.

The thundering gunfire seemed to go on forever, as I pressed my back to the mast... but in reality, it was probably mere seconds. The barking gun abruptly halted; heavy bootfalls followed, as the pirates disembarked to take advantage of the cleared quarterdeck. I dared a glance and saw that well over a dozen bodies now littered the deck—friend and foe alike. A few of them still writhed in pain. A greater number were far too still.

In the space of an instant, I was the only defender left on the quarterdeck.

The new Reavers on the quarterdeck split their forces—some moved to secure the stairs to the main deck, while others joined the battle there. A few used the high ground to take shots into the melee below. The longboat's gunner—satisfied with his grisly work—turned his attention back to the skies in order to fire upon Miss Brighton's harried longboat.

A pair of veteran pirates thudded onto the deck nearby. One—a leathery skinned, heavy-set northern man—had foregone the others' heavy armour in favour of dark goggles and a battered old coat. The other—a stockier hobgoblin woman in rust-red armour and crimson war paint—stole most of my attention; she looked as though she could have easily won a wrestling match with my bosun.

I tossed my hat aside, praying that the winds wouldn't take it from me—then turned and aimed my recovered blunderbuster at the hobgoblin woman.

The firearm bucked in my grip—but the woman moved at the last moment, and my shot went tragically wide, clipping her left side. Her resulting snarl looked more like a fierce smile than a grimace. The man with her was still drawing his pistols as I left cover, but the woman didn't bother going for any of the firearms she wore at her side; she barrelled directly at me, forcing me into a panicked backpedal as I cracked open my blunderbuster to feed it new shells, cursing myself for not having reloaded earlier.

As it turned out, however, there was at least *one* other defender left on the quarterdeck.

Wood creaked and groaned around us. The heavy-set woman staggered heavily partway through her charge—and slammed face-first into the deck. Her head made a loud *thunk* as it bounced off the planks.

I didn't wonder what had happened; I'd had Syrene on board long enough to recognise her work.

The woman struggled to right herself, with blood dripping down her nose—but the wood of the deck clung to her like mud, sucking at her feet with every step. She flailed to pull herself free, confused at the resistance and unable to see what had grabbed her.

Unnatural, chiming laughter echoed softly on the wind. To a creature like Syrene, the chaotic violence on deck probably seemed like good, clean fun.

"May the Everbright bless you, Syrene," I gasped out. I chambered the last shell in the blunderbuster and snapped it shut. I raised my firearm to take aim at the inconvenienced hobgoblin woman—just before a bullet whizzed past my ear.

The northern man with her had barely missed me the first time—but his second shot clipped my right shoulder, jarring my blunderbuster's aim down towards the deck. I clutched at the fresh injury, staggering back... and found myself staring down the barrel of an enemy gun.

The male pirate's pistol was aimed squarely at my face.

I dropped my blunderbuster and lifted my hands slowly. It was hard to make out the man's expression behind those dark goggles... but his yellow, gap-toothed smile told me that he had every intention of firing on me.

"Where's yer cap'n gone, gob?" he spat at me.

I stared at him for a moment, dumbfounded.

The slur 'gob' didn't faze me in the way that it normally would have done, compared to the gun in my face. No—it was the slow, dawning realisation that neither of these pirates knew I was the captain of this ship. They'd mistaken me for a *deckhand*, solely because I was a goblin.

I am not, as a rule, very fond of goblin stereotypes. But sometimes, when an enemy has his firearm pointed right between your eyes, it's worth stifling your indignation and catering to people's mistaken prejudices.

I threw both hands higher into the air. "Cap'n is dead!" I yelled hastily. I kept running my mouth on pure instinct, aware that he might pull the trigger and move on if he thought I was of no further use to him. "Krig surrenders! Krig gives you engine sequence!" I dug into the goblin cant of my youth, uniquely identifiable for the way its speakers refer to themselves by name. It had been far too long since I'd last been in Morgause, and I knew my Coalditch accent was slightly *off*—but there weren't any other goblins on this ship right now, and the pirates weren't familiar enough with Coalditch to pick out the oddities. Between the cant and my horrifically tattered coat, I presented a convincing picture of some desperate lower-class scab from Morgause, hired to swab the deck.

The bearded pirate's yellow grin widened at my apparent capitulation, though he kept his gun carefully trained upon me.

The ship swerved minutely—then righted itself. Syrene had been forced to take back the wheel. The deck finally released the heavy-set woman next to us; she clambered to her feet with a spooked expression. "Somethin' unnatural about this ship, Cap'n Griever," she hissed, wiping at her bloody nose. "Let's kill 'eh gob an' get this air wae."

I stared at Captain Griever and his gun, holding my breath. "Nah," he said. "Gobs can be useful. Ain't ye useful, gob?" He diverted his pistol from me, gesturing it towards the longhorn. "Get on th'longhorn an' gie them engine boys the good word," he ordered me. He glanced sideways at the hobgoblin woman. "Man the 'elm. We're takin' the whole ship."

Gears worked furiously in my head. I needed a decisive change in fortune if I was going to escape these two without a weapon in hand. I still had my hand axe, but they'd riddle me with holes long before I reached them with it. I shuffled across the deck towards the longhorn, doing my best to project a terrified obeisance as I pulled down the chatterbox and changed its frequency to match Dougal MacLeod's outflyer.

"Calling engine room!" I said into the chatterbox. "Cap'n says slow down! Slow the engine down!"

"What?" Dougal's voice crackled back, momentarily confused.

"The captain is *busy!*" I emphasised. I flicked my fingers over the device, tapping the button that opened and closed the line. Three short bursts, followed by three long ones, capped with another three short ones: an SOS. "Cap'n says: Stop what you're doing right now!"

A lengthy pause followed. Sweat trickled uncomfortably down my spine.

In another life, I'd have made an excellent actor.

The hobgoblin woman cursed loudly behind me. "Wheel willnae move, Cap'n!" she gritted through her teeth. She tugged fruitlessly at the helm, which resisted even her impressively bulging muscles. "What've they done tae it?"

Dougal chuckled suddenly. I heard a familiar sound in the air above us, drawing steadily closer. *"S'a good thing ah was already on ma way back then,"* he said. *"By the way... Ah'd duck."*

I blinked—and then, very sedately, I turned towards Griever, offering out the receiver. "For you," I offered.

The pirate frowned and took the chatterbox from me.

The moment he did, I took off sprinting. I vaulted over the bannister, landing heavily on the main deck—just as Dougal's battle-scarred, gull-winged ship dived at the *Rose*.

The outflyer's engines screamed defiance as the aether-powered forward guns snapped off three short bursts of aetheric rounds, each with its own sharp report. The first burst howled wide, sweeping past the ship entirely. The second caught Griever in the shoulder, snapping him upright. The third slapped into his chest with enough force to pluck him from the deck and send him tumbling off my ship. Dougal's outflyer finished its pass over the ship, barely twisting aside to avoid the canyon wall.

The hobgoblin had taken cover behind the wheel—but now, she snarled with fury, abandoning the helm. She grabbed her fallen captain's pistol, turning it in my direction.

But my view of the hobgoblin was suddenly obstructed.

Syrene rose up between us, forming her body once again from the bloody deck. Her wooden flesh dripped with scarlet; the halo of lavender which made up her hair freed itself from the braids on her head, snapping like a nest of serpents. The wind rose sharply, howling around her with otherworldly fury. That palpable rage spread to everyone in her immediate vicinity. Syrene's utterly expressionless, inhuman countenance bore into the pirate woman.

In a staring competition, my money was on the faerie.

The woman shrieked and scrambled back in raw terror. Her fear rippled out, spreading through the other pirates in a chorus of horror. Syrene's will pressed around us with a dreadful intensity. Even I found myself taking a step back.

The gunner on the longboat swung the mounted repeater around in a fit of panic, opening fire on Syrene. There was no experience or finesse involved—no disciplined, steady burst-fire. Instead, the pirate unloaded the weapon's top-mounted drum completely, desperate to destroy the creature in front of him.

Bullets struck Syrene—but her wooden body didn't chip or splinter. Instead, each bullet struck with a staccato *tock*, embedding into Syrene's trunk-like form with little to no effect... until finally, the gun clicked empty.

Syrene levelled her unblinking gaze on the wide-eyed gunner and his pilot. *Leave,* was the message that she radiated.

She did not need to voice the sentiment aloud.

Between the death of their captain and the sudden arrival of that bloody apparition, the pirates' morale shattered. The most sensible ones were already fleeing back to their longboats. The hobgoblin woman on the quarterdeck chose the better part of valour and scrambled to join them. The closest longboat turned to flee in a blind panic—leaving its dead and wounded behind without so much as a second thought.

Syrene watched them go, with blood still dripping from her branch-like fingers. Beneath the howling winds that surrounded her, I heard a slight stutter in Dougal's outflyer.

Now that the northerner's ship was closer, I could see that he'd damaged his wing and cracked his viewport—presumably in his initial skirmish with the *Revenge*. Even so, Dougal flipped the outflyer about in an impressive manoeuvre, skirting towards the longboat that still plagued Lenore and the marines. The armoured boat hurriedly switched targets, returning small-arms fire. Dougal danced around the longboat and let loose a torrent of aether. The volley ripped apart the enemy longboat's starboard engine in a fiery burst.

The *Rose*'s crew cheered in triumph. A vindictive satisfaction rose within me, matching the sound, as I realised that the gunner who'd mowed down my crew was dead—but I had no intention of standing by while the rest of the pirates escaped.

I hurried up the steps of the quarterdeck towards the longhorn, dialling in Dougal's frequency; it picked up in a matter of seconds.

"Already on your way back, eh?" I said. I tried to sound cross with him—but the words came out relieved instead. "I ordered you to stay back until signalled."

"Ye dinnae pay me tae follow silly orders, lad," the veteran pilot replied smugly. *"Ah've got yer six."*

I grinned. "They've overextended themselves, don't you think?" I observed. "Rip 'em apart, MacLeod."

"Don't mind if ah do," Dougal said.

The northerner pivoted away, angling his outflyer to begin an attack run at the *Revenge*'s unprotected engines. A chattering burst of aether lit the valley, tearing at the *Revenge*'s aft. Dougal's aetheric guns weren't enough to cause any serious damage to that thick armour plating, but the engines on the *Revenge* still coughed and began to make strange, unpleasant sounds amidst the rest of their screeching.

Dougal pulled up just enough to flirt with the top deck of the *Revenge*. Shots that had been only marginally effective against the ship's hull were far more devastating against the crew. He finished his pass, twisting to fly between the canyon wall and the *Revenge* at a nerve-wracking angle and speed. I held my breath as I watched—but he barely made the gap. Dougal continued his flight safely past the damaged pirate ship, just as the remaining crew scrambled to reorient their guns towards him. They took a few wild shots his way—but I heard his laughter over the channel as they missed by great lengths.

I took some altitude with the *Rose* as the *Revenge* slowed. Syrene claimed the wheel as we levelled out, and I stepped aside to pull my spyglass, surveying the state of the *Revenge*. I soon realised just why the pirates hadn't altered their trajectory: MacLeod's strafing run had ripped the main deck apart, and the quarterdeck was a shredded mess. I saw the helmsman's corpse slumped over the ruined wheel.

By now, the *Revenge* was in the throes of panic, with its captain dead and its chain of command in tatters. Lenore's boat sidled along the *Revenge*, reminding the brigands that turnabout was fair play. She and the marines opened fire on the remaining pirates. My gunnery chief led the charge, felling another brigand with every shot of her rifle. Lenore and her people boarded the ship with ruthless efficiency —but their ultimate target wasn't the pirates onboard. Instead, they made a daring run for the cannons on the main deck of the *Revenge*. Very soon, their true objective became clear.

The gunnery ladies knew very well how to work a ship's cannons. The *Revenge*'s main guns popped and roared, one by one—all aimed with perfect precision at the canyon wall.

It wasn't a full broadside. But it was enough to thoroughly piss off a mountain.

Lenore and the marines bolted for their longboat, hooting and laughing. Dougal flipped back around to lend them cover fire, and I heard his own triumphant whooping in my ear over the longhorn.

I spun the *Rose*'s wheel, frantically navigating us away from the hobbled *Revenge* and its immediate vicinity. Lenore and the marines sped back towards me in their longboat, haphazardly pulling in to dock.

Great cheers went up as my gunnery chief came back aboard. I yanked the lever beside me, commanding Mr Finch to give us more speed. The deck rumbled beneath my feet; the sails snapped forward, and the aether took us upward. I pushed the *Iron Rose* as quickly as I could. I didn't dare let us dwell in the canyon with the pirate ship.

With morbid fascination, and no small sensation of vindication, I looked over my shoulder to the doomed *Revenge* and its crew.

A rumbling avalanche began on Ironspine's slopes—a furious cloud of earth, stone, and exposed iron. The thunder of the avalanche soon morphed into a hungry and terrible howl; as I watched, the cloud shifted into a great wolf the size of the *Rose*. The earthen creature leapt from the edge of the canyon, catching the *Revenge* in its rusted iron jaws like a faltering bird and bearing it down onto the mountainside. Ironspine's rusty teeth savaged the ship's metal bones, seeking the aether-powered heart inside.

The *Red Reaver's Revenge* would find revenge no more.

I took us out to open skies, more shaken by Ironspine's howling than I dared to show. The fate of the *Revenge* could so easily have been our own... but for today, at least, the Lady of Fools had favoured us.

Far behind us, there came a hollow explosion and a great roar, as Ironspine's teeth closed upon the ship's engine.

An uncanny nausea followed that explosion. Ironspine's victorious howl turned to one of sudden agony; all around me, the crew staggered and moaned. A few people ran for the railing to vomit over the side of the ship. The winds that still surrounded Syrene let out a shriek of terror, and I saw the faerie double over in pain.

I had seen more than my fair share of aether engines detonate during my time in the Sundering War. None of those engines had ever exploded like this. The hulking wreck of the *Revenge* spilled forward into the canyon; its rusty hull splintered like cheap kindling. That hull ruptured into an oily mess—a sickening black cloud that rippled through the air like spilled ink.

The true horror was the effect of that strange discharge on Ironspine. The mountain's snout and jaw sloughed off like mud, eroding away at the touch of the black substance. Ironspine writhed in pain, slamming itself against the canyon walls in an attempt to wipe the black spots from its body. None of its efforts seemed to do any good; the great creature now looked like a barghest rotted with mange. Even as I watched, Ironspine melded back into the earth, searching for an escape.

But the mountain continued to buck and moan.

I forced us to take more altitude—as much as we could afford. Avalanches wracked the mountainside. Behind us, a black scar ate at the land, withering trees as it grew. Syrene's fear and horror radiated at the rest of *Rose*'s crew like heat from a small sun.

Finally, the mountain fell utterly silent. All that remained was the creaking of the rigging and the lonely howling of the wind.

I staggered to my feet and turned towards our navigator. "Syrene," I croaked out. "What—"

The faerie was already gone from sight.

The *Rose* faltered in the air, and I realised that Syrene had ceased piloting. I leapt for the helm to steady the wheel, shoving down the fear and queasiness that still lingered in my veins.

Never in my life had I heard of a faerie being *afraid*. I hadn't really believed that it was possible.

In the following moments, the rest of reality came crashing down upon me. My body trembled. The cries of the wounded and dying on the deck filled my ears. It was hard to distinguish between the voices of my own people and those of the wounded pirates the *Revenge* had left behind. Crew rushed the quarterdeck, sifting through the wounded savaged by the *Revenge*'s gunner in the hopes of finding some still alive.

Little made his way towards me. He'd tied up a nasty cut on his upper arm with Evie's neckcloth. His nose was plainly broken, and blood had long since drenched through the makeshift bandage. He signalled slowly and painfully with both hands.

You all right, Captain? he asked.

"Perfectly fine, Mr Little," I said. I forced a smile over my shivers.

I could tell that Little dearly wanted to ask about the ruckus below —but Little was a man of action, and there were practical, immediate concerns on our plate.

The enemy crew? he asked me.

"A bullet or the brig," I told him. I paused. "We'll want to keep at least one to ask some questions about this mess."

Little nodded—though he paused a moment later and flashed his bloody hands. *Cutting it a little close with MacLeod, weren't we?* I saw concern clear upon his face.

"All part of the plan, Mr Little," I assured him. It wasn't *entirely* a lie.

After a few seconds of my confident, unwavering smile, Little seemed to accept the answer.

"Be a good man and see the wounded to Physicker Holloway, will you?" I asked.

Little nodded. He paused as he turned though, looking behind us towards the stretch of blackened earth that wounded the Ironspine's slopes. *Any idea what that was about?* he asked finally.

"No idea," I confided. I clapped him on his good shoulder, doing my best to sound unbothered. "Best we focus on the here and now. We'll scratch our heads over that little detail later."

Little tore his eyes away from the Ironspine. He forced a nod and a half-smile, despite his pain. If I wasn't terrified about the fate of the *Revenge*, then surely, Little didn't need to be terrified either.

As I said before: In another life, I would have made an excellent actor.

* * *

SYRENE'S FEAR stayed with us all the way to New Havenshire. Normally, Strahl had an uncharacteristic way with the faerie—surely due to their mysterious bond, and not due to his dubious personality—but even he found it impossible to lure Syrene out of the ship. Eventually, he gave up.

"Might as well try to command the Four Winds," Strahl told me. "She'll come out when she's ready. Probably for the best, given the mood she's in."

I nodded uneasily. As unnerved as I was by recent events, the last thing we needed on top of everything else was a confrontation with an unstable faerie.

"Not a single word about that strange engine," Lenore announced, stomping her way up to the quarterdeck. Her scowl could have melted steel. "Those pirates are either more petrified of Red Reaver than they are of us, or else they really haven't got a clue. They said if anyone had answers, it would be Captain Griever."

I glanced towards the railing, where Griever had gone overboard. "Oops," I muttered.

Behind us, Dougal's outflyer still bobbed along, backlit by the late afternoon sun. He followed us at a light engine burn, trying to protect what was left of his wing's dubious integrity. I'd tried to argue Dougal into docking back onto the *Rose*, but he'd stubbornly refused. The *Revenge* might have other friends nearby, he'd said, and he wanted to keep a vigilant eye out for them. There was no reasoning with Dougal once he dug in his heels, so I'd given up the fight and slowed down the *Rose* to match his outflyer.

As we entered New Havenshire's airspace, Evie picked up the longhorn to speak to the port authority. He sent word to have a physicker and some lawmen waiting for us at our designated landing area—the former to help with the wounded and the latter to remove our unwanted guests from the brig. Our destination was the massive two-tiered bluff where the airfield was nestled; a lone watchtower, perched on the higher tier, afforded the port authority a commanding view to guide us along. The snow-capped watchtower glistened in the sunlight, high above New Havenshire's sprawl.

I took us in for a graceful landing on the dock, settling the *Rose* onto one side of the U-shaped wooden pier.

"Why, um, thank you," Evie said on the longhorn. "That's... that's very kind of you, Dougal. I'll see you shortly." His expression was perplexed. Evie held the chatterbox out towards me. "It's Dougal, Captain," he said.

I winced and pried my fingers away from the wheel. I'd had my hands on it for so long now that my fingers felt as though they'd frozen into claws. I massaged a few times at them, then plucked the chatterbox from Evie's hand, pressing the receiver to my ear.

"There's the hero of the hour!" I declared with gusto. "We've got a lovely airfield waiting for you, MacLeod. And I think I owe you a few more drinks, after all that fancy flying."

I was met with windy silence.

I knew the line was open—I could hear the rattling engine and the sharp whistle of wind from the cracked cockpit's canopy. "Dougal?" I asked carefully.

Finally, I heard the creak of his seat. I turned to watch the outflyer dip and bob against the sun, flying towards the airfield.

"Sorry, Cap'n," Dougal slurred. *"Just a bit tired, s'all."*

Something was wrong. I suspected I knew what it was.

"You were hit," I said finally. "Weren't you?"

Dougal chuckled. The sound was a pale imitation of the vibrant, deafening laughter that always made my ears ring. Evie stared at me; worry dawned upon his features as he listened on.

"You stubborn, airheaded *idiot!*" I snapped. The fear that pounded through my pulse manifested as fury.

"Cap'n—" Dougal protested.

"How bad is it?" I snarled, as the outflyer began its wobbling descent. The people at the airfield immediately saw that something wasn't right. Already they scurried aside, fearing that the ship would crash.

"Hard tae say, lad," Dougal mumbled.

"Holloway!" I bellowed.

The crew had noticed Dougal's drunken flying as he descended for the landing strip. A few glanced my way as I raised my voice at him. Evie hurried to the railing—his eyes were wide, and his breathing was quick. Fervent prayers stumbled from his lips as he went.

"Dougal, you listen to me," I said sternly.

"Never was good at that," Dougal chuckled hoarsely.

"Damn it, MacLeod—" I stammered.

"Ah was thinkin' the day, lad," Dougal said softly, *"Ah'm glad ah did what ah did. Ye turned out just fine. Thought ye ought tae know that."*

Tears welled in my eyes. I slammed the chatterbox onto the longhorn with a violent clatter. I took the steps to the deck two at a time, searching for my ship's physicker.

Holloway was still kneeling on the blood-soaked deck, stitching up the injured. He hadn't yet noticed the ruckus with Dougal's outflyer.

"Holloway!" I shouted. The fear in my voice cut through his focus. The physicker snapped his one-eyed, monocled gaze towards me. He only needed one look at my face. Holloway snatched up his valise and hurried towards me.

Evie came hot on my heels—but I whirled on him, speaking with more venom than I should have. "No!" I snapped. "I don't need a damned priest!" I gestured at my bosun. "Strahl, get over here! Little—the ship's yours!"

I dimly registered the injury on Evie's face and the anger in Little's expression—but just for the moment, I didn't care. I fired up the engines of the longboat, just as Strahl and Holloway leapt aboard. I sped us forward so sharply that the other two stumbled, clutching the sides of the longboat for dear life.

"Don't you dare," I muttered, rushing us towards the landing strip. "Don't you *dare* do this to me, MacLeod!"

Dougal's outflyer dipped towards the airfield's runway—but the landing gear lowered too late. The ship hit the hard-packed earth with a rude bounce, nearly nose-first; the prop on the nose snapped where the blades clipped the earth. The outflyer belatedly corrected itself and landed on its belly once more, but the damaged wing snapped off as it slid to the end of its landing. Slowly, the ship spun to a halt.

I landed the boat as close as I could, leaping out towards the fallen craft. I don't remember calling out Dougal's name as I approached—though it would explain why my throat hurt so much.

I clambered haphazardly over the wreckage. Inside the cockpit, I saw the pilot slumped in his seat; the inside of the ship was badly scored by the damage of Dougal's first firefight with the *Revenge*. I took my hand axe to the canopy, striking at the damaged joint that kept the ship closed off—but my strength was only enough to dent at the metal.

Strahl yanked me aside with powerful hands. He slammed a pry bar into the joint with violent precision. The veins in his neck bulged as he leaned upon the bar, until the hatch gave way with a final snap. Strahl cast aside the length of iron and shoved the canopy open, waving away the fumes that had filled the interior.

Holloway rushed past me. As he caught sight of the cockpit, he and Strahl shared a dreadful look. The hobgoblin squeezed himself just far enough inside to reach a hand down, pressing fingers to the underside of Dougal's chin to search for a pulse. His shoulders sank, and my heart lurched in my chest. I tried to surge forward, but Strahl intercepted me with a firm hand on my chest.

"Cap'n," he said calmly. "He's—"

I punched him in the nose.

Strahl stepped back, more surprised than injured. In fact, I *knew* I'd hurt my fist more than I'd hurt his face, but I didn't care. I shoved past him and clambered past Holloway, climbing onto the one unbroken wing to look into the cockpit.

There sat Dougal MacLeod, his beaten old coat and proud golden kerchief spattered with blood. His comfortable gut had been punched through with debris from an unlucky hit. What skin I could see beneath his goggles and his mane of white-streaked red hair was deathly pale—but there was still a smile frozen on his lips.

My eyes fogged with tears. A mewling sound coughed out of me. I reached out to shake his shoulder several times. But I knew that he would never wake up.

"Damn it, MacLeod," I whispered.

4

THE RIGHT HAT - SAINT EVERETT - THE UNWELCOMING COMMITTEE

"He was dead before he hit the strip, Captain. Judging by the bleeding."

Long after the others had dragged me back to the *Rose*, I was still in a state of numbness. For the general safety of everyone's spirits, I had allowed Physicker Holloway to take me captive, though he was forced to sit me in a corner of the infirmary for a few more hours as he tended to other people's more life-threatening injuries. I barely noticed the passing of time.

The corpse of my coat hung on a peg nearby as Holloway's deceptively gentle, calloused hands cleaned my wounded shoulder and patched it up. Fortunately, the bullet had glanced off the bone there, rather than shattering it.

I remembered the first time I'd found myself in this position, sitting at the edge of a cot with the physicker towering over me. I was just a cabin boy then, desperate to earn the world's respect by way of my uniform... but by the blue skies, I wanted to be *just* like Holloway one day. There was something about the hobgoblin—so large, gentle, *educated*. Somehow, he had transcended the stigmas associated with his race, becoming recognised for his skill and dedication. When he spoke, others *listened*.

"Captain," Holloway said again.

As I said. *Others* listened.

I blinked and looked his way. Holloway had barely changed since that dreadful day above the capital. Certainly, his coal-black hair had given way to great swells of natural silver, but this had only added to his existing air of distinction. Holloway's left eye was now a milky pool of white, and he'd traded his spectacles for a cunning monocle, which currently dangled from the chain attached to his vest pocket.

The surrounding room was nothing like the expensive, elaborate sickbay we'd had aboard an Imperial ship of the line. But it was neat. Pristine. Organised.

Safe.

Holloway gave a disappointed sigh and fixed me with the sort of look that never failed to turn me back into a cabin boy.

"We should have—" I began.

"I'm going to stop you right there," Holloway interrupted me.

An ugly little beast had burrowed its way into my heart, tearing away at the softness within it and filling it instead with ill humours. That beast snarled and reared up to lash out—but the open heartache on Holloway's scarred, aged face stopped it cold.

That bitter, complicated grief was a mirror to my own. I couldn't rage against it.

"Dougal MacLeod did whatever he pleased on this ship," Holloway said softly. "You'd never dare to give him a real order, and he knew that." His voice was thick, but curiously steady. "Every choice he made up until today was just that—his choice. If he'd wanted to live a safe life, he'd have stayed in Pelaeia."

My stomach churned with sickness at the words, though I knew they should have been comforting.

"I took the job," I whispered. "I knew it was dangerous, I *knew*—"

"And so did the rest of us," Holloway said. "Everyone here knows what Ironspine does to ships. We rolled the dice. The Lady of Fools loves you, Wil... but even you can't win every gamble." He smiled painfully. "But more importantly... you're not the only one upset right now."

Holloway kept looking at me, silent and patient. I knew his expression was meant to imply something, but I wasn't a mind reader. And I was in no state to—

No. I *knew* what he wanted. He wanted me to apologise to Evie.

I almost opened my mouth to defend myself with an ill-conceived excuse... but I knew in my heart that I had done wrong, and that there was no point in trying to fool either of us.

Even as I brooded on the idea, I became aware of a different low-key panic clutching at my heart. I'd ordered Evie and Little off the quarterdeck *right* before the pirates' gunner had opened fire. Had I made a slightly different choice—had I delayed just a bit too long—I would be mourning two extra people right now.

I hopped stiffly off the edge of the cot, slipped on my mess of a shirt, and grabbed my battered coat from the nearby peg. I failed twice to put my left arm through the correct hole in the sleeve before I finally managed it.

"You're right," I mumbled. "Of course you're right."

Holloway's smile turned oddly misty. He patted me gently on my uninjured shoulder. "You're a good lad, Wil," he murmured.

My throat closed up at the observation. I remembered Dougal's last words to me, over the longhorn. *Ye turned out just fine,* he'd said. The hobgoblin in front of me would have understood just how awful and how comforting those words were.

It was hard to feel right now as though I'd turned out fine. But Dougal had made a point of reassuring me that I had his good opinion —and so, the only recourse left to me was to be exactly the sort of person Dougal thought I was. That sort of person would face down his mistakes with honesty and humility.

Holloway watched me as I turned to go. I thought he would leave it at that. But he interrupted me before I could open the door.

"Wil," he said softly. "If you need anything..."

The gentle offer made my heart twist in my chest once again. I wasn't sure, at first, how to respond. Part of me wasn't sure that I *could* respond without breaking down into tears. But even as I shook my head at Holloway, a stray thought tugged at my mind.

I couldn't remember the last time I had hugged Dougal.

Holloway was cleaning himself up and tucking away his effects. I walked back towards him. "Horace?" I said. His name was thick on my tongue.

He faced me again, with visible concern. "Yes, Wil?"

I threw my arms around him in a fierce hug, despite the burning pain of my wounded shoulder. I was keenly aware in that instant that Holloway could disappear from my life just as quickly as Dougal had done. *All* of them could disappear, without so much as a moment's notice.

Holloway stiffened with surprise. He was a man generally unaccustomed to obvious emotion. But soon, he wrapped his enormous arms around me and hugged me back.

✲ ✲ ✲

I wandered below deck for a time, asking after Evie. The answers I got sent me back topside on a merry chase. By the time I reached the main deck, I was right as rain—or so I kept telling myself. With my hat upon my head, I was a changed man. I was confident. Sure. Commanding. I had hit my stride once more.

With the right hat, anything is possible.

My crew had not been idle while Holloway administered to me. I found the cargo doors open; my crew had already begun to unload our precious containers onto the pier. Though night had fallen, something darker hung over the work—there was no laughing or singing, as I'd normally expect. My newly composed expression wavered a bit in the face of that stony silence.

As I approached, I heard Mr Finch's voice fretting as the crew raised the cargo from below. "Careful now, *careful!*" he called. "Are you certain the netting is safe? These are marked as extra-fragile!"

"We've got it under control, you bloody scarecrow," Strahl drawled back at Mr Finch. My bosun stood by the gangplank, looking over the damaged rigging. He kept one eye on the crew as they worked, though, acting as Little's voice when my first mate flashed his hands.

Little caught sight of me as I approached, and his hands slowed a step. He did *not* look happy with me. I knew I deserved that anger, to some extent, but I also found it tiring. Most of the time, Little was a very easy-going man—but on the few occasions where his anger got the better of him, he tended to bottle it up and avoid addressing the problem until it finally exploded. I was going to have to force the matter out into the open at some point. If I was lucky, Little would admit to being angry and accept an apology. If I was *less* fortunate, he'd assure me he was just fine, and I'd have to re-approach the conversation several times.

Not now, I thought. *We'll do the easy apology first.*

I headed over towards my chief engineer, intent on asking after Evie.

Mr Finch was a timeless creature—so much so that I believed he belonged in a museum. I never could determine his age, but I had ultimately decided that he must be somewhere in his thirties or forties. His hair was black as pitch, shot through with veins of gleaming silver white—though whether this was due to aether exposure or graceful ageing, I couldn't tell. Because Mr Finch insisted so often on wearing gloves, however, he'd managed to keep his sepia skin untouched by the bright blue veins that so often afflicted other aether engineers. His usual expression suggested that he was perpetually upon the edge of a headache, and he reserved the lines on his face solely for the act of scowling.

By some unknown art, the man remained eternally immaculate. I had never spotted so much as a mote of dust upon him, let alone the greasy stains one might normally expect from an engineer. This was partially because Mr Finch kept the engine room every bit as spotless as he kept himself. His jaw was always clean-shaven; the shaving mixture that he used left behind a faint smell of sandalwood. Mr Finch was the only fellow aboard the *Rose* to sport a proper morning coat—indeed, he had several. On this particular night, he'd paired his coat with a double-buttoned vest and dark gloves.

Mr Finch's piercing, grey-eyed gaze fell upon me. Shortly

thereafter, he turned about with an indignant sniff, clasping his hands behind his back.

I approached Strahl, careful to offer Little an extra bit of room. Still, I felt my first mate's stewing anger keenly upon my skin.

Excellent, I thought bleakly. *I've managed to upset a record number of my crew in the space of a single day.*

Strahl caught me watching Mr Finch's back. "Oh, it's not what you think," he said, with a faint grin. "Your little manoeuvres broke his new tea set."

I cringed. "You mean to say... the tea set I *just* bought him? To replace the *old* one that broke?"

Strahl nodded sagely. "Looks like you'll be needing to buy a replacement for your replacement," he observed.

I let loose a plaintive groan.

Down below us on the pier, dockworkers began unloading what they thought were crates of tea. This, more than anything, set my teeth on edge; though the crates were marked as extra-fragile, the workers had no idea the volatile stuff they were handling. Mr Finch wasn't entirely wrong to be worried. If just one canister were to shake loose and break, igniting the others... I shuddered at the thought.

I watched them work for a time, standing next to Strahl and Little. We were all eager to rid ourselves of our deadly cargo.

"MacLeod and his ship?" I asked the two men quietly.

The resulting pause stretched uncomfortably between us. Though Strahl and Dougal had managed to work together, there had always been a deep friction between them. There was a rule aboard my ship that no one was allowed to speak positively of the Avalon Imperium. Strahl had agreed to that rule, and I knew he truly believed that the Imperium was better off dead—but he still *felt* more like an Imperial soldier than the rest of us did. All of his stiff military habits grated constantly on Dougal's nerves in subtle ways.

I wasn't sure that Strahl would miss Dougal MacLeod. I shouldn't have *needed* him to miss Dougal—it didn't make sense that everyone on the ship would mourn the man equally. But the idea that Strahl might find the ship *more* pleasant without Dougal bothered me more than I wanted to let on.

Strahl coughed into his fist. "MacLeod's onboard, Cap'n," he replied. "Syrene's looking after him."

As soon as the last of the cargo is off, I'll get the outflyer on board and into the hold, Little signed. *Finch is already looking into how to disassemble it.*

A small bit of tension left my body at the reassurance. No matter how upset we all were, I knew I could trust my crew to see to Dougal. One way or another, we'd get his ship home so his clan could make use of the salvage.

As the dockworkers made it halfway through the next load of cargo, I remembered what I'd originally come topside for.

"I'm... um. I'm looking for Evie," I said finally. I tried to make it seem like a captainly question, but I knew I sounded chagrined. "I need to speak with him. Have either of you seen him?"

Strahl shook his head. Little fixed me with his dark-eyed gaze, behind which burned a well-deserved anger. His eyes weren't red-rimmed. No—those tears would come later, when the work was done.

Evie is on the pier, Little signed my way grudgingly. *He's talking to some woman.*

I flashed him a quick *thank you* with my hands. "As you were, gentlemen," I said aloud. I glanced towards my bosun. "Oh, and Strahl. About the, uh... about your nose." I winced as I remembered the crack of his nose beneath my knuckles.

Strahl scratched at his jaw. "Oh?" he asked idly. "It's fine. Physick says it's not broken. Just bumped it in the fight, Cap'n. Nothing to worry about."

I blinked. Before I could respond to the uncommon moment of charity, Strahl stepped away, heading down towards the hold to chat with the crew.

I glanced at Little, but he didn't seem to have noticed any strangeness in the exchange. In fact, my first mate had already turned away, settling his features back into a cool expression. I didn't relish the thought of the conversation I owed him—but we'd have it when time permitted.

I tipped my hat with a sigh and moved onwards. The gangplank rattled beneath my boot heels as I left the *Rose* behind.

Evening had now descended upon New Havenshire in earnest. A crisp wind danced across the top of the bluff—a pervasive chill that found all the holes in my coat and raised goosebumps along my flesh. The night sky was sharp here, with far more stars than fleeting clouds.

I found my halcyon under a row of flickering aetheric lanterns upon the pier. Evie was dressed in his formal best. He wore his fine blue coat—but he'd left it open to display the cerulean sash that marked him as a priest of the Benefactor, which meant that he'd probably been out plying his mercies again.

The moment I saw the woman he was chatting with, I knew that we were doomed.

Mercy was the Benefactor's greatest virtue, and Evie believed in it wholeheartedly. On a good day, the halcyon was already prone to picking up the first charitable cause to cross his path. But when Evie was feeling *particularly* wretched, his proclivity for mercy expanded. On those days, I could swear that Saint Everett Seymour went searching intentionally for the most pathetic sob story he could find.

Today, he had found a gem.

The distraught woman in front of Evie was smaller than average—even given my unimposing height, I suspected that she would come in a hair shorter than me if we were to stand side by side. This smallness made her seem even more wretched as she nursed her left arm, which was currently encased in a plaster cast and pinned to her chest in a sling. Her hair was a warm shade of chocolate brown, tied atop her head in a neat, well-woven bun. Though she was clearly in the younger part of her twenties, she wore a conservative, high-collared dress with a quaint cameo fastened at her pale throat. Despite the fact that she was forced by necessity to show the bare fingers of her broken arm, some silly, modest impulse had compelled her to wear one blue satin glove on her other hand.

I spied a carriage waiting a short distance behind her. The driver puffed away on a pipe, with his hat tipped over his face. Even as I watched, the woman dabbed at her watery eyes with a handkerchief and thanked Evie profusely.

The halcyon leaned forward to pat her gently on the shoulder, and I stifled a groan. There wouldn't be any talking him out of this one.

"Good evening, Halcyon," I said pleasantly. I marched up to the two of them. "Preaching His fair word even at this late hour?"

"Especially at this late hour," Evie replied, without skipping a beat. I met his eyes and saw there an absolute dearth of anger or judgement. Unlike Little, Evie had probably forgiven me the very instant after I'd snapped at him. The realisation only intensified my shame, especially as I noted his puffy eyes. "Captain," Evie said gently, "may I introduce you to the lovely Miss Hawkins."

I turned my attention to the woman next to him and took a deep breath. Evie might not have held a grudge against me—but I knew he'd just introduced me to his apology of choice.

"Cap... Captain?" Miss Hawkins stuttered. She pressed her other hand to her mouth belatedly, as though to cover her surprise.

I forced myself to swallow the sarcastic quip that threatened to escape me at that: *A goblin captain? Don't be absurd! I'm the ship's errand-boy.*

I shot Evie a long-suffering look, just to let him know how seriously I was taking this apology.

"Indeed, Miss Hawkins," I said loudly instead. "Captain William Blair of the *Iron Rose*, at your service." I swept my hat off my head with a flourish and offered a slightly exaggerated bow. I immediately regretted the gesture, as it reminded me sharply of my wounded shoulder.

I straightened once more, masking the pain with a smile that was more grimace than pleasure. I took a step towards the woman and offered out my hand. Miss Hawkins squirmed in place, eyeing my fingers with the sort of wariness most women reserved for spoiled food or skittering insects. She forced herself to smooth her features, however, and reached out to take my hand delicately. *Aren't you glad you're wearing a glove?* I thought at her acidly.

"Seeking passage aboard our craft, then?" I asked, with a cheer I didn't really feel.

"Y-yessir, Captain Blair, sir," Miss Hawkins stammered.

I held onto her hand a *bit* longer than was strictly necessary, just to see if she would snatch hers back... but Miss Hawkins kept her hand dutifully in mine until I let her go. I knew she was coming aboard, given Evie's interest in her case—but I decided to run her through a few of the questions that had niggled at my mind, regardless.

"I find that decision interesting," I said. "We haven't picked a destination yet, you see."

Miss Hawkins blushed. "Well," she said reluctantly, "given the weather of late, I suspect that you won't be travelling any further northwards. I doubt you would be headed to Carrain or to the Emerald Spires, as they've started skirmishing again. And, well, given the *Rose's* reputation—"

"*Reputation?*" I barely stifled my indignation this time.

The lady's mouth dropped a bit as she realised her faux pas. "F-for... um. For *discretion*, Captain, sir," she amended hastily. "And, um... expediency. I have heard your ship mentioned before, at least in passing. And when I heard that you had come into port..." She trailed off uncertainly, tucking a loose strand of hair behind her ear. "South-easterly is my heading. And also yours, by my estimation."

I narrowed my eyes at her. I was a *bit* impressed, but I didn't particularly want to show it. We hadn't settled on our next destination yet, but her reasoning was sound.

"All true, Miss Hawkins," I admitted slowly. "Though we have one slight detour to make in the north-easterly direction first. It *will* add a few days more to our travels, but if that isn't a bother..." I paused, considering. "Did you have an ultimate destination in mind?"

"Oh," Miss Hawkins said. "Um. So long as it takes me closer to Lancet, sir. I am bringing several effects to the university there. I'm a student, you see. I study the sciences." She searched my face. "I can pay, Captain. Please."

There was desperation in her grey eyes, as definite as the day had been bright and murderous. I glanced back towards the pier near the

Rose, where Dougal's broken outflyer still waited to be brought aboard. Some of the crew had started carefully removing its other wing so that they could safely stow the ship in the cargo hold.

"Miss Hawkins..." I began. "I would be remiss not to inform you that there *is* danger in coming aboard my vessel. Not from my crew, but from those who would wish us harm. You could find yourself in their crosshairs." It was a sober, sincere warning. As much as the judgmental woman irked me, I knew I'd feel awfully guilty if she ended up on the wrong side of Red Reaver's pirates.

Miss Hawkins shook her head quickly. "Oh, believe me, sir," she replied. "I wouldn't have sought passage aboard your ship unless matters were already dire."

Evie winced behind her.

My face must have been quite something, because Miss Hawkins' smile vanished, and she hastened to correct herself. "I mean, I... I know that *discreet* vessels such as yours aren't exactly known for their respectability."

The halcyon reached up to pinch at the bridge of his nose, embarrassed. I set my jaw. Every word out of Miss Hawkins' mouth only made me regret the situation further.

"I assure you, Miss Hawkins," Evie interjected smoothly, "Captain Blair is one of the finest men that I have ever known. Reputation aside, he has a formidably kind heart. And, in my experience, he has always insisted on repairing his mistakes." The halcyon smiled tiredly at me, and I looked away uncomfortably. I knew that he meant every word—and that this was, moreover, his way of accepting my apology while we were still among awkward company.

Miss Hawkins looked me over dubiously. I couldn't entirely blame her. I was still wearing my thoroughly stained, torn-up, decrepit excuse for a coat. She settled her features into a soft smile, though, which she directed towards Evie. "I don't mean to be difficult," she assured him softly. "I appreciate your generosity, Halcyon. And... you as well, Captain."

Evie's sheepish look confirmed my suspicions—he'd already promised Miss Hawkins that he would find her a place on the *Rose*.

Miss Hawkins reached her blue-gloved hand into the purse at her side. "I'll entrust this to your care until I depart, if you don't mind, Halcyon," she said. Miss Hawkins pinched out a folded-up note, which she handed over to Evie. She snapped gloved fingers for the carriage driver's attention. He tilted his hat back and emptied his pipe, before hopping off the front to open the doors of the carriage and retrieve her effects.

Five valises, two hefty satchels, one steamer trunk, and five large messenger tubes later, he finally closed the carriage doors again. Evie and I stared at the tall pile of luggage.

At least the cargo hold is mostly empty now, I thought.

Evie sneaked a glance down to the note in his hand. The number he saw there inspired a thoughtful expression. I suspected the payment was reasonable enough to justify the woman's passage, though perhaps not quite as high as I'd normally prefer. Evie nodded my way and tucked the note into his coat pocket for the moment.

"Well," I said with forced cheer, "that settles that, doesn't it? Would you help the poor woman with her luggage, Evie? I'd like a moment with you when you're done as well, if you please."

"Aren't you helping?" Evie asked. He shot a wary look towards the growing mountain of luggage.

"Oh, I'm afraid I can't," I told him blithely. Perhaps I'd accepted the woman on board… but I wasn't about to go lugging her baggage onto the ship. I tapped meaningfully at my wounded shoulder. "Physicker's orders."

Evie sighed—but he didn't pause long before rolling up his sleeves and grabbing for the first valise. I turned back for the ship and gave a few whistles to catch the crew's attention. A few hand signals later, some of them headed down to help Evie with the luggage.

As they worked, I found myself unwillingly drawn to observe the progress on Dougal's outflyer. Watching as it was rapidly dismantled felt almost more final than the sight of his body had been. A saw chewed off the ship's one remaining wing with a shower of sparks, leaving only a foot-long stump in its place. Part of the tail came off next, clattering loudly to the ground. Finally, a crane swung slowly about, so the crew could prepare the remnants of the outflyer to be hauled into the *Rose*. Some irrational part of me kept hoping that Dougal would hop out of the cockpit with that booming laugh of his—but as the crew carted away the ship's separate pieces, that vision dwindled away by necessity, until I had fully confronted it and laid it to rest.

It was a deeply personal moment. Perhaps that's why I didn't notice the raised voices that were headed my way until they were nearly upon me.

An armed city watchman shoved me rudely aside. He and several fellows in their dark coats moved alongside the dock workers, directly headed for our unloaded cargo. The sight shocked me back to the present, and I scrambled to regain my bearings.

Evie was halfway up the gangplank with another bundle of Miss Hawkins' effects. The lady herself had settled nervously at the foot of the ramp, watching as Strahl and a deckhand headed up with the steamer trunk between them. Little and a few of the others were still handling Dougal's outflyer.

Judging by the watchmen's stony faces, we were about to be greeted by the unwelcoming committee. I stepped hastily forwards, holding up a hand to calm my crew's sharp glances.

"Excuse me, gentlemen," I said, "what seems to be the problem?" New Havenshire's constabulary continued to shoulder past me, ignoring me entirely. "Now see here!" I demanded, less calmly this time. "This cargo is meant for the mayor. I have documents!"

Already, several of the watchmen had started attacking the crates with their prybars. They fished through the bricks of tea as though they knew just what they were looking for, casting them aside to bring up the containers of smuggled aether. The intense floral aroma of broken tea wafted towards me—though another, much less pleasant smell beneath it made me wrinkle my nose. I exchanged a look with Strahl on the gangplank and turned to face the crew, masking my hands from the city watch with my body.

Get ready for a hasty departure, I signed.

The watchmen removed one of the containers of aether from a

crate and placed it upon the pier. My mind ran through the possibilities as I searched for some way to charm or trick our way out of the... *misunderstanding*. But as I saw the first canister of aether, something gave me pause.

I was used to seeing aether canisters made of silver and steel; aether reacted with most other materials. The canister that the watch hauled out onto the pier, though, was a thing of heavy rusted iron, which landed on the ground with an ominous *thunk*. As it landed, I caught a stronger whiff of the stench that had been lurking beneath the rich smell of tea.

That canister stank of rot and bile.

An uncomfortable shiver went down my spine. I wasn't alone—even the watchmen took a moment of pause. The ones closest to the canister covered their noses and mouths and made noises of disgust.

"Open it," one of them ordered, with authoritarian certainty. Judging by his hat and his obnoxious manner, he had to be the fellow in charge.

The watchmen hesitated. The officious one shoved one of his men forward. "Now!" he emphasised.

"Gentlemen, please," I tried again. My stomach churned. "If I can just speak with the lord mayor, then all of this—"

The watchman in charge backhanded me hard enough that I stumbled back. My hat tumbled off my head, falling upon the pier.

A gloved hand snapped out to catch me, steadying me on my feet. I glanced back towards Miss Hawkins in surprise. Her grip was stronger than I'd expected, and her stance was solid. There was a worried look on her face—but it wasn't directed at me. Rather, I saw that her eyes were fixed upon the watchmen.

"I think you should listen to the captain, sir," Miss Hawkins said. I felt her weight shift through the hand that she had on my shoulder, and I wondered if she intended to try and *stop* them.

The watchman who'd been ordered to open the canister moved towards it, reaching for its valve. Miss Hawkins stepped forward sharply, but the officer interposed himself, shooting her broken arm a disdainful sort of look. "I *will* ruin your evening, ma'am," he told her. "Back away."

Behind him, a reddish black vapour screeched into the air.

It was a vile, oily cloud—it came with a wave of overwhelming nausea that sent me down to my knees and left my scalp tingling with a feverish sensation. I knew instantly that this was the same awful substance that had fuelled the *Revenge*. The plume of inky darkness moved like a thing alive, shifting between myriad bruise-like colours. It caught the poor watchman along the side of his face.

I wasn't surprised when he started screaming.

The watchman stumbled back from the open valve, clutching at his face. Dark vapour continued to hiss into the air, licking at its surroundings. The bricks of tea around the canister shrivelled. The wooden pier dried out and slowly began to rot.

The flesh on the left side of the watchman's face was melting. One of his eyes had gone black as night; shadowy veins grew away from it, eating at his skin. He stumbled towards his comrades, spitting out yellowed teeth onto the pier. The other watchmen backed away, horrified, unwilling to touch him.

The canister's valve was still open. The small cloud continued to grow as I stared at it, heart pounding in my chest. The rest of the watchmen had backed away entirely; no one seemed willing to get close enough to shut the valve again.

I pulled away from Miss Hawkins, scrambling for the canister. One of the watchmen snatched belatedly at my arm—but I heard a solid *thunk* as Hawkins slammed her plaster cast into his chest.

I hopped over the crates, skimming around behind the miasmic terror that had begun to spread across the pier. I came at the canister from behind the valve, painfully aware that an unlucky shift in the wind would leave me in much the same condition as the watchman that still screamed in agony.

With trembling hands, I reached out to grab the valve... and twisted it shut.

The unearthly screeching halted. The inky cloud lingered, thick and malevolent... but I could tell that it was ever-so-slowly dissipating into the air. I fell back onto the pier, staring at it with dread.

Rough hands dragged me back to my feet, holding me tightly in place. I caught sight of Evie on the gangplank; his face was gaunt as he stared at the dwindling cloud. His lips formed silent, fervent prayers.

The watch-captain advanced on me in a terrified rage. "What in the Four Winds was that!" he demanded. He gripped my jaw painfully with one hand. "What. Was. That?"

"That," a voice rasped from further up the pier, "is Unseelie aether."

5

BARSBY'S BARGAIN - A GREY GLOVE - THE SILVER LEGIONNAIRE

Unseelie aether.
    I had made a promise to transport a gift from the enemies of our Seelie gods—the stuff of nightmares incarnate. I had carried that stuff in my *hold*. Several of my crew had given their lives for it.

No wonder Evie was praying. We had just committed heresy of the highest calibre. Treason, too, for anyone who still cared about that sort of thing.

The two watchmen that currently held me between them weren't really necessary. My knees were jelly. I wasn't sure I could have stood on my own even if I'd been allowed the dignity.

The raspy voice that had spoken was distantly familiar. I turned to search for its source, still reeling from the revelation of what I'd done. Just beneath the feeling of that blasphemous aether, I registered the odious presence of a nearby Oathbreaker; the unpleasant aura rasped against my soul like ragged cobwebs, setting me on edge.

A tall, lean man had approached us while we struggled—it was he who carried the broken Oath with him. He wore a black, neatly fitted coat, more finely made than the attire of the dark-coated watchmen he'd brought with him. A fashionable half-cape over his left arm partially hid the rapier at his side, though it left the pistol riding on his right hip bare to see. There was no fashionable neckcloth to hide the hideous scars around his throat, which had warped his voice beyond my recognition. The single eyepatch that he wore sent a flare of ice through my veins.

After all, I'd picked it.

"Good evening, Barsby," I greeted the dead man. "Clearly, rumours of your death were grossly exaggerated."

Barsby grinned at me. A golden tooth gleamed in the lantern light of the pier. His sandy blond hair was more neatly combed than I remembered; his blocky face retained a bit of its old roguish appeal, but his skin had darkened from countless hours in the sun. He looked a far cry from the criminal and occasional broker that I'd once known so well.

"Death didn't take," Barsby replied, with great satisfaction. His leather gloves creaked as his hands clenched and unclenched. I knew he wasn't happy to see me, but for some reason, he'd put on a smile.

Keep him talking, I thought wildly. Barsby always had enjoyed a good gloat. I just needed to buy the crew enough time to get into position to leave, in case we needed to beat a hasty retreat.

"It may be best for you to stay back, sir," the watch-captain said quietly to Barsby. "If you get a face full of that aether, I'm the one who has to explain it to the lord mayor."

My gut sank.

Oh. Oh *no*.

"Take care of your man, Watch-Captain," Barsby said magnanimously. "Let me worry about my own duties." He clapped the fellow on the shoulder. Most would have seen the gesture as a respectful dismissal, but I caught the patronising glee on Barsby's face. He enjoyed having power over these people. He definitely enjoyed having power over *me*.

"Working for the lord mayor directly?" I observed. My mouth went dry. "Well. That's a change in circumstances, isn't it?"

Barsby widened his smile as he stalked around the pier. He headed towards the crates, which the watchmen had begun cracking open one by one—this time with far more care. The watchmen now looked fearfully at every crate as though the aether inside was coiling itself with conscious malevolence, just waiting to devour them.

"In a roundabout way, William, I've got you to thank for it," Barsby told me. "Your betrayal—"

"More of a mutual betrayal, wasn't it?" I corrected him. "Considering the bounty hunters."

Barsby conceded to that with a shrug and a boyish grin. "I go where the Winds of Fortune blow, William," he said. "The bounty on your head was finally too good to pass up. And I will hand it to you— you *do* have good taste." He tapped his eyepatch and chuckled, as though sharing an inside joke with me. As though we were still friends... or ever had been, really.

I forced a nervous laugh. "Clearly, you escaped the rope," I said. "Done marvels for your voice. Gives you a kind of, uh. Air of menace. Must be quite the daring story."

"Maybe we could trade botched execution stories later, William," Barsby said, with a catlike smile.

I hadn't realised he'd heard about what happened in Lyonesse. My, I really *was* getting something of a reputation.

"So... there *will* be a later, then?" I observed. My heart skipped a beat. Maybe, just *maybe,* we'd be walking out of here. Barsby followed the Winds of Fortune, after all. And this haul was good business.

"That all depends," Barsby sighed, holding out his hands in a helpless gesture. "This... cargo, William. If this were the Imperium, you and your crew would be found guilty of the highest treason. As representatives of this city's leadership, we can't simply overlook that."

"Excuse me?" I asked flatly.

Barsby meandered closer, resting one hand on the pommel of his sword. "Well," he said, "you can't expect me to let such an *egregious* violation go unpunished, can you? The Imperium may be dead, but we're all still Seelie-fearing folk."

I struggled against my captors, seething with helpless fury. "You miserable, rotten bastard!" I accused him. "This cargo is for *you*, isn't it! What have you got yourself tangled up with?"

My captors forced me down, kicking out my knees from under me. Barsby loomed over me, smiling as he placed a hand on my shoulder. My *bad* shoulder. He must have seen me flinch, because he gave it a friendly squeeze. I winced away the pain, choking down my cry. I didn't want to give him the satisfaction.

Barsby leaned forward like a confidant, throwing his voice into a genuinely dreadful whisper. "I do mean it, William," he said. "If it weren't for you, I wouldn't be enjoying all that this new life has to offer. And imagine my joy when I found out the *Iron Rose* had swooped in to save the day with my cargo. So, here's where we stand: I am confiscating your smuggled goods. And, out of sheer benevolence, I'll square you off—if you do one little job for me. I just need you to pack this all back up and take it to Morgause. I have a client waiting there for the delivery."

I grimaced, fighting down my anger. "So," I gritted out, "why wait until it's almost unloaded to come to me with all of this?"

"Because I'm a petty man, Blair," Barsby told me in a friendly tone. "And inconveniencing you makes me feel warm and fuzzy on the inside."

He was just close enough that I could have head-butted him and bloodied up that stupid, infuriating grin. I suppressed the impulse... with effort.

Barsby's grin soon faded of its own accord, however, as confusion leaked into his expression. He stared at me more closely, as though trying to unravel a mystery. A moment later, I realised what had distracted him: He was searching for the lingering shame of my broken military Oath.

Of all people, Barsby knew that I should have been Oathbroken. We'd broken our Oaths on the same day, for the same reason. Barsby's broken Oath still surrounded him like a disgusting, invisible miasma, unsettling my stomach... but my honour had somehow been repaired.

Only an Oath's original counterparty or an exceptionally powerful faerie could forgive its betrayal. We'd both sworn our Oaths in the name of the emperor himself... and he was a *very* dead man.

"What *have* you been up to for the last few years, William?" Barsby murmured.

I ignored him.

"I was promised further payment, Barsby," I growled instead. "I also need fuel. Repairs. You can't expect me to fly on empty tanks and empty stomachs."

Barsby narrowed his eye at me, and I wondered whether he might forcibly divert the subject back to my Oath. But he pushed past it instead, refocusing on the matter of our heretical cargo. "Don't you worry your... *fine* coat over that," he told me, inspecting the large tear in my left sleeve. Barsby's croaking voice dripped with venom from behind that pleasant, gold-toothed smile. "I'll see you outfitted. Tell you what—you hand me over that outflyer, and I'll even toss you a little extra."

Fury blossomed across my face, and Barsby grinned wider. "No?" he asked me.

It took every ounce of self-control I had not to spit in his face. "*No,*" I hissed.

"I suppose I should say I'm sorry for your loss," Barsby offered, wholly insincere. He was playing a dangerous game, and he knew it. But the miserable wretch just *had* to twist the knife.

"Dougal died fighting Red Reaver's pirates for your cargo, Barsby," I hissed. Something ugly and dangerous slipped into my words, and I looked him in the eye. "One more word about him, and I'll make you eat one of those canisters before your men gun me down."

Barsby took just one step back at that. Maybe it was my tone. Maybe it was the mention of Red Reaver herself. *Maybe* he still had one tiny ounce of affection for Dougal, smothered at the bottom of his shrivelled black heart. On a better day, I might have believed the last one—but today, I was out of sympathy.

Barsby masked his moment of hesitation with a callous shrug. "Well," he said, "it occurs to me that I'm going to need some collateral. And since I know what a *loyal* captain you are to your crew..."

He turned away from me, snapping his fingers and signalling the watchmen towards the gangplank. "...I'll be taking some of them on as *guests* at my humble abode," he said loudly. His tone made it clear that this was an order and not a request.

Barsby nodded at the men that were holding me. They tossed me aside, throwing glares over their shoulders at me as he gestured towards my crew. "I'll have four of them," Barsby ordered. "I seem to remember there's a few charming ladies below deck. Why don't you go grab them for me, gentlemen, so we can get reacquainted?" Barsby shot me an oily smile. "We'll be very accommodating, as long as they come without a fight. You can collect them when the job's done."

His searching gaze fell next upon Miss Hawkins, who stood nearby, shocked and pale. "She's new," Barsby noted idly. "Gentlemen —take her too."

"Barsby, no—" I snarled.

"Sir, please!" Miss Hawkins begged, backing up a few steps. "I'm just a passenger, I swear!"

"She signed on just a few minutes before you arrived," I snapped, staggering between Miss Hawkins and the inbound watchmen. "She has nothing to do with us, Barsby." The movement caught everyone off guard—the dark-coated guards paused, uncertain how to proceed. Miss Hawkins blinked at me, as though seeing me for the first time.

The watchmen looked back to Barsby. The smile slipped from his face, and he sneered towards Miss Hawkins: "You should have picked a better ship."

And you should have known better than to threaten my crew, I thought. It was the last straw. I was willing to endure plenty of indignities in the name of protecting the people on my ship—but the gunnery ladies were liable to shoot the watchmen on sight, even if I *were* silly enough to try ordering them along quietly.

I figured I might as well start up the violence early.

I reached for the weapons at my belt—but a grey-gloved hand placed itself delicately upon my forearm. Miss Hawkins glanced over at me, her face resolute.

Wait.

A grey glove. I could have sworn she had been wearing a *blue* glove before.

My heart raced as I met her gaze. Miss Hawkins had stern, grey eyes, utterly devoid of colour. As though they had been washed too many times... or exposed to large amounts of aether. *That*, I realised, was why she had been loath to shake my hand—she had been worried about leaching the colour from my clothing and giving away her abilities.

The guardsmen's footsteps drew closer behind me. It was time to gamble.

"Get us out of here," I told her, beneath my breath, "and I will fly you anywhere."

"Anywhere?" Miss Hawkins asked. Her dull grey eyes sparked with acute interest. The edges of her brown wig were slowly streaking silver before my eyes. I could smell the aether now, wafting from somewhere on her person. I heard the faint hiss of it being injected into one of her foci beneath her outfit.

She *was* an aethermancer!

"I'll have your Oath on that, Captain," Miss Hawkins whispered.

I closed my eyes and stifled a groan. I should never have congratulated myself on escaping an Oath to Picket. Clearly, I'd only baited Noble Gallant into sending another one my way—and this time, Miss Hawkins had an impossible amount of leverage on me.

I didn't have the time to bargain. An Oath to Miss Hawkins, whoever she was, was still leagues preferable to letting Barsby have his *collateral*.

"My Oath to Noble Gallant," I sighed morosely, "or I'll never kiss the clouds again."

The chains of fate snapped around my soul, briefly choking the air from my lungs. A slow smile curved across Miss Hawkins' lips as she felt the Oath take. She gave me the slightest nod. The constables approaching us paused as they felt the Oath manifest, put off by the unexpected spiritual weight which settled in around me. They had to be wondering what I considered so crucially important, at a time like this.

"All right, Barsby, wait!" I called out. I dragged out each syllable with put-upon reluctance.

Barsby stopped in his tracks. He turned around, watching me with barely disguised contempt. Slowly, a smile grew across his face. He knew that he had won. He had known it since the beginning of our encounter; he'd just wanted me to *say* it.

"You drive a hard bargain," I sighed. "Obviously, you have the upper hand."

The whine I'd heard from Miss Hawkins slowly levelled off, and I smiled.

"—and so, after careful consideration," I said, "I regret to inform you that you are *still* a snivelling, opportunistic parasite—and the most contemptuous scum I have ever had the displeasure of dealing with."

Barsby's smile vanished. Murder crept into his gaze, and a dark, ugly cloud danced across his face. Slowly, he retrieved his pistol from its holster, holding it menacingly at his side. The city watchmen followed his lead, drawing their guns and pointing them in my direction. There were more than half a dozen of them, in addition to Barsby himself.

"And just what do *you* intend to do about it, Blair?" Barsby hissed. He emphasised each word with careful elocution. In all honesty, being nearly hanged to death had done marvels for his intimidating manner—an honest shudder raced down my spine at the rasp in his voice.

"What will *I* do?" I repeated. "Oh. Nothing." I placed a hand on my chest and offered a gallant smile. "*She*, on the other hand..."

All eyes turned towards Miss Hawkins.

A high-pitched whine rose from her left arm, still cleverly wrapped in its sling. Hawkins tore the arm free and thrust her left hand at Barsby. Aether erupted, in a blinding flash of blue-white light. A bright lance howled through the air, slamming into Barsby's chest. The blast threw him clean off his feet, tossing him from the pier tail-over-teakettle. I had only a moment to relish his wide-eyed look of shock before he fell from sight.

A steel and silver gauntlet now peeked through the broken plaster on Hawkins' left arm, venting bright-burning aether into her palm. The watchmen gathered their wits quickly. One of them shouted the obvious—"Aethermancer!"—and some of them ducked for cover. But a few of them fired their weapons at us.

I dived for cover—but I needn't have bothered. Miss Hawkins stepped in front of me and brought her left arm up. Blue-white aether flared once more, forming a fortification several feet wide. Bullets slapped against this intangible aegis with all of the destructive force of wet paper. Each time a bullet hit the shield, concentric rings of opalescent light rippled out from the point of impact, and an odd, reverberating hum buzzed through the air.

I had encountered a handful of aethermancers in my time—but I had never been privileged enough to have one on my side. There was something indescribably satisfying about standing *behind* an aethermancer, rather than before one.

"What's the plan, Captain?" Hawkins asked me. The nervous creature she had so masterfully portrayed before was abruptly gone, replaced by a professional, steadfast presence.

"Make for the skies," I managed. "In one piece, preferably."

"*That's* your plan?" Hawkins asked. A hint of exasperation leaked into her tone, though she did not yet sound hard-pressed.

"Would you rather we depart in *several* pieces?" I retorted. "Perhaps we could stick around for breakfast!"

Gunshots cracked above us, as the crew of the *Rose* began taking potshots at the watchmen. The engines purred back to life, and the telltale churning of the drives filled the air. That was a good sign. All we had to do was get on board and get out of here before someone got the bright idea of firing up the city's anti-air defences.

My eyes fell upon the crane. Its straps were still latched onto Dougal's outflyer. Little hid behind the vessel along with a handful of my crew, using it as cover against the watchmen. I needed to get my people back onto the ship... along with the outflyer. I wasn't bringing Dougal back to his family without his ship.

"The lanterns nearest to the crane," I said to Hawkins, pointing. "They're aether-powered. Can you knock them out?"

"I can," Hawkins said crisply. "But I would need these men to stop firing at me."

As though on cue, the *Rose's* cannon ports opened behind us. Rifles poked through the ports; the guns barked neatly, one after another. Three of the firing watchmen staggered back. One of them toppled over the pier, and I could swear I heard Lenore's hard laughter float over the air.

Hawkins seized the opening. The aetheric shield in front of us wavered and winked out as she flashed her hand towards the lantern at the end of the pier. The lanterns flared and burst in a popping wave, collapsing in puffs of aether and shattered glass. That area plunged into darkness, turning my crewmen into indistinct shadows behind the bulk of the damaged outflyer.

"Haul that thing up, and let's get out of here!" I shouted to my crew.

"Haul *that* up?" Hawkins snapped at me. "We don't have time!" I heard the growing reluctance in her voice. Already, she'd begun to back herself towards the *Rose*.

But I wasn't leaving that outflyer behind.

I drew my hand-axe and my blunderbuster. "We'll *make* time," I told Hawkins.

I didn't wait for a response. I charged forward—and leapt atop the open crates of Unseelie aether.

The nearby watchmen levelled their weapons at me—but none of them fired. They might not have been the brightest fellows, but it hadn't been *that* long since they'd all seen their comrade get his face eaten away by the blasphemous aether in those canisters. None of the men wanted to chance hitting them at such a close distance.

I aimed my blunderbuster upwards and shot once. The gun bucked in my hands, bursting the lantern just above us. Darkness rushed in.

Goblins have a dubious reputation for enjoying gloomy, disgusting places. In all honesty, we dislike the muck as much as anyone else does... but it *is* true that we can see in the dark.

My sensitive eyes adjusted to use the dim starlight overhead, picking out each watchman in turn. I watched them fumble for cover, clearly aware of their sudden disadvantage.

I didn't particularly want to have a second encounter with the

Unseelie aether beneath my feet, either—which is why I slipped my firearm back into its sling. I leapt off the pile of crates towards the first watchman, lashing out with a vicious heel-kick. He reeled back, clutching at his nose, and brought his club around in a blind swing. It was a clumsy attempt; I ducked beneath it with ease. I hooked my axe behind his knee and gave it a sharp yank. He fell to the ground with a pained shout, dropping his club behind him.

I didn't have the chance to follow up on my advantage. Another watchman had followed the sound of the fighting in the darkness. I rolled aside just as his club came after me. The club slammed into the man I'd just downed instead, and I heard a low, strangled groan behind me.

I snatched up the first watchman's club with my free hand, turning to parry a second attempt at the back of my skull. The second watchman's eyes had adjusted somewhat—he followed my figure through the darkness with difficulty. I used the club's longer reach to swat aside a few more blows, wincing as my injured shoulder twinged in protest. As underwhelming as I felt, however, it occurred to me that the watchmen must have seen the situation very differently. I could only imagine how sinister I seemed—a goblin in a ratty coat and bloodied shirt, red eyes alight in the half-dark of the cluttered pier, laughing as his hand-axe danced in the night.

For the second time in as many days, I embraced the overdramatic approach.

"Come on, then," I hissed at the man in front of me. "I hope you've got a good story for Death Victorious."

The watchman let out a soft yelp; his next swipe went slightly wide. I parried the wild swing, ignoring another painful flare in my shoulder, and sank my hand-axe into his clubbing arm. As he stumbled off balance, I dropped the hand-axe to take a two-handed swing with the borrowed club, cracking it over his head.

I had to hit him twice, actually. He was a headstrong fellow.

Once I was convinced the fallen man wasn't getting up again anytime soon, I tossed the club aside and retrieved my axe from his arm. For a moment, I looked around, expecting to find more watchmen—but Hawkins had reluctantly followed my cue, just as I'd hoped she would.

She was brawling with *four* of them.

One of Barsby's personal goons had closed the gap as her... *whatever* it was continued to cool down from the last blast. The burly man snatched her by the hair, while a dockhand moved in to take a nasty swipe at her head with a pry bar. Hawkins screamed in pain— and for a moment, I worried that I had dragged my new ally into more trouble than she could handle. But she ducked and tore herself free just in time. The hair came free from her head—and Barsby's goon was left holding a wig for the space of a single, puzzled breath.

Hawkins rolled deftly aside and raised her left hand. The sharp whine of aether filled the air. Another flash of blue-white light illuminated the area, highlighting her ghostly figure as she blasted both men off the pier.

In that flash, I saw Hawkins with her true face unveiled. There it was: a headful of jaw-length, ivory hair, bright in the moonlight of the darkened pier. Her pale skin now shimmered with bright blue veins as aether circulated through her system. During the fighting, she had torn the skirt from her hips to reveal trousers, all leather-strapped with various aethermancer's trinkets. There were fortified aether containers with tubes that fed to gadgets still hidden on her person, and several arcane-looking silver devices stored in easily accessible holsters. Hawkins slipped one of these devices over the knuckles of her right hand and rolled seamlessly into a bout of fisticuffs with the last two watchmen.

Miss Hawkins probably weighed less than half of what my bosun did—but she removed men from the fight with the same terrifying alacrity. Each time she landed a punch, those silver knuckles flashed with light; the force of her blows made men stagger back as though they'd been struck by someone Holloway's size.

I moved to aid Hawkins—a bit halfheartedly, I'll admit, given the regular bursts of aether she kept putting off. I halfway expected to get blasted off the pier myself, if I got in her way. But as I came closer, I realised that the crane wasn't moving.

Little and the others had made it to the underbelly of the *Rose*, where drop-lines hung down from the main deck. Little had prioritised the crew over Dougal's ship—a perfectly reasonable decision, and one which I *should* have expected. The understanding still hit me like a bullet to the chest. The *Rose*'s engines whirred, jumping to the next phase of ignition... but the outflyer hung in the air, tantalisingly close to the ship.

Further down the pier, watchmen climbed the anti-air towers. They'd decided to blow us out of the sky as soon as we cleared the docks.

"We have to *leave*, Blair!" Hawkins shouted. "We don't have time!"

I knew she was right. In a better frame of mind, I'd have taken the loss, no matter how painful it was, and prioritised our escape.

But Dougal's death had turned back the clock. Today, I was a stupid, terrified cabin boy in a very fancy coat. That ship was as much a piece of Dougal as his beloved aviator's coat was, and I couldn't bring myself to leave it behind.

"*Please*," I begged Hawkins. Tears choked at my voice. "It's MacLeod's ship. I can't leave without it."

Hawkins backhanded one of the men in front of her with the silver gauntlet on her arm. The metal made a dull, sickening noise as it struck bone. She turned to narrow her flat, colourless eyes at me.

A boot scraped, just behind me. I spun reflexively, sweeping my axe in front of me. The movement barely knocked aside the keen point of a thrusting rapier. Barsby had crawled back onto the pier; his remaining eye was alight with pure malevolence. He lunged again without missing a beat, and I backpedalled wildly. I tried once or twice to reach for the blunderbuster at my side—but the rapier darted and slashed, pressing me inexorably. Even with one eye, Barsby was a sharp duellist, and his longer arms and the reach of his weapon only made things worse. I hopped back awkwardly, trying desperately to gain some room.

"I'll see you dance the gallows jig, Blair!" Barsby hissed raggedly. "Mark my words, I'll wring your damned neck!"

I jumped back, evading another blow by the skin of my teeth. "Which is it?" I gasped.

"What?" Barsby snarled.

"Which... is it?" I repeated breathlessly. "Are you going to hang me, or are you going to strangle me? It can't be both, Barsby. Don't be ridiculous."

Barsby swiped again with a furious growl. As his rapier swept past me, I switched tactics, diving inside his guard to swipe at his leg with my hand-axe.

Barsby twisted at the last moment, flicking the rapier to block the blow. He yanked the blade beneath the axe's head and forced it upwards with his greater strength, locking both weapons and slamming them against one of the dock's wooden posts. I scrambled to hold on to the axe with both hands, knowing that I was an inch away from losing it entirely.

"You've always been a fast talker, Blair," Barsby hissed at me. Blood flowed into his remaining eye from a nasty cut on his forehead. "But that's all you're good at. It's pathetic, really."

Any moment now, those flak towers would turn towards the *Rose*. I knew I'd made the wrong decision—that I should have joined the *Rose* when Hawkins had first insisted on it. But there was no going back.

So I went for the low blow.

"At least I'm a pathetic captain with a real crew," I gritted out. "No one wanted *you*, Barsby. So what does that make you?"

Barsby's remaining eye widened in fury. He wrenched at his sword, loosening the lock on both our weapons. I tried to haul back and extract my hand-axe—but Barsby surprised me with a vicious jab at my wounded shoulder. My arm exploded in fiery pins and needles. For just a second, my vision went black; it came back just in time for me to see him lunging at me with his rapier. I stumbled clumsily back, reaching for my sidearm in the hope that I could get a shot off in time.

I never got the chance to find out which of us was quicker.

Blinding aether arced between us. I heard a clattering of steel; I smelled the sickly stench of burnt flesh.

Barsby stumbled back, clutching at the stump of his right wrist where his hand had once been. His hoarse scream was equal parts pain and sheer terror as he fell back, staring up at Hawkins.

"You are in my way, worm," Hawkins snarled. "I am *done* being nice."

There was a sword in her hands—a white blade of pure aether. It was elegant, ethereal; it burned like a small star, lighting up the entire pier. Hawkins pointed the blade down towards Barsby, whose mouth worked in soundless fear.

In that moment, I shared his horror.

I hadn't just sworn an Oath to an aethermancer. I had bound myself to a Silver Legionnaire.

6

ECHOES - WRAITHWOOD & VERDIGRIS - A PARTING GIFT - MY FAIR LADIES

Career airmen always said northerners were a wild lot. Old legends claimed they were brash mountain folk so hot-headed that their hair grew red. Northerners lived upon the rocky, white-capped slopes of Pelaeia—a once-living mountain, now dead. Every one of them was born to the open skies.

The northern clans had been the Coalition's fiercest proponents. And they had suffered for it commensurately.

It was a northern ship, the *Freewind*, that had taken us onboard. Evie, Little, and I were confined to the lower decks of the vessel, ordered to help Physicker Holloway tend to the injuries of Coalition soldiers—always under the watchful eye of at least one well-armed rebel. We were lucky, we came to learn; the *Freewind*'s surgeon had perished in the battle when a broadside ripped apart their starboard hull. The lack of a surgeon made Physicker Holloway more welcome than he otherwise would have been.

It was still a very chilly, angry sort of welcome.

The *Freewind*'s captain worked Holloway around the clock. Eventually, it became clear that this was a different sort of vengeance —that the rebels meant to keep the physicker on his feet until he collapsed. But our unlikely protector, Dougal MacLeod, did indeed keep faith. He argued down the captain in an explosive, undisciplined sort of shouting match, the likes of which we never would have seen on a proper Imperial vessel. We heard only bits and snatches as we cowered in the surgeon's quarters, expecting the worst. Over and over, the name Pelaeia came up. *Remember Pelaeia!* one man yelled. *Who will pay for Pelaeia?* another one demanded.

To this day, I don't know what Dougal said to convince the others. But eventually, the shouts died down to a weary murmur. Dougal returned and told us all to get some rest.

Some of the northerners on the ship still looked at us with sullen anger. But most of them now just looked... tired. I found the lack of jubilation confusing. The Imperial Navy had always encouraged us to celebrate the Imperium's victories; whenever word came back of a major rout, they doled out extra rations and toasted the fallen. More than once, I'd heard the officers laughing about the rebels they'd thrashed. Every once in a while, I'd laughed with them, imagining our enemies fleeing with their tails between their legs.

The Coalition had achieved the impossible; if there was such a thing as total victory, then they had managed it. But on this ship, at least, there was no joy.

For a long time, Dougal MacLeod was the only man to talk with us—and even he had only so much time to spare. Eventually, however, the ship's halcyon crossed that invisible line.

Elfa Goodhollow—one of the small folk known as a nisse—was even shorter than I was; I was constantly surprised to find myself looking down at someone thrice my age. Elfa had a naturally pleasant-looking face, with a button nose, broad dimples, and plenty of freckles. Like everyone else on the ship, though, her eyes were haunted, and exhaustion clung to her in an ever-present shroud of misery. Her uniform consisted of a ragged jumpsuit and a Carrain-cut militia overcoat. She wore her cerulean halcyon's cloth around her shoulders like a shawl.

I hadn't met many nissar, growing up in Morgause. Any nissar who *did* wander into the city often ended up quietly chased out of the community in order to prevent others from following them. The industrial overseers there called nissar 'halflings'—since they were half the size of most folks. They believed that nissar made poor workers due to their natural irritability. *Halflings don't take orders well,* I'd heard a foreman say. *Half the time, they don't do half the work! And whenever one of 'em gets mad, you end up dealin' with all of 'em.* I'd always imagined that nissar were twice as spiteful as those twice their size, because they had to fit the same amount of bile into an even smaller body.

Elfa Goodhollow didn't *look* angry to me. In fact, the first time I met her, she brought biscuits.

I had to ignore the dried, bloody handprints on her sleeve, courtesy of the injured and the dying. Everyone on board looked like that, to some extent or another. Washing clothing was a waste of water, and the *Freewind* still had a ways left to go before her crew would be able to replenish her stores.

I was predisposed to mistrust nissar... but Elfa *seemed* perfectly sweet. Besides which, she was a halcyon of the Benefactor—perhaps, I thought, His mercy had tempered her otherwise-irritable nature. She asked us careful questions over biscuits: Were we injured? Did we have a warm place to sleep? I took turns with Evie giving short, wary answers, most of which seemed to satisfy her. Little said nothing; ever since our fateful last day on the *HMS Caliban*, he'd endured our daily existence with a vacant gaze and a troubling, uncharacteristic silence.

"Do you have any questions for *me?*" Elfa asked, once we'd demolished her miniscule bounty.

I hesitated. I *did* have questions—many of them. My instinct was that those questions would get me into trouble. It was hard to ask too many questions in the Imperial Navy without seeming insubordinate.

I was starving for a friendly face, though, and Elfa had been nothing but kind. My question spilled out of me before I could stop it.

"What else do they want from us?" I asked the halcyon. I meant the words to come out strong and defiant—but I was still a twelve-year-old boy, and they came out desperate instead.

Elfa blinked at me slowly, as though trying to absorb the question.

"They've beaten us!" I quavered. "We've surrendered. They

destroyed the *Sovereign Majesty*, and the capital, and they killed the emperor. What else do they want?"

Elfa heaved a long, heavy sigh. She gave me a pitying look.

"The Coalition didn't destroy the *Sovereign Majesty*," she said. "Best as we can tell, someone sabotaged the *Sovereign Majesty* from the inside. But our faction—Carrain and the northern clans—we had nothing to do with it." She softened her tone as she continued. "As to the rest... the people of Pelaeia want their families back. They want their homes back. But they cannot recover either. Their hearts shall yearn for the impossible for the rest of their days."

Evie clutched at the copy of the Word that Holloway had given him. He hadn't dared to put the book down; he carried it with him everywhere we went. "I don't understand," he said. "We didn't take anyone's home from them."

I knitted my brow. "There was... a battle at Pelaeia," I said slowly. "The Imperium won. It was a decisive victory."

Elfa dropped her eyes to the book in Evie's hands. "There was no battle," she said calmly. "There was a slaughter."

The words hung in the air. I felt them try to penetrate, but my mind refused to accept them.

Evie cleared his throat uncomfortably. "But they told us... Wraithwood and Verdigris led the charge. It took a Silver Legionnaire and an Armiger to win Pelaeia."

I closed my eyes, remembering. I thought of how we'd cheered when news reached us that the Imperium had crushed Pelaeia—the largest clanhome of the north. Gone were the great shipyards that had once manufactured outflyers and frigates by the dozen. Fearsome Wraithwood and noble Verdigris had clipped the northerners' wings at last.

I had toasted the fall of Pelaeia, just as I had toasted every other victory. I had indulged in wild fancies that night, dreaming that I was a powerful aethermancer, so loyal and respected that Emperor Lohengrin himself had given me a silver sword and made me a Silver Legionnaire. As I slept, I imagined myself charging into Pelaeia next to Wraithwood, cutting down vicious, faceless northerners by the score. As I returned home, triumphant, people watched me pass with awe and confusion. *A goblin Legionnaire,* they whispered. *We were so wrong to spit at him before.*

I doubt I was the only cabin boy to dream that way. But I knew in that moment that I was the only cabin boy who should have known better.

"The Imperium sent a Silver Legionnaire and an Armiger to *raze* Pelaeia," Elfa said. "It was meant to send a message—to crush the northerners' spirit. They destroyed the shipyards... and then, they slaughtered the workers. They killed whole families. They bombed the slopes of the mountain with aether, and cut down the northerners as they fled its destruction." She paused. "I left the Imperium's service that day. Every other halcyon I know did the same."

"No one ever told us," Evie whispered. His hands were white on the Word in his hands. "They said that we won the battle. They said that the halcyons were too soft-hearted, and..." He winced at the understanding. "...and they had to leave."

No one, of course, had told us that the halcyons had *chosen* to leave. We'd been told that the Imperial Navy had removed them from active service. The official word was that there was a place for mercy—and that place was on the ground, far away from the practicalities of war.

"The Benefactor *is* soft-hearted," Elfa said. "How could He be otherwise? He's the source of all our mercy." Her expression flattened into exhaustion, once again. "We tried to convince the other three orders to support us—to send a unified message. But the other Tuath Dé care nothing for mercy. The only thing we managed was to exile ourselves."

Some part of me still didn't want to believe it. But days later, we finally descended the gangplank of the *Freewind*... and the truth was suddenly inescapable.

Pelaeia was *still* burning.

Perhaps my memory is being overdramatic. Either way, swaths of the mountain were still a smoking ruin. Gutted remnants of the city expanded up the sharp, rocky slopes, limned in eerie licks of aether-light. An entire portion of the upper district had collapsed in an avalanche, wiping out at least a third of the city below it. Ramshackle buildings and landing areas barely stood in the lower levels amidst the debris. The burnt-out husks of fighter ships and larger vessels dotted the mountainscape. Over it all fell large, fluffy flakes of ash.

I'd expected to find tents or ships-turned-homes fielding many of Pelaeia's wounded... but if there *were* wounded, then they were few in number, tucked away where I couldn't see them. As I stepped off the gangplank, it dawned on me that the crewmen from the returning northern ships outnumbered the survivors that had huddled on the slopes of that mountain.

The wind howled—and for a moment, I thought I heard a ghostly wail upon it, carried down from the ruins above us. I shuddered and stared. The sound was too persistent to have been my imagination, which could only mean one thing.

Echoes.

Growing up around miners had exposed me to plenty of ghost stories—many of them true. To the best of our scientific knowledge, echoes were spectral apparitions made of ambient aether, doomed to replay their final moments in an endless cycle.

I'd never actually seen an echo before; only those who died around large amounts of aether tended to leave behind such imprints. But between exploding ship engines and aetheric cannons, I realised, the Sundering War was bound to have left behind whole swaths of echoes.

Was Pelaeia an entire *city* full of echoes? I couldn't fathom it. The sheer scale of that horror was beyond my understanding.

Dougal caught me looking. "Aye," he mumbled. "Echoes linger in Pelaeia. They always will. We dinnae dare even go and collect the dead. Figure we'll have to get'n aethermancer's help eventually, but..." He trailed off, staring at the city with a pained expression. "After what Wraithwood did, we'd sooner no have any ae their kind nearby."

Our group fell into a horrified silence as we went, crunching over ash and snow. The cold shadow of that eerie, burning mountain swallowed us on all sides. My impressionable young mind imagined that Death Victorious had spread out their black cloak, and that this darkness was merely its edges, peeking out into the mortal world. At any moment, I thought, that dread Tuath Dé would come for my soul.

They say that when Death Victorious comes to spirit you away, the featureless shadow within that cloak shall demand the story of your life. In the shadow of burning Pelaeia, I began to recount the things that I had said and done... and I trembled at their weight. When Death Victorious came for me, I knew that I would have to tell the faerie that I had cheered the atrocity before me; I would have to recount my fantasies of butchering northerners next to heroic Wraithwood and noble Verdigris.

It was a religious experience, in the truest sense of the phrase.

Let me live, I begged the mountain's corpse. *Please, don't let this be my story. I will do better. I will do everything differently, I swear.*

The mountain only wailed.

The sun was nearly gone. As it dipped behind the slopes entirely, the aether that still limned the city glowed ever-brighter, back-lit by the bloody sunset. Holloway slowed his step. His undamaged eye was half-fixed upon the sight; I heard him muttering prayers beneath his breath.

"Oh, don't go prayin' tae the Benefactor," Dougal said to the physicker. He'd spoken softly to me before, but his voice gained a harder edge as he addressed Holloway. "It was His empire that did this. Elfa's a good sort, but we don't keep her on board 'cos ae her merciful Tuath Dé. He can go an' hang Himsel'."

I cringed at the open heresy in these words—but none of us dared to contradict Dougal, with that awful graveyard still in sight.

"They hammered the shipyards first," Dougal said grimly, breaking the guilt-ridden silence. "Wraithwood, an' a whole regiment ae aethermancers. They slipped in at night, cripplin' our defences. By the time we realised what was happening, they brought their dreadnought up the mountain an' started bombing the clanhome." He watched my face in particular as he spoke. "People tried tae flee. But Verdigris an' they Imperial troops were waitin'. They cut our people down. Workers, children, elders. They did it aw disciplined an' efficient. Just how the Imperium does everything."

I stacked the stories I had heard against the brutal reality before me. On the one hand, there was Wraithwood the bandit-killer; Wraithwood, wyvern-slayer and protector of the realm; Wraithwood, who had once saved the young prince from terrible assassins. Wraithwood, with his mysterious mask and his blazing silver sword.

And Verdigris—the grand Armiger, called by the name of their wargear. I had never learned the nature of the pilot inside that great machine, I realised now. Whoever they were, stories said they'd hunted the fearsome hydras of the Greymire, and faced down the marauding wartracks of the Rustland Corsairs.

But there had been no bandits or hydras in Pelaeia.

I was crying. That was why Dougal had looked at me. Tears froze upon my cheeks and eyelashes, harsh against my skin.

I was too young and selfish to mourn Pelaeia—a city I barely knew, full of people I'd considered enemies. In that moment, I mourned the death of the image I had crafted of myself: a brave and righteous soul, labouring under the unfair yoke of the world's prejudices. I cried because I was not a noble soul, but a thoughtless child soldier, idolising butchers in my dreams. I cried because I had to bury my heroes upon the slopes of Pelaeia.

In the years to come, I would learn to mourn the people that had died. But mourning myself... that was a start. The hideous self-loathing that soon followed was a necessary first step on the road to becoming someone better.

* * *

OF COURSE, mortals make their plans, and the Lady of Fools laughs at them.

Twenty years later, a terrible apparition glared down the edge of her monstrous blade at Barsby. Her gaze was cold and shimmering with iridescence. Her pale hair danced along aetheric winds.

"You have one chance to flee, coward," Hawkins told Barsby, in a voice as chilly as the grave. Wisps of blue-white light escaped her mouth with every word. She hadn't used a focus to create the sword, I realised. She'd broken one of her aether vials and *inhaled* the stuff directly, foregoing the mechanical buffer that most aethermancers used to protect their mind and body. I had scrapped with aethermancers before—but none of them had ever dared to touch the gift of the Everbright directly like this.

Truly, Silver Legionnaires were a cut above the rest.

What have I done? My mind sputtered like a whirligig, refusing to process the horror of my situation. For twenty years, I'd done everything in my power to recant my crimes and foreswear the Imperium... and now, I'd sworn an Oath to one of its greatest champions.

Barsby scrambled back with a croaking, gurgled cry. His sword—and his hand—lay forgotten on the pier.

Hawkins turned those empty, glowing eyes upon me. "That ship is very important to you, isn't it?" she asked me. Aether spilled from her lips as she spoke... but there was an odd sentimentality in her tone. "You shall have it, Captain. But no more delays. You gave your Oath."

Dougal's outflyer still dangled unsteadily from the crane. There was no way we would get it into the hold in time. Hawkins' sword had done the unthinkable: It had driven all thoughts of Dougal's ship from my mind. Revulsion roiled in my guts as I realised I had contracted a *Silver Legionnaire* to save his vessel.

Dougal would have been horrified.

And yet—Hawkins sighed and released the aether around her. The blue-white light disappeared; her foci whirled once more and died.

Hawkins headed for the crates and reached down towards one of those terrible canisters. I widened my eyes and staggered forward to stop her—but before I could take more than a few steps, she opened the valve once more.

Black rotten aether hissed out from the spout in a vile cloud. I was sure, in that moment, that the woman before me would dissolve into a hideous mess upon the pier—but Hawkins sucked in her breath and flexed her grey-gloved fingers. The inky vapour froze in midair, shivering like some amorphous, nightmarish creature.

Hawkins gestured violently towards the outflyer. The Unseelie aether leapt to her command, winding its way around the ship in shimmering bands of night. The outflyer lurched free of the crane—or no, I realised, the Unseelie aether had *eaten* through the crane's straps and let the ship loose. The craft jolted its way down towards the pier... and settled itself directly before us.

"Hop aboard," Hawkins ordered me. "Now."

Her voice shook on the words. Her body trembled beneath the strain, and I knew then that this was no casual parlour trick, even for a Silver Legionnaire.

Kill her now, a panicked voice within me insisted. *Now, while she's weak. Whatever she's doing here, it can't possibly be good.*

It was true that I had sworn an Oath that Hawkins would make it safely to her destination. For most people, that would have been the deciding factor. But I had broken an Oath once before—and under the right circumstances, I knew that I could live with the consequences.

It was her expression that stopped me. There was a raw, knowing grief there—an uncanny twin to the misery in my own heart. I knew in that moment that Hawkins had buried someone dear to her, not long ago at all.

I could always kill her later.

I clambered onto the stub of the outflyer's hacked-off wing. Hawkins followed, with effort; I heard her laboured breathing beside me, as dark, shifting aether lifted us from the dock. I balanced on the wing, gripping the edge of the cockpit with my hands until my knuckles turned white. There was a sudden sensation of falling *upwards*; the hiss of aether; the smell of spoiled, rotten filth...

White aether flashed abruptly. Hawkins gasped in pain, releasing her grip on the ship to clutch at her right hand, which still held the silver sword. Something about the Unseelie aether had destabilised the sword. Even as I stared with alarm, the skin of Miss Hawkins' hand began to burn.

The silver sword winked out, plunging us back into darkness.

The ship floundered; I yelped and clutched more tightly to the edge of the cockpit. Miss Hawkins gritted her teeth against the pain, however, and slowly—drunkenly—the outflyer righted itself, stuttering through the air.

The ship bounced roughly against something. Darkness cleared, and I saw the *Rose*'s hold rising up to meet us with alarming alacrity. I remembered, far too belatedly, that perhaps a quarter of our heretical cargo still lingered there. If the outflyer hit those crates, it was likely that none of us would survive long enough to worry about New Havenshire's flak guns.

The outflyer caught the edge of the deck, catapulting me entirely off the side and down into the open hold. I saw my crew's ashen faces out of the corner of my eye and heard their panicked shouts.

If I survive this, I thought to myself, *I am never smuggling aether again.*

I hit the deck, and darkness took me.

* * *

THANKFULLY, this story does not end quite so ignominiously. Though I am sure that Barsby would have had quite the laugh if it *had*.

I awoke sometime later. That was a welcome surprise—until the headache returned. This time, I hadn't even had the pleasure of drinking an entire bottle of fire-rum beforehand.

Warm light pressed against my eyelids. A hammock swung gently beneath me; the welcome sound of the *Rose*'s engine hummed through the wood that surrounded me. A wet rag pressed against the ghastly, throbbing bruise at my brow.

I groaned, and someone smacked me in the thigh. Hard.

"Are you sure you're not hiding a red cloth somewhere, Captain?" Lenore snapped. "I could swear you've pledged yourself to the Lady of Fools directly."

I cracked open my eyes and found myself staring down the barrel of a fully loaded, scolding finger.

"I'm not a Fool," I assured my gunnery chief, with a weak smile. "I mean... not a proper one, at least. I'm certainly an *everyday* sort of fool."

Lenore narrowed her eyes at me in the flickering lamplight. "There is nothing everyday about your foolishness, Cap'n," she sniffed. I heard a slight waver in her voice this time. Footsteps sounded nearby, and three other ladies poked their heads into view.

"Captain's awake?" Martha asked worriedly.

"Of course he's awake," Navi grumbled. "Why else would Lenore have smacked him?"

"Oh, Captain!" Mary fawned, reaching out to pat my sleeve. "We had such a fright when you fell into the hold!"

A hollow, miserable feeling tugged at my stomach as the past few days came flooding back to me. I didn't deserve this sympathy.

The *Red Reaver's Revenge*. Dougal. Barsby. Hawkins. I had bungled everything I'd touched—and we weren't even done paying for it yet.

The gunnery ladies continued clucking over me, unaware of my gloomy thoughts. Martha stood hunched over me, still clutching her needlepoint hoop in one hand. She was the tallest woman I'd ever met, looming easily above the other three. In the full light of day, her skin was a dark brown—but in this light, it looked more like rich ink. Her hair was pulled back into thick locks, tied with an old, fraying kerchief. Her full lips pursed with relief as she looked down at me. Her head tilted slightly askew, as it always did—Martha had gone near-deaf in her right ear a few years ago, due to a misfired cannon.

In another life, Martha had been a carpenter's daughter, soon to be wed. The war had claimed her father, though, and burdened her would-be husband with an awful temper. I never did find out exactly what happened to her betrothed... but Martha had been clear that she needed passage out of town in a hurry, and I'd been careful not to ask too many questions. She'd been a reliable fixture on the *Rose* ever since.

The steaming scent of hot porridge filled my nose. My stomach remembered that it was a mortal thing in need of sustenance, and it awakened like a ravenous beast. Martha smiled wryly and passed me a bowl. "Have mine, Cap'n," she said. "I can just go grab more."

I was too hungry to argue. Still, I wasn't so far gone that I forgot my manners in front of Lenore. *Thank you*, I signed politely. A dozen unfamiliar aches and pains protested as I reached for the bowl, and I winced. Lenore reached out to guide me upright. As I pressed the bowl to my lips, she brushed absently at the dust on my shirt, scowling at it as though it had personally offended her.

Mary leaned forward to catch the damp cloth that fell from my forehead as I sat up. Her brown eyes flickered golden in the lamplight as she draped the cloth over the top of my head instead. One of Mary's many precious adventure novels—*Jack Blue's Last Laugh*—sat bookmarked in her lap. It was rare indeed that Mary offered her undivided attention to anything *other* than Jack Blue, and I found myself touched by her sudden focus upon me.

Sixteen-year-old Mary was wide-eyed, petite, and still so painfully young. Though she was often severe and fond of utilitarian clothing, the crew of the *Rose* still considered her our darling. Mary wasn't actually related to anyone on the crew, but her dusky complexion was so conveniently ambiguous that she'd pretended more than once to be someone's sister, daughter, or cousin. Lenore occasionally convinced Mary to let her weave a few bright ribbons into her dark hair; currently, there was a reluctant green bow at the base of her braid.

Lenore had brought Mary onto the ship with her when she'd arrived, and she'd been as good as family ever since. Mary had clever, talented fingers, which she put to use in a hundred different ways— she'd been a natural addition to the gunnery ladies' knitting circle, and she'd even helped out Holloway a time or two as his assistant nurse. Unfortunately, Mary had also spent a very long time using those clever fingers to survive as a pickpocket—and every once in a while, when meeting someone slightly too wealthy and slightly too insufferable, Mary still got it into her head to relieve them of whatever happened to be in their pockets. She called these ill-gotten gains her "book fund."

Mary had *many* books.

Presently, Mary had put her talents to work upon my ragged coat. I saw it draped across a nearby stool; the hole in the shoulder was already stitched back together. Mary had done the best she could with it, but I could tell that the coat was starting to consist of more stitches than material at this point.

Navi fretted on my other side. Her aged, imperious face held more wrinkles than I last remembered, and her ebony hair was threaded with more silver. Her fingers worried absently at the edges of her elegant blue sari. "What spectacular tomfoolery that was," Navi scolded me. "I swear, Captain, one of these days you're going to end up like my youngest son did."

I winced at the reference. Jahnavi Varma, a kumari of Aarushi, had lost nearly a dozen family members to the war, including her father, her husband, and her sons. Most of them had been noble airmen. After so many years, the lady had mostly tamed her grief; she now had a habit of telling fond stories of her deceased relatives whenever the situation reminded her of one. The stories were sometimes oddly enlightening, in fact; Navi had picked up an incredible amount of knowledge regarding weapons, politics, and ships-of-war. Had they allowed women to serve in the Navy, I daresay she would have made an excellent admiral.

Navi had lost everything: her estate, her affairs, her family. There was a bittersweet freedom in her loss, however—for finally, she had made her way to the rickety airship of her dreams. Our ageing, erstwhile kumari now spent much of her time maintaining the ship's mounted guns with all of the love she'd once afforded her own children. She had names for every one of them.

"Your youngest son was... Sameer?" I guessed faintly.

"Sameer was the second-youngest," Navi corrected me with a sniff. "Hassan was the youngest. He died when the ship's munitions blew up around him. Poor, dear Hassan was very brave... but tragically dim." She somehow managed to state this matter-of-factly, with the benefit of twenty years of distance.

"Ah," I said dimly, in between gulps of porridge. "Yes, that does sound like me."

Mary fidgeted with a nearby book, though she didn't open it. "Mr Holloway said you'd only cracked your head a bit," she told me. "He had to see to the lady, so he told us to watch you for now."

"The lady?" I mumbled. I knitted my brow, forcing thoughts to fit together. "You mean Miss Hawkins? Did something happen to her?" I forcibly squelched the small part of me that thought this might not be a *bad* thing. A dead Silver Legionnaire on my ship still wasn't ideal—but it was far *more* ideal than a live one. I wasn't actually certain whether Hawkins dying on my ship would break my Oath by default. I wanted to believe that Noble Gallant would understand why I couldn't ask a dead woman where she wanted to go...

But who was I kidding? His priests were called *judges*.

"She used that black aether," Martha said grimly. I forced myself to return my wandering attention to the conversation. "It went down about as well as poison, apparently. The physick's trying to flush it out of her system, but he's not sure she'll survive it."

I winced at that. Hawkins wouldn't have used Unseelie aether at all, if I hadn't insisted so wildly on bringing Dougal's ship with us. Silver Legionnaire or not, I knew I owed her more than just my life.

It was all so damned complicated. Once upon a time, I had convinced myself that if I ever saw the shadow of the Imperium again, I'd know it for the evil that it was. The next time around, I thought, I wouldn't be taken in. But I had managed to forget the reality of it all—how the very same people who committed atrocities against little children could also be kind and sympathetic and even self-sacrificing, given the right circumstances.

How on earth am I supposed to feel about this? I wondered.

Maybe, I hoped, the choice would be taken away from me entirely. Perhaps Hawkins wouldn't survive at all. It was a coward's hope.

"Why did an aethermancer trouble herself on our account, Captain?" Lenore asked me carefully.

It occurred to me then that no one else on the ship had got a close look at the sword that Hawkins had drawn. From up above, it must have looked like just another bit of aethermancy. It had been very *powerful* aethermancy, of course... but there was no way the rest of the crew could have guessed at the truth. Even I found it unbelievable—and I had *been* there.

"I made an Oath to Miss Hawkins," I said slowly. "I promised to take her anywhere she wanted, in return for her help."

Lenore let out a long breath. "Well then," she said sardonically. "I hope Miss Hawkins doesn't intend to go far—given that we never capped off our fuel in New Havenshire."

I closed my eyes and groaned.

Damn you again, Barsby, I thought.

"We'll have to stop at Pelaeia anyway," I mumbled. "Maybe we can make a deal there." I opened my eyes again and struggled up to my feet.

"Captain!" Mary scolded me, in her best nurse-like tone. "You're supposed to be resting."

I shot her a wry look. "I'm headed up to see our physicker," I told her. "I expect that's worth the trip."

I didn't tell her that I intended to make a few extra stops along the way.

7

FORGIVE ME, HALCYON - A LITTLE DISAGREEMENT - WHAT'S OWED - SILVER'S LEGACY

The sun was just beginning to rise as I climbed up to the main deck. I pulled my coat more tightly around myself, scowling at the way its weak sleeve pulled across my arm. Mary had suggested I ought to just get a new coat... but I'd lost an awful lot in the last few days, and I was determined at least to cling to my old, familiar coat.

Navi had thrust yet another ghastly knitted scarf upon me before I left, insisting that I needed it for my health. Soon, I reflected, we'd all be sporting warm clothing, given our northeasterly heading—but we always had it in spades because of the gunnery ladies and their itchy knitting needles. Even now, somewhere below deck, there awaited an entire trunk full of gloves, hats, and scarves—all monstrously colourful. To be given a knitted hat or scarf was a rite of passage aboard this craft; it meant that the ladies approved of you.

Worries careened through my mind as I paced across the deck. How long would it take Barsby to recover from the shock of his lost hand? Would he send *friends* after us, once he regained his bearings? And, blast it—we were going to have to burn New Havenshire from our list of welcoming ports. In addition to the Silver Legionnaire we were carrying, we still had a quarter of that blasphemous cargo in our hold—could we safely dump it off somewhere? Or maybe, if we got particularly desperate, we could use it for fuel—

No. I might be a fool sometimes, but even I knew better than to try *that*.

The truth, of course, was that these were all problems for the future Captain Blair. I was trying to distract myself with overwhelming problems of the sort I might not even be able to solve... because I still had something very straightforward and very difficult left that I needed to do.

I moved along the main deck, nervously tipping my hat to the crew members on duty. Slowly, I sneaked over towards a group by the railing that currently faced westward, away from the rising sun.

"...You gave us Your love, and You asked us for nothing in return but to love one another," Evie intoned in solemn prayer. "May we always remember Your request, Most Merciful of Faeries. Let us remember mercy when we are tired. Let us remember mercy when we are angry. Let us remember mercy when we are grieved."

I squirmed in place, though I had already managed half of an apology for my behaviour and received the equivalent of forgiveness. This was a common prayer to the Benefactor—but it felt perhaps a bit too on-the-nose this morning. Surely, Evie hadn't changed his sermon as I approached? No, I decided; he was probably reminding *himself* to be patient and merciful, even as we all grieved. That was Evie's way.

I saw Little standing at the helm, out of the corner of my eye. If it hadn't been for my absence below deck, I knew he would have been with the others, listening to Evie. Little wasn't a *religious* man, exactly, but he'd once confided in me that Evie's prayers made him feel safe and calm. In truth, I suspected that Little worshipped his husband more than he worshipped the Benefactor—but I couldn't really grudge him the sentiment. The Benefactor might have been theoretically loving, but He was a terribly distant figure. By comparison, Evie had been Little's constant and caring companion for more than twenty years.

I returned my attention to Evie as he finished his prayers. He offered his hand to one of the kneeling crew and helped the man to his feet. The two of them then turned to two others, and helped *them* to rise—and so on, until all were upright. Hugs and cheek-kisses and gentle words of affirmation followed as people milled about for a spare moment, enjoying the lingering feeling of camaraderie.

I wish I could have found the same sort of solace that they did. But the ugliness of the war had affected me far differently than it had affected Evie. Mercy and I had a very complicated relationship these days... as evidenced by my internal conflict over the aethermancer on my ship.

Some of the crew spotted me, and I offered a few weak nods. Evie shot me a bleary smile, and I knew that he hadn't slept very well at all. "It's good to see you topside again, Wil," he said. Normally, he would have called me 'Captain' on-deck, but I could tell that he needed the comforting familiarity today. "And on your feet this time, too," he added, with a hint of tired humour.

I managed a lame sort of laugh at that. "Only fire-rum can fully vanquish me," I said. I stumbled over my next words. "I was hoping to... maybe have a moment. With you. Er—*alone*."

Evie's smile became a bit easier. He settled his hand on my shoulder, as light as a sparrow, and ushered us both aside. He was wearing his blue sash openly again; I found that whenever he did, it granted him an unusual amount of strength and confidence. I might have been the captain of the ship—but Evie was the captain of our souls.

The halcyon led us up to perch upon the quarterdeck, apart from the rest of the ship. I leaned against the railing, staring at the wake of our ship and the mountains below us. Finally, I cleared my throat uncomfortably.

"I realise now that I never really said *sorry*," I started. "Or... I suppose I should say, *forgive me, Halcyon, for I have wronged a friend—*"

"—you apologised very kindly, Wil," Evie interrupted me gently. "And I forgave you."

I turned back towards him, frowning dimly. "I did not," I told him. "I know I hit my head, Evie, but my memory is still quite sharp on that point."

Evie squeezed my arm reassuringly. "Actions speak louder than words," he said. "I know you didn't want a passenger, Wil. But you took Miss Hawkins aboard anyway, because I asked."

I let out a breath at that. Evie must have caught the brand new conflict in my manner, for he raised an eyebrow. "She's been a rather more... *exciting* passenger than I originally expected," he admitted. "But isn't that all for the best, given that she helped us in our hour of need?"

I dodged the subject for the moment. "I didn't come here to talk about Miss Hawkins," I said. I barrelled onwards into the conversation I had originally meant to have. "When we ran to check on MacLeod, and I yelled you off, Evie... all I could think was that if you came with me, it meant that we needed you to... to speak for him. That I'd be..."

"That you'd be admitting he was already dead," Evie finished softly. "I understand, Wil. You wanted a physicker more than you wanted a priest, because that meant he might still be alive."

I nodded mutely. There was still an awful, hollow place in my chest where my heart ought to have been. But my eyes were dry, at least.

"I have to rectify that now," I said. "We're going to have to see Dougal off. When we do... I'd greatly appreciate it if you spoke for him then."

The little tension that remained between us drained away at that. "Of course I will," Evie said. He held out his arms, and I embraced him as tightly as my injured shoulder allowed. There was a hint of desperation to the hug, as there had been with Holloway; we were both keenly aware of the possibility that we might lose one another at any moment. Last night's dubious heroics certainly hadn't helped with that feeling.

"You had us scared," Evie mumbled at me.

"*You* were scared?" I scoffed. "You do remember that I was the one getting shot at?"

"I remember," Evie said ominously. For just an instant, I saw a dark cloud cross his face. "For a moment, I'd hoped that Barsby might have found himself a pleasant path, out there on his own. But he's gone above and beyond this time. After all of the chances we gave him—"

"Mercy measures the giver and not the receiver, Halcyon," I reminded him wryly. "At least Barsby didn't get away unscathed. He's lost his hand, and a good part of his shipment. And I hazard he'll think twice about harassing meek-looking young women from now on."

A ghost of a smile flickered across Evie's lips. "I shouldn't be so pleased about that," he admitted.

"You can be a *little* pleased," I told him, with an answering grin.

We paused at the helm. My hands itched for the wheel, but I restrained myself. Little looked over his shoulder, already narrowing his eyes—but his quiet anger eased as he saw our smiles.

Little turned his glance towards Evie and locked the wheel in place, in order to free his hands. *Did he apologise for being an ass?* he signed.

I raised an eyebrow. "I'm standing right here, you know," I said.

"Yes, he did," Evie replied comfortably. "I told you that we'd work it out."

I cleared my throat. "Still right here," I reminded them both.

Still rude, Little observed.

"And ignoring someone isn't?" I insisted petulantly.

Evie laughed, glancing between us. "It's fine, Sam," he said. "Really."

"Goodness!" I exclaimed. "I must have died after all. I'm haunting my own ship!"

Little rolled his eyes and finally acknowledged me. *Still angry with you, Captain,* he warned. But he held out a fist in my direction, and I knocked mine obligingly against it.

An awful remaining tightness in my chest loosened at that. On top of everything else, trying to navigate Little's silent, ongoing anger had felt like a weight on my shoulders. But Evie had gone out of his way to bring that anger into the open, where I could at least handle it in a straightforward manner.

"I'm... genuinely sorry," I said. "I'd be angry with me, too."

You didn't yell at me, Little signed grudgingly. *Evie forgave you. I guess I'll get over it.*

"We all know Evie's required to forgive everyone," I said ruefully. "Anyway... it's all for the best. You'd have to get in line if you decided you want a piece of me. It seems I've made all kinds of enemies this week."

Little signed Barsby's name, along with something obviously angry—but I couldn't make out the gesture. I blinked and looked at Evie, who snorted. "He just called Barsby a *cyclopean weasel*," the halcyon translated for me.

I chortled at that and tried to repeat the gesture so I'd remember it for posterity. Little shook his head, but I saw him try and fail to hide a small smile.

"Well, that cyclopean weasel is going to need a bit of time to recover from Miss Hawkins," I said. "He might still send people after us—but if they follow us to Pelaeia, they won't enjoy what happens next."

"And what about Red Reaver?" Evie asked quietly.

I faltered at that. It was a fair observation. We'd ducked one of Red Reaver's ships—but the pirate herself was still out there somewhere. Someone had dared to steal Unseelie aether from her... and if Red Reaver ever found out that the *Rose* had been involved, we'd never fly the south again without looking over our shoulders. On top of everything else, we'd gone and destroyed one of her ships.

"We'd better hope none of her crew made it back to her," I muttered.

That was a very angry mountain, Little offered hopefully. *Maybe it killed the stragglers.*

"No," I sighed. "We're never that lucky. We'd best assume she'll hear about the *Iron Rose* eventually." I shook my head. "For now, we're headed north. Reaver's never travelled that far before, and I don't figure she'll dare it now, either. She's made enemies of both Carrain *and* the Emerald Spires. The northern clans don't seem to want her back home, either."

Evie frowned. "We still don't know who actually wanted that stolen aether," he observed. "Surely, it wasn't Barsby?"

I chewed on the inside of my cheek. "No," I said slowly. "Barsby was a middle-man. We only ended up with his cargo by luck. When he saw it was us, he decided we ought to go the rest of the way to Morgause, in order to hand it over to his client." I pondered this for a long moment. "Barsby might be petty, but he's not stupid. Why would he risk sending a shipment like this with someone who didn't want the job, instead of overseeing it himself?"

Little shot me a grim look from over the wheel. *What kind of client wants Unseelie aether?* he asked. At my surprised reaction, Little jerked his chin towards his husband. *Evie overheard Barsby. We haven't said anything to the crew yet.*

I grimaced at the revelation, but moved past it for now. "Whoever *did* order this... particular shipment... I'm sure they're a dangerous customer," I observed. "Barsby's always been a cowardly little rat. It doesn't surprise me that he'd rather have us risk that meeting in his place."

"Well, good luck to him now," Evie said with a shrug. "He's angered Red Reaver, burned his last bridges with us, *and* lost part of his cargo." A sanctimonious glint came into his eyes. "Barsby should have paid more attention to his prayers. He might have learned how little Noble Gallant loves a weasel."

A cyclopean weasel, I signed emphatically.

Little beamed at me for a moment, before he regained control of his features.

"Well," Evie said. "Good riddance to Barsby, then. You said we're headed to Pelaeia, in the meantime?"

"We are," I said. I glanced at Little. "Have we started in that direction already?" I asked him.

We have, Little confirmed. *I assumed that was our heading. I couldn't ask you while you were out cold, but we've got Dougal's outflyer in the hold for a reason.*

"You assumed right," I replied. "We're taking MacLeod home. First, we'll see him off proper—and then, we beg, borrow, and sell whatever we can in order to get back in the air."

The two men nodded.

"We still have the note from Picket, for half payment," Evie said, "and another note from Miss Hawkins, worth a tidy sum. They're admissible in most provinces, if we sail to a city with a bank. But maybe someone in Pelaeia will be willing to buy one of them off us at a discount."

And where are we taking Miss Hawkins? Little asked. Or at least, I *assumed* he was talking about Hawkins. He'd used the sign for *miss* and created a new sign after it, which I took to be his name for her.

I drew in a deep breath at this. I'd been trying to decide how to broach the subject of *Miss Hawkins* for the last bit. But I knew that I owed my two best friends—and eventually, my entire crew—the blunt truth.

"About Miss Hawkins," I said in a low voice. "She's not quite the woman that she first represented herself to be."

Little snorted. *What was your first clue?* he signed.

I winced. "Yes, *obviously* she's an aethermancer," I said. "But I'm afraid that's not all. While I was fighting Barsby, she... she summoned a silver sword."

Evie and Little replied to this observation with stunned silence.

I figured I may as well tear off the bandage all at once, before they regained their bearings. "Before I knew what she was, I swore an Oath that I'd take her anywhere she wanted to go, in exchange for her help," I added wearily.

Evie planted his face into his palm.

Little moved his fingers into a very delicate question. *And where is it, precisely, that this Silver Legionnaire wants us to go?* he asked.

"She didn't say," I replied, with a calmness that I did not feel at all.

Little threw up his hands.

Evie let out a tremulous breath. "I'm so sorry, Wil," he said. "I had no idea—"

"I know you didn't," I said. "There's not a single person on this ship that would knowingly deal with a Silver Legionnaire. But Miss Hawkins is here now, and I've made my Oath. So I need to make some important decisions before we reach Pelaeia."

We can't take a Silver Legionnaire to Pelaeia, Little signed furiously.

I held up a hand. "I still don't know if she *is* a Silver Legionnaire," I said. "Not all of the Legionnaires survived, and most of the swords aren't accounted for. But, Oath or no Oath, I don't intend to help Miss Hawkins pursue any Legionnaire business. So... *if* she survives, then I'll be having a bit of a heart-to-heart with her. I'm not making any more decisions until then. I just wanted to start making people aware."

Little levelled a flat look at me. *Or—we could dump her off the ship before she wakes up,* he suggested. *Oath or no Oath.*

"I'm talking with her, Sam," I said stubbornly. "We owe her that much. It was going to get messy down there. And between MacLeod, and the others we lost to the *Red Reaver's Revenge*... I'm just starting to feel like I've seen enough death for one week. Whoever she is, Miss Hawkins *did* step in for us—so she'll get a fair hearing. No more and no less."

Little forced some of the tension out of his shoulders. He nodded in reluctant agreement.

"On that note," I said, "I have to go and see a physicker. Keep us on a steady course, Sam."

Aye-aye, Cap'n, Little signed back at me. *Go get your head checked out.* A small, morose smile ghosted across his face at the double-meaning.

"I doubt the good physicker can fix *everything* that's wrong with my head," I replied wryly. "But we'll see what he can do."

I headed back down below deck, tromping my way towards Holloway's quarters. But as it turned out, I was far from the only person on the ship with an interest in the woman inside.

Strahl was waiting just outside of the physicker's quarters. He leaned against the wall, eerily back-lit by the blue aether lantern that swung from the ceiling. His faded grey arming jacket was stained and patched, but still quite serviceable. Even on the ship, his weapons hung from a heavy belt around his waist. Strahl crunched into an apple as I watched; his eyes flickered towards me, and he shot me a strangely wary salute.

"Mr Strahl," I greeted him politely. "It's funny meeting you down here. I was under the impression you were the ship's bosun, and somewhat... *necessary* up top."

Strahl shot me an unpleasant smile, before sinking his teeth into the apple again. After he'd swallowed down the bite, he said: "That woman. The one with the silver sword. She's trouble."

I stared at him.

Strahl had been up on the deck of the *Iron Rose* when Hawkins had drawn that sword. I'd seen him there during the chaos. He'd had the same viewpoint as the rest of my crew—and none of *them* had recognised the silver sword from that distance.

"You're guarding her," I said slowly. "Or... no. You're guarding the rest of us *from* her."

Strahl didn't respond to this directly. "The Legionnaires were assassins and mercenaries, even when they still had a master," he said. "Now, they don't even have *that* leash. That woman's got a silver sword, and no Oath to bind her."

I watched Strahl's face carefully. I'd speculated more than once that my bosun had been in the Imperial Army as a younger man—but whatever role he'd served in the Imperium, he'd somehow dodged swearing the Oath that the rest of us had broken by default. I knew that Strahl regretted his service. It was the only thing that every crewmember on this vessel could agree on: The Imperium had deserved its death. But Strahl and I had never discussed any particulars, past that very important point of agreement. Like many of the rest of the crew, Strahl was looking to make a clean break from his past.

Strahl's stone cold face betrayed nothing. But I believed in my heart that he spoke from a place of concern for the rest of us.

"There was only one female Legionnaire, the way I remember it," I said. "I could recite you facts about the other dozen from memory, but... I never took an interest in her, for some reason." I mumbled the last part. It was obvious, in hindsight, why I'd never cared about Sweet Laurel. I couldn't imagine myself wielding a woman's sword... so there was no point in obsessing over her.

Young William Blair had been awfully full of himself, in more ways than one.

"She's not Sweet Laurel," Strahl told me. "Sweet Laurel was around thirty-five years old when the war ended. This woman's barely in her twenties. Can't you tell?"

I flushed at that. "The white hair makes things difficult!" I said defensively. "I have enough trouble telling new humans apart as it is." Strahl arched an eyebrow at this, and my flush deepened. I'd complained to him more than once that humans seemed to think all goblins looked alike. I breezed very quickly past the subject. "So, she's not a Legionnaire. She got her hands on one of their silver swords though, and she knows how to use it."

"She knows how to use it *well*," Strahl said grimly. "A real Legionnaire trained that woman. If I'm wrong, I'd eat your hat."

I reached up instinctively to defend my hat, even as I spoke back slowly. "You seem to know an awful lot about Legionnaires, Mr Strahl." I looked just past his head as I said it, careful not to imply a confrontation.

Strahl levelled a furnace glare at me. "Just what I've heard, Cap'n," he emphasised. His tone wasn't very convincing—but then, it probably wasn't meant to be. He took another violent bite of his apple. "You know—the physick says she's still sick from the aether. Be a shame if she didn't pull through."

Strahl sounded perfectly at ease as he said the words. He spoke in the same bored, casual tone he normally affected.

My bosun had killed a lot of people in his time.

I closed my eyes with a groan. I should have anticipated, perhaps, that I wouldn't be the only person on board to entertain the idea of hastening Miss Hawkins' demise. We'd all seen the war, from one angle or another. None of us wanted any part of the Imperium's remnants.

"Holloway is caring for her," I emphasised wearily. "Miss Hawkins will be fine."

It was not the answer Strahl had been hoping for. My burly bosun set his jaw and looked away.

"Syrene would've torn that aethermancer to bits already, if it wasn't for me," Strahl said darkly. "That woman used Unseelie aether. The Fair Folk still call that sacrilege. Come to it, Syrene's not too happy about us taking Unseelie aether on board either. She was in the mood to tear your arms from your sockets for a little bit, once she found out."

I felt another presence, then—a black, murderous, *violent* loathing that sank into my gut and flooded my veins. It was a hatred so feral that for a moment, I wanted to sink my teeth into Strahl's neck and butcher him for his arrogance. Syrene's face peered from the wall just behind Strahl, staring at me with unblinking black eyes.

I clenched my teeth against the irrational surge of fury. "Is that a threat?" I growled. I wasn't sure whether I ought to address the question to Strahl or to Syrene... so I asked the both of them at once.

The air grew thick between us. Syrene stared back at me, eerily expressionless. I felt the strands of her alien emotion wind around me, like the web of a sinister spider. Syrene pulled her body free of the wall, laying one long-fingered hand upon Strahl's shoulder with cryptic grace.

"Not a threat," Strahl said quietly. "Just a reminder."

"A *reminder*," I repeated slowly. "Then allow me to remind *you*, Mr Strahl, that if it weren't for me, you'd have hung from the gallows years ago—and Syrene would still be trapped in some aethermancer's trophy case. I remember what you said to me the day we all risked our necks to break her out. Do you?"

Strahl turned his stony visage away at the reminder. Before he did, however, I caught a flash of regret in his eyes. Both Strahl and Syrene had promised to follow my orders, so long as they were aboard the *Rose*.

"I made no contracts with the Evernight," I said to Syrene. "I was told the canisters were aether—and if I'd opened one up to check what *kind* of aether they were, then I'd be dead right now, anyway." Something plucked a nervous string in my soul as I forced myself to meet her inhuman eyes. I wasn't sure whether the nervousness was mine or whether she'd engineered it herself. "If there's to be any punishment, then it falls on the heads of those that pacted with the Unseelie. Isn't that right?"

Syrene went utterly still. There was no breeze below deck... but the strands of her lavender hair still danced upon a phantom breeze as she contemplated my argument.

Slowly, the furious bloodlust abated. Warmth and affection flooded back with jarring suddenness. Syrene's body shifted too—that arachnid, predatory grace gave way to a more fluid and feminine composure.

"We agree with the good captain," Syrene said, in a voice like pleasant wind chimes. "We remain grateful to him for his efforts on our behalf." A cunning undertone slipped into her cheerful voice. "We would *also* be quite happy to tear the heart from the woman who stinks of the Unseelie."

I shivered uncomfortably. I was reminded of a child begging for sweets.

"Miss Hawkins falls under my hospitality," I told Syrene. "For *now*." I glanced towards Strahl. "That goes for you as well, Mr Strahl. As long as the two of you are on my ship, you respect my rules. You agreed to that."

Silence stretched between us. Strahl met my eyes, and I could see him measuring his words carefully.

"...this is a mistake," he said finally. He shook his head in defeat, though, as he took another bite from his apple and turned to lumber away.

Syrene followed after him, melting away into the *Rose* itself.

I let out a sigh of relief, before I could stop myself. That had been an... unexpectedly *bracing* conversation.

I waited another moment for the trembling in my body to relax. Once it had mostly gone, I knocked at the good physick's door.

Holloway's heavy footsteps sounded on the other side. As he opened the door, I noted his tired features; the physicker probably hadn't slept since treating both me and Hawkins. Still, his gruff face relaxed as he saw me walking around under my own power.

"I see Miss Mary did her job admirably," Holloway said. He

stepped aside to let me into his quarters. "Still. Let me take a second look at you."

I closed the door behind me, glancing surreptitiously around the room. Several injured crew still rested in bunks on one side of the clinic. On the other side, in a more secluded corner, Holloway had tucked Hawkins away in order to keep an eye on her personally. Her pale figure stood out like a ghost in the dim light—and I found myself thinking about Strahl and his own bleached colours. Perhaps, the thought struck me, my bosun really *was* an aethermancer? But I discarded the strange idea almost as soon as I'd had it. Strahl could barely work the sword he'd stolen off an aethermancer in Lyonesse, even with Mr Finch's clever engineering tricks to help him.

"Look at me, please," Holloway said, interrupting my thoughts. He tucked his fingers beneath my chin and angled my head upwards so that he could inspect my eyes. Whatever he saw there, it seemed to satisfy him—for he dropped my chin again. "You don't seem much worse for the wear," Holloway observed. "Very fortunate."

"The Lady smiles on a fool," I mumbled self-consciously. I glanced towards Hawkins again. "How is our passenger doing?"

"Her outlook is... positive," Holloway said. He stepped away from me to grab a tumbler of whiskey. The good physickers always kept a bottle on hand, for more reasons than one. "I was a bit at a loss as to her treatment, at first, but Walther offered his expertise on the matter."

"Mr Finch?" I asked in surprise.

Holloway raised an eyebrow at me. "Walther is certified to teach theoretical aethermancy," the physicker said. "He hasn't taught a class since before the war, of course, but he is still quite the formidable academic. Especially considering some of the more..." He paused. "*...sensitive* material he stumbled across, during his tenure at university."

Mr Finch was perhaps the last man anyone would suspect of being a rebel. In some ways, that was part of his charm. During the Sundering War, my upstanding, tea-obsessed chief engineer had pretended to be an obedient scholar and professor. Right up until the end of the war, however, Mr Finch had used his academic access in order to pass the Coalition sensitive information about the empire's latest ships, weapons, and aetheric research.

"And what does Mr Finch's theoretical aethermancy suggest about Miss Hawkins' condition?" I asked carefully.

"Fortunately for Miss Hawkins," Holloway said grimly, lowering his voice, "Walther had occasion to browse some of the empire's most restricted records. There are still old papers on the effects of Unseelie aether, dating back to the last two Breachings."

I sighed heavily. Perhaps it shouldn't have surprised me how many people had figured out the truth about our cargo, given its horrifyingly distinctive effects. "Miss Hawkins should count herself fortunate that our chief engineer is such an unruly academic magpie," I muttered.

"Quite," Holloway agreed. "Apparently, Unseelie aether lingers within the body unless it is specifically flushed out. Post-Breaching medical records suggest treatment with diluted Seelie aether. Walther and I borrowed some of Miss Hawkins' extra aether for the purpose, and I've been administering it in small, regular doses. Of course, Seelie and Unseelie aether do not react particularly well with one another, so there are bound to be—"

Hawkins bolted upright in her bed, clutching at her stomach. Holloway dropped the tumbler back onto his desk and reached for a bucket just next to her cot. Hawkins grabbed at it blindly—whereupon she proceeded to be violently ill.

"—side-effects," Holloway finished.

I winced at the sight. Hawkins was sickly pale and sweating with a fever. Thin threads of darkness threaded visibly through her veins just beneath her skin, where Unseelie aether still lingered within her.

Hawkins spent the next minute heaving and trembling over the bucket. Eventually, however, she sank back against her cot with a soft groan.

The charitable half of me wanted to give the poor woman time and space to recover. But we were on our way to Pelaeia—and I had no intention of bringing her with us unless she had something truly remarkable to say to me.

"Mr Holloway," I said, "would you mind giving me a moment alone with Miss Hawkins?"

Holloway shot me a startled look—but I had always been blessed with an uncommonly loyal crew, for reasons I had yet to fully understand. He nodded curtly and turned away, towards his other patients.

"I don't foresee any difficulties," Holloway told me. "But I'll be nearby, if she should take a turn for the worse."

He drew the hanging curtain closed, in order to give me some privacy with Miss Hawkins.

Hawkins took a few shuddering breaths. I could tell from her face that she was still trying to gauge whether she had more in her stomach to throw up.

"We need to talk, Miss Hawkins," I said. "And I'm afraid it really can't wait for a more convenient time."

Hawkins steeled herself. I watched it happen—the way her posture straightened and her breathing levelled out. It shouldn't have surprised me how quickly she regained her composure, even in the middle of that wretched sickness. All of the best aethermancers had a cold iron will. It was how they maintained control of the aether they wielded.

"Are we still being chased, Captain?" she asked.

I settled myself carefully onto the stool next to her bed. As I did, I checked the room surreptitiously for any signs of aether or foci. I saw only the aether-lantern above us and a single vial of wispy-looking aether upon the far table. The aether in that vial was the diluted stuff that Holloway had mentioned; it was probably of even less use than the stuff in the aether-lantern.

"We haven't seen any signs of pursuit just yet," I said. "But that doesn't mean there won't *be* any pursuit. We still have that unholy aether in our hold, after all."

I watched Hawkins carefully as I said this. Since waking up, I had thought back on the sequence of events that had brought her to our ship. Hawkins had shown up in need of passage at the exact same moment that we had arrived with our cargo. What's more, she had *known* that we were carrying Unseelie aether; she had flinched and tried to warn off the watchmen as they cracked open the crates.

"I was thinking we should dump the stuff as soon as possible," I said slowly. "Do you know of a safe way to destroy it?"

Hawkins stiffened at the suggestion. "I would ask you not to destroy the aether in your hold, Captain," she told me shakily. "Not *yet*, at least."

I narrowed my eyes at her. Already, this conversation was trending in a direction that suggested I ought to have let Syrene have her pound of flesh. "You want us to *keep* Unseelie aether?" I asked.

Hawkins must have read the darkness in my expression. She clenched her jaw. She was sick and blurry-minded, and she knew it. There was little way for her to control this conversation the way that she probably wanted to do.

"You made an Oath to me, Captain," she told me. "I went above and beyond to fulfil your needs—"

"—and you could still hare off and murder a whole slew of people, and it would still be on my head," I finished for her. "Look at me, Miss Hawkins. I saw Pelaeia only a week after it was razed. No amount of honour or personal fondness will ever convince me to contribute to something like that again."

Hawkins blinked at me in confusion. I felt a moment of disconnect between us—as though I'd just turned her world upside-down.

"You're an... anti-Imperialist?" Hawkins asked me. Her tone was utterly bewildered. "I thought you were ex-Navy."

I flushed with displeasure—and no small amount of shame. "I suspect that you are about to have a very disappointing day, Miss Hawkins," I told her coldly.

Hawkins shook her head slowly. "I think there has been a misunderstanding, Captain," she said. Curiously, she now sounded more confident than she had before. "I asked for passage on your vessel because I intended to foil this shipment. An Imperialist faction has paid for this cargo. I have other uses for it... but they are scientific in nature. Above all else, however, this aether must not reach the people who have paid for it. I *would* destroy it, before I allowed such a thing to happen."

Now *I* was feeling perplexed.

My first instinct, of course, was that Miss Hawkins was lying to me once again. And why not? She had disguised herself and misrepresented her intentions when she'd asked for passage on our ship. She had a silver sword. Strahl was convinced that she had been trained by a Silver Legionnaire.

But Miss Hawkins had only misrepresented herself when she'd thought that she was talking to an ex-Imperial captain. Moreover... she was of necessity working in opposition to whichever dangerous client Barsby was too afraid to face—whoever it was that had commissioned the theft of Unseelie aether.

The enemy of my enemy is sometimes a war criminal too, I reminded myself grimly.

"Why do you have a silver sword?" I asked her bluntly. "And what do you intend to do with this Unseelie aether?" Hawkins forced a neutral expression onto her face. I saw her prepare to put me off—so I made myself a little more plain. "You're going to answer these questions," I told her. "And I'd better believe the answers. Because if you don't convince me you're something other than a proud new Silver Legionnaire, Miss Hawkins, then I swear, I will throw you off the side of this ship."

Hawkins narrowed her eyes at me. "You swear?" she repeated in a chilly voice. "And how much is *that* worth, Captain Blair?"

I clenched my jaw. "I'm not in the mood to argue theology," I told her. "Either you believe me or you don't."

Hawkins considered me calmly. I saw her glance towards the aether-lantern; and then towards the vial of diluted aether. I knew she was assessing whether she could overpower me with what she had on hand. And perhaps she could—she was, after all, a fantastically skilful aethermancer. But what then? She'd still be sick and weak, on a ship full of antagonistic people.

It didn't take her long to come to the conclusion I hoped she would.

"I will remember this, Captain," Hawkins said.

I crossed my arms and waited.

Another shudder wracked the woman's body as I watched. She heaved into the bucket next to her with a choked sound of frustration. I might have believed she was trying to buy time, if not for the miserable tears in her eyes.

Once she'd recovered, Hawkins reached for a waterskin next to the cot and took a long drink. The steel went out of her spine. The haggard look returned.

"I was trained by a Silver Legionnaire," Hawkins croaked out finally. "By luck, Captain, more than anything else. I lost my family to pirates. I would be a slave right now, and not an aethermancer at all, if Jonathan Silver hadn't rescued me."

A remnant of my old hero-worship fluttered within me—immediately tempered with nausea. "Jonathan Silver," I whispered. "Then, the sword you hold—"

"I carry the sword Galatine," Hawkins finished dully. She glanced down at her heavily bandaged right hand. "He... Jonathan passed the sword to me before his death."

The grief on her face was instant, and fresh. Sympathy surged inside me once again, no matter how I tried to quash it. Jonathan Silver had been no saint. Rot and ruin, he had been a pirate himself, before the emperor had offered him a silver sword and a letter of marque.

But Hawkins had clearly loved the man.

"He wanted to atone," Hawkins said softly. "It was all he ever talked about. He's been researching... he *had* been researching a way to send on the echoes that linger from the war. Now that he's gone, I'm the only one who can do it for him."

The weight of her statement struck me like a blow. I found myself briefly at a loss.

Was it true? Could it possibly be true? As far as I knew, Jonathan Silver hadn't had anything to do with the razing of Pelaeia... but he'd been active in the war. Surely, the ex-Imperials on my ship couldn't be the only ones that regretted their past, now that the truth was common knowledge and the propaganda had been stripped away?

Pelaeia had been rebuilt—but it was still a pale shadow of its former self. So long as the tortured spirits of the war remained, there would always be areas that were dangerous, off-limits. There would be families who could never retrieve the bodies of the fallen. Every evening, when the wailing grew louder, the clanfolk were reminded that the ghosts of their loved ones would never truly rest.

No one could ever fix the razing of Pelaeia. But if this was true—if Hawkins really could accomplish what she said she could accomplish—then the clans could at least be allowed some respite from its horrific aftereffects.

"You need Unseelie aether for this?" I asked softly. I tried to keep my tone suspicious… but I already knew that I halfway believed her. I *wanted* to believe her.

I wanted to believe that I had been offered a chance at atonement, no matter how slight.

"Seelie aether created those echoes," Hawkins said quietly. "They might have been an unexpected side-effect, but they're still of a Seelie nature. Unseelie aether is putrid, it's true… but it is inherently opposed to everything that the Seelie create. With the right instruments and intentions, and with a strong enough will, I believe that I can safely unravel the trap that the Seelie aether has created and allow those echoes to move on. At least… all of the theory points in that direction."

By the Benefactor's merciful hand, how I wanted to believe her.

"You're in luck, then," I said stiltedly. "As it turns out—we're headed to Pelaeia now."

Hawkins blinked at me uncertainly.

"Rest up, Miss Hawkins," I told her. "I'm going to give you a chance to prove the truth."

8

NO OATHS - AESIR MACLEOD - UNWELCOME NEWS

The survivors of Pelaeia didn't want us.

I didn't blame them, even back then. The Imperial Navy hadn't treated its Coalition prisoners with half as much care as we'd been shown. We were exiled to the edge of the ragged encampment in Pelaeia's shadow; Elfa settled there to watch over us, since no one else wanted to do so. But we were fed, and we had straw cots and heavy blankets to keep us warm in the cold northern air. Every morning, Holloway left to see to the sick and injured, while the rest of us stayed with Elfa. She did her best to find us useful work, which we performed with all of the desperation of guests who knew that they were unwelcome.

Evie took to following around the halcyon like an anxious duckling. Every spare moment that Evie wasn't diligently working on chores or worrying over the rest of us, I saw him reading the Word of the Benefactor, scouring it with soul-deep urgency. Sometimes, I saw him look at the burning mountain that overshadowed us, and I knew the exact thoughts that ran through his mind: *How can I be a good person again? Is it even possible? Surely, if anyone would know, it would be the Benefactor.*

Little still hadn't said a word since that fateful moment on the

HMS Caliban, but Evie had coaxed him into rudimentary communication using some of the Imperial Handsign we'd learned by watching the officers. It was such a relief to see that Little hadn't completely broken. There were so few people willing to talk to us, and some days, it felt as though all we had was each other.

Dougal MacLeod visited once or twice, in the evenings. His presence was always stilted and uncomfortable. I knew on some level that he didn't want to be there—that he only came because he felt a responsibility to see through his decision to spare us. But I had developed a pathetic, inexplicable need for his approval, and so I often found myself talking at him with far more enthusiasm than he might have liked. I couldn't stop myself, no matter how uncomfortable he looked; I had never known such a bone-deep desire for anyone's good opinion. I desired it more than I had desired smiles from Physicker Holloway or accolades from Vice-Admiral Wakefield.

It was during one of these evenings after dinner, as I babbled about the way we'd made up hand signs for each of our names, that Dougal interrupted me.

"It's a warm night, lad," he said. "Why don't we walk an' talk, outside?"

My heart stuttered in my chest. I cut myself off mid-sentence, caught halfway between hope and fear. Surely, I thought, the big man was going to take me aside and tell me in private that I ought to leave him alone—that just because he'd spared my life didn't make him my friend. But I nodded nervously and pulled my coat more tightly around me, carefully gauging the proper distance at which I ought to follow him.

It was not actually a warm night. There are very few warm nights on the slopes of Pelaeia. But the stars were bright and clear, in a way that reminded me of the view from above the clouds. The scene would have been beautiful, if not for the flickering aether-light of the moaning mountain before us.

Dougal walked for a long while in silence—long enough that I began to wonder if I was supposed to say something. But eventually—

a good ways down one of the game trails—he settled himself onto a broad rock.

There was no other convenient rock next to him, but that didn't matter. I sat down on the cold, hard ground next to him, glancing worriedly up at his face.

I wasn't sure what to make of the expression there. I'd been expecting anger, or annoyance, or regret. But it was just a weary sort of sadness. Dougal MacLeod struck me in that moment as a man who'd gone past normal grief.

"Ah'd like to ask ye a question, lad," Dougal said finally. He stared up at the sky, in the opposite direction of the mountain behind us. "But ah'd like ye tae give me a true answer, if ye can, an' no just one ye think ah'd like to hear."

I had started to tremble at some point, and not from the cold. I would have told Dougal MacLeod anything he wanted to hear... but the truth? I had a feeling that whatever truth he wanted, I'd be loath to give it to him.

Still. I couldn't bring myself to disappoint him. I nodded slowly.

"Why'd ye join the Navy?" Dougal asked me. His eyes fixed upon those distant stars with a hint of confusion. "What made ye take the uniform an' go aff fightin' the Coalition?"

My mouth went dry. I knew the answer to this question—I didn't have to think about it for even a moment. But it was a stupid reason, and I knew that too.

Dougal glanced down towards me. I saw the disappointment in his face, the longer that I stayed silent. It drove me to speak, though the words hurt coming out of me.

"The sky," I said, in a raspy, faltering voice.

Dougal frowned at that, and I could tell he didn't understand. I struggled to keep going—but he didn't interrupt me, or try to rush me.

"I grew up in Morgause," I said. "You don't see the sky there, almost ever. There's always smog. But one day, the wind picked up just before a storm, and I saw..." I swallowed. "I saw a blue patch of sky. And I just knew I had to get closer to it, no matter what it took."

Dougal rocked back a bit at this. It clearly wasn't the answer he'd been expecting.

"The Navy was recruiting," I told him. The words spilled out of me in a rush, as though a dam had broken. "I tried to volunteer, but they told me they didn't take goblins. I should've left it at that. But I sneaked aboard the first Navy ship I could find, just before they deployed." I smiled ruefully. "They found me in storage. Probably would've thrown me over the side, but... Mr Holloway said I was his nephew. Goblins and hobgoblins aren't related at all, except in the name—but they pretended to believe him, I guess. They made me a cabin boy and gave me a uniform."

Dougal watched me as I spoke. I saw in his features the same fierce studiousness that Evie had displayed while reading the Word of the Benefactor—as though he was trying to discern the answer to a great mystery from the details of my story.

"Ye were proud ae that?" he asked me. He kept his tone carefully even, but I still flinched at the question.

"I... yessir," I said, in a small voice. "I'm sorry."

Dougal gave a pained, startled sort of laugh. "Ye're sorry?" he asked me.

"I am," I said desperately. "I am... so sorry. I thought I was doing a good thing, sir, I really did. I worked hard, and I did everything I was told. I knew I might die if we got into a fight, and I thought I was brave to be there anyway."

Dougal shook his head. That pained laugh dimmed to a bewildered chuckle. "Did they tell ye *why* ye were fightin'?" he asked me.

I swallowed. "Because... the rebels were traitors," I said softly. "It's our duty to send soldiers to Arcadia, to defend everyone from the Unseelie. But the rebels refused to go." I looked down. "Vice-Admiral Wakefield said the rebels were being selfish. He said the rest of us sent Tithes, but the rebels thought they were too special to send their own."

Dougal nodded along with this, as though it was more along the lines of what he'd expected to hear. "Oh, aye," he said. "We refused at some point." He sighed heavily. "We sent our Tithes, lad. We did it wae pride. There's no greater duty than tae join the Seelie in their battle, tae protect our world. But the empire kept... askin.' More an' more Tithes, they asked for, 'til we'd little left to give. We'd wives wae no husbands an' children wae no fathers. Crops died in th' fields for lack a' hands tae harvest 'em. Come winter, people starved." He crossed his arms over his chest with a grim sort of thoughtfulness. "The favoured provinces like the Emerald Spires never got asked twice. But Pelaeia got asked a third time. It was a death sentence for our families. So we said no... an' when the Emerald Spires had the gall tae threaten us, we took from their shipments tae feed our people for the winter."

I knitted my brow at this. My first instinct was that this was new information to me... but I'd promised Dougal to be truthful, and I realised on some level that I *had* known this already. Back in Morgause, I'd overheard conversations about the distant civil war. It had been a topic of mild interest, and occasionally a topic of sentiment. A few people *had* harrumphed and said how the Emerald Spires was full of hypocrites, and perhaps something less violent could be worked out if people would just *talk*.

But most people had been of the opinion that the Coalition had to follow the rules just like everyone else. Surely, the Coalition had broken the rules, and that was why we were fighting them. The rebels had attacked first, which made them wrong. And the Imperium wouldn't have fought a war for *bad* reasons.

Even as young as I was, I thought I was wise and world-weary. I knew that people didn't enjoy thinking very hard—and that they especially didn't enjoy thinking very hard about other people in trouble. I'd begged for food and received kicks and insults instead. I'd advanced to pickpocketing, just to survive.

But somehow, I'd assumed that the empire as a whole was different from its citizens. For... what reason? Because it was old and vast? Because it had always been there, so it had to work? I wasn't sure now. Why did I think that the people who ran the empire were any different from the people who walked past me with their eyes straight ahead every day of my life?

The rebels had starved. And then, they'd gone to pickpocket food from people who wouldn't miss it.

"I knew that, I think," I told Dougal. Misery threaded through my voice. "I didn't believe it. I didn't *want* to believe it. I don't know why. The Imperium never did anything good for me, but... I still wanted to believe they were right."

Dougal rubbed at his face. "I cannae understand it for ye," he admitted. "Part ae me doesn't *want* tae understand, ye know?" He turned to look at me, and I saw the exhaustion in his shoulders. "Ah won't lie, lad. It would've been easier tae let ye die an' let Death Victorious sort ye out. An' truth be told, ah understand why Cauldwell wanted tae shoot ye. He lost his father an' his wife an' his babe in Pelaeia. Ye were old enough tae serve an' shoot at us, an' there's a view that says that means ye're old enough tae die fer it."

I stared at him. My body froze; my breath caught in my throat. There was no keener terror in the world than to hear the man that had saved my life question whether I ought to die after all.

But Dougal shook his head at me. "Ah made my decision, lad," he said. "Ye dinnae know why ye believed the empire. An' me... Ah dinnae know why ah hurt another man tae protect ye. But ah needed t'do it fer some reason, an' ah'll see it through now."

My body fell to trembling. I wasn't sure if it would stop until I was back in my cot, buried beneath the blankets.

"Did you lose family in Pelaeia?" I whispered.

Dougal nodded. There were no tears in his eyes—but I suspected that was because he had already cried too many. "Lost ma sister an' ma niece," he said. "Ah've taken up raisin' ma nephew. He's a wee lad—barely talks just yet. But he's lost his arm. An' he knows what happened, even if he cannae describe it yet."

"I'm sorry," I said again. I knew it was inadequate, but it was all that I had. My throat choked up with tears. "I'm sorry. I wish I could take it back. I wish I'd been better."

Dougal smiled wanly at me. "There's some that'd say it's easy t'be sorry after ye've lost the war," he told me. "But it means... *somethin'* to me, lad. A wee bit." Something about my tears stirred an answering lump in his throat. "Cauldwell needed vengeance tae feel whole, ah think. But ah needed… ah needed tae believe ah could make sense ae it. Ah want tae think we can learn a lesson that'll stick, an' that maybe next time, someone puts their foot down an' says *there won't be another Pelaeia*."

I seized upon this immediately. "There won't be," I said. "Not in front of me. I'll put my foot down if it kills me, Mr MacLeod, I'll give you my Oath—"

"Yer Oathbroken, lad," Dougal reminded me gently. "Ye cannae give Oaths anymore."

I closed my mouth—abruptly reminded of my fresh new shame.

"Wouldn't want yer Oath anyway," Dougal told me. "Oaths dinnae mean anything tae me. Tyrants force Oaths on people—poor people, people who can't say no. An Oath is just another kind a' chain." He met my eyes steadily. "Make me a promise from yer heart, instead—because ye mean it, an' because ye truly believe it."

I clenched my fingers into fists. I desperately wished that I could have sworn to Noble Gallant. I wanted Him to hold me accountable, so that I needn't fear that I would lose my nerve to cowardice.

But Dougal wanted me to hold *myself* accountable. That was the apology he wanted. And I knew in that moment that it was the most generous thing that anyone would ever offer me. Because what I *deserved*, without a doubt, was the bullet that Cauldwell had meant for me.

Dougal had offered me the sort of mercy that no one should ever ask for.

"I promise," I whispered. "You didn't spare me for nothing, Mr MacLeod."

This time, I did see tears in Dougal's eyes. They welled up and spilled over, mixed with a painful, bittersweet relief.

The big northerner reached out to hug me. He held onto me because I was the only one there, I think, and because he needed emotional purchase. But I took a comfort from that hug that I knew was also undeserved.

Evie had gone searching for the meaning of mercy in the Word of the Benefactor. But it was a heretic named Dougal MacLeod that made me understand just how precious and how terrible mercy can be.

* * *

TWENTY YEARS LATER, New Pelaeia looked somewhat less like a camp of ragged refugees and somewhat more like a real city. The lower districts had been mostly rebuilt, and newer areas had been constructed on the lower slopes of the mountain. Some of the vessels that had landed near Pelaeia at the war's conclusion had been turned into more permanent fixtures: pubs, inns, homes, and even one lonely, rarely used shrine to the Benefactor. These odd ship-buildings mixed freely with wooden homes built from great logs, dragged up from the forests below.

The contrast between old Pelaeia and New Pelaeia was even starker from our viewpoint in the air. The Upper District, already devastated, had withered further under decades of ice and snow, unchecked by mortal oversight. That awful, immortal aether-light still burned upon the mountain. I knew that unless someone had executed a miracle in my absence, at least two-thirds of the old city remained cursed by echoes. Aethermancers had offered before to study the phenomenon... but they were always rejected. Wraithwood had not left the people of Pelaeia with a terrible fondness for aethermancy.

Aethermancers weren't *illegal* in Pelaeia, exactly. They were just... unwanted. Strahl always attracted sideways glances when we visited, given his aether-bleached appearance. Clearly, he hadn't earned an "honest grey", as some northerners liked to say. Hawkins, however, was an even more obvious taboo without her disguise. I worried at first that she might chafe at being told to stay on the ship for an extended period—but Hawkins surprised me with a hearty dose of common sense and agreed that this was for the best. This gave me a bit more faith in my decision to pursue her strange research; it has been my experience that great power and common sense rarely keep company.

We weighed anchor at the lower dock in the late afternoon. My weary crew began to settle us in, quietly cursing Barsby's name. I cringed as I passed the grumblers. Picket's jobs were normally reliable money—but because Barsby had kept us from the bank in New Havenshire, there wasn't any money to share this time. This job wasn't the first time we'd lost good people... but it was certainly the first time we'd done it for free.

Those with money still squirrelled away took their leave to relax; a few of those without decided to stretch their legs away from the ship. As for me—I had grim business in town.

I didn't particularly want to address that business alone. But I needed Little to remain with the ship in my absence. Evie would have been a comforting choice, but he had stepped in as Holloway's backup nurse while Mary rested.

Miss Lenore Brighton greatly desired a stiff drink, however. And since the person I was searching for was likely to be at a pub by now, we found ourselves in each other's company.

The mountain air was chill, especially in the shadow of the great peak. My breath came in silver plumes as I headed into town with Lenore. We both dressed in knitted layers we'd acquired from the gunnery ladies over the years. Lenore could have knitted her *own* outerwear, of course, but it was an unspoken rule that no gunnery lady ought to knit her own things. In fact, Lenore's lopsided scarf had come from young Mr Billings, who'd only just learned enough about knitting to hold his own.

"Is Mr Billings technically a gunnery lady?" I mused aloud.

Lenore arched an eyebrow at me. "He's proven he can knit," she said. "I suppose that means he won't be leaving."

I nodded my agreement. "Oh, yes," I said. "Certainly, he's *staying*. I was just wondering whether he minds being called a gunnery lady, or whether we ought to find a different name for you all, on his account."

Lenore twitched her lips. "Trust I already asked him," she told me. "Mr Billings doesn't want the name changed. He worked hard to earn his place. He said if we changed the name, people might think we'd lowered our standards for him."

I snorted.

The streets in the Lower District were coated with a light dusting of snow, but it had already been mostly trampled away. We caught a few curious looks between us—me with my green skin, red eyes, and pointed ears, and Lenore with her pretty face. This far north, established settlements were mostly populated by humans and stony-skinned hobgoblins, with the occasional nomadic cervitaur wandering in from outside; goblins were a rarity outside of the industrial heartlands of the former Imperium. I'd always noticed that people softened their suspicions of me when I was with a woman, though, since they assumed I was a servant. Lenore's presence made me seem 'cute' and 'subservient', rather than 'shifty'. I wasn't fond of the implications either way—but at least this version of things led to less open trouble than the narrative that I was a natural-born troublemaker.

Lenore scowled and pulled her scarf up over her mouth. "Northern manners," she muttered. "Someone ought to teach these people not to stare."

"We're in Pelaeia," I said grudgingly. "They've got a right to worry about newcomers. The other northern cities are a bit friendlier."

Lenore shifted her shoulders, as though to shake off the weight of those glances. "I don't like *friendly* people either," she retorted. "I like people who mind their own business."

I smirked despite myself. "Northerners mind their own business," I said. "They *also* mind everyone else's business. They're very talented minders, I've always thought."

Lenore narrowed her eyes over her lopsided scarf. "We're looking for one in particular, I take it?" she said.

"Aesir MacLeod," I replied glumly. "Dougal's nephew."

Nephew didn't quite convey the depth of their relationship, of course. Aesir had lost both his parents and his arm to the atrocities in Pelaeia at a very young age. Dougal had been forced to raise his nephew like a son—a circumstance which hadn't suited either of them terribly well. Certainly, they'd loved each other... but Dougal had probably been a better uncle than he was a parent, judging from the way they'd clashed.

"And you think we'll find Aesir MacLeod in a bar?" Lenore asked.

I squinted at the darkening sky. "Winter is just starting up," I said. "The pubs here always make sure to keep the fires stoked high. Aesir does salvage work and ship repairs, mostly outdoors. He'll be right next to the fire with a warm cider, if he can manage it."

The Lady of Fools had certainly got Her fair share of laughs over the course of my early life. Somehow, I'd managed to forge a more cordial relationship with Aesir than he'd had with his own uncle. We weren't *close*, mind you, but we'd found some common ground while growing up together.

I'd spent a lot of time feeling guilty about Aesir's missing arm—and even more time trying not to show it. Not everyone in Pelaeia wanted my guilt, I had learned. *The men of Pelaeia want their families back,* Elfa had told me. My guilt was a poor substitute for that.

Rather than guilt, I suppose, I'd given Aesir a few warm ciders and a bit of company.

The source of those ciders soon came into view. MacGregor's Anchor was a sturdy structure: equal parts stone, wood, and steel scrap. The titular anchor—a huge, battle-scarred chunk of steel beaded with melted snow—stood proudly out front.

Lenore craned her head to blink up at the anchor. "I don't think I understand northern art, either," she admitted to me. "What is *that* supposed to be?"

"*That* is MacGregor's anchor," I explained. "Captain MacGregor's ship ran out of munitions during a battle, so he decided to weigh anchor on an Imperial ship instead. I'm not sure how true the story is, but northerners say he pulled *that* ship into *another* ship, and all three of them went down off the Lackland Coast." I shook my head at the idea. "Some enterprising sort salvaged the anchor and brought it back to Pelaeia and decided to rename the pub—because, they say, if you're going down in the drink, you may as well bring some folks with you."

I couldn't make out Lenore's mouth beneath her scarf—but I

thought I saw her eyes sharpen with vicious glee. "There's a man after my own heart," she said.

I looked away uncomfortably. Lenore hadn't been a part of the Coalition... exactly. Her husband had left home to join the cause, though, and he'd died in the war. Everyone on the *Rose* had made their peace with the past, more or less... but every once in a while, we couldn't help but remind each other of our once-cluttered loyalties.

Loud cheering broke out inside the pub, cutting through the awkward moment.

The door opened—and a man tumbled out onto the slick cobblestones.

He rolled on the ground a few times, gaining an impressive distance from the pub before he came to a thudding stop. Still, he looked more shocked than injured; he soon shook his head and wobbled to his feet.

I recognised him more by his stained mechanic's jumpsuit than by his features. I find it embarrassingly difficult to tell humans apart sometimes, and most northerners here had the same broad shoulders and thick head of fiery red hair. It had been a few years since I'd seen Aesir MacLeod, and even in the half-light, I could tell that he'd aged out of his awkward phase into a well-muscled man in his prime. He'd cut his hair short—odd for a northerner, but not entirely unexpected. Aesir had often complained that his long hair had a tendency to catch in little places while he worked; it would be just like him to lose his patience one day and cut it all off. A new blaze of white on the right side of his head stood out sharply. I was sure it hadn't been there, the last time I had seen him.

"Is that all ye got?" Aesir called out towards the pub's open door, with only a hint of a drunken slur. "Ah'm still standin'!"

"So much for a quiet drink," Lenore muttered.

Aesir had barely stormed back in when a boot drove into his gut, shoving him backwards. Said boot was attached to an old northerner, who stomped out after Aesir. The older man's hair was mostly blond, with only the faintest embers of rusty red remaining; it reminded me of the last vestiges of paint on an otherwise barren hull. Despite his age, the northerner was still strong and hale. His powerful arms filled out a dark old jacket. A faded golden Coalition kerchief hung around his neck.

Part of the man's face was horribly scarred, melted like pale candle wax. Bright blue veins shimmered beneath those waxy burn scars. I would have bet my hat that scar had been caused by aetheric flames. He was far drunker than Aesir, judging by his stagger. A dark fury clung to him as he moved—the sort you could only find at the bottom of a bottle.

"Tha's 'nough outta you, whelp!" the older man slurred. He took a powerful swing at Aesir with his fist—but the younger man quickly danced out of reach.

"Ye've had enough tae drink," Aesir snapped back warningly. He pointed a warning finger at the raging drunkard. "Shut yer gob an' go hame, Hamish. Ye're makin' an arse ae yersel. Ye'll wake up embarrassed tomorrow, mark ma words."

Hamish screwed up his face, dimly furious. "Nae respect!" he spat. He took another wild swing at Aesir—somewhat better aimed, this time. Aesir brought his arms up into a boxer's defence, just in time to protect his head. "Ah was *there*, boy!" Hamish growled. "Ye dinnae get tae talk to me that way!"

Hamish's swing had put him just within arm's reach of Aesir, however. The younger northerner lashed out with his left hand to grip at a fistful of Hamish's braided beard. Aesir yanked the beard sharply downwards, introducing Hamish's face to his right fist.

The impact made a loud metallic *clang*. Hamish rocked back on his heels, stunned by the blow.

Light glinted off Aesir's mechanical right hand as he pulled it back. I stared at the arm with fascination. It, too, was a new addition. Though it had clearly been pieced together from scrap, it had five distinct fingers—all the right length and size—and it worked very nearly as a hand should do.

Hamish shook off the punch. The old man straightened as best he could, raising his hands into an aggressive stance.

Aesir sighed heavily, and stuck him again.

Clang.

This time, I heard the man's jaw crunch very slightly.

Hamish dropped to his knees with a groan. He tried one more time to throw himself at Aesir's knees—but the younger man simply stepped aside this time. Hamish lost his balance and tumbled to the ground, instead.

"Ye're so drunk, ye don't even mind who ye're talkin' tae," Aesir said. "Where'd ah lose my arm, Hamish?" His lip curled in weary disgust. "Bein' at Peleaia disnae give ye the right tae be a bastard. When Finley says ye've had enough tae drink, ye've had enough tae drink. An' if ye ever raise yer hand to her again, I'll make sure ye've got to wheel yersel hame in a wheelbarrow."

A few other northerners had crowded near the door of the tavern, watching the fight warily. Aesir raised his eyebrows at them, and two of the sturdier men filtered out, mumbling words of gratitude at him. They dragged Hamish upright, despite his protests, and hauled the groaning man away. The rest of the crowd disappeared uncomfortably back inside, leaving us alone with Aesir.

I cleared my throat.

"Er—Aesir MacLeod?" I said carefully.

Aesir blinked at us, as though just noticing our presence. A moment later, he seemed to recognise me. "Blair!" he said, with obvious surprise. "Well... been a while, hasn't it?" He dusted off his hands, before hooking his thumbs through the belt loops on his jumpsuit. "Sorry 'bout that. Hamish's been... more an' more ae a problem lately. Everyone's tae much ae a coward tae tell aff a *survivor*, so he just goes on 'til it's tae much tae stomach."

I looked at Aesir bleakly. "So they make you do it instead?" I observed.

Aesir flashed me a hopeless smile. "Perks ae survivin' just keep addin' up, the older ah get," he said flatly. "Nae one *tells* me tae do it. They just... stand back 'till ah have tae."

A tired, furtive expression stole across his face at the statement. But he buried it quickly, forcing on a roguish grin that reminded me painfully of Dougal. "Who's the lady?" he asked. The question was halfway addressed to Lenore, herself. It carried an overly interested tone that made me wince.

"The *lady* is not interested," Lenore said shortly.

A drunken laugh bubbled out of Aesir at that. "Understood," he said. "Shame. Ye look like fun."

Lenore relaxed a bit at the easy acknowledgement. She glanced at me sideways. "I'm getting my drink, Captain," she said. "You know where to find me." She stepped past Aesir for the door of the pub, slipping quietly inside.

She'd clearly decided that this was supposed to be a private moment. Coward that I am, I briefly wished I'd asked her to stay.

Aesir watched her go with vague interest. As Lenore disappeared, he glanced back towards me. "Where's the old scoundrel, then?" he asked. "Don't tell me he's back oan the ship."

I thought I had been ready for that question. I *wanted* to be ready—to say exactly the right words for the situation. But my mouth opened, and... nothing came out. The words choked in my throat.

Aesir's forced smile drained from him, all at once.

"I'm... I'm sorry, Aesir," I finally croaked.

Aesir shook his head violently. For the first time, the alcohol in his blood showed in a nasty way upon his features. "Don't apologise," he spat. "Makes sense, doesn't it? The old man decided tae kick off, 'stead a face me."

The words were brutal—but the sentiment behind them was nothing I hadn't heard before. Bewildered grief hovered beneath the surface, overwhelmed for the moment by shock and drunkenness.

"I..." I swallowed heavily. I wasn't sure how to respond to that ugly mixture of emotions. I found myself forced to fall back upon the things I'd prepared to say in advance. "I brought back... him and his ship. So the clan can have the salvage for a proper wake."

"Ah don't care." Aesir fumbled the words, even as he spoke them. "Don't care. They'll do what they want. Some old, stupid tradition. Maybe they'll even have a halcyon talk nice about him." He laughed hollowly at that. "Nevermind how much he hated the Benefactor, aye?"

Every sentence only made me wince harder. I had already asked Evie if he would speak for Dougal. It hadn't occurred to me, somehow, that Dougal might have found the idea abhorrent.

"I just thought... he'd have wanted to come home," I said miserably.

Aesir staggered back against the pub's wall. The weight of the news seemed to have caught up with him, to some extent—because he slid down into a seated heap at the base of the building.

"He left as soon as he could," Aesir said dimly. "Left *me*. Why in rot an' ruin would he want tae come back, when he worked so hard tae escape?"

Silence fell between us.

I was perhaps the worst person in the world to deal with Aesir's complex feelings about Dougal. Holloway was right in that I'd never really been able to give the man orders—but it was worse than that. Deep down, I'd never been able to *think* badly about Dougal, even when he might have deserved it. Some part of me shied away violently from the idea, every time I tried.

I didn't have the right to disagree with Dougal MacLeod. I certainly didn't have the right to tell him so, even if I *had* disagreed with him.

"I'll... try to talk the chief down from having a halcyon," I said thickly. I mentally apologised to Evie, hoping he would understand. "I have to ask her about something else anyway."

Aesir raised his head to look at me. An odd light had kindled in his eyes, as though he'd had a personal revelation. I wasn't sure I liked that look.

"Ye're leavin' again soon," he said. "Back oan yer ship."

I shifted warily on my feet. "I am," I said carefully. "But not yet. I have... it's complicated."

Aesir squinted at me from his place on the snowy ground. "Uncomplicate it fer me," he said.

I worked my mouth helplessly for a few seconds. After the display I'd just seen, the very *last* thing I wanted to do was bring up the past. But Aesir's expression was suddenly fiercely focussed, and I knew I wasn't going to get away without telling him at least some of the truth.

"I have an aethermancer on my ship," I said finally. "She says she has the technology necessary to put the echoes to rest. I... halfway believe her. But I need to ask for permission if we're going into old Pelaeia."

Aesir chewed this over with far more calm than I had expected.

"Ye're goin' tae old Pelaeia," he said. "An' then ye're leavin'."

"Yes...?" I said. Aesir seemed far more focussed on the latter fact than he was on the former. I wasn't at all sure what to make of that. "I mean, we're staying for the wake, obviously—"

Aesir clambered to his feet, unsteady. "Chief's inside," he said. "Ye could talk tae her now, if ye wanted."

"I don't... I don't know if now is the right time," I stuttered. "We've only just got here, and—"

"—an' sooner is always better," Aesir finished firmly. He stalked over to grab me by the arm, dragging me towards the pub. "Everythin' wae Old Pelaeia's a big decision. An' it takes time to put a wake together. May as well let her know the now."

I heard the ulterior motive underlying Aesir's voice—but I wasn't clear-headed enough to figure out just what it was. Either way, I couldn't gin up the courage to protest as he dragged me into the pub behind him.

* * *

THE INSIDE of MacGregor's Anchor was a chimaera of heavy logs, sturdy stone, and bits of scrap from old ships. Everything here was a building block; the northern clans respected old bones and twisted steel. They preferred to build on top of history, so that its skeleton showed through at the edges.

The tables and chairs inside were just as varied as the structure's building materials—though they all had a well-worn, comforting look to them. The hearth inside crackled with an inviting fire, spreading a bit of warmth through the ramshackle public house. Beneath the heavy smell of wood smoke, I caught the sharp scent of MacGregor's infamous cider, and my stomach gurgled with sudden longing.

Lenore had already seated herself at a table in the corner, as far from company as humanly possible. Aesir wove his way towards a different table, however, pushing through the busy pub with drunken determination.

I recognised the woman at that table, though we hadn't spoken for quite some time. Chief Crichton was nearly as old as Dougal had been—but time had been far kinder to him than it had been to her. Her hair, once dark red, was now a stark blonde. Her legs were missing below the knees; a pair of stiff-looking mechanical implements served in their place. A few of the fingers on her left hand were similarly missing. Crichton's hawkish eyes, once bright green, had dulled to a pale, lustreless shade—but those eyes had lost none of their sharpness. She turned her gaze upon us in a peremptory glower, even as Aesir dragged me behind him towards her table.

"MacLeod," she said, in a stern, cracking voice. "Ah'm *relaxin'* the now. Whatever business ye've got, it can wait 'til the 'morra."

"Dougal's dead," Aesir told her. Nearby conversations died, and all hope of a quiet, private conversation evaporated abruptly. Shocked grumbles rippled through the nearest tables, as I squirmed under the redoubled attention.

The glare on Crichton's face melted away into a stony, businesslike expression. I remembered that expression from the few official clan meetings to which I'd been allowed. It was the look of a woman who knew all too well how to handle tragedies in her community. She was, I think, an unparalleled expert on the matter of untimely deaths.

"Where's his body?" Crichton asked.

Aesir glanced back at me. "Blair brought 'im home," he said. Somehow, he managed to keep the bitterness from his voice, this time.

Chief Crichton turned those sharp eyes upon me, and her gaze hardened subtly. The chief and I did not have fond memories of one another.

"Blair," she said, in curt acknowledgement.

"Ma'am," I greeted her back, as respectfully as I could manage. The word still came out of me in a small voice. There's a special discomfort involved in being hated for good reason. It's a helpless, incontrovertible state of being—knowing that you did something to deserve that hatred, and that nothing you do will ever be enough to wipe it away. I had spent several years in my youth helping to build New Pelaeia... but that still felt like a paltry penance, all things considered.

"He still in one piece?" Crichton asked me. "Good fer a wake?"

The question hit me like a club. I'd forgotten how straightforward Chief Crichton could be. I had to work to recover my voice. "He's... yes," I managed. "It should be fine. I brought his ship back, too."

Crichton nodded, silently checking an item off her list of funerary preparations. "Ah'll send some ae the boys tae collect him tomorrow," she said. "We'll want tae sort the wake sooner, rather'n later."

I hesitated, knowing that what I had to say wouldn't go over very well—but I'd promised Aesir that I would try. "I know Dougal would prefer no priests—" I started.

"Not your decision, bluejacket," Chief Crichton said coldly. "These are clan matters. None ae your concern."

Aesir snorted. I glanced at him in surprise, and saw that he was shaking his head. "No worth the fight, Blair," he told me. "Dougal should've warned ye no tae bring him hame." A scathing note entered his voice.

"Ah'll overlook that tone fer now, MacLeod, as yer currently grievin'," Chief Crichton said. "Ye'll keep a civil tongue in yer head fer the rest a' this conversation, though, or ye'll leave an' come back when ye're under control."

Aesir clenched his jaw. I *felt* him working to smother the helpless, injured fury inside himself. But he'd had years of practice being angry at Dougal; he forced an unnatural calm into his voice. "Ye'll do what ye'll do," he said. "But that's not everything." He glanced towards me, weighing something in his mind. "Blair's got an aethermancer on board. Says they can send on the echoes in Old Pelaeia."

In reply to this, a dreadful silence stretched across the pub. A pin drop might have sounded like a grenade.

Chief Crichton stiffened in her chair. "They won't be tryin' any such thing," she said. She speared me with a vicious look. "Keep yer aethermancer oan that ship, Blair. Mark my words, Ah won't be responsible fer what happens to 'em if they step aff it."

Dark murmurs now trickled through the tables around us, breaking the stillness. Threatening glares dug beneath my skin, and I had to resist the urge to take a step back.

"Why?" Aesir measured the word out with exaggerated calm, as though to demonstrate his civility. "Why don't we let someone *try*, Chief? We don't tinker with foci. We barely touch aether, other'n fer ships. Long as we're afraid ae aether, we're sure not goin' tae put anyone to rest oursels." He rested his mechanical arm upon the table, and I realised the obvious—it was powered with aether. "Can't make things worse fer those souls, Chief. Every night, they scream. Some ae us hear family screamin'. An' maybe we're ready fer it tae stop."

Crichton's stiff posture caved against that unnervingly calm statement. She looked away from Aesir, suddenly very tired. Every person in the pub was haunted by the ghost of that mountain—but Aesir had lost both his arm and his family in Pelaeia. He had watched, up close, the awful moment of its birth.

"...ye trust that aethermancer?" Crichton asked quietly.

I opened my mouth to tell the truth—*no, not at all*—but Aesir beat me to the punch. "Sure do, Chief," he said.

I didn't dare contradict him. I certainly didn't now dare to mention that this particular aethermancer carried a *silver sword*. I wasn't sure just what Aesir was playing at... but he knew I didn't have the spine to call him out for it. Not with our history. Not with Dougal freshly gone.

"I'll be watching the aethermancer the whole time," I said instead. "If she tries anything beyond what she's claimed, she won't be leaving those slopes alive."

"She won't for certain," Chief Crichton said softly. "As ye won't be the only one goin'." She turned her hard eyes upon Aesir. "Ye want an aethermancer in Old Pelaeia, lad? I'll allow it. But *you're* goin' wae 'em."

In the seconds which followed this statement, nothing dared to make a sound. Even the wind, it seemed, was silent.

I stared at Aesir, unable to hide my horror. I knew the chief had just thrown down a gauntlet she didn't expect him to take up.

If I'd expected anyone present to protest on his behalf, or volunteer to take his place, then I was swiftly disappointed. The people in the pub averted their eyes or sipped at their drinks in discomfort.

But Aesir gave the chief a stilted, painful nod.

"So ah will, then," he said. The fury he'd been holding onto cracked into the words, and he shot a hard look at me. "We'll go tomorrow, Blair," he said. "Ye'd best be ready."

9

THE GHOST OF OLD PELAEIA - COFFEE & CONSIDERATIONS - SHADES & TATTERDEMALIONS - A WEAK SIGNAL

"What in the world were you thinking, Aesir?" I hissed.

I hurried after him as he left MacGregor's Anchor. Darkness had already fallen outside. I'd forgotten how quickly night swallowed up Pelaeia, especially towards the end of the year. A cold wind pinched at my cheeks, blistering at my skin. I had to set a swift pace just to catch up with Aesir's longer legs; as I did, I grasped at his flesh and blood arm, trying to slow him down.

Aesir turned a bleary, bitter expression upon me. "Chief is plannin' the wake," he said. "Ye'll be goin' to Old Pelaeia. What else do ye want, Blair?"

I had to resist the urge to throw my hands into the air. "You don't know my aethermancer!" I told him. "You have no idea who she is or whether she's trustworthy. Why would you—"

"Who bloody well cares, Blair?" Aesir demanded. He tugged his arm free of my grip, staring down at me. "What's the worst she's gonna do? Make the mountain scream *louder?*" He laughed incredulously. "Ah'm tired ae this graveyard. Ah'm sick tae death of it—if it doesn't kill me, livin' in this shadow, it'll turn me intae Hamish." He pressed his hands upon my shoulders, forcing me to meet his eyes.

"Look at me, Blair. Either Old Pelaeia goes, or else ah go. Elsewhere, ah mean. *Anywhere* else."

There was an unmistakably desperate look in Aesir's eyes. At first, I thought it had to be new—but as I thought back, I realised it had always been there, lurking quietly beneath the surface.

From high up on the slopes above, a wandering scream drifted our way. We turned our heads in unison, watching as flickering werelight echoes winked into life in the misty ruins above. Tormented screams filtered down upon the wind, eerily familiar; the echoes still sounded exactly as they had over a decade ago, during those sleepless nights I'd spent in Old Pelaeia's shadow.

The encroaching night was already bitterly cold… but the chill that raced down my spine had little to do with the temperature. I drew in a shuddering breath and looked back at Aesir. "You're going to have to walk into Old Pelaeia," I said. "You should never have agreed to that. It wasn't fair of Chief Crichton to ask it of you."

Aesir spun away from me with a disgusted noise, tearing his eyes away from the haunted slopes. "Don't tell me what ah should an' shouldnae be doin', Blair," he said. "No yer call tae make." He paused, with his back to me. "If Dougal wanted tae go to Old Pelaeia, ye'd have said *yessir* an' got outta his way."

My heart twinged painfully at the fresh mention of Dougal. I tried to find words to respond—but my mouth worked soundlessly instead. I knew that he was right.

"Ah don't want ye to treat me like ye treated him," Aesir added. "But don't ye go actin' like him, either. Ye're no ma uncle, Blair. An' a good thing that is, too—we wouldnae get along, otherwise." He started down the snowy street, once again. His boots crunched on the thin layer of snow. "Ah'll see ye at the *Rose*, first thing in the mornin'. Echoes won't bother us durin' the day. Figure ye don't want tae meet 'em at night, when they're *real* upset."

I helplessly watched him go.

A light dusting of snow drifted on the cold winds. A wave of distant screams rippled across the mountainside. I crammed my hands into my coat pockets, forcing myself to stare at the moaning ruins. I knew it was only the beginning of Old Pelaeia's nightly death knell.

The native clanfolk walking through the streets ignored the wails. They'd lived here long enough that their faces remained cold and hard... but none of them had the stomach to look up at the ruined city as the echoes of their loved ones cried out for mercy.

Footsteps sounded from behind me; a hand came down on my uninjured shoulder, and I realised belatedly that Lenore had left the pub to come after us.

"Still good with people, I see, Captain," Lenore observed.

I reached up to rub at my face. "That was sarcasm, wasn't it?" I asked. "I just want to be certain—since I'm doing so well with nuance tonight."

"That was sarcasm," Lenore assured me, with a straight face. "And what exactly are you doing in the morning?" Clearly, she'd heard at least the tail end of my conversation with Aesir.

I looked up at the haunted slopes and sighed heavily. "Something very stupid," I replied.

* * *

NONE of us slept well as Old Pelaeia was slaughtered again. The first few hours were the worst: Shrieks of fear rose and fell with the wind. But the screams were punctuated by periods of sudden, eerie silence, as echoes met their temporary demise. Inevitably, they always rose again to repeat the awful pageant.

The Imperium had gutted Pelaeia and left it to die in the dark. Now, the Imperium was dead—but Pelaeia still begged for mercy.

I managed only a few hours of fitful sleep before I abandoned my bed. The air was even more frigid than I remembered it; then again, I had once spent nights in Pelaeia next to a crackling hearth, rather than in my quarters aboard the *Rose*. My breath billowed out in pale clouds with every shivering breath. Every scrape and bruise on my body ached stiffly.

I dressed as quickly as I could, swaddling myself several layers deep. Finally, when I ran out of clothing to add on top, I donned my hat and opened the door to the main deck.

An eerie stillness had swallowed the world outside of my cabin. Frost had crept across much of the *Rose* in the twilight hours. A deep muffling mist made it difficult to see more than ten feet away. The rigging creaked; lanterns swayed. The wind moaned... though it was hard to tell if it was *only* the wind.

The rest of my crew were even more uneasy than I was; they spoke among themselves in unusually hushed tones, as though worried they might draw the attention of the echoes in the gloom above us. The newer people on board had never been to Pelaeia before, and had therefore never heard the howling at night. Mr Billings, in particular, kept shooting terrified glances at the mountain, as though expecting the screams to return at any moment. I buried my troubled feelings about Pelaeia beneath years of practice, doing my best to display an outward confidence as I performed my morning rounds.

Eventually, after a miserable eternity, the faint light of dawn crept across the mountainside.

The sombre mood slowly evaporated with the mist. A pillar of smoke drifted up from an exhaust pipe on the main deck, carrying with it the smell of breakfast. My crew's niggling fear gave way before their hungry stomachs; even existential terror was no match for the promise of a warm meal. I briefly considered nipping down to fill my own stomach before company arrived—but just as first light broke upon the horizon, a single figure headed up the gangplank.

Aesir MacLeod had bundled up against the weather; his grease-stained jumpsuit was gone, replaced by homespun wool layers and a large, eclectic greatcoat. Given our conversation the evening before, I was expecting Aesir to be miserable and hungover—but he was instead bright-eyed and unnervingly cheerful.

"Blair!" Aesir called out buoyantly. "There ye are! Hope yer ready for an adventure!" His long legs ate up the distance between us in several strides. As he came closer, I noticed his red-rimmed eyes—but I knew it was best not to comment on them.

"Aesir," I greeted him, with a tired nod. "You're rather, er... punctual."

Aesir looped his arm around me in a way that made my injured shoulder protest. "We'll want as much daylight as we can manage," he said, as I gritted my teeth against the pain. He paused next to me, searching through the other people on deck. I didn't realise just what he was looking for, until he said: "Where's yer aethermancer, then?"

"Below deck," I replied. I wriggled out of his grip with great difficulty, rubbing gingerly at my shoulder. "Most of the crew is still... waking up. Would you like some tea or coffee?"

"*Coffee*," Aesir sighed. He said the word with the same sort of reverence most people used for the Tuath Dé. "Don't get much ae that in these parts."

"This way," I told him, nodding towards the stairs below deck. "She'll join us in the galley."

Aesir raised an eyebrow, as he followed me down below. "She?" he asked politely.

I glanced his way suspiciously. Aesir's expression *seemed* perfectly innocent—but he'd used the same tone with Lenore, just the night before.

"I *did* mention that previously, yes," I said warily.

Aesir grinned. "Wasn't quite masel last night," he said. "Must've forgot that wee detail."

I paused in the corridor, with a sinking feeling. Miss Lenore Brighton had been a poor subject for Aesir's flirtations. Miss Hawkins—a Legionnaire-trained aethermancer with a silver sword—was even worse.

"Aesir," I said warningly, "I know I don't have any right to tell you what to do—"

"But yer gonna try," Aesir mused idly.

"—but *please* believe me when I say you want as little to do with Miss Hawkins as humanly possible," I finished.

Aesir shot me a sideways glance. Perhaps he'd picked up on the worry in my tone. He considered this, long and hard. Finally, he nodded at me.

"I believe ye," Aesir said.

I sighed in relief.

"—that *you* want as little tae do wae her as possible," he added.

I palmed my face, stifling a groan. It was clear there would be no reasoning with him on the subject. Perhaps, I thought, Aesir would change his mind as soon as he saw Miss Hawkins and her pale, somewhat terrifying appearance.

I conjured up an image of the woman in my mind... and shook my head in despair. I kept forgetting what a pretty face Miss Hawkins had, in light of the complicated emotions her silver sword instilled within me. Strip away the stern expression and the aethermancer's foci, and you were left with a rather charming young woman, with a straight-backed posture and a cute little button nose.

I couldn't help noticing, either, how heads turned as we walked towards the galley. The *Iron Rose* has always had an abundance of women on board, and several of them seemed to appreciate Aesir's tall form and cavalier smile. Martha and Navi interrupted their existing conversation for a giggle as we passed; Martha wiggled her fingers at the younger MacLeod, and he tossed them both a wink.

To be fair, I had spent the morning expecting *some* manner of looming disaster. But I can't say that the problem of MacLeod the Younger's rugged charm had ever crossed my mind.

Physicker Holloway was the first to greet us as we entered the galley. The hobgoblin had traded in his waistcoat for an itchy-looking woollen sweater with the sleeves rolled up to his elbows. Sailor's ink and peppered scars wove sleeves of their own on both of his thick forearms. Holloway looked up at us from the goose-necked coffee pot. As his eyes fell upon Aesir, a flicker of somewhat stunned recognition skipped across his broad face. Aesir was his own man... but the ghost of Dougal MacLeod was clear upon his features, even so.

"Some coffee for myself and Mr MacLeod, if you wouldn't mind?" I asked the physicker.

Holloway inclined his head and poured two cups, walking over towards us to offer them out. He hesitated in front of Aesir, looking at him with uncertainty.

"I'm... very sorry for your loss," Holloway told Aesir softly.

I saw the struggle behind Aesir's face as he heard the words. At first, I worried that he might make a point of his lingering grudge with Dougal, right then and there... but he swallowed the words and simply nodded. "Thank ye," he said. Then: "Fer the coffee, too." He smiled and swiped the cup from Holloway.

I commandeered one of the nearby tables and sent one of the gunnery ladies to find Miss Hawkins. If we'd been back in the Imperial Navy, we probably would have dined in my cabin, to maintain a separation between the officers and the crew.

Then again, if we'd been back in the Imperial Navy, I never would have been a captain at all.

Some of the crew did shuffle aside, in order to give us some privacy—inasmuch as the area could provide any privacy. Physicker Holloway produced a tin cup of coffee for me, then went to secure us some biscuits and marmalade. The invigorating tastes and scents were nearly enough to dispel the sense of foreboding that still hung over my head. I'd barely finished my second biscuit, however, when Aesir suddenly stopped eating, with his biscuit halfway to his open mouth.

"Good morning, Captain Blair," Miss Hawkins said from behind me.

I turned, drowning my dreadful sigh with hot coffee.

Miss Hawkins stood perfectly upright this morning—if the pale woman still suffered any illness from her direct brush with Unseelie aether, none of it now showed in her manner. The dark veins had all disappeared, replaced once more with the bright, uncanny blue of a normal aethermancer. Her crisp, militaristic clothing was comparatively dark, though I could see where it had greyed in places over time. Her bob of neatly kept silver hair and dishwater grey eyes stood out starkly against her otherwise sombre attire.

Miss Hawkins had layered herself for the weather with a borrowed jacket and heavy boots—though I noted that none of the gunnery ladies had offered her any knitted accessories. She wore none of her foci that I could see, but there was absolutely no mistaking her for anything other than an aethermancer.

"Miss Hawkins," I greeted her back, vaguely uncomfortable. I rose to make formal introductions—but I was a bit too slow.

Aesir swept to his feet and stepped between us, offering out his mechanical hand. "Aesir MacLeod," he introduced himself. "What a pleasure it is to meet ye, Miss Hawkins. Blair mentioned yer research... but he somehow forgot tae mention how *pretty* ye were."

Miss Hawkins blushed. The bright red colour was painfully apparent on her cheeks. I had a moment of dissonance, as I tried to square the deadly sword I knew she carried with the way she fumbled through her response.

"I... er... well, I'm sure that isn't the sort of thing which often comes up in conversation," Hawkins stammered. She reached out to take Aesir's hand—only to realise an instant later that it was made of something other than flesh and blood.

For just a moment, I worried that I might witness a repeat of my first cringeworthy introduction to Miss Hawkins. But even as I watched, her features lit up with a strangely transcendent delight, and she gave a wondering gasp.

"My goodness," Miss Hawkins breathed. "That's... what a *construct!* The fingers are fully articulated? And there's barely any leakage from whatever aether source it's using. This is... well, it's a piece of *art*, isn't it?"

"So the ladies tell me," Aesir said cheekily. But there was an uncommonly pleased tint to his voice that I hadn't heard as he'd flirted with Lenore. He turned his hand in hers to face his palm upwards, allowing Miss Hawkins to examine the prosthetic's fingers in more detail. "Ah made it masel, actually."

Hawkins glanced up at him sharply. "You did?" she asked. The surprise in her voice soon bled into outright awe. "It must have taken forever! And... you worked one-handed, as well?"

"Oh... it's mostly just spare parts," Aesir said, with badly veiled pride. "Trial an' error, y'know. More, uh, error'n trial. But ah suppose ah worked it out eventually."

I cleared my throat uncomfortably. "Er," I cut in. "As I was... about to say. This is Miss Hawkins—an aethermancer, obviously, and currently our passenger aboard the *Rose*." I looked between them warily. "Miss Hawkins, this is Aesir MacLeod. He's our late outflyer pilot's nephew, and the reason we're being permitted to enter the ruins of Old Pelaeia."

Miss Hawkins' smile faded very slightly. "I... see," she said softly. "I'm very sorry for your loss—"

Aesir pulled his hand back with a heavy sigh, shaking his head. "Let's no, Miss Hawkins," he requested tiredly. "Ah'll be gettin' it fae everyone fer weeks. Ah'd rather talk about yer equipment, if y'please."

Hawkins looked away. I caught again the flash of fresh grief on her face, and I knew she'd been hoping to commiserate somewhat. But she nodded slowly. "I can explain some of the theory if you like, Mr MacLeod."

Aesir smiled warmly again, as though someone had flipped a switch inside him. "Ah'd love tae hear it," he said. "Here, have a seat—"

A pale movement caught my eye, several feet away from us. Strahl had settled himself at another table. He had the wretched appearance of someone who hadn't slept a wink. Between his weariness and his grey washed hair and eyes, he looked positively ghoulish. Still—Strahl glanced towards Miss Hawkins more than once, and I knew that he had decided to continue his watch on her as a potential danger.

I excused myself from the table—not that either Aesir or Miss Hawkins particularly noticed my departure amidst their animated discourse—and moved to approach Strahl.

My bosun kept his eyes upon the two people I'd left behind, even as I sat down in front of him, sipping at my coffee.

"I'll need you to accompany us into Old Pelaeia," I said quietly. "If you're not too tired, that is."

Strahl stiffened at the suggestion. It was hard to tell, exactly, but I thought he might have gone a shade paler at the idea.

"I don't think that's a good idea," Strahl said.

"I'm going," I told him, speaking the words into my cup. "*She's* going. And she's bringing Unseelie aether with her." I paused grimly. "You've killed aethermancers before. If she's lying, and she decides to do anything *untoward* in Old Pelaeia... I'll need your expertise."

"I killed that aethermancer with Syrene's help," Strahl muttered flatly. "And Syrene isn't setting one single root of hers in those ruins, Cap'n."

I considered him over my cup. Most people would have been frightened to try and kill a Silver Legionnaire... but Strahl wasn't most people. The day I'd first met Strahl, he had been set to be hanged for the murder of a powerful aethermancer—and the idea of his own imminent execution hadn't bothered him terribly much.

It seemed highly unlikely to me that Strahl was any more frightened of dying on a silver sword than he had been of dying at the end of a rope. But there was, nevertheless, a strange, uncharacteristic fear behind his eyes.

"You're not afraid of Hawkins," I said softly. "What *are* you afraid of, Mr Strahl?"

Strahl swallowed heavily. He looked away, unable to meet my eyes. "Those ruins," he whispered. "They're... I shouldn't walk there."

A horrible thought occurred to me, then. Pure, nauseating terror snapped at my spine, and I straightened in my seat.

Strahl had probably been a high-ranking officer in the Imperial Army. It had never occurred to me, though, that he might have been *involved* with Pelaeia.

"Did you... were you *here* when it happened?" I whispered hoarsely.

Strahl snapped his eyes back up to mine. "No," he said. "No, I was elsewhere." He sounded dimly bewildered by the assumption. "But I was important enough to..." Strahl shook his head, suddenly haunted. "I should have tried to stop it. I should have *known* to stop it. It's not right for me to set foot there."

I let out a long, awful breath. "Must be nice," I said. "Having the choice to walk away." I shrugged bitterly. "I don't have that choice, Mr Strahl. Someone's offered a little bit of peace to Old Pelaeia. I'm obliged to try and seize that. Stewing in my own guilt is just self-pity, compared."

Strahl flinched at the words. He looked away, ashamed.

"If you're too tired to join us, I'll find someone else," I said.

I sipped my coffee in silence, watching Aesir and Miss Hawkins discuss theoretical aethermancy only a few tables away from us.

"I'll need to put some gear together," Strahl finally replied. "When are you venturing out?"

"As soon as possible," I said. "Aesir says the echoes get more active at night... so we'll want to be back before sunset."

Strahl shoved slowly to his feet. "You've got an eye on her?" he asked me reluctantly.

I half-turned my head towards him and tipped my hat. "I'll handle Miss Hawkins if she decides to attack the coffee," I assured him wryly.

Strahl shook his head and turned back for the exit. As he left, I rose to rejoin the other two.

At some point, the solicitation on Miss Hawkins' face had transformed to frustrated bewilderment. "—but you surely understand why Caliban's Base Principle of Aetheric Equivalence applies to the situation?" she asked Aesir, with a hint of desperation.

Aesir held up one mechanical finger. "Actually," he said, "er... no. No in the least." He smiled sheepishly.

Miss Hawkins looked crestfallen. "I see," she said. "I don't suppose anything I've said in the last few minutes has made any sense at all, has it?"

"Ah'll be honest," Aesir admitted, "ye've been haverin' since ye sat down. But ah loved listenin' tae it."

"Havering?" Miss Hawkins asked.

"Talking nonsense," I informed her, as I took a seat at the table with them.

"Well... but..." Miss Hawkins went pink again as she looked at Aesir. "Why didn't you say something?"

"Ye just looked so excited," Aesir said apologetically. "Felt rude tae stop ye."

Miss Hawkins wilted in disappointment. "Oh," she said in a small voice. "It's just that this expedition would have been... far simpler, with a second set of hands. I'm used to having help with the device." She looked down at her lap. "I'm afraid I got ahead of myself. Given Mr MacLeod's—"

"—call me Aesir," the man across from her interjected, with a winning smile.

Miss Hawkins flustered again at that. "Er, yes, *Aesir*," she corrected herself. "Given Aesir's obvious skill at engineering, I'd hoped that he might be able to assist me. But I'm afraid that his understanding of aetheric principles is..."

I raised an eyebrow at Miss Hawkins, warning her about the foot she was about to insert into her mouth.

"...his understanding is more *practical* than academic," Miss Hawkins corrected herself quickly. She shot Aesir an apologetic look. "Your work is... well frankly, it's incredible. But I'm missing the shared terminology I would need in order to explain this device to you in such a short period of time. At the very least, I would need someone who can read classical engineering schematics—"

"—I'm terribly sorry to interrupt," Mr Finch cut in. "This will only require a moment." At some point during our discussion, my chief engineer had joined the crew in the galley for breakfast; now, he had appeared next to my chair. "Captain—thank goodness I caught you this morning! We are nearly out of tea—er, well, technically we have those bricks in the hold, but I checked them in a desperate moment, and they're quite literally rotten. I was hoping to buy some proper tea in Pelaeia, but I'll need whatever petty money we have left on hand."

I turned slowly in my chair to consider my dapper chief engineer.

Mr Finch frowned at me. "...Captain," he said warily. "Why are you all looking at me like that?"

* * *

"I FAIL to understand why it is you require *my* presence for this excursion!" Mr Finch hollered. He had to work to make himself heard over the wind, as Aesir's flatbed salvage-boat chuffed its way up the slopes of Pelaeia.

"Because you're a genius, of course!" I yelled back at him. "We require only the best, Mr Finch!"

The salvage-boat was larger than the four-person craft we kept on the *Rose*, but it only had one passenger seat. I held onto the side rail of the flatbed, while Mr Finch clung for dear life just next to me. Miss Hawkins' equipment took up most of the space in the boat, crowding Mr Strahl against the side opposite to me and Mr Finch. Aesir had offered the sole passenger seat to the lady herself, in order to enjoy her ongoing conversation; he piloted the salvage-boat with a deft hand, seemingly immune to the existential dread that consumed the rest of the passengers on-board.

"But this is suicide," Mr Finch quailed. He clutched at the back of Miss Hawkins' seat, as though the stiff wind might blow him away.

"No," Miss Hawkins assured him with quiet determination. "This is *science*." Her grey eyes stared out over the approaching ruins with a critical eye.

"Does that make me a scientist?" Aesir mused, over the chug-chug of the boat's engine.

"Why is he here again, Cap'n?" Strahl grumbled. His voice crackled with a tinny, mechanical quality as it filtered through his helmet's chatterbox. His heavy armour rattled and clanked beneath the words.

"You heard Blair," Aesir replied flippantly. "Ye needed geniuses."

"Chief Crichton was very explicit on the matter," I called over the wind. "Miss Hawkins is only allowed in Old Pelaeia so long as Aesir is with us. And he *did* volunteer."

Miss Hawkins smiled gratefully at Aesir. I wondered idly if that smile had taken some of the sting out of entering the old city.

Mr Finch shook his head incredulously. "Mad," he muttered to himself. "You're all stark raving mad."

"And yet," I observed, "here you are." I pried one hand from the side rail, reaching over to clap my chief engineer on the shoulder. "Thank you, Walther."

For all of Mr Finch's quailing, he had ultimately *chosen* to come along. Perhaps I shouldn't have been so surprised. Though Finch hadn't fought on the front lines of the Sundering War, his crimes against the Avalon Imperium had been serious enough to earn him a theoretical summary execution. It took a special sort of courage, I supposed, to sabotage an empire from within.

Mr Finch gave me a stiff, careful nod. His gaze drifted past me towards the ruins, though, and he muttered a prayer (or a curse) to the Lady of Fools beneath his breath. As I turned to look upon the desolation, I felt inclined to join him.

The thick city walls of the lowest tier were only halfway standing. Those parts which hadn't been shattered by Imperial bombardments were smeared with ash or half buried by snow. The main gate, a thick set of iron doors, had been peeled open like a can of sardines.

Silence descended upon the boat as we entered through the broken jaws of that gate. About ten feet past it, Aesir slowed the vehicle to a halt, staring at the blackened rubble that surrounded us. The Imperial fleet's bombardment of the city's upper levels had caused great landslides, burying swathes of less-fortunate districts beneath them. Shattered buildings poked through the snow in places, along with the carcass of a single burned-out ship. It was one thing to look at Old Pelaeia from below... and quite another to be *there*, drinking in the sheer scope and scale of the butchery.

I dared to glance at Aesir's face—and instantly regretted it.

There was no pain there. Instead, where there should have been pain, there was only a terrible blank mask. The smile that Aesir had pasted on his face had died away, replaced by a hollow, empty-eyed look.

Some part of him, I thought, was processing the surrounding wreckage. But the greater part of him had simply switched off, unable to handle the sight of it.

Mr Finch shivered next to me. Miss Hawkins glanced from horror to horror, with her hands clasped over her mouth.

Strahl wanted to look away. I could tell, even with his helmet on. But he forced himself to take in the sight. I knew he was etching it upon his bones in the same way that I had done with the dark mountain's silhouette, nearly two decades ago.

Even as I forced my attention back to the scene before us, though, my eyes fell upon the snow, and a spike of alarm shot through my spine.

There were footprints. Everywhere.

Dirt and snow were smeared across the half-buried street; every so often, I could see where a distinct footprint had left its mark. In fact, it looked as though a fresh conflict had happened just the night before.

...probably because it had.

Every hair on the back of my neck stood up at once. I couldn't help feeling as though there was a presence nearby. At first, I wondered if it was just my imagination, reacting to the tableau in front of me... but then, the snow on the ground shifted, some fifteen feet away from me. A low rasping noise whispered across the wind.

Something I couldn't see was slowly dragging itself towards me through the snow.

"We need to move," I said, breaking our horrified silence. "Now." The words sounded strangely loud in my own ears. My heart hammered in my chest.

Aesir turned to look at me—but the blank look on his face suggested that he hadn't actually processed the words.

Slowly, a spectral figure formed within the whirling snow. It rose from the ground in wisps of blue steam—a piteous mass of warped aether-light, barely humanoid in shape.

It was missing the entire lower half of its body.

The others followed my gaze. Mr Finch let out a strangled, high-pitched noise. Miss Hawkins froze, briefly panicked. Aesir lost what little life was left in his expression. Wherever his mind had gone, it clearly wasn't *here*.

That was a problem, seeing as he was our driver.

"Aesir!" I said—louder and more insistent, this time. "*Move!*"

Metal clanked—and Aesir cried out in alarmed pain. Strahl had reached out to slap him upside the back of the head with an armoured glove.

"Drive!" Strahl snapped, in his booming voice. The harsh order cut through that haze of choking fear that had gripped us all. Aesir sucked in his breath, lunging for the boat's controls. We lurched forward with sudden speed.

The thing that had been dragging itself towards us quickly fell behind. There was no way that it could have kept up, given its struggling pace—but that hardly mattered. The hideous terror it had inspired stayed with us, long after it had dropped out of view. Strahl scanned the area around us as we sped along, searching urgently for signs of other echoes that might reach out for us with long-dead hands.

He found them, in spades. Shimmering wisps dotted the landscape before us. Some were more solid than others. The weakest of the echoes looked like wandering motes of light, but there were also vaguely shifting figures, coalesced from the dirt and the snow.

They were few and far between, but it didn't matter. They had us surrounded.

Surrounded... but for what? The thought struck me suddenly.

There was no *pattern* in the way the echoes moved. They weren't closing in on us. They were just... fleeing. And dying.

I had known that would be the case, on some level. But here on the mountain, seeing them lurch to ghostly life, it had been all too easy to forget.

I forced a few calming breaths into my lungs, letting the cold air sting me back to sensibility. I searched the cold snow around us and finally pointed. "Over there!" I called out to Aesir. "No footprints there."

At first, I worried I might have to yell it again—but whatever sense Strahl had knocked into Aesir had yet to drain away again. Aesir wheeled the vehicle around at my direction, coasting us towards a stretch of pure, undisturbed snow.

Slowly, we came to a stop. The salvage-boat's engine hummed beneath our feet, as distant echoes glimmered on the mountain snow.

"I thought you said they wouldn't bother us during the day," I managed slowly. I glanced at Aesir questioningly.

Aesir swallowed. "Ah didn't know they'd be here in broad daylight," he rasped. "Ah don't... Ah've never came up here before."

Miss Hawkins sucked in a breath. The sharp motion seemed to break the horrified spell that had come over her. "Echoes should be... *less* active in the hours opposite of their death," she said. She tried to speak with authority, but her tone wavered on the words. "Though, admittedly, that does not mean *inactive*."

I swallowed too. "They don't seem upset at us specifically," I acknowledged carefully. "I suppose this does still count as *less* active."

Nothing was wailing at us, at least.

As it slowly became clear that no echoes would be springing into existence near our current patch of snow, Miss Hawkins unbuckled her seat's harness and made her way to the nearest of the lashed-down crates that contained her equipment.

"Could you keep us steady please, Aesir?" Hawkins asked. "This equipment is... delicate. Mr Finch—would you be so kind as to help me for a moment?"

Strahl and I scanned the environs warily, while Mr Finch assisted Hawkins into a harness with a bulky aetheric battery, wired to a pair of burdensome goggles. Miss Hawkins armed her left hand with the foci I'd seen her use on New Havenshire's docks, but she pulled a strange, clunky sort of glove onto her right hand and equipped a different device to her right forearm, just atop it. Several meters danced frantically upon her arm, until she made a few adjustments to settle them.

I looked out over the wreckage of the city. "In layman's terms," I asked slowly, "how does this work? What happens next?"

Miss Hawkins turned to face me, lifting up the heavy goggles so they rested atop her head.

"I mostly learned from someone else's research," she said uncertainly. "But... if we're correct, then echoes are not actually *individual* aetheric disturbances." Her foci hummed with aether. The inside of her goggles glowed against her pale hair, shimmering blue atop her head. "Echoes are the manifestations of a single, aether-induced traumatic cluster. Which does not *preclude*, of course, a trauma which involves only a single individual. But more often than not—"

I turned towards my chief engineer. "In layman's terms, how does it work?" I repeated, this time to Mr Finch.

He blinked at me owlishly. "A single source of aether—like an aetheric bomb—can catch several people within its sphere of influence," he translated slowly. "It is the aether which creates echoes, and not simply the... the individual deaths themselves. Thus, all echoes caused by a single source of aether would naturally be connected." A hint of awe slipped into his tone, as though the concept had never occurred to him before.

"That *is* what I said," Miss Hawkins noted, with a hint of annoyance. "Well... more or less." She tapped the goggles atop her head. "This spectraetheric visor will allow me to see active aetheric activity which is normally invisible to the eye. The visor's range is limited, but it should suffice for our purposes. The glove will allow me to pull on any active aether in order to gather a reading."

"Like a compass?" I hazarded.

"Almost," Mr Finch corrected me, this time without prompting. "Think of the glove as a longhorn, searching for particular frequencies."

"And instead of chatter," I said slowly, "it detects these... aether clusters?"

"Yes," Hawkins agreed with a nod. "Every aether cluster has a nerve centre that holds the pattern together as a whole. We call that central knot a 'fetter'. Pelaeia should have several fetters. This is our first practical test, so we'll want the smallest fetter we can find."

Aesir's face had recovered a bit of its life, but he now looked at Hawkins with a hint of unease. "An'... what are ye gonna *do* wae that fetter when ye find it?" he asked her.

"Ideally," Miss Hawkins said, "I should be able to dissolve the aether which underlies its construction, and release that which has been trapped within its net." She looked uncertainly to Mr Finch, as though expecting another translation—but my engineer merely nodded. "It's more complicated than that, of course," Hawkins added. "But I've described the process as simply as I can."

Aesir nodded slowly. I had the impression that he'd understood more of the previous explanation than I had, for all that he wasn't an academic. There was still discomfort on his face, but it was tempered with the benefit of first-hand knowledge. More than anything else so far, that gave me hope that the woman on this boat with us might truly mean well.

"I'll need you to take us out slowly, so that I can get some readings," Miss Hawkins told Aesir gently. "By definition, we'll have to get rather close to the echoes, but... they don't seem hostile so far." Her brow knitted with worry, and I knew that she had picked up on Aesir's distress. "Will that be all right, Mr MacLeod?"

I had never before seen Aesir MacLeod look any *less* all right. But he flashed a weakly flirtatious smile at the aethermancer. "Only if ye call me Aesir," he reminded her again. "That's very important."

Hawkins coloured beneath the shifting blue light of her goggles. "Very well then, Aesir," she mumbled sheepishly. She pulled the goggles down to hide her eyes, and Aesir's lips twitched with satisfaction. At least, I thought, the banter gave him something else to focus on.

Hawkins wasn't able to sit in the passenger's seat, with that bulky pack on her back, and so she relinquished the seat to Mr Finch. She clambered into the flatbed with the rest of us, holding her arm out over the side of the salvage-boat to take readings as Aesir drove us back out into the once-populated areas of the mountain. As we went, she called out numbers to Mr Finch, who scribbled them down clumsily, clutching a pencil between his gloved fingers.

It wasn't pleasant, driving so close to the echoes—but just as Miss Hawkins had predicted, few of them paid us any real heed. I tried to detach myself from the understanding that these vague blue wisps had once been living people. I focussed instead on the dry, overly-complex explanation that Miss Hawkins had offered for their existence. These were not people, I thought. They were a scientific phenomenon. A *cluster* of aetheric reactions.

But though the echoes did not scream at us in the daylight, we soon discovered that they did *whisper*.

As Miss Hawkins directed us towards a distant blue shimmer, I heard a woman's voice upon the wind, crackling like a broken signal from a longhorn.

"*...it'll be awright, my sweet,*" she murmured. "*Yer mama's got ye. It'll all be over soon.*"

The whisper hit me like a blow to the chest. My mind blanked, and in between blinks, I found myself on my knees, still clinging to the rail above me.

I couldn't see Strahl's face, behind the helmet he wore. But his straight-backed posture folded slightly against those words, as though they were an anchor pulling him down.

Miss Hawkins had an aethermancer's iron will. She held her arm out before the flickering wisp of light as we approached it, checking the readings on her meters. But she soon moved us onward again, shaking her head against the wind.

Echoes were not the only thing we found on that mountain.

I should have expected the bodies. I knew no one had dared the old city long enough to collect them. Most of them were mercifully caked in dirt and snow, but some were sheltered enough by the debris that I could make out their features. The cold had preserved them unnaturally well, even after two decades.

The bodies were mostly too small to be fully grown northern men —but I should have expected that too. Between the Tithes and the rebellion, Pelaeia had already lost most of its fighting men at the time of the attack. These echoes would be mostly women, children, and the elderly.

Miss Hawkins paused us several times—sometimes directly in front of an echo, and sometimes in front of nothing at all. But as the day waned and the sun dipped further down in the sky, I began to sense her frustration.

"It's gettin' late," Aesir observed finally. His eyes tracked the sun with a sharp-edged wariness. "We've got tae start back."

"We could always come back tomorrow," Mr Finch offered carefully. The sights and sounds of Old Pelaeia had been no more kind to him than the rest of us, and I was surprised by the implication that he intended to join us for a second time.

"No," Miss Hawkins said softly. "It won't matter." She slumped back against the railing, cradling her stiff right arm.

"What do you mean, *no?*" I demanded. "You said this would work. You dragged us all the way out here, when *none* of us wanted to face this—"

"I know!" Miss Hawkins said. Her voice took on an awful, miserable edge, and I knew suddenly that the reality of the mountain had got to her after all. "I... I *know*," she said again, more softly this time. There were unshed tears beneath the words, trapped halfway in her throat. "The readings are just too weak. There's aether lingering everywhere here. I can barely get a signal against the background noise."

"Oh," I whispered. My stomach sank into my boots and curled against my toes.

"You're saying it's impossible, then?" Strahl asked, in a stiff voice.

"No," I said, with bone-deep trepidation. "I don't think that's what she meant."

"We..." Miss Hawkins sucked in a steadying breath. "We need a stronger aetheric signal—"

"We need to wait until nightfall," Mr Finch translated, in a horrified whisper.

10

FOR FETTER OR WORSE - HISTORY REPEATING - MISS HAWKINS' CURIOUS CONTRAPTION - SILENT

"I'm no doin' this again," Aesir said quietly. His hands trembled where they rested on the wheel.

I didn't blame him in the least. Frankly, I was surprised he'd stuck it through so long already.

Miss Hawkins closed her eyes. A series of emotions flickered across her face in short order: Disappointment. Frustration. Shameful relief.

I felt them all with her. But if anyone had the right to call this off, it was certainly Aesir MacLeod.

"All right," I said. "Turn us around, then—"

"Did ah say ah was turnin' back?" Aesir asked sharply. He turned in his seat, looking between me and Hawkins. "Ah said ah wasn't doin' this *again*. We're doin' it the night. Ah'll stay wae the lady. Am ah bringin' the rest ae ye back tae the front gate?"

"No," Strahl and I said.

"Yes, please," Mr Finch said, nearly at the same time.

Several people turned to look at him. After a moment, Mr Finch gave a groan and slumped in the passenger's seat. "No," he corrected himself mournfully.

The sun had already plunged nearly to the horizon. Long shadows stretched hungrily across the slopes of the mountain. The dark corners of the ruins deepened. Slowly but surely, lights winked into existence in New Pelaeia, below us. For just a moment, I imagined I was looking down at a second sky, full of twinkling stars.

That was the land of the living, far below us. But we had chosen to walk among the dead, in the underworld above.

"We don't want to stay any longer than necessary," I said. "Let's choose the right place the first time. Something with a big enough signal to get this done."

Aesir nodded grimly. "I'm guessin'... more echoes means a bigger fetter?" he asked.

"Yes," Miss Hawkins replied, in a tremulous voice. "We'll want... more than half a dozen echoes. Preferably less than a score. Anything more than that would be exceptionally dangerous. I don't yet know how they'll react to the use of aether in their presence, but I expect... something."

Mr Finch squinted down at his notes through fogged glasses. "We had some potential signals," he said. "There was that collapsed lighthouse. Or perhaps that large building we found, about an hour ago."

"The front gates," Strahl said.

I swivelled to look at him. I wasn't the only one.

"The moment that lighthouse toppled, it was no longer of interest," Strahl said flatly. "Imperial forces would have ignored it. That means we'd only be dealing with echoes from the initial bombardment." He paused, as though to fortify himself for the next statement. "The building we passed was burned down by Imperial pyroclasts."

"Aethermancers with fire-projecting foci—" Mr Finch began to clarify.

"I know *that*," I interrupted him, with a hint of exasperation. I'd served in the Imperial Navy, after all.

Strahl nodded grimly. "That's what caused those melted bubbles in the stone. I guarantee, we *don't* want to deal with that."

The bleak confidence in his voice made my stomach churn.

"The front gates," Strahl repeated grimly.

"Ye gettin' enough air in that helmet?" Aesir asked incredulously. "You *saw* that place when we came in, didn't ye?"

"Aye," Strahl replied patiently. "There might be too many echoes there. But most of them will be *inside* the walls. And this way, we can have an open escape route right behind us."

Miss Hawkins was the closest thing we had to an expert on the matter—dubious though her credentials might have been. I looked at her questioningly. She weighed the risks silently... and nodded, very slowly.

"We've mostly dealt with shades so far," Hawkins said softly. "They're less substantial—made of aether, and little else. They can be dangerous in their own way if you let one touch you, but they're fairly easy to avoid. I'm sure the front gates will have what we dubbed tatterdemalions, especially once the sun goes down. They'll have bodies, of a sort; made up of whatever debris is closest. They'll be exceedingly dangerous, even if they don't *intend* to hurt us. But Mr Strahl is correct. We need the escape route."

"Then I guess we're headed back to the gatehouse," I said. "Can we get back there before dark, Aesir?"

"*Can we get there before dark,*" Aesir repeated with a scoff. "Hold onto yer bonnets. We'll be there in nae time."

We turned back in silence, as twilight crept in around us. Soon enough, my keen eyes adjusted to the dim light. The aether that still burned upon the mountain grew more and more visible in the darkness, casting stark blue shadows upon the snow. Slowly—before our eyes—Old Pelaeia began to burn again.

As that light strengthened, so too did the echoes. Their wispy outlines steadied into vaguely humanoid shapes.

The whispering grew louder.

Aesir had promised to pick up the pace—but he had to swerve sharply as echoes manifested out of thin air, dancing with fresh agony. Frantic, breathless curses spilled from his lips as he veered away from the aether-ghosts, searching for a clear path. More than once, I thought he'd overturn our cumbersome vehicle entirely—but Aesir had learned more about piloting from Dougal than he probably cared to admit. Somehow, he kept us upright and in one piece.

Ruins whipped past us at breakneck speed, kindling with eerie light. Agonised voices whipped into a frenzy around us. Some small, detached part of me couldn't help but wonder at the ephemeral display, even as the rest of me quailed in horror.

Aesir made good on his promise. Just as the last of our daylight disappeared, we reached the twisted front gates of Old Pelaeia. But even the humans on that boat no longer required daylight in order to see—because the thoroughfare that led down to those broken gates was burning with phantom aether-light, too.

We skimmed to a halt just outside the gatehouse, in an area with slightly less disturbed snow than the rest. I pulled down my goggles, staring up at the broiling city. Aesir and Strahl pulled crates of equipment from the flatbed with urgency, while Miss Hawkins and Mr Finch began to assemble a squat, sturdy-looking tripod on the ground.

Partway through their work, the first screams ripped through the night, high up on the slopes above. They cascaded through the city in a rolling wave of sound. That concussive wave of shrieking was deafening here, and unnaturally real. Aetheric lights bloomed in countless silent detonations, as the phantom battle for Old Pelaeia's top tier joined in earnest.

Miss Hawkins' curious contraption came together behind me, constructed upon the tripod. It consisted mostly of a tall spire, as thick as my wrist, with several adjustable antennae and a control panel. It *looked* an awful lot like a portable longhorn, with its multitude of dials and switches—but it also had a slotted opening at its base, which I knew to be exactly large enough for the small canister of Unseelie aether that Hawkins had brought with her to Old Pelaeia.

"Ah'll keep the boat runnin'," Aesir shouted at the two of them. He had to work to make himself heard over the nightmarish din, as he hopped back into the boat and into the driver's seat. Even as he did, a movement caught the corner of my eye.

The ambient, burning aether that had risen upon the mountain now swirled into a humanoid form, only ten feet to my right. But this was no weak, half-manifested shade, like the ones we'd encountered earlier that day. It was far more solid.

And far more *real*.

Clumps of scrap, dirt, and snow pulled themselves together around the aether to form a rough body, with eyes like ragged, burning pits. The being made of rubble stumbled to its feet. It looked as though it should have been clumsy and bulky, but I was shocked by how naturally it moved. This, I realised, was the thing that Hawkins had termed a *tatterdemalion*.

"Strahl!" I shouted in warning, gesturing wildly towards the fresh echo.

The tatterdemalion turned to face me, as though it had heard me. Its mouth opened, spilling forth licks of blue aether; it spoke to me directly, in a strange and resonating voice.

"Brace yersels, lads!" it shouted at me. *"Get to cover!"*

The words were distressingly clear and coherent, compared to the whispers we'd heard earlier.

The echo rushed for the ruined stairs that lead up to the top of the wall. More of them soon swirled to life around us, coalescing in fits of clattering wreckage and snow. They moved with far more purpose than the drifting wisps of aetheric light had done. Soon, a host of tatters and glowing shades formed fighting ranks on the wall, to wage the same hopeless battle they had fought and lost for more than two decades now.

Strahl stared at them, reaching for the aether-charged sword over his shoulder. "What in rot and ruin…" he managed.

Miss Hawkins stood among the burning, restless dead, with her right arm outstretched. Threads of tenuous aether drifted towards the glove she wore, feeding the meters on her forearm. She'd lowered the goggles over her eyes; they lit her pale face with their ambient light, so that she almost seemed like a ghost herself. The sight set a chill into my bones.

"Incoming!" one of the echoes called out.

The warning shout was so universally known among soldiers that Strahl and I immediately ducked for cover.

Artillery blasted apart several of the gathered echoes on the wall... or rather, it *seemed* as though it had. I had to squint to realise that the section of the wall in question had *already* been missing, and that the only thing that had burst was the echoes themselves. Brief, horrifyingly realistic shrieks of pain came and went. Chunks of scrap and dirt from the vanquished tatterdemalions rained down, pelting us from above. Other echoes remained on the wall, just out of sight, screaming in agony.

"Man down! Someone help!"

"Open fire!"

"Hold! Hold fast!"

We already knew that the defenders of Pelaeia were doomed. Every echo we could see had died, by definition. It occurred to me, though, that there were odd gaps in the echoes where more people should have been. Something other than aether had killed the defenders who should have filled those gaps.

The answer to that mystery dawned on me, just as the sounds of the battle took a sudden shift.

Raw fear rippled through the apparitions.

"*Wargear!*" someone called out. The word came with a hysterical edge.

Echoes turned their attention to the twisted front gates. Some of them took shots at the empty air in front of the gatehouse. Scrap shot like bullets through the night, and I was suddenly very glad that we'd set ourselves up at an angle to the gates, rather than at the centre of the action. Even in our less central position, dangerous shrapnel hissed past our heads, such that we had to duck for cover behind the rubble.

Miss Hawkins and Mr Finch continued their work, through it all.

It was curious and horrifying how few the echoes were, directly near the gates. Most of the scene was so visceral and clear—but everywhere that the wargear Verdigris had passed, there were only large swaths of silence and stillness. The towering wargear's pilot had not used aether, after all, to tear open those gates; they would have simply wedged the wargear's great hands between the doors and torn them open from the outside. Such was the strength of the Tuath Dé's *other* gifts to Avalon.

We didn't see the defenders that Verdigris tossed aside like dolls. But beyond the gates, the ground churned, and more than a score of tatterdemalions coalesced. Their hands rose from the dirt and snow; even as they clambered to their feet, I caught sight of their real bodies, twisted and broken beneath the disturbed ground. I barely had time to wonder which source of aether had killed so many people, before the next scream went up.

"Aethermancer!"

It was an awful word; the sort that presaged plenty of death. The woman who screamed it *knew* what it meant. I heard in her tone the certain knowledge of her own impending doom.

"Legionnaire!" another voice cried hoarsely.

"It's Wraithwood!"

My blood ran cold.

The large throng of echoes fell, one by one—cut down with chilling grace and speed. Stone limbs clattered to the ground, carved away by the memory of an invisible silver sword. Silver light flashed within the aether that bound those tattered bodies, like lightning bursts in a storm cloud. Snow, dirt, and aether spewed every which way, and it sickened me that I didn't know how much of that was meant to be blood.

This, I thought, was the dream I had once had; I imagined myself now in place of that phantom Wraithwood, wielding a bright and deadly silver sword. The horror of it nearly made me empty my stomach—but I caught myself against the debris where I'd sheltered from the shrapnel, steeling my resolve.

That wasn't who I was anymore. I wasn't here to join in Wraithwood's atrocities—I was here to undo some small part of them.

"Hawkins!" I yelled. "Aren't we here to *stop* this?"

Somewhere during the chaos, Miss Hawkins had fallen to her knees. She clutched at the machine in front of her, staring at the destruction with such soul-deep horror that I knew the eyes behind her goggles were wide with tears. I knew then, with utmost certainty, that the aethermancer we had brought with us was no Silver Legionnaire. She might have had the sword; she might have had the training. But Miss Hawkins was missing the merciless instinct required to perpetuate the slaughter before us.

I knew then why it was that she had cut off Barsby's hand. As terrifying as she was with that sword, Miss Hawkins couldn't bring herself to kill with it. She was no Jonathan Silver, nor was she a Wraithwood in the making.

The knowledge steadied me in a way that nothing else had done so far. I risked the open ground between us, sprinting towards the machine where Mr Finch had thrown himself to the ground and where Miss Hawkins stared ahead.

I lunged forward, dodging shrapnel to grasp at her shoulders. "Hawkins!" I repeated. "You can end this! You can *stop* him! You have everything you need! You just have to turn on your machine!"

It was more complicated than that, of course; I knew that it was. But the sentiment cut through the haze that had held Hawkins spellbound. She sucked in a shuddering sob, straightening in my grip. Her iron will snapped into place once again, and she lifted her right arm. Strands of visible aether wafted towards her fingertips. The meters on her forearm leapt wildly. As alarming as the sight was, it seemed to be exactly what she was looking for.

Hawkins turned her goggles upon the battlefield. Azure light burned behind that visor, fixing upon a single spot among the chaos.

"It's there," Miss Hawkins breathed. Wonder tinted her voice, despite the tears that still lingered there. "We were right. There *is* a fetter."

"There is?" Mr Finch gasped. He peered up at us from the place where he lay prone on the ground. "That's wonderful! Your theories were all correct, then—"

"Yes, wonderful!" I cut him off urgently. "Now what do we *do*, Miss Hawkins?"

Hawkins snapped her eyes towards the machine, upon its tripod. "We have to move it," she said. "I need to be next to the fetter."

"Lead the way," I told her. "Mr Strahl—I need you with us!" I glanced down at Mr Finch. "Coming, Walther?"

Mr Finch made a small noise of distress, somewhere in his throat. But he climbed back up to his knees, straightening his bulky coat with bizarre dignity.

I eyed the tatterdemalions that still fought near the gates. "What would a blunderbuster do to one of those things, Miss Hawkins?" I asked her. "Would it... *hurt* them?"

Miss Hawkins swallowed. "Technically," she rasped, "it... it would simply disrupt the aetheric bonds that hold its body together."

"You might temporarily turn it back into a shade," Mr Finch supplied helpfully. "It would become weaker, like the echoes we saw earlier today."

I nodded grimly. Absolutely no part of me enjoyed the idea of *attacking* one of these echoes. But Miss Hawkins needed protection if she was going to operate that contraption in the middle of that battlefield.

"Aesir!" I called back. "We're going in! We need cover—can you bring the salvage-boat around in front of us?"

Aesir was looking even more pallid than before; but the stress of the situation had kept him on his toes, at least, and he nodded grimly. The boat's engine roared, and he swung the vehicle around, just in front of the machine. Clods of dirt pinged against the side, even as Hawkins and Mr Finch hoisted the tripod between them to carry it.

Strahl settled in on the other side of them, as I pulled my blunderbuster. I gave Aesir a grim look. "Hawkins says guns won't really hurt these things," I yelled at him, over the din. "But it won't be pretty. You might want to look away."

Aesir shook his head at me. "Blind pilots aren't useful, Blair!" he hollered back. "Do what ye 'ave tae!"

My stomach dropped. I had already hated almost everything about this afternoon. But the prospect of blowing apart Pelaeian tatterdemalions in front of Aesir was easily the *worst* thing I could think of.

There was nothing for it. Hawkins needed room to work. And we'd all committed to this, one way or another.

We moved forward, closer to the chaos. Aesir led the way with the salvage-boat, hunched behind the wheel for cover. Our advance was painfully slow, as Hawkins and Mr Finch carried the tripod between them and Strahl and I covered their flanks. Freshly churned snow and debris made the path even more treacherous. I tried not to think about what else might lie beneath our feet as we stumbled along.

If there were any small mercies to be had, it was that the fetter Miss Hawkins had identified did not lay fully beyond the gates. A few feet in front of them, she signalled Mr Finch to help her set down the machine.

Perhaps I was imagining it, but I thought there was a subtle eddy in the air. The screams of Pelaeia distorted unnervingly around us—faintly muffled, as though we'd stepped into the eye of a phantasmal storm.

A single body lay there, beneath our feet—the first northerner to die by Wraithwood's silver sword. A tatterdemalion had crumbled atop it, blanketing its outline with snow and stone.

Miss Hawkins consulted the readings on her forearm one more time; but then, she reached around to unclip her harness in several spots. The aether battery packs on her belt and harness came free, and she held them out to me.

I goggled at her in disbelief. It hardly seemed like an appropriate time for our aethermancer to *disarm* herself.

"Put these on the boat!" Miss Hawkins urged me. "I learned my lesson on the pier in New Havenshire. I can't mix any of this with the Unseelie aether; I was lucky to have survived the first time." Her foci hissed all at once, venting a cloud of prismatic aether into the air around us. Some of it caught on my skin, tingling with an electric high. The fabric of her coat bleached grey before the wind picked up the aether, carrying it away.

I remembered the unfortunate way the Unseelie aether at the

docks had interacted with Miss Hawkins, and I winced. Somehow, it hadn't occurred to me until now that she would need to touch that stuff *again*.

"Are you going to be all right?" I asked.

The question came out before I really had the time to think about it. I *was* concerned for Hawkins, I realised. I had walked onto this mountain still worried that I might have to kill her... but I no longer entertained any notion of asking Strahl to end her life. Hawkins, I thought, had truly come to Old Pelaeia in order to do something good. Perhaps she had other motivations as well—certainly, I was under no illusions that she'd told me everything. But I had seen the evidence of her humanity and her empathy, and I had begun to suspect that she was indeed possessed of a certain amount of altruism.

Miss Hawkins attached a small tube to the glove on her hand, fixing its other end to another slot in the machine. She shook her head at me. "It won't be pleasant," she said. "But I'm not carrying any other Seelie aether this time—and the device *should* act as a buffering foci. I don't think it will kill me."

I noticed, of course, the lack of utter certainty in that statement. But we had come too far for me to question things now.

"You're a Fool's fool, Miss Hawkins," I informed her. I reached over to clap a hand onto her shoulder. "But at least you're in good company!"

I clambered partway up the side of the salvage-boat, carefully setting the batteries down into the passenger's seat. Even Seelie aether was volatile stuff; there was no point in being careless with it.

Before I could turn around, I felt the device activate. The air around us hummed with a prickling feeling; the ambient, burning aether around us swayed oddly, as though drawn in by a new source of gravity.

The echoes around us halted in their tracks. Their voices lifted as one in a single, keening howl that made my hair stand on end.

Floating shades and writhing tatters turned in unison towards Hawkins and her device, and I remembered then that she had said the echoes would react to aethermancy.

Miss Hawkins had retained the glove on her hand; as I watched, she lifted it into the air. Before, Hawkins had drawn power from her aether batteries—but now, having discarded them, she exerted her will directly upon the ambient aether surrounding us, spooling it around her fingers. Though her goggles had gone dead and dark, her eyes glimmered iridescent within them. Those tethers of shining light threaded across her gauntleted hand like cobwebs... and I saw that each one was connected to a different echo.

Beneath the sound of the screaming echoes, the device gave a high-pitched whine that left my ears ringing. Mr Finch doubled over the machine's console, calling out readings, but I couldn't hear them.

The web of aether in Miss Hawkins' hand sparked, flashing with silent lightning. The aether that burned around us rippled, coruscating with opalescent colours. A few of the tatterdemalions twitched violently; their corporeal forms stuttered uncertainly. One of the echoes on the ground reconstituted its missing legs, pushing itself back to its feet to stumble towards her. Another tatterdemalion slammed the stump of its arm into a nearby pile of wreckage, forming the gnarled limb from sharp, rusted steel.

"Aethermancer!" one of the echoes cried.

"Legionnaire!" another one repeated.

"It's Wraithwood!"

I widened my eyes in sudden understanding. The echoes had mistaken Hawkins for their killer.

I was perched unsteadily upon the salvage-boat—but Strahl still stood next to Miss Hawkins, and he had realised the woman's danger at the same moment I did. He stepped out from behind the salvage-boat and drew the sword from the scabbard on his back, activating its aether-charge. The blade's edges blossomed with golden light; the super-heated metal steamed against the frigid evening air.

Strahl didn't attack with that sword, though. Rather, he stood in place, holding it before him like a beacon.

The tatterdemalions turned towards him, as the sword's minor stores of aether flared and bled off into the night.

"Strahl!" I screamed. "What are you doing?"

Echoes turned towards Strahl, staring at him with their empty gazes. Between Strahl and Miss Hawkins, it was clear which figure better approximated a Silver Legionnaire. Strahl's tall, imposing figure cut a frightening picture against the night—even as the sword in his hand bled white-hot aether.

Strahl knew exactly what he had done by drawing the echoes' attention. But he stayed where he was, even as they howled towards him in a wave of fear and agony and twisted debris.

I leapt from the salvage-boat, pulling my blunderbuster. Despite my earlier reservations, I didn't hesitate: I squeezed off a shot at one of the charging tatterdemalions.

A crack split the air; dirt and scrap showered onto the snow. The tatterdemalion didn't even seem to notice I'd blown a fist-sized hole in its chest; it continued staggering forward, now somewhat more ungainly. Part of its torso crumbled as it moved, revealing the roiling aetheric form beneath. I'd managed only to inconvenience it.

I changed tactics, turning my blunderbuster upon the tatterdemalion's knee. Another burst of the firearm caught its leg. The limb crumbled back into dirt and snow. The echo pitched forward into another tatterdemalion, forcing it to stumble. I fired my third shot at the second tatterdemalion, clipping off its jagged, rusty arm at the elbow.

The tatterdemalions pressed forward, utterly ignoring me.

I cracked open my blunderbuster, forcing its smoking shells from the chamber. I fumbled for shells in my coat pocket with numb fingers, far clumsier than I would have liked.

As the first echo reached Strahl, he brought that aether-charged sword down upon its arm. The searing blade sizzled as it carved through snow and aether—but worse by far was the way the tatterdemalion screamed.

The violent reaction made Strahl stumble back in surprise. The echoes hadn't even flinched as I shot away at their limbs—but this particular assault, so similar to the one that had murdered them the first time, seemed to trigger their death throes all over again.

The tatterdemalion clattered to its knees before Strahl, clutching at its missing arm.

"*Mercy!*" it sobbed. "*Please, have mercy!*"

Strahl froze. The sword trembled in his hands.

The other echoes didn't hesitate, however. One of the tatterdemalions tackled Strahl from behind. The sheer force of the collision knocked the sword from his grasp; the burning aether along the blade snuffed abruptly as he released the activator on the hilt. The two figures, living and dead, rolled through the snow, and I saw the tatterdemalion deal Strahl several vicious blows. I prayed that his armour would absorb the worst of them.

More hands burst from the snow to grapple at Strahl, burning with aether. Several echoes piled onto Strahl's armoured form, screaming in desperation. Pelaeia's dead fought for their lives all over again—but this time, I realised, they had a very good chance of killing the man they believed to be their murderer.

"Strahl!" I tried to shout. But my voice barely managed to cut through the screams. I finished reloading my blunderbuster, snapping it closed over the fresh shells. But I couldn't get a clear shot—not without hitting Strahl himself.

"Finish it!" Strahl bellowed. "Hurry!" His booming voice overtook the screaming din for a moment, before the echoes drowned it out again.

Hawkins pulled on the web of strands that twined around her fingers. I saw the struggle in her movements; her face strained with effort as the aether-tethers pulled upon her, both physically and mentally. But she planted her feet and exercised that iron aethermancer's will, hissing something to Mr Finch just behind her.

Mr Finch fumbled with a small, rusted iron canister of Unseelie aether—and slotted it into the device.

It occurred to me, in the moment just afterwards, that Hawkins was currently *surrounded* by ambient Seelie aether. With it, she had spun around herself an entire web of bright aetheric lines. Even with the aether batteries safely stowed in the salvage-boat, she was about to have a very bad night.

The unified wail of the echoes grew louder. The tethered lines of aether writhed upon her fingers. Ugly reddish black smudges of Unseelie aether crawled along that bright web, bruising it with darkness. Echoes writhed and staggered in strange, violent fits. Shadows pooled within the aether that constructed their bodies.

In that moment, Hawkins and the echoes screamed as one.

One of the tatterdemalions fell apart. The bright blue fires of its shade flickered madly... and then, it winked out, with a silent sort of sigh.

I felt its absence—a lessening of the awful psychic weight that surrounded us. It hadn't been merely discorporated. It was *gone*.

"By the Winds of Fortune," I breathed. "It's *working*."

The machine whined again, high-pitched, as Mr Finch worked the controls, tuning them to different frequencies. Echoes twitched and warped in random fits; the pile of tatterdemalions that still clawed at Strahl rippled unsteadily.

Abruptly, the machine found the right pitch; it rang a note of sudden harmony, clear and beautiful. Miss Hawkins lifted her hand in triumph, gritting her teeth through the pain. Her eyes darkened into black pools, drawing in the light around her.

But a harsh silver light burned against her glove, wavering oddly. Unseelie aether hissed against her right hand, like butter on a hot skillet. Hawkins hadn't summoned her silver sword—but it was still there all the same, fighting with the Unseelie aether. Her hand jerked violently, as though fighting an unseen force.

Several of the ghostly strands snapped, destabilised by the sword's struggles. Hawkins staggered in place as her control wavered dangerously.

One of the freed echoes turned its inhuman gaze upon Miss Hawkins and abandoned Strahl. It let out a cry of blind rage, stumbling towards her.

I stepped into the way, levelling my blunderbuster. The gun roared, kicking back against my shoulder; it blew apart one of the tatterdemalion's legs at the knee. The echo lurched and lost its balance, clattering against the ground.

Silver light and writhing darkness both flared behind me. Hawkins redoubled her focus, forcing new threads of midnight power into existence, despite the silver sword's protests. One of those tethers caught at the downed tatterdemalion, holding it where it was.

The other strands of aether-light began to unravel, burning like lit wicks. Reddish black aether hissed along the bindings. As it reached the echoes, it tore at the blue light within them, making it gutter. Clumps of debris fell from tatterdemalions as their forms began to collapse. Shades dissipated into the mountain winds.

Then—all at once—the echoes around us gave a collective sigh.

And the burning aether at the gates to Old Pelaeia guttered out.

Hawkins doubled over, retching on the ground next to her. She clawed at her goggles with her left hand, holding her right arm close to her chest. Argent light still flickered angrily along that arm, steaming against the night—but slowly, that too began to calm itself. Mr Finch hurriedly switched off the device, cutting off its flow to her glove.

Everywhere above us, the echoes of Old Pelaeia still screamed and died... but the gates, at least, were silent and empty, except for our presence.

I rushed for the broken pile of debris that had collapsed upon my bosun. My heart hammered in my chest; I was vividly reminded of Dougal's downed outflyer, and the body I had found within it.

Snow and rubble shifted, however... and Strahl's form burst through the surface. His armour was pitted; there were whole pieces of it missing, where it had been clawed away. As my sensitive eyes adjusted to the lack of aether-light, I noted dark stains on the clothing beneath, where blood had soaked through it.

I dropped my blunderbuster to tear at the remaining detritus, grasping at his gauntleted hand. Strahl hauled himself up, nearly bowling me over in the process.

"What were you *thinking?*" I demanded, with a hint of hysteria.

Strahl groaned painfully—but he turned away from me, even so, to fish through the rubble. Shortly, he found the sword he had lost there, and stashed it back across his back.

"With all due respect, Captain," Strahl told me, "now you know what the rest of us feel like when you get one of your so-called brilliant ideas."

I worked my mouth soundlessly for a moment. I *wanted* to argue with that statement... but I couldn't.

Somewhere behind me, Aesir had leapt from the salvage-boat to rush for Miss Hawkins. I turned and saw that he had pulled her arm around his shoulder, hauling her to her feet. He said something to her that I couldn't hear—soft, and gently reassuring. Hawkins nodded dimly, using him as a crutch to stumble her way towards the salvage-boat.

I turned to Mr Finch, feeling torn and ragged.

"Mr Finch," I said, "please tell me you know how to disassemble this contraption."

"Naturally," my engineer scoffed. His face was drawn, and his hands trembled as he worked at the tower. As he set one of the antennae down in the snow, however, he paused and turned to look at me. "Captain," he said hesitantly. "About... about that money, for the tea..."

I sighed, and started rummaging through my pockets.

11

NEFARIOUS DESIGNS - JUST LIKE DOUGAL - THE FIRST RULE - HOMEWARD BOUND

"I do wish you would stop bringing me such interesting new injuries," Holloway sighed at me.

The physicker threaded a fresh needle, as I helped Strahl gingerly shuck his bloody undershirt. Ugly gashes showed along his skin, and I knew he'd soon be subjected to several nasty medications, given the rusty metal that had pierced him.

"Nonsense," I replied, in a voice far more cheerful than I felt. "I'm just trying to keep you busy, sir. We wouldn't want to put you out of a job by being too safe now, would we?"

Miss Hawkins, so recently free of the sickbed in the corner of the infirmary, had returned to it once again. Her nausea had passed more swiftly this time, and she seemed overall less physically wretched... but the veins of her right arm were red and livid, and I had the sense that the trials in Old Pelaeia had left a far more lasting mark upon her psyche than upon her body. In fact, she had barely said a word since we'd returned.

Aesir—none too steady himself—had nonetheless insisted on keeping Miss Hawkins company as Holloway dosed her with more of the diluted Seelie aether. The younger MacLeod now sat next to her, holding her good hand as she curled into the thin pillow beneath her head.

I knew Holloway had things under control with Strahl, so I nodded once at them both and headed over to speak with the bedridden aethermancer. Miss Hawkins looked dazed and haggard, and I knew it wasn't all due to Unseelie aether.

"Your device worked as intended," I observed quietly. "I would have thought you'd be at least somewhat pleased."

Miss Hawkins swallowed, and I saw her tighten her hand on Aesir's. "I didn't realise…" She trailed off, looking shell-shocked. "I thought I knew how terrible it was. But I was wrong." She looked away from me. "Wraithwood. He was there? He did… all of *that?*" Tears pricked at her eyes. "How many more echoes did he leave behind there?"

I frowned. "I thought it was common knowledge by now," I said. "Wraithwood and Verdigris led the charge on Pelaeia, after the bombs fell." I glanced at Aesir questioningly.

"Well, aye, ah figured it was common knowledge an'aw," Aesir said. "But ah was there, so… no like ah spent much time askin' *other* people questions about it."

Miss Hawkins jerked her hand abruptly from Aesir's grip. Horror crossed her features, before she could fully suppress it. I realised then that no one had thought to tell her just *how* Aesir had lost his arm.

Hawkins opened her mouth—but she failed to find the words she was searching for. Finally, she shook her head and said, in a small voice: "I think… I need to speak with you, Captain Blair. Privately."

Aesir frowned. There was far too much concern on his face for Miss Hawkins—a near-stranger—given the severity of what he'd just relived. But it occurred to me belatedly that Aesir probably *needed* someone else to focus on, to distract himself from the obvious. Everything from his earlier flirtations to his current consideration was a helpful excuse against examining his own state of mind too closely.

I wasn't sure just what would happen, once that excuse was no longer available.

"Would you mind going to the galley and finding something bland for Miss Hawkins to eat?" I asked Aesir.

Aesir nodded slowly, and pushed himself to his feet. "Need tae stretch ma legs, in any case," he assured us both. "Ah'll be back."

He headed for the door of the infirmary with only a hint of reluctance. As it closed behind him, I pulled at the nearby curtain to afford some privacy to my conversation with Miss Hawkins. I'd barely sat back down, however, when the aethermancer spoke to me.

"We need to leave," Miss Hawkins said. "Now."

I rocked back at that, as though she'd slapped me across the face. "Now?" I repeated incredulously. "Miss Hawkins, I have a wake to attend. And—for that matter, several of my crew are going to want to be there, too. I'm sure your business can wait one more day—"

"Captain," Hawkins interrupted, "your Oath to me—"

"—was to take you anywhere!" I snapped. "And I *will* take you anywhere you want to go, Miss Hawkins. But you never specified the haste with which I was required to do that."

Hawkins flinched, and I immediately regretted my tone. I hadn't meant to be quite so harsh—but the day's events had unravelled me, and my nerves were raw and strained.

I took a deep breath and subdued my voice, with effort. "If you tell me *why*," I added carefully, "you may find me more amenable."

Hawkins swallowed. She cast one last glance in the direction of the door, beyond that curtain... and sighed.

"Someone else stole the schematics for that device," she explained softly. "The *real* device. What I have here is merely a small-scale prototype. If they receive that shipment of Unseelie aether... they'll be able to use the machine."

I scratched at my jaw, frowning. "And that's... bad?" I asked warily. "What would they be able to do with it, other than banish echoes?"

Miss Hawkins shivered as she forced herself upright. A long, slow-burning panic danced beneath the surface of her face. I *felt* it radiating from her, as she searched for the strength to speak her fears aloud. "Captain," she continued, "that device was built to forge a connection between an aethermancer and a fetter. I needed that connection, in order to fully discorporate the entities trapped there."

"Right," I said, nodding slowly. I knew there was a terrible twist coming, of course, but I had yet to see the problem.

"With that connection," Hawkins told me, "a less ethical aethermancer could *control* those entities, rather than set them free."

My mouth went dry.

I replayed the evening's events in my mind. I remembered Hawkins, standing at the centre of that twisted black net of aether; I remembered the dozen or so threads, each connecting her to a different echo.

I tried to imagine how differently the night could have gone, if she had been as false as I had feared. Those echoes had piled onto Strahl; without Miss Hawkins' intervention, he surely would have died. And then, she would have been free to turn those tattered spirits upon the *rest* of us.

My horror must have showed on my face—for Miss Hawkins nodded ominously. "I felt it," she whispered. "In that moment when I gained control of them... the Unseelie aether made them docile, unthinking. Like blank slates for my will."

Silence fell between us.

"...I take it back," I said. "I didn't want to know about this."

Hawkins clenched her jaw. "I need to get to Morgause," she told me. "I have to stop this." She took a breath. "I loved Jonathan like a father. I *know* he wasn't a good man, but he gave me... everything. I know how much this meant to him. I know how horrified he would be at the idea of someone using his invention to commit another horrible act."

Miss Hawkins had already confided in me that the stolen Unseelie aether was headed to an Imperialist faction. The Avalon Imperium hadn't hesitated to raze Pelaeia. I knew with certainty that the empire's remnants would have no qualms about using this device for terrible ends.

I wanted nothing more than to stay just one more day. I *needed* to be at Dougal's wake. I needed to remember him with others, to remind myself of the long life he had led, and of the difference that he'd made in *my* life. But that was purely selfish of me. Dougal probably hadn't wanted this wake at all. In fact, he'd *told* me what he wanted from me, several years ago, and I had made him a promise from my heart.

This can't happen again, I thought.

"Just get me to Morgause as swiftly as you can," Hawkins urged me. "I can handle the rest, Captain. I *will* handle the rest."

I rubbed a hand across my tired face. "I'll talk with the crew," I told her. "We'll leave as soon as we can."

I left her to rest behind the curtain. Holloway was still stitching up the last of Strahl's gashes; as he looked up at me, I sighed. "I need some air," I told them both. "I'll need to talk with everyone soon, though."

I departed the infirmary in search of Aesir MacLeod and the cold night air.

* * *

The evening was haunted by Pelaeia's mournful shrieks—but tonight, at least, I knew that the voices in that chorus were a handful fewer. The idea gave me a small amount of solace.

A few minutes after I made it to the starboard railing, I heard steady, plodding footsteps behind me. Aesir leaned his mechanical hand against the wood with a soft *thunk*. He joined me in silence for a time, as we both looked out at the great valley beyond Pelaeia. It wasn't always easy to enjoy the great beauty of the world with a dead mountain howling at your back... but we tried anyway.

"I take it you left some food for Miss Hawkins," I said finally.

"Ah did," Aesir agreed. "Even looked like she might keep it down."

Well. At least there was that. I didn't expect Miss Hawkins would have an easy time of things in Morgause if she was still poisoned with Unseelie aether by the time we arrived.

"Ah'll want tae tell Chief Crichton about what we managed," Aesir added. "Though... ye know, I'm no even sure she'll believe me. She sure won't believe *you*." He glanced at me sideways. "Nae offence intended."

"No offence taken," I assured him. I gave a dry laugh. "I was there, and I barely believe it myself."

Aesir nodded dimly. "It, uh…" He hesitated. "It wasnae any better the second time 'round, Blair. But we… we *did* something. That matters."

A dull hope flickered behind his eyes. I felt horrible knowing that I had to quash it.

"Miss Hawkins… shared some troubling news with me," I told him. "I'm Oathbound to see her to her destination, and time is of the essence." I swallowed. "I desperately want to stay for the wake, Aesir. But what she's asked for *is* more important. I'm sorry."

Aesir turned an incredulous look upon me. "But her machine, it… it *works*," he sputtered. "What's mare rottin' important than that? We finally let an aethermancer into Old Pelaeia—one who knows what she's doin' there—an' she's just… leavin'?"

"I don't know what to say," I admitted. "I keep hoping someone will ask me to make an easy choice this week. Hasn't really happened yet." I rubbed at my face. "I have every confidence that her request will turn into yet another disaster, if it makes you feel any better. We're certainly not going sight-seeing. But I'm going to make certain that she lives, so she can come back here and finish what she started."

Aesir ran his good hand through his hair; the pale blaze along his right temple was bright in the moonlight. A loud, frustrated sigh escaped him.

"Fine," he said.

I frowned at him. "Fine?" I asked. It was in no way the answer I had been expecting.

"Let me join yer crew," Aesir said, without skipping a beat.

"That is—*not* fine," I stammered quickly. In fact, I surprised *myself* with the swiftness of my response.

Aesir's cool expression dissolved into anger. "Ye *need* an outflyer, Blair," he argued hotly. "An' if this business is dangerous, then ye need one even more'n ye did before."

"Aesir—" I tried.

"Ah've got ma own ship," Aesir insisted. "Bought it off one ae Uncle Dougal's old squad mates fer a real sweetheart deal. Ah mean, granted, she still needs a few tweaks—but if ah can salvage a few parts from Dougal's ship, ah know ah can have her up in the air in no time. You'n Miss Hawkins need ma help."

"Aesir, if this is about trying to impress Miss Hawkins—" I began warningly.

Aesir rocked his head back. "Impress Miss Hawkins?" he sneered. "Ye think ah'm doin' this tae chase a skirt?" He placed his hands on my shoulders, forcing me to stare into his eyes. "I told ye, Blair—either Old Pelaeia goes, or ah dae. An' if ye're no stayin' tae fix Old Pelaeia, then that means ah'm *goin'*. That means ah need a ride... an' you've got one."

Aesir released my shoulders to stand upright once again, hooking his thumbs into the pockets of his greatcoat.

Aesir was right, though I hated to admit it. We had made plenty of dangerous enemies in the last week alone, and flying without an outflyer pilot left me feeling plenty vulnerable.

But the idea of bringing Aesir with us—of giving him an expressly dangerous role on the ship—made my stomach twist with nausea. I felt, suddenly, as though I had a weight on my chest. I leaned into the railing, gulping in a few quick, surreptitious breaths. The sky above us spun, and it took a second before I felt able to speak at all.

"How many hours of combat flying do you have?" I asked him tightly. I already knew the answer to the question—and I saw in his face that I was right to ask it.

"Well, ah've... plenty of hours of *flying*," Aesir replied evasively.

"How many aircraft have you shot down?" I pressed, talking over his cagey response. Aesir grinned triumphantly, opening his mouth to reply, but I lifted a finger. "In an *outflyer*," I added.

Aesir's grin faded to a glower, and he closed his mouth.

"You're not experienced enough," I told him hoarsely. "We've picked up some terrible enemies, Aesir. There won't be any time for learning on the job. Red Reaver's people took down Dougal, and he was one of the best pilots in the Coalition. What do you think they'll do to an amateur, if they catch up with us?"

I'd raised my voice a bit too loudly. Some of the crew on the evening watch glanced our way, clearly eavesdropping. I sucked in another deep breath, trying to still the sky that still wavered above me.

"Red Reaver," Aesir murmured. The name penetrated his stubborn anger. I heard a healthy dose of trepidation in his tone. "That's who shot him down?"

I nodded, working my way through the knot in my throat. "Not... Red Reaver herself, obviously," I said. "But we helped steal her fuel and downed one of her ships. She'll be after us, even if we *do* somehow manage to drop off Miss Hawkins without incident." My voice trembled, despite my best efforts. "I'm barely keeping myself together right now, Aesir," I told him. "I know I can't stay for the wake, but I'm trying my best to do what Dougal would have wanted otherwise. He wouldn't have wanted you on the *Rose*, with all of this trouble gunning for us."

Aesir stiffened at that. I glanced at him too late, and saw an unexpected fury in his eyes.

"So that's it, then," he said coldly. "The old man kept me fae leavin' when he was alive. An' now, ye won't let me go wae ye because he's dead." He slammed his mechanical hand into the railing, in a way that made the wood creak dangerously. "First, he said ah couldnae survive without an arm. Well, ah fixed that, Blair. An' you know what he said then? He said *Pelaeia needs you here*. He said ah was part of a *community*." Aesir spat over the side of the railing. "Dougal wanted out, an' he got out. But he was too much of a coward tae let me do the same—because *he* couldnae handle it. An' what I wanted never did figure in."

The sheer vitriol in his tone made me quail. The stars above me swam again with anxiety. I gulped in another steadying breath. "Aesir, I... some of the crew will likely be staying for the wake," I managed. "We'll be coming back for them, once I take Hawkins to Morgause. We'll... we can talk about it again, when we get back—"

Aesir jabbed a metal finger into my chest. "An' now we're on tae the empty promises," he snarled. "Yer *just* like 'im, Blair. Bet ye must be real proud ae that."

He whirled away from me—and stalked for the gangplank. Soon, his long legs took him off the *Rose* and out into the night.

I watched him go, feeling helpless and confused. Helping Miss Hawkins was so clearly the right thing to do... but everything else I did seemed fraught with unintended consequences.

Aesir couldn't know how wrong he was. At that moment, I wasn't proud of much of anything.

* * *

Though it was the last thing I wanted to do at that particular hour, after the evening that we'd had—I called an emergency officers' meeting.

I held the meeting in the engine room, mainly so that we could avail ourselves of the heat at the mechanical heart of the *Rose*. The engine room was much like its custodian, Mr Finch: forever impeccable, and ceaselessly hardworking. Thick steam pipes ran across the walls, connecting up to the multitude of careful additions our chief engineer had made to the original ship. There was a music to the chamber, made up of rattles, hisses, clanks, and thrums, contrasted against the gentle creaking of the ship's wood. An aetheric core purred soothingly at the centre of the room, from behind thick sheets of silver-lined steel.

The heat from the steam pipes seeped slowly into my limbs as I sat down to wait for the rest of my officers. I rubbed at my hands, wincing at the growing pain in my fingers as cold numbness finally gave way to better circulation. Given the lateness of the hour, Mr Finch had yet to replace our stores of tea—but he fished out the very last of his personal stash of chai as a matter of principle, steeping it with water from a kettle he'd boiled upon the surface of a pipe.

Mr Finch set out a lovely ceramic cup for me and poured it halfway full. I closed my hands around it gratefully, settling my ratty, fingerless gloves against its warm surface. The spicy scent of the tea tickled pleasantly at my nose. I distantly noted the long crack running down the side of the cup. I was, unfortunately, the primary cause of broken crockery on the *Iron Rose*—a fact which Mr Finch well knew, and which he had prepared for accordingly by giving me something already partly broken.

"You'll find this more savoury than your usual floral preferences," Mr Finch advised me loftily. "If you can't abide the strength of flavour, I'd advise a bit of sugar."

I hadn't had a taste for tea, until Mr Finch had joined the crew; I'd always thought it was an acquired taste. Mr Finch, of course, had acquired more than enough taste for all of us combined. He only seemed to forget his habitual peevishness, in fact, when he was recommending new flavours of tea to his fellow crewmates. His careful, drawn-out plan to addict us all to his personal vice of choice had worked—as evidenced by the petty change currently in his pocket.

Holloway had cleaned himself up in the time it took for me to call the meeting. The physicker joined me first, carrying some of the leftover biscuits and marmalade. Mr Finch poured Holloway a slightly larger cup of tea, evincing his subtle fondness for the only other well-mannered gentleman aboard our vessel. Mr Strahl appeared not long after Holloway, leaning against the wall just next to the door; livid bruises had begun to creep along his skin, peeking out from beneath his loosened shirt.

Miss Lenore Brighton joined us sleepily, sitting upon a wooden step ladder as primly as she could manage while still blinking awake. Evie and Little came last of all. I felt a faint stab of envy as Evie leaned himself back against Little's broad chest, using his husband's heat to ward off the cold. I'd never desired a relationship of the sort that they shared—my ship was and always would be my only love—but sometimes, by the Everbright, I *did* desire the convenience of a large human heater.

As Mr Finch doled out the last of the tea for the latecomers, I took one last sip... and settled into the unpleasant business before me.

"Let's cut to the quick, shall we?" I said. "I'm already falling asleep. I know I'm not the only one."

Lenore yawned delicately behind one hand. Evie shook himself, and forced himself to sit up a bit within the circle of his husband's arms.

"Today, a small group of us ventured into Old Pelaeia with Miss Hawkins," I began, "in order that she might prove a scientific claim. She *did* prove that claim. Miss Hawkins used the device that she brought aboard with her, along with a small amount of Unseelie aether, to successfully banish several of the echoes in Old Pelaeia."

Little straightened in shock. Evie blinked quickly, suddenly fully awake. Lenore narrowed her eyes with contemplative suspicion.

Holloway's monocle slipped from his eye and fell into his teacup with a wet *plop*.

"Unfortunately," I continued, "the device in Miss Hawkins' possession is merely a prototype. An Imperialist faction has stolen her research, and may have built a fully developed model from her schematics. They do not intend to do anything benevolent with that device. Miss Hawkins says that she intends to stop them, and I believe her story."

Evie, Little, and Holloway had barely begun to grapple with all of the implications regarding the echoes of Old Pelaeia. All of us had lived, both physically and spiritually, in the shadow of that mountain. I was careful not to describe just *what* a proper villain might do with Miss Hawkins' machine, of course—much as I trusted my crew, that seemed like a secret best kept by as few people as possible.

But Lenore pursed her lips. "That's fine and dandy for Miss Hawkins," she said, "but what does any of that have to do with *us?*"

"As some of you are already aware," I continued carefully, "Miss Hawkins' assistance in New Havenshire came at a price. I swore an Oath to see her to any destination she desired. That destination is Morgause."

"That's... where Barsby wanted us to ship his cargo, wasn't it?" Evie asked slowly. The expression on his face suggested he had yet to fully digest everything I'd said—but his mind worked ahead of him anyway, picking out connections.

"In return for holding *some* of us hostage," Lenore said, with a disdainful grimace. "Not that such a plan would have worked out very well for him."

I nodded at Evie. "Barsby is tied up in this misery too," I answered. "He'll be trying to get the rest of his cargo to Morgause, however he can. But our business—er, *Miss Hawkins'* business—is with Barsby's client." I glanced at Mr Finch. "I know we didn't have the chance to refuel in New Havenshire. How low *are* we on fuel? Could we make it to Morgause?"

Mr Finch frowned deeply. He pushed to his feet, wandering towards a nearby bulkhead, above which were affixed several large tubes, each with their own dangling strings. Mr Finch reached up for one in particular, pulling it down to reveal a neat—if outdated—map of the continent.

Mr Finch snatched up a ruler from a neatly kept cubby, measuring out from Pelaeia to Morgause, at the heart of the duchy of Mavra. He scribbled a few calculations on scrap paper, while the rest of us sat in foreboding silence.

Finally, he said: "At best... if the weather is with us... we could make the trip fairly quickly. At worst, we could still stretch the fuel by using float and sail. But... in either case, we're going to have a problem. Either we refuel in Morgause, or..."

Mr Finch trailed off grimly.

Or Morgause becomes the end of the line, Little finished, with a dour flash of his fingers.

Mr Finch sighed. "I did have a chance to inquire about refuelling *here*, before I was conscripted into Miss Hawkins' endeavours," he muttered. His tone did not sound positive.

"Pelaeia's kept rather minimal stores of aether since the war," Holloway observed quietly.

Mr Finch nodded. "Understandably," he said. "But it's worse than that, I'm afraid. There have been rumblings in the south—significant delays in trade. Something has disrupted the supply chain of aether leading north. Aether is suddenly very scarce."

"That doesn't bode well," I muttered. I reached up to rub at my face. "But there's nothing for it. Miss Hawkins needs to get to Morgause, posthaste. I'll drop her off, and we'll figure out some aether afterwards."

Little cleared his throat. Evie coughed lightly into his hand.

I arched an eyebrow at both of them. "Yes?" I asked.

Little smirked tiredly. *With all due respect, Captain,* he signed, *we all know you're not just dropping off Miss Hawkins.*

"I—" I paused, still trying to parse his meaning. Slowly, I knitted my brow. "I have no intention of involving myself in Miss Hawkins' affairs any further than I already have," I said adamantly.

Evie sighed long-sufferingly. "Wil," he said patiently, "I have known you for over twenty years. You are patently incapable of *uninvolving* yourself."

It's your best and worst quality, Little agreed.

"If I'm not mistaken," Lenore observed, "we're currently discussin' a matter which would cause grief for both Barsby *and* a bunch of rotten Imperialists." A cold, cunning glint came into her eyes. "I can't say as I'm not tempted to involve *myself*."

"I am *not* dragging us all into Miss Hawkins' dangerous affairs," I reiterated stubbornly.

"You are," Strahl grumbled, "and it doesn't much matter. What's the first rule aboard this ship, Captain?"

I sucked in a deep breath.

"The Avalon Imperium deserved to die," Holloway said softly. He rubbed gently at his tea-covered monocle. "We all agreed when we came aboard, William."

My stomach twisted into a knot. The tea in my cup had tasted almost sweet at first—but now, it left a burning taste at the back of my throat. Maybe I should have used some sugar, after all.

I *was* going to get involved in Miss Hawkins' affairs. I'd tried to convince myself otherwise—mostly so that I could convince the rest of the crew to stay out of it themselves. But everyone here knew me far too well.

"We brushed up against Imperials in Lyonesse," Strahl said. "You acted like a fool then, too. I know it's not my job on this boat to think, but give me some credit, Captain."

"We'd have to leave before Dougal's wake," I observed. I said it with an eye towards Little, Evie, and Holloway. And I *did* see flinches at the suggestion. "But anyone who wants to stay for the wake can do so. We'll return after Morgause, as soon as we can."

An awkward, painful silence followed.

"I'm coming," Strahl told me. "Obviously." He fixed me with a flat gaze. "We keep Syrene out of this, though. She stays on the ship at all times."

There were heavy implications which Strahl *didn't* speak among the rest of our company.

At least one Imperial nobleman in Lyonesse had recognised Strahl. Strahl had swiftly repaid that recognition with unrepentant murder; it was why he'd been set to be hanged in the first place. But whoever Strahl had been in the Imperial Army—however important he might have been—Syrene was another matter *entirely*. Strahl had called Syrene a symbol of the Imperium. If Imperialists were ever to get their hands on her, he'd told me, the consequences could be dire.

"I'm still coming with you, Wil," Evie said softly. He forced a smile at me. "Elfa is still in Pelaeia; I saw her today. She can handle Dougal's wake."

I knew what it cost him to say the words. But I *also* knew that steady look in his eyes. He wasn't going to budge.

What time should I get us ready to depart? Little signed. I didn't bother asking him for clarification; if Evie was going to Morgause, then surely, his husband was going as well.

"As soon as we possibly can," I sighed. "I thought about waiting until morning, but..." I shook my head helplessly. "The clock is ticking."

Lenore shrugged. "Ain't none of us sleepin' with all that racket outside anyhow," she said. She pushed up to her feet. "Count me in. Purely outta spite, of course."

I glanced at Lenore curiously. There was a small smile on her lips that suggested her decision wasn't... *purely* out of spite. But Miss Brighton rarely liked to admit such things out loud.

"There are more interesting injuries in your future, I'm sure," Holloway sighed heavily. He cast a glance at Mr Finch. "And you won't be getting far without an engineer."

Mr Finch looked down into his teacup, forlorn. "No," he said piteously. "No, you really will not." At first, I thought Mr Finch's miserable expression was evidence of his unwillingness. But then, he said: "I suppose we *won't* be buying any more tea before we leave."

I blinked.

"Mr Finch," I remarked, "I must take a moment, amongst all of this madness, to openly admire your dedication to supplying us with tea. It really is unfathomable."

Mr Finch shot me a look of mild irritation. "All things are possible with a good cup of tea, Captain," he scoffed. "I detest attempting the impossible without it—but one must make do, when extraordinary circumstances threaten."

I smiled helplessly at him. "I meant it as a compliment, Mr Finch," I assured him. "You keep reminding me lately that you're far more than a meek, retired academic. Only a proper Fool would be brave enough to worry over tea at a time like this."

Mr Finch grimaced. "I've never been especially fond of the Lady of Fools," he muttered.

"Every one of the Seelie has their place in our lives," Evie assured him gently. "The Lady of Fools grants us courage in the face of difficulty. Proper Fools accomplish great things, Mr Finch." He disentangled himself from Little, offering a hand back towards his husband to help him up in turn.

A heavy weight had settled onto my shoulders over the last week. But that weight lightened somewhat at the realisation that everyone from my dearest, oldest friends to my rough and recent crew had volunteered to leap into this stupidity right alongside me.

I tried to clear my throat surreptitiously—but a small, un-Captainly sniffle escaped me, nevertheless.

"I've never had a problem waking anyone up," Strahl observed dryly. "Miss Brighton and I will rouse people and spread the word. Give us an hour, and the only people left on board will be the ones coming with us."

"I'll clean up this mess and prepare us for departure," Mr Finch declared.

Officers filed out of the engine room, one by one. But Holloway remained in his seat, staring down into his teacup. Though Holloway had volunteered to come with me, I knew that the grief of Dougal's passing still tore at him deeply in a way that Evie, Little, and I might never really understand. The idea of leaving before Dougal's wake surely didn't thrill Holloway any more than it thrilled me.

Lenore paused on her way through the door. Her lips curved into a concerned frown. And then—to my surprise—she doubled back to place a gentle hand on Holloway's arm.

"After all this excitement, I don't figure I'll be sleepin' anytime soon," Lenore told him. "Once we're in the air... you mind if I impose on you a bit? I thought I might borrow one of your books."

Holloway looked up at her, blinking. "Oh," he said. He cleared his throat quickly. "Erm, yes. Yes, of course. By all means."

"Much obliged, Horace," Lenore thanked him gently.

She turned her head to raise an eyebrow at me. Belatedly, I realised that I had stopped to stare.

I turned away quickly, knowing it was a bit too late to pretend I was minding my own business. I draped my knitted scarf around my neck and pulled back on my mittens, heading for the door.

Evie fell into step just next to me, as I left.

"Wil," he said quietly, "about Dougal's wake..."

I flinched. "I know," I mumbled. "I know I asked you to speak for him—"

"That's not what I wanted to say," Evie cut me off. There was an odd tone to his voice. "I was thinking... when all is said and done, maybe those of us on the crew ought to remember him *his* way. It might be nice if we poured some drinks and shared some stories, just between us." He smiled tiredly. "I think in this case, I'd like to remember him as myself, and not as a halcyon."

I slowed, staring at him. My heart clenched in my chest.

"I'd…" My voice broke slightly, before I recovered it. "I'd really like that, Evie. I think that's a perfect idea, actually."

Evie looped an arm around my shoulders. I leaned into his embrace with a hard, exhaled breath.

After a few moments, Evie pulled back to look down at me. "You're so cold," he observed, wrinkling his nose with apprehension. "You should ask the gunnery ladies for another jumper."

"I'm already wearing *three*," I grumbled. "Goblins weren't meant for cold weather, Evie."

Evie rubbed at my hands with a rueful smile. "I suppose it's a good thing we're headed to Morgause, then," he said. "Less snow and more smog."

I pictured the soot-stained skyline in my mind—as clear as the day I'd finally flown away from it, on the deck of the *HMS Caliban*.

"Yeah," I mumbled ironically. "Home, sweet home."

12

WAR ON THE HORIZON - THE JUDGE - INSPECTION

The next few hours were a gruelling effort. Leaving port in the middle of the night was never pleasant, but our encounter in Old Pelaeia had worn me to bits. Still, I felt obliged to oversee our departure, given that I was the one who'd declared it. The air was even colder, up among the clouds—and by the time dawn finally came, I felt ready to sleep for a week. I retreated wearily to my cabin, while Little took over the journey.

It felt like only seconds after I closed my eyelids before I opened them again. But there was something strange about the light in my cabin—and as I blinked more fully awake, I noticed that it was *earlier* in the morning than when I'd gone to bed. Little, I realised, had conspired to let me sleep through the entire day.

I rolled out of bed, groaning at the protest in my sore muscles as I dressed for the warmer southern weather. Finally, I pulled on my coat and headed out onto the deck to give my first mate a stern talking-to.

There were more crew hanging about on the main deck than I was expecting for the hour; some of them had clearly decided to linger after their shift change. A small group had gathered on the starboard side of the ship, staring out over the railing.

A toxic scent wafted over the air towards me—and soon, I heard a thundering in the distance. I joined my silent crew, and discovered a battle being waged on the horizon.

An entire city burned in the distance, fighting for its life. From my vantage point, it looked like a second, smaller sunrise. Great pillars of smoke rose up, marking its place upon the landscape. Another sullen detonation echoed across the distance between us. Streaks of light arced across the sky as the city's anti-air towers raked at passing outflyers. Rippling broadsides illuminated the shadowy outlines of naval ships above the city. Flashes of light danced on the open ground beyond the city as armies clashed.

The sight made me sick to my stomach. I couldn't watch it for more than a few seconds.

I found Little on the quarterdeck, observing the battle through a collapsible telescope. The helm behind him moved of its own volition, informing me that Syrene had the wheel. As I approached, Little slid the telescope closed and turned to face me. His expression was grim.

What's going on over there? I signed.

I think that's in Carrain, Little replied. *The invading ships look like they're from the Emerald Spires. They've got dreadnoughts in the sky, and plenty more troops on the ground.*

I let out a breath. "I know Carrain and the Spires aren't *friendly*, but this seems extreme."

I don't even want to speculate, Little signed bitterly. *But it looks serious. This isn't one of their little border skirmishes. I ordered a wide berth, as soon as I saw it. Thankfully, we're almost across the border into Mavra.*

I nodded appreciatively. "Good call," I commended him. I paused. "Couldn't help but notice *someone* allowed me to sleep through all this ruckus."

You needed your beauty sleep, Little told me. He smirked, giving me a once-over. *Still do.*

I chuckled lightly. The rumbling in the distance killed the moment of humour, though, and I shook my head, clapping Little on the shoulder. "Go and get some breakfast, Sam. I'll take it from here."

As he departed, I tipped my hat to our unseen faerie navigator. "Good morning, Syrene," I greeted her. "If I may?"

Meeting no objections, I took back the helm for the next leg of our journey.

We'd left the great snow-capped mountains of the clanhomes long behind us. Before us sprawled the rolling hills and sweeping plains of the duchy of Mavra. The region was notoriously overcast and grey, even at the best of times. Today, however, dark clouds choked the sky, and the rising sun soon became only a faint suggestion behind their cover.

In spite of that, I knew the very moment that we reached the border. I knew this namely because of the line of Iron Guard that currently stood vigil along Mavra's perimeter in a humbling show of force.

My home province, Mavra, was a centre of industry; primarily, its industry was war. Before I'd left, Mavra had supplied the Imperium's military... but since then, it had sold weapons to the highest bidder, all across the shattered Imperium. Not all of Mavra's production output made it outside of the duchy, however; the province maintained its own impressive military, known as the Iron Guard.

Today, we saw the Iron Guard on full display, mobilised against the possibility that the battle beyond might spill across the border. Large, ugly dreadnoughts lingered menacingly in the air; outflyer carriers hovered behind them, ready for deployment. There wasn't a single ounce of elegance to the Iron Guard, but there didn't need to be —it was an unrepentant threat of pure, destructive power.

Civilian traffic still flowed through the military lines, however; Mavra never did close for business. The *Iron Rose* was allowed to approach closer. As we did, a pair of black-striped Shrike outflyers buzzed overhead, swooping close enough that I knew they had given us their complete attention.

Not long after their departure, a giant, lumbering ship descended from the clouds ahead of us. It was a merciless brick of battle-scarred metal—technically, it was only a bit larger than the *Rose*, but it made such a stark impression that it *felt* far bigger. The other ship's belly-mounted cannons were already levelled towards us in silent threat.

When the longhorn rang, I answered it *very* quickly.

"*Unidentified vessel,*" a woman's voice drawled over the line. "*This is the warship Gallant Challenger, of Mavra's Iron Guard. Identify yourself and state your business.*"

I drew in a deep breath, rearranging my mind and my mouth in order to reclaim the dialect I'd spent so long trying to shed.

"The *Iron Rose* hears you, *Gallant Challenger*," I answered, chewing each word. "She carries cargo'n a passenger to Morgause. She's gots her papers'n all."

The style of speech marked me clearly as a lower-class native from Mavra's capital city, Morgause. It wouldn't garner me any *respect*, of course, but it would hopefully result in less suspicion.

"*Have those papers ready, Iron Rose,*" the woman on the longhorn replied. "*You will cut your engines and prepare to be boarded for inspection. Any hostility will be met with extreme prejudice.*"

"Understood, ma'am," I answered, in a voice slightly higher and more strangled than I'd hoped.

The longhorn's line closed at the other end.

I dialled the longhorn to blast an order to all internal frequencies at once. "All hands on your best behaviour!" I ordered. "We are being boarded for inspection. Engineering—please bring us to a full stop. I'll require Mr Mendez and Halcyon Seymour topdeck immediately."

I set aside the chatterbox and turned down the quarterdeck. "Mr Strahl!" I called out. "Please see that both you and Miss Hawkins are dressed for polite company!" I gestured briefly towards my own face. There was nothing *wrong* with having an aethermancer on board, as far as I knew—but aethermancers *did* get a great deal more attention than your average traveller, and I had a feeling that Miss Hawkins didn't wish to explain her true business in Morgause.

The *Gallant Challenger* did not leave us waiting for long. A bulky, armoured longboat angled out of the clouds within the minute, bearing down upon us. The crew were still lining up on deck as the longboat docked with the *Rose*, dropping a ramp across the gap with a sharp hiss of steam. A gunner in an armoured coat sat atop the longboat at a heavy repeater, training the weapon cautiously upon us.

I was uncomfortably reminded of the *Revenge*'s gunner and the havoc he'd wrought on the quarterdeck. I tried not to dwell on it.

Four figures drew my attention as they marched down the ramp towards our ship. Three of them wore polished breastplates over ashen surcoats, with argent-tasselled epaulettes atop their shoulders. Silver foci gleamed upon each of them, while featureless helmets shrouded their faces. I tried not to shiver as I saw them; clearly, Mavra's military meant business if they were dispatching aethermancers for routine inspections.

The last figure, an ambiguous humanoid with a short, trim frame, stood out starkly against the others. They wore a short-sleeved greatcoat over a more stylised, engraved breastplate; a helmet and an armoured bevor conspired to hide most of their head and face. Unlike the aethermancers, this figure carried a sabre on one hip and a large aether-pistol on the other. A grey capelet draped across their left shoulder, stitched with a white shield denoting their religious dedication to the Tuath Dé known as Noble Gallant.

Judges—Noble Gallant's priests—served commonly within bureaucracies of all sorts, and especially within the military. Those who served Noble Gallant were supposedly more dutiful, more impartial, and more difficult to corrupt than the average mortal. I'd lived long enough by now to question that assumption... but I'd also lived long enough to keep that questioning safely inside my head.

The judge crossed the ramp and then stopped a few paces later, lifting a hand and beckoning behind them with one finger. A short, lanky goblin in an ill-fitting grey and brown uniform hurried across the ramp from the transport. A box-like portable desk dangled around his neck by a leather strap.

I felt a strange pang of emotion, looking at the younger goblin's green skin and red eyes. Morgause was full of goblins, but we were somewhat rarer outside of Mavra. Every time I returned, I abruptly remembered what it was like to be around my own people—to be one of many, rather than a standout oddity. But the disdain for goblins was also differently flavoured in Mavra, if no less pervasive—a contempt born from familiarity, rather than from ignorance.

The goblin paused to salute the judge, and I found myself wondering whether his obedient manner was sincere or else tinged with secret resentment. The judge continued staring straight ahead, ignoring the goblin.

"I am Judge Lindholm," the judge informed us. Their helmet's chatterbox garbled their voice, but I could still make out each word clearly. "The captain of this ship will declare themselves and step forward to present their papers."

I glanced sideways at Little and gave him a tiny nod.

Little stepped forward. *I am Captain William Blair,* he signed to the judge.

Sweat trickled down my spine. I didn't *enjoy* having Little pretend to be captain, but I knew it was the best way to avoid unnecessary trouble in dangerous situations like this. That was a very big ship, and those soldiers were very ready to commit violence. They were far more likely to accept answers from a tall, good-looking human like Little than they were to accept them from *me*.

The judge did not immediately respond. Mystified confusion flickered between the rest of the boarding party as they looked at Little.

"What is he saying?" the judge asked flatly. "His Imperial Handsign is atrocious."

"I'm afraid the captain only knows a smattering of the official signs, Your Honour," Evie cut in, with an apologetic smile. "We've had to make do over the years and fill in the blanks with our own... well... dialect. He can hear you well enough, though."

Judge Lindholm turned to consider the other Iron Guards. "None of you can understand him?" they asked. When none of the soldiers volunteered, the judge turned back to us with an air of faint displeasure. "I'll require you to translate for me, Halcyon," they said.

"I'm afraid I only know a small amount of it myself," Evie lied, with a hint of apology. "But our helmsman is quite fluent." He made a gesture to indicate that he was talking about me.

Judge Lindholm turned towards me. I doffed my tricorne in greeting, careful not to meet their gaze directly. "Your Honourship," I mumbled, butchering the address. "The cap'n just said he's Cap'n William Blair." I looked at Little, signing back at him: *Please say you hid the canisters while I was asleep.*

No, Little signed back at me. *We were worried they'd rot the hull.* He paused. *Evie must've said a hundred prayers over them, if it helps.*

"Well?" Judge Lindholm asked me.

"Cap'n tells Berkin t'give yous our papers, with 'is compliments," I said. I fumbled for the papers in my interior coat pocket, offering them out—but Judge Lindholm inclined their head towards the goblin aide next to them, instead.

I passed the documents to the goblin, who clipped them onto the portable desk, looking over the seals that Evie had so recently forged for us. I missed some of the conversation behind me, but I did hear Evie introduce himself.

"Halcyon Seymour, at your service," Evie greeted the judge. He tapped both fingers over his heart, drawing attention to his cerulean sash.

The judge turned that intimidating gaze upon Evie. "Where are you from?" they asked. The question didn't feel particularly friendly.

"I'm originally from the province of Loegria," Evie replied. "I've spent most of my life travelling, though. I've only been back home once or twice since the Sundering War." If the judge's coldness bothered Evie, he managed not to show it. He continued the conversation in a warm tone.

The judge made an enigmatic, contemplative sound. "Have you spent much time in Carrain, by any chance?" they continued.

"About as often as anywhere else," Evie said honestly. "We've had business there a handful of times. Why do you ask?"

The judge didn't answer the question directly. Instead, they said: "It seems you're behind the times. I'll advise you to avoid the Emerald Spires for the near future, Halcyon."

Evie knitted his brow. "I appreciate the advice," he assured the judge. "But... may I ask why? I know we skirted a battle there. Are things that dangerous?"

"Carrain and the Spires are at war," Judge Lindholm replied evenly.

"For now, it's mostly border clashes. But they're escalating quickly." The judge glanced once towards the goblin, who still checked over our papers, scribbling notes onto a separate piece of paperwork. "The Church of the Benefactor has split. Only the Emerald Halcyons are welcome in the Spires now. The province has scattered their traditionalist halcyons to the four winds and told them not to return. If you show up in the Spires without a state licence, you'll be confined to your ship, at best. At worst, you might end up fined, imprisoned, or...otherwise."

Evie and I both stared at the judge, utterly flabbergasted. The Emerald Spires had never evinced a great love for the Benefactor—the Emerald Halcyons, a state-sponsored splinter branch of the faith, preached such wildly different interpretations of the Benefactor's Word that few people outside of the Spires considered them to be real halcyons at all. But outlawing traditionalist worship was... ridiculous. The threat of *execution* was even more outlandish. The abrupt escalation made it seem as though the Spires had lost all reason, overnight.

"And His Grace, Lord Evergreen gave these orders?" Evie clarified slowly.

Though I couldn't see the judge's face, I felt their disgust at the mention of the name. The Duke of the Emerald Spires had broken his Imperial Oath in the worst way possible by ordering his men to betray and murder Emperor Lohengrin. To say that judges were not fond of Oathbreakers would be an incredible understatement—and Lord Illyrian Corbinec was one of the most notorious Oathbreakers of all.

"News out of the Spires suggests that his son, Aurelius Corbinec, rules now in all but name," Judge Lindholm replied in a clipped tone. "He's always been a religious boy."

The judge's flat intonation made it impossible to tell whether they were being facetious or not. I wracked my memories in search of anything I might have heard about Aurelius Corbinec—but came up blank. I wasn't exactly up-to-date on the finer points of politics in the Emerald Spires.

I hated the idea that I might soon be forced to learn all about those politics.

"Thank you for the warning," Evie told the judge carefully. "I suppose this business between Carrain and the Spires has something to do with the aether shortages we've heard about? We were hoping to refuel in Morgause."

"I'm afraid you'll have to get in line," Judge Lindholm replied coolly. "Someone waylaid the most recent aether shipments on the Copper Road—probably Carrain, trying to starve the Spires. Only the very lucky and the very rich are getting fuel right now." The judge moved on briskly, holding out their hand. "Your manifest, please," they asked.

Little handed over the logbook to the judge. I forced myself back to the present moment, looking back towards the goblin aide who still peered over our travel papers. Normally, I had the utmost faith in Evie's forgeries, but it occurred to me that it might be best to hedge our bets and make friendly with the help, either way.

"All this trouble, just so's we can get back to Morgause," I griped, shaking my head. "S'a rottin' pain, innit?" I let my dialect slip even further.

The goblin aide chuckled dryly, flicking his eyes towards me. "Goblin's got the whole world at his fingertips, but he comes back 'ere, right?" he mumbled quietly. I grinned as I caught his familiar accent.

"Can take the goblin outta Coalditch, but it always drags him back," I offered with a sigh.

The aide raised his eyebrows at me. "Lockit's from the Ditch too," he said, pressing a hand to his chest. Say what you will about goblin cant, but introductions are far more efficient when everyone refers to themselves in third person.

"Berkin too," I replied. Berkin *was* the name I'd been born with; it felt just a bit awkward on my tongue.

Lockit peered a little more closely at something on the page—and I cleared my throat. "Hey," I said. "They still has that bakery up on Septimus Street? The one with them lavender'n honey cakes?"

Lockit looked up at me again. "Bloomington's?" he said. "Nah.

Bank took it over. They owns the whole street now." He reached into the desk to pull out a stamp, and officialised our papers. He held the new paperwork out to me with a rueful smile. "Not sure what they *wants* it for, but we all knows Ol' Smythe, don'ts we?"

I took the papers, grimacing at the reminder. Colridge & Smythe was the premier—the *only*—bank in Morgause. The city's inhabitants cursed the institution loudly and often... but everyone important still had little choice but to do business with Ol' Smythe.

"May the bankers all rot, by th' Benefactor's mercy," I said, with an ironic tip of my hat. "Berkin's thanks."

Judge Lindholm had just stepped aside to interrogate Miss Hawkins—once again a meek and proper academic in her wig, her dress, and her gloves. I held my breath as I watched, worried that the judge might notice something out of place at any moment... but the armoured priest turned away, apparently satisfied, and returned to speak with Little.

"You there," Judge Lindholm said, pointing at me. "With us. I'll require you to translate again."

I nodded obligingly, hurrying over with the newly stamped travel papers. "Yes, Your Honourfulness," I said.

I saw Lockit smirk lightly at the title, out of the corner of my eye.

We descended into the ship in a small group. The judge and the aethermancers grew tense as we entered the cramped corridors below, keenly aware that they were further away from their fellows on the longboat. I suppose they were worried about a potential ambush... but as we went deeper below, it was the *smell* that suddenly overtook all other concerns.

The damp, mildewy stink walloped us all, the moment we opened the door to the cargo hold. I quickly covered my mouth and nose— but the Iron Guard had to do their best to look professional and unaffected.

"What *is* that?" Judge Lindholm asked. Their breath wheezed slightly behind their helmet. "Your manifest said you were carrying tea."

"Definitely tea," I assured them. I tried to sound confident as they moved into the room. One of the aethermancers slipped a pry bar into one of the crates. It cracked open a bit too easily. A stronger, more nauseating scent welled out of it. The aethermancer groaned with disgust, leaning away from the crate.

"That is a revolting tea," the judge observed. They waved a hand at the other crates. The other aethermancers moved to crack open further containers, clearly begrudging. Each open crate only intensified the smell. It occurred to me as I watched that the aethermancers seemed particularly affected by the stench. I wondered if the hint of Unseelie aether on the air was bothering them as well.

I glanced uncomfortably at Little—but my first mate didn't seem prepared to offer any fantastic ideas. I shifted once on my feet... and then, inspiration struck me, encouraged by my several conversations with Mr Finch over tea.

"It's fermented!" I told the judge.

"Fermented?" Judge Lindholm repeated. I heard a soft gagging noise behind the helmet.

I forced myself towards an open crate, where one of the aethermancers had started prodding at the contents with their pry bar. I knew the Unseelie aether was buried at the bottom; thankfully, the aethermancer had little interest in digging too deeply.

I grabbed a sodden brick of the rotting tea leaves. My skin crawled, despite the glove I was wearing, but I tried to keep a smile on my face as I waved the blackened brick before the judge's helmet. "Aye," I said, with an enthusiastic nod. "Judge would be surprised how much them toffs at Colridge & Smythe'll pay for the stuff. Proper rank, yeah? Rich people has such funny tastes." I shoved the brick insistently at the judge. "Cap'n says you can has one. Crew's got more'n enough."

The judge stared me down, trying to seem unflappable. But I could tell that their constitution was of a lesser quality than their integrity.

"That won't be necessary," Judge Lindholm said. They turned on their heels to march from the cargo hold, gesturing towards the aethermancers. "We're done here."

The aethermancers stopped their work instantly, with obvious relief. They left the crates behind them, clearly desperate for the fresh air of the main deck.

"The *Iron Rose* is cleared for travel into our borders, Captain Blair," Judge Lindholm informed Little, as we returned to the surface. "Welcome to the duchy of Mavra." They added a final stamp onto the paperwork I carried, barely pausing on their way back to the transport. The other members of the Iron Guard pulled subtly away from the aethermancers as they returned to the longboat, reacting to the pungent fragrance that still clung to them.

Little gave a courteous half-bow. Evie offered the judge a friendly smile, as they headed back onto the ramp. "Fair winds and blue skies, Your Honour," our halcyon intoned, by way of farewell.

We watched as the transport pulled up its ramp and slowly departed.

Once it was safely out of view, I burst into motion, ripping off the glove that had touched the tea and flinging it over the side of the ship. I danced uncomfortably on the spot, with a sound of manic revulsion.

"Ugh!" I groaned. "I can't believe I *touched* that stuff." I held the offending hand as far away from myself as possible. "Mr Little—please get us moving. Physicker Holloway—do you have something I can use to disinfect my hand?"

The physicker looked at my hand and wrinkled his nose in disgust. "Perhaps we ought to consider amputation," he said.

13

THE COLD IRON CROWN - TOLD YOU SO - OL' SMYTHE - ROCK BOTTOM

No further military lines bothered us as we headed deeper into Mavra. But as we sped past once-golden fields, it soon became clear that we were approaching Morgause. There was a change in the air—a pungent stench of a different sort than the rotted tea in our cargo hold. The closer we came to Morgause, the more the smell of industry assaulted us. A great black cloud hovered ahead of us, just visible on the horizon.

The faint smell of lavender stood out all the more starkly against that polluted air. I felt Syrene's queasiness knotting at my gut, making my head swim. The faerie's outline surfaced slowly in the mast, and she fixed her jet black eyes upon me.

"These are ill winds, Captain," Syrene whispered. "We do not like this place."

"I don't think *anyone* likes this place," I told her bleakly. "Least of all the people who live here." I didn't bother to hide the bitterness in my voice.

"The winds... do not speak here," Syrene murmured. Her tree-like body shuddered. "The earth screams. Why have mortals allowed this desecration?"

"The Seelie keep asking for Tithes in order to help fight their war,"

I replied. "Unless you want us showing up to fight with pointy sticks, we've got to make our weapons *somewhere*." I rang the nearby bell until Little headed up the steps to meet me.

Yes, Captain? he signed.

"Let everyone know to get ready," I ordered him. "We'll be arriving within the hour."

Going through that storm? Little asked me. He hooked a thumb over his shoulder, towards the dark clouds in the distance.

"That's not a storm," I corrected him. I adjusted our course and locked the wheel into place, just long enough to snatch the mask from my belt and slip it over my face. "Gas masks and goggles, Mr Little. Welcome to Morgause."

* * *

An untrained eye might have mistaken the great rolling dunes in the dead fields around us for filthy snow. The flakes of puffy ash that drifted on the air would have quickly corrected the notion.

Morgause—a dark behemoth of a city—slowly swallowed the horizon, the closer we came to it. The city was a sprawling mass of steel, hunched upon a wide-open pit in the earth. Local stories had it that Morgause had started as an Imperial mining town a few hundred years ago, conveniently situated such that its inhabitants could dig out iron from sunup to sundown. Whatever the truth, I'd looked down on that iron pit for much of my childhood, knowing that it would eventually swallow me up; it was my fate to join the miners down below, or else to crawl through machinery at one of the many factories which made use of Morgause's iron.

Towering stacks surrounded that cavernous maw, belching soot and smoke. The coal-powered foundries rarely ceased production these days. The rest of Morgause was a rat's nest of industry, twisted through with steam pipes and enormous clockwork factories. Locomotives snaked their way to and from Morgause on tangled tracks, chuffing like mechanical beasts of burden. The entire city growled with the endless cranking of gears, the whistle of billowing steam, and the hammering of distant miners.

People who had never been to Morgause liked to say it was the shining jewel of the duchy of Mavra. People who actually lived there called the city Mavra's cold iron crown.

Ships hovered over the city like blowflies on a corpse, flashing their lights in the smog. We flared our own aether-lamps as we approached, keen to avoid an unexpected collision. Evie called the port authorities on the longhorn to request docking space, while I navigated us into the city. I knew we'd soon be gouged for the privilege. Evie may have forged us a renewed port licence, but Morgause's bureaucrats always required a little extra money underneath the table.

Our destination was the Aviary—a stacked collection of platforms and hangars where ships of all sizes came to roost. The Aviary was relatively safe from the sweeping torrents of ash and soot... if you could afford it, of course.

The pier's docking arms embraced the *Rose* with a rude mechanical jolt. We rattled to a halt, and I pulled a kerchief from my inner coat pocket to wipe the grime from my goggles. I didn't really need my goggles to shield me from the sun in Morgause—the ever-present haze of smog clouds did that all on its own—but I knew the air would burn my eyes after too long if I took them off.

I already longed for a patch of blue sky. The *Rose* would be filthy with the touch of Morgause by the time we left. Everyone on the ship would be filthy, too; the city had that effect on people.

Rot and ruin, how I hated this place.

Grey-coated watchmen observed us from below as we lowered the gangplank. Those new to the city might have mistaken them for soldiers, but I knew that they were little more than armed bribe-mongers in service to Colridge & Smythe. Locals called them 'grims', for their harsh attitudes and bleak apparel. The pair of grims soon walked up the ramp onto the deck, and I headed down from the helm to join them. Evie fell into step next to me, with our forged papers in-hand.

"Which one of you is the captain?" the smaller watchman asked. The filthy gas mask that hid his face occluded his voice.

"That'd be me," I replied, as I strode out ahead of Evie.

The grim who'd spoken chortled as though I'd made a joke.

I've got enough sense of self-preservation to take that sort of insult from a ship full of aethermancers and a judge—but these two-penny toughs were no aethermancers. The watchman's laughter slapped me in the face, aggravating the indignity to which I'd just subjected myself on the way here. Hot fury welled up inside me, like blood from a wound.

I stared the grim down flatly. As I stood there, waiting in silence, his laughter slowly died. Though I couldn't see behind me, I knew that Evie was staring at him, too; in fact, a great number of eyes on my ship had levelled upon the man with decided displeasure.

That swell of righteous anger at my back soaked into me, bolstering my sense of self. What did it matter if a professional shakedown artist from Morgause had a low opinion of me? I had a loyal crew. I was the captain of my ship because they got up every day and decided to believe in me.

The grim who'd laughed cleared his throat uneasily. "Captain," he said finally, with an uncomfortable nod. "Your... documents, then?"

I nodded shortly at Evie, who still carried our papers—but I kept my eyes focussed on the watchman who'd cracked the joke. He squirmed subconsciously beneath my gaze, and I felt a bolt of brief, vindictive satisfaction.

"Here you are, sir," Evie said. He passed the documents over to the second grim, pointedly ignoring the first one as he did. "Along with our... compliments."

The quieter grim took the paperwork, along with the few paper crowns Evie had slipped between the pages. He barely glanced at the writing—most of his interest lay with the bills, which he shoved openly into his breast pocket.

I inclined my head at him. Maybe he would share the bribe with his partner, and maybe he wouldn't. Either way, it wasn't my problem. I'd paid Morgause's unofficial toll.

"Welcome to Morgause, Captain," wheezed the grim with the paperwork. He jerked his head at his partner, then turned down the gangplank to leave. The other grim followed, casting uneasy glances over his shoulder at the crew.

I didn't realise how tense my body had become until they were gone. My hands unclenched. I stopped grinding my teeth. As that fury drained away, its absence left me lightheaded and twitchy. I took in several deep breaths, trying to ignore Morgause's noxious stench as I did. My calm returned, even as I coughed on the smog.

I cleared my throat, breaking the tense silence which the grims had left behind them. "We have some bank notes to cash, everyone," I rasped. "There's at least a day of shore leave, while we sort out our aether and look for jobs. We've got a few spare gas masks—use them whenever you can. Your lungs will thank you for it."

As I spoke, Miss Hawkins swished her way up to the main deck. She was, once again, the meek and overburdened passenger I had taken on at New Havenshire. I saw signs of the woman beneath the disguise, now that I knew to look for them: the extra makeup to hide her bright blue veins; the layers of billowing cloth, to hide her foci. If I listened closely enough, I could even hear the rattle of her aethermancy accoutrements beneath the fabric of her dress. Hawkins had dyed her wig a dark brown once more, and had hidden her dishwater grey eyes behind some goggles.

Miss Hawkins picked me out and soon headed towards me. "Captain," she addressed me, "you've held up your end of the bargain." She offered out one gloved hand. "I hold your Oath to be fulfilled."

I took her hand, even as the air around me released the terrifying, leaden weight I had been carrying. The fulfilment of my Oath was uncomfortably abrupt, such that I barely had time to process it before Miss Hawkins finished her handshake.

Most people are rightfully afraid of becoming Oathbreakers... but since the day Syrene had repaired my honour in an arguable flight of fancy, I had lived with a far more intimate knowledge of what might happen to me if I broke an Oath again. Some fatalistic part of me had assumed that I was doomed to be Oathbroken again as soon as I'd sworn to Miss Hawkins at all. Instead, I found myself blinking back confused relief all at once, as that Oath I'd made to her melted off my shoulders in far too casual fashion.

If Miss Hawkins noticed how badly the moment had shaken me, then she ignored it. "We seem to be here in good time," she said instead, with a hint of relief. "I'll need to do some investigating to see if the ship I'm looking for has arrived."

I swallowed down my conflicted emotions, dimly aware that Miss Hawkins had just told me something I hadn't known before. "You know the ship you're looking for?" I asked her, trying to keep the question professionally disinterested.

Miss Hawkins released my hand. "It needn't be any of your business, Captain," she said gently. "I suggest you find some fuel soon and make your ship scarce. I've left some of my extraneous equipment with Mr Finch—it should sell for a sizable amount, as long as you let him haggle the price. Hopefully, it will be enough to get you back into the air."

I sharpened my attention on Miss Hawkins. The sudden generosity felt... ominous. "You're not expecting to survive this business of yours," I observed darkly.

Miss Hawkins heaved a sigh. "It is *dangerous* business," she said. "It comes with the distinct possibility of violence. Either way, I am about to cause quite the ruckus, and I would prefer if you weren't tangled up with it, given that someone might figure out which ship brought me here. I know what you sacrificed in order to get here in good time. I won't repay that with further trouble."

I narrowed my eyes. A sense of contrariness rose within me, despite her solicitous tone. "Miss Hawkins," I said, "I am used to being the biggest troublemaker in town. I'm not certain I like the suggestion that you're about to outdo me." I paused, then added: "Pelaeia *needs* you to return. You know that. If there's anything I can do to help—"

Miss Hawkins turned away from me—but not before I saw the flash of guilt in her expression. "Sort out your fuel, Captain," she told me. "I don't know when the hand-off will occur—but as soon as it begins, I'll have to get involved." I knew it was meant to be a dismissal.

I rarely take dismissal very well.

I smiled pleasantly at her back, readjusting my plans. "May the Lady of Fools bless your errand, Miss Hawkins," I said.

Miss Hawkins started down the gangplank. Even as the top of her wig disappeared, I sought out Evie on the main deck.

"Halcyon," I said conspiratorially, "I would greatly appreciate it if you made certain that charming young woman wasn't accosted on her travels in Morgause. And if you *happen* to overhear the ship she's looking for while doing so, then I would be obliged to hear its name."

Evie raised an eyebrow at me. Nearby, Little flashed his hands at me with grim humour.

Told you so, he signed smugly.

"Yes, yes," I sighed. "You all told me so." I paused. "In any case, we're going to need to exchange some bank notes in a hurry. But I'll be damned if we're going to sell any of that equipment. Miss Hawkins is going to survive her little errand, and *then* she's going to return with us to Pelaeia to finish what she started."

We still need aether, Little observed. *We don't want to be caught flat-footed when the fireworks begin.*

I nodded wearily. "I know," I said. "I... I *think* I can get us some. But I'll need to shop around."

I didn't linger for any further questions. None of them would be questions I wanted to answer—in fact, I knew that they'd be questions that I really *shouldn't* answer.

Instead, I sought out some of the gunnery ladies, along with our esteemed physicker, to let them know that they would soon be needed at a bank.

* * *

It was something of a walk from the Aviary to the magnificent bank that made Morgause run.

Colridge & Smythe wasn't so much a pillar of the community as it was a rotten foundation—but everything about the great edifice suggested respectability, nonetheless. The bank's stone steps and thick colonnades were a shocking, pristine white against the rest of the smog-stained block. The building's enormous brass doors were polished to a perfect shine. Its delicate stained glass windows looked as though they belonged in a temple. Every morning, I knew, an army of workers got up before dawn to spray every inch of the bank's walls and windows with clear, clean water. The result was a seemingly magical, untouchable symbol of money and power.

Armed guards stood vigilant watch over the bank, with trained barghests by their side. The guards were oddly faceless behind their gaunt air masks; they looked nearly identical, in their stiff grey uniforms and gleaming black boots. High-powered aether rifles glowed a sullen azure against their backs, warning off any would-be troublemakers.

The barghests were an even stronger discouragement than the aether rifles, though. The huge, wolf-like creatures came easily up to my waist, even while settled onto their haunches. Large, crooked teeth protruded from their mouths, too big to fit behind their lips. Red eyes looked out from their sharply defined, skull-like faces, watching us intently as we passed. I'd had nightmares about barghests when I was far younger; feral packs of them still roamed the Pityards and the warrens of Undertown, snatching people off the streets at night. These particular barghests looked well fed, at least, and less likely to attack the bank's well-off customers out of hunger.

Kumari Jahnavi Varma strode ahead of me, holding Mary's hand in hers. The two of them had dressed in formal black mourning attire, befitting a wealthy widow and her granddaughter. Holloway walked next to me, behind them; I'd sheepishly asked him to discard his usual, more gentlemanly attire in favour of rougher dress. Instead, our physicker wore a thick wool jumper and a beaten old sailing coat. Without his monocle, Holloway's scar and damaged eye stood out more keenly, lending him an unearned air of menace.

We paused by one of the many lampposts in front of the bank, whereupon the other three pulled off their masks and straightened their clothing.

"I've never worn anything so... *itchy,*" Holloway complained softly. He reached up to tug at the high collar of his turtleneck.

"But you look so cunning, Mr Holloway," Mary told him, with a winsome little smile. She twirled her parasol with great pleasure. Though Mary was sixteen years old now, she'd been the ship's darling for far too long, and we only asked her to come on jobs with us very rarely. Despite the fact that Mary was technically considered a gunnery lady, I'd yet to allow her a firearm of her own—a matter of ongoing and increasing conflict between us.

"You're brilliantly intimidating," Navi added. "Stylish. Aloof. A hint of roughness around the edges. A perfect protector for this distraught widow. You remind me rather of Augustus."

Holloway blinked. "Er... pardon," he said. "Was Augustus one of your grandchildren, my lady? I fear I don't recall."

"No, dear," Navi said with a chuckle. "I meant the character from *Honour and Humility.* You've read it, I think?"

Holloway straightened and pressed a hand to his heart. "Madam," he said, "you flatter me."

"I do," Navi agreed. "But it's still an apt comparison." She took Holloway's arm and glanced back towards me. "You're not coming in with us, Captain?" she asked.

I shook my head slowly. "Ol' Smythe wouldn't let me in even if I wanted to come," I told her. "You don't need my help. I trust you'll eat those poor clerks alive."

Navi smirked. "I *am* feeling rather peckish," she said.

"They'll try to hold the funds for a few days," I told her—mainly for Mary's benefit, as our younger gunnery lady had never had to deal with bank notes before. "We can't afford to wait for that. I trust you'll get your way as usual, Kumari."

Navi inclined her head imperiously. "I cannot imagine the sort of monster who might refuse to give a grieving widow her husband's funds," she said. She paused, and added: "Dear Mary might well cry."

Mary grinned at me, still twirling her parasol. "I might," she agreed. "It'd make an awful big ruckus."

I snorted behind my mask. "I have every confidence in you," I assured her. I tipped my hat at Holloway. "Sir," I said, "I leave these poor, defenceless ladies in your care."

Holloway somehow kept a straight face. We both knew Lady Navi was carrying a firearm somewhere on her person—and that she was likely a better shot with it than he would ever be.

"I sure *feel* defenceless," Mary said archly. She crossed her arms at me meaningfully. "Maybe if someone had given me a gun—"

"We'll talk later, Mary," I said quickly. I didn't want to have this conversation here.

Mary narrowed her eyes at me. She snapped her parasol closed and turned for the steps of the bank with a sullen sniff, marching away from us in a huff.

"She'll grow out of the attitude, darling," Lady Navi assured me. "They always do."

I sighed. I hadn't *meant* to end up as an awkward semi-parental figure to an adolescent girl... but somehow, it had happened anyway when I wasn't paying attention. "I miss the hugs," I grumbled.

Navi patted me on the shoulder. "I know, dear," she said. She smiled over at Holloway and straightened her posture. "Shall we, Mr Augustus?" she asked him.

Holloway inclined his head at her. "Indeed, ma'am," he rumbled gruffly, affecting a character voice. "But only if you'll kindly call me 'Gus'." The two of them followed after Mary, up the steps of the bank.

I turned away reluctantly, fading back into the crowd on the street.

Morgause had changed superficially since my last visit... but underneath it all, nothing had *really* changed. Flowing rivers of unwashed masses in grime-caked overcoats choked the streets, trying to ward off the smog. Visitors to Morgause dotted the crowd, painfully obvious with their bright splashes of colour as they cowered beneath parasols and broad-brimmed hats.

Somehow, though, I'd managed to forget the *noise*. In the middle of the day, the racket in Morgause was positively deafening. Raised voices shouted in a dozen different dialects, trying to make themselves heard over the army of workers that trundled through the streets. Massive pipes hissed and leaked. Trams and heavy machinery thundered.

There was a smothering, pervasive energy to Morgause—a frantic, angry impatience, as though the entire city was running late and you had put yourself in its way.

Locals shot me strange, wary looks as I walked alone. Goblins weren't unheard of in the wealthy business districts, but we were supposed to be toiling at menial jobs around this hour. Worse, perhaps, was my lack of grime—I'd been gone so long from Morgause that none of my clothing held even the memory of smog. I wound my way swiftly out of the area, intent on avoiding the patrolling grims who turned their heads with suspicion as I passed.

Some of the tension relaxed as I transitioned into a less wildly affluent part of town. One might be hard-pressed to claim that Morgause had a true middle-class—but at least the people here weren't fodder for the mines. Here, the buildings were closer and the layers of soot were thicker; but street lamps burned brightly against the smog, pushing back the unnatural darkness.

I crossed through a small marketplace, where throngs of people pressed even closer than before. More than once, the crowd jostled me; someone hissed at me to mind where I was stepping. I thought longingly of the way people in Shackleton had parted before my bosun—but I knew that the presence of a tough like him would rankle some of the more *territorial* locals. And I needed all the goodwill I could muster.

Butchers, blacksmiths, and tinkerers jostled for attention, just outside of their cramped shops. A gorgon fortune teller hissed at me from a ragged tent on the street corner, warning me of my bleak future; the snakes beneath her hood followed me with their eyes as I passed.

Maybe it was just my imagination—but it felt as though the further I walked, the stronger that ever-present tension in the people of Morgause grew. People strode past me with violent purpose, as though every moment counted. Several of the locals who passed me juggled freshly bought necessities; some of the shops had closed up entirely, even in the middle of the day, with prominent signs warning the crowds gathered outside that they were 'SOLD OUT' of everything from bread to gas masks.

Morgause had become a tinderbox—one spark away from mass hysteria.

"Extra, extra, read all about it!" A young newsie hollered over the crowds, perched atop a crate. He brandished a newspaper in his hand like a weapon, thrusting it high into the air. "Emberhill strikes again as Peacekeepers plunder the Copper Road! Fifty thousand crown bounty for Carrain's most notorious aethermancer, dead or alive! More aether delays expected!"

At least the muckrakers were making a mint off of the frenzy, I thought faintly. The Morgause in me had to appreciate the hustle.

I skirted warily around the panicked crowds, taking shortcuts through the side streets. And finally, I began to see the goblins.

Most of them were streaked with grime, fresh off some gruelling factory shift. Some of them lit the street lamps that fought back the daytime darkness. A few of them sat on street corners, begging for money.

There were several reasons why I didn't like coming back to Morgause. The breathless guilt was one of them.

Through a combination of foolish daring and sheer dumb luck, I'd somehow managed to escape this smog-infested hole. I'd bucked fate, fleeing the promise of empty factory work and probable industrial injury.

There was a reason no one in Mavra seemed willing to believe that I was a captain. Maybe there was no law against it... but goblins simply didn't rise that far. The crushing weight of profit, prejudice, and merciless bureaucracy was normally enough to keep us down in the muck, all on its own. The greatest irony of my life, I knew, was also the greatest tragedy: By participating in the Sundering War, I had ended up taken prisoner in a place that offered me infinitely more opportunity than my own home.

Though the Imperium was long dead, the walls I passed were plastered with other opportunities. Posters along the street urged citizens to 'ENLIST IN THE IRON GUARD TODAY!', promising wages far more enticing than those offered by the average factory. Other flyers were sprinkled with advertisements, company slogans, and pro-company rhetoric. 'NEVER TOO YOUNG TO WORK HARD!' one declared. 'NO HONOUR IN IDLE HANDS', another chastised. Though I hadn't seen these specific posters before, their tone was mostly familiar.

But the further I went, the more those eye-rolling old slogans were overtaken by newer, more uncomfortable fare.

Someone had gone to great trouble in order to cover up the rest of the posters with rows of large, bright green flyers—as though determined to conquer the caked-on layers of advertisements, once and for all. Every picture depicted the identical silhouette of a halcyon in a green sash, holding their hand over their heart.

'MERCY IS FOR THE TRUE', said the posters.

It took me an extra second to process the error in the text. Admittedly, I'd never *read* the Word of the Benefactor—but Evie had quoted it to me so many times that I could swear I knew the entire thing by heart, even if I couldn't recite it in chronological order. Endlessly, one of my dearest friends had told me: *Mercy is for the afflicted.*

I slowed to stare at the image. As I came to a stop, a delayed shiver of disgust slid down my spine. Suddenly, I found myself especially glad that Evie wasn't here—I had no idea how he might react to such heretical propaganda.

Clearly, the Emerald Spires and its attitudes had trickled outside of any formally defined borders.

I reached for the edge of the poster on instinct, prying at the edges. Paper and glue both frayed beneath my fingertips as I peeled away a strip of emerald green. I don't know what, precisely, I intended to accomplish—there were so many of the posters here that I could never have torn them all down, even if I'd spent the entire day trying to do it.

I clawed away the right-hand side of the flyer, taking several layers of other posters with it. Years unwound themselves in literal fashion, all at once, as I accidentally revealed a faded blue image far beneath that emerald heresy.

Half of a massive wargear showed through where the halcyon once had been, waving an Imperial banner in one hand and thrusting a blade into the sky with the other. Legions of uniformed soldiers charged ahead of it, while proud warships sailed overhead.

'—IGHTS ON!' read the poster. The rest was still covered by the halcyon's head, but I already knew what the words would say.

'THE IMPERIUM FIGHTS ON!'

It occurred to me, as my throat closed up and my stomach churned, that the faded blue ink in the soldiers' uniforms made them look rather like echoes.

The poster struck me like an accusation. I took an involuntary step back from it, forcing myself to breathe.

You can't change the past, I reminded myself faintly. *All you've got is now.*

I whirled away from the wall, avoiding nearby glances as I strode away with my pulse racing. No one chided me or tried to stop me; whoever had put up those posters, they hadn't stuck around to defend their work. Small mercies, I suppose.

It wasn't very long at all, though, before I found myself in the dingiest, most industrial area of the city: Coalditch.

Home, sweet home.

A warren of shanties rose up around me, woven together in a chaotic mess of scrap, junk, and colour. Pedestrian traffic thinned; instead, goblins loitered together in open groups, sharing bowls and stories around barrel-fires. Maybe it was just my imagination, but I couldn't help thinking that Coalditch was simultaneously bigger and less vibrant than when I'd been a child. The smiles were strained; the folk were thinner, and their belts cinched tighter. Still, warm trickles of laughter echoed behind me, suggesting that a shred of something kinder still remained here underneath the layers of misery and grime.

Here, where goblins lingered openly, it was easier to pick out those from northern Mavra, with black striations on their green skin. There were more Rustlands goblins than I remembered, too—those with red clay skin and bright yellow eyes. A few tall, broad-shouldered hobgoblins had even been informally adopted into the area, though they still stood out like sore thumbs.

Any city that got big enough ended up with its own version of Goblintown—a small district where goblins naturally congregated together for safety and mutual aid. In Morgause, Coalditch was our Goblintown. As a young orphan, I'd leaned on its sympathies several times for a leaky roof over my head, for a place to sleep next to a warm oven in the winters, or for one of the stale old lavender honey cakes that the goblin baker from Bloomington's sometimes brought back to hand out.

Bloomington's is closed, I remembered dimly. The judge's goblin aide had told me it belonged to Ol' Smythe now.

I had considered—oh so briefly—seeing if I could get the help we needed in Coalditch. The truth was, we needed a small miracle if we were going to find enough fuel for our ship before Miss Hawkins implemented her plan. But Goblintown was a place for meeting basic needs, and not a place for well-dressed goblins searching for a tank full of aether. In fact, I felt miserably guilty only seconds after having the thought.

I wasn't a local here anymore. I had abandoned all of these people in order to put on a shiny uniform and sail the skies. I didn't deserve to come back here begging for help.

No—I hadn't come to Coalditch in search of warmth and stale old cakes. I'd known from the moment I set foot here whose tender mercies I would be entreating.

I headed off the beaten path, into more dubious, shadowed alleyways. Soon enough, I heard what I was searching for: the rattle of loose coins in a small tin cup.

"Sir gives Gella some change?" The soft whine came from a goblin in dire straits. She was young and pitiful looking; filthy enough that I knew she'd intentionally exaggerated her condition with extra soot. She'd lost one pointed ear—maybe to sickness, or maybe to a violent quarrel. Her braids rattled with nuts and bolts, clinking softly against rounded shards of glass. The bandage over her right eye was a nice touch, but I could tell that it was purely cosmetic.

No one with half a mind would ever have set up begging *here*, where foot traffic was so sparse.

I pulled a coin from my inner pocket and flicked it into her cup.

"Ooh, sir is so full o' mercy," Gella sighed at me. "Benefactor will loves sir. Lady of Fools will blesses sir."

I sank down onto my haunches in front of her.

"Berkin Nim needs a favour," I said quietly.

Gella narrowed her eye at me, and I held up a hand quickly. "Not *that* kind of favour," I added. "Berkin has… hit rock bottom."

Gella smiled slowly at that. The expression showed a gap between her teeth. She looked down into her cup, and then back up at me. Her red eye twinkled. "Not yet, he hasn't," she assured me softly.

I sighed and fished out another coin. I tossed it into the cup with another *clink* against the tin.

Gella shoved up to her feet. She had a legitimate limp—her foot had been mangled, probably in some mechanical accident. But, like a gentleman, I let her lean on my arm, knowing that she might take it as an opportunity to peruse my pockets.

She led me further back into the alleyway, ducking us through a series of steam pipes that wouldn't have admitted the average human being. Soon, we came to a sewer grate that was a bit too loose to be properly secured.

I removed my hat, knowing what was about to happen.

"Let's get on with it," I muttered.

Someone threw a stinking sack over my head. I heard the sewer grate squeal as it yawned open before me.

A new, unseen goblin escorted me down into the foetid sewer below—the one place in Morgause where no human would ever willingly go.

14

THE UNDERLORDS - RATS - A FOOL'S PROMISE - NEW FRIENDS, OLD ENEMIES

The warrens of Undertown were a nightmarish maze, legendary for their sheer impenetrability. The city's bowels were so twisted that had Morgause been a living being, it would have surely died of complications.

Down, down, down we went, into that impossible, stinking labyrinth. More than once, I knocked my head upon a low-hanging pipe, much to the amusement of my new monosyllabic guide.

Colridge & Smythe controlled much within the city of Morgause... but the bank would never truly control what it didn't fully respect. Goblins who fell on hard times certainly weren't going to ask Ol' Smythe for help—how could they, when the bank rarely let them through its doors for anything other than janitorial work?

No, indeed. When the goblin miners and lamplighters and beggars of Morgause needed more help than meagre Goblintown could provide, they went to their own powerful institution—and its reach was far greater than any banker probably knew. Goblins, after all, were *everywhere* in the city.

Many people in Morgause scoffed at the notion of an organised goblin underworld. But what they didn't believe in could still definitely hurt them.

We travelled for the better part of an hour before my boots finally scraped against raw stone. Above me, I heard the hammering heart of Morgause—the enormous steam vents which thrummed with the city's lifeblood. Before me, I heard a riot of voices—dozens upon dozens of them, in a jumbled, lawless mess.

Someone yanked the black sack from my head... and suddenly, I was a child all over again.

I stood within a large patchwork tent, erected within the confines of a roughly hewn cavern. Dozens of swaying lanterns cast feeble light across the wild tent. Shadows danced merrily among the many red-eyed goblin-folk before me—a gathered host of the most long-lived scoundrels that Morgause had ever known. I shuffled in my spot, duly intimidated by the dangerous dignitaries in front of me.

Before me sat the Underlords, in the heart of their place of power. And from the looks of it, court was in full session.

I'd stood in front of the Underlords only twice in my life—before the uniform and the puffed up pride and the terrible realisations which soon followed. As a child, I'd understood that the Underlords were dangerous people, but I'd looked upon them with a mixture of fear and awe. They were, in their own way, somewhat glamorous.

Now that I was an adult, the shimmering glamour had fled. Underneath it was the cold, hard understanding that these goblins were like smiling, trained barghests. They were good at killing, good at hurting people, good at controlling everything they touched. If ever I convinced them I was troublesome, their smiles would drop, and they would tear me into little pieces.

But they were definitely capable of giving me the things I needed.

There were five Underlords here today—more than I remembered from my youth, though I still recognised a few of them. Each of them kept their own demesne within the court, surrounded by their preferred comforts and hangers-on as they conducted business.

The notorious Archrogue Highprofit currently reclined upon a hand-carved bed, bedecked with silken sheets and a rainbow of decadent curtains. He was every bit the green-skinned, red eyed Morgause goblin I was. Highprofit had doubled in size since I had last seen him; I wasn't surprised, given that he was missing his entire right leg from the knee down. Technically, he had a wooden leg which he could use at his leisure—but he was well past middle-aged now, and he had declared his intention to fully enjoy the comforts available to him in his twilight years. Today, a gaggle of goblin ladies hand-fed him, while another attendant massaged at the stump of his knee.

The archrogue was the closest thing the Underlords had to royalty —his great-great-grandfather was the man who'd first united the disparate criminal goblins of Morgause beneath one banner. Highprofit himself had pulled off a truly legendary score in his youth, though it had ultimately cost him his leg. He never allowed anyone to forget that it was his crew and his plan that had once breached the vaults of Colridge & Smythe. A stolen bust of Colridge stood proudly on display beside Highprofit's bed—now improved with the addition of a wig and a painted-on moustache. If I wanted money, then Highprofit could lend it to me... at a *very* steep rate of interest.

Not very far away from Highprofit, Ginny Glazier batted at tossed teacups, swinging her rusty crowbar with frightening precision. The shattered remnants of vases, plates, and porcelain statues surrounded her. Her shock of black hair was tied back into a practical ponytail, but there was a wild look in her red eyes. She wore a weathered leather jacket over a grime-stained jumpsuit; neither one completely concealed the black tattoos which snaked up from her collar and along her throat. Ginny was close to my age, and I remembered her dimly from our mutual childhood. Never one for subtlety, she had started her illustrious criminal career by smashing in shop windows in busy districts and taking what she liked.

It wasn't about the things she stole. Ginny had admitted that to me one night, as we huddled together in front of a stove in Goblintown. She didn't want those things for their own sake—she simply wanted to know that she had *taken* them from the people who would never normally sell them to us. She wanted to break what mattered to them, to force them to acknowledge her existence. Even as a little girl, Ginny had burned with a wild, deep-seated anger that sometimes frightened me. I understood it better, now that I was older; she'd simply seen everything a bit more clearly than I had, at the time. The forced misery and the unfairness and the lack of opportunity had festered within her, until she'd finally found her version of an outlet for it.

There was a certain charisma in that open rage of hers. Ginny's current entourage looked at her with a strange, bewitched sort of loyalty in their eyes. Hoots of satisfied laughter rose as her crowbar came down upon a shining crystal goblet, spraying the floor with glimmering shards.

If I needed someone who specialised more in breaking than entering, I suspected I knew who to go to. But I wasn't strictly certain that I wanted to risk Ginny turning that famous fury upon me when she realised who I was.

The last Underlord I recognised was the infamous Gentleman Sharper. The stylish goblin had reclined himself in a hammock, strung up between two transplanted marble pillars. I was perhaps unduly proud of my captain's hat and my heavily patchwork coat—but Sharper's greatcoat, with its gleaming brass buttons, made me feel like a guttersnipe by comparison. Sharper wore a highwayman's hat pulled down over his eyes as he watched his hangers-on, who sat at a bevy of lordly tables nearby. The goblins that surrounded him played high-stakes games with stacks of gems, bank notes, deeds, and other illicit goods piled high.

Gentleman Sharper was a legendary gambler, and an even shrewder businessman. Everyone who was anyone knew that Sharper ran the Cinderhouse—a high-stakes gambling hell that never set up in the same place twice. Once upon a time—or so the story went—he had forcibly settled a bloody turf war between the Hammerton gang and the Steel Street toughs by inviting both leaders to the Cinderhouse for a very special, very *final* game of roulette. The incident had earned him an instant invitation to join the Underlords. Ever since then, people said, Sharper had accumulated so much money and so many favours that he might as well have been a faerie.

Almost every goblin in Morgause wanted to be Gentleman Sharper… and those who *didn't* want to be him were probably lying.

By now, my guide had left me among a small crowd of fellow supplicants. I was far from the only desperate goblin in need today; in fact, Morgause had a way of manufacturing desperate goblins, much as it manufactured weapons and warships. I was a bit taller than the average goblin, but I still had to crane my neck to peer over the rest of my fellows as I turned my attention to the last two Underlords, both of whom were utter strangers to me.

The sheer size of the next Underlord drew my eye. He was a sturdy-shouldered, bull-necked, rust-skinned giant of a goblin. As I listened in on the ruckus, I heard someone address him as Kura Coal. Kura's clothing seemed strangely familiar to me, though it was ragged and worn. It was only after a good five minutes of study that I realised his coat had been stitched together from the bloodied uniforms of grims. The jacket made a striking statement: Neither Kura Coal nor his people feared Ol' Smythe's reach.

Kura had settled himself on a raised chair overlooking a sparring match; a pair of chained barghests lazed beside him, chewing on meaty bones. Other goblins crowded around to watch the match, passing bets and cheering on their fighter of choice. The commentary surrounding me suggested that this was a sanctioned duel. Kura Coal, I deciphered, was to the Underlords as Mr Strahl was to my ship—he had taken on the job of maintaining order here, at least partially through violence. Had I needed some muscle, Kura Coal might have been my best option... but I was obviously hoping that it wouldn't come to that.

The last of the Underlords lounged upon a truly massive divan of laughable proportions. Several goblins with lacquered fans chatted idly next to her while she painted her nails. I muttered an inquiry to the goblin in front of me in line, and learned that she was properly addressed as Abbess Boblin. The abbess was a woman of stunning beauty—and she clearly knew it well. Her midnight black hair piled atop her head in a lady's braided bun. A tailored, gold filigree corset openly hugged her figure; the only thing the abbess wore atop it was a strand of expensive pearls. A theatrical porcelain half-mask adorned her face, setting off the yellow streaks in her rich olive green skin. Big, golden eyes peered out from that half-mask with keen interest.

Abbess Boblin, I was told, ran the Cadmey—an 'institution' for wayward souls who hoped to learn the fine art of companionship. She had her finger on the pulse of the city's courtesans and their respective establishments... a position which also gave her access to a surprising amount of information. Like Gentleman Sharper, the abbess had managed to stretch her influence into parts of the city which normally wouldn't welcome goblins. If I had good information to barter—or perhaps a pretty face—the abbess would be willing to hear me out.

I observed the Underlords for the better part of a loud, tumultuous hour, turning my options over in my mind. Which Underlord would have the means to secure me an entire fuel tank of aether? My gut told me I would have the most luck with either Highprofit or Gentleman Sharper, but I knew it was a big ask. No rational goblin would volunteer to nick aether in the middle of a shortage like this.

At the end of the day, the Underlords were just like any other insular criminal family, balancing their power and control against a certain amount of community goodwill. I was no longer a part of their community—which meant that they'd almost certainly be gouging me for the help. As a captain with my own ship, I had a few bargaining chips on my side that many of the other goblins here didn't... but I was also about to ask them for the means with which to flee Morgause entirely.

This was going to go hard for me. But one way or another, Miss Hawkins was about to dive straight into trouble... and I intended to make sure she had a ship to fly her out of it again. In fact, I intended to fly her straight back to Pelaeia.

Slowly, the rough sketch of a plan fell into place in my mind. Eventually the burly goblin who'd been wrangling the line nudged me along to an area near the centre of the tent, where I could easily reach any one of the Underlords' seats.

"Which Underlord is the goblin seein'?" he asked me shortly.

"All of them," I declared. The other goblin blinked owlishly.

If there's one thing a good fool knows, it's this: Grand gestures can accomplish a lot. Granted, they might accomplish your instant, painful demise... but either way, you're bound to get a reaction.

I squared my shoulders and stepped forward, slapping on my best, most charming smile. "My fair Underlords!" I called out.

I had to force my voice over the chaotic din—but I'd spent years now shouting orders into the wind, and I had the lungs to do it.

I earned a few curious looks from the assembled company within the tent, along with some disdainful sneers. Importantly, however, I saw the Underlords turn their heads towards me. Some of them looked intrigued. Some of them looked ready to gut me. But all of them *looked* at me.

Though I'd been expecting it, the weight of all those important eyes threw me off balance for a moment. Five ruthless, powerful criminals had now taken an interest in me—here at the centre of their domain, where I was utterly at their mercy. The cunning words I'd been planning curled up and died on my tongue. Sweat trickled down my spine, and I cleared my throat hesitantly, searching for my voice again.

"Um," I greeted them. "Er. Hello."

I know. Hardly a masterstroke of inspiring rhetoric.

Silence slowly fell within the tent, stretching out into a painful pause. Then—all at once—the Underlords burst out laughing.

Ginny howled. The archrogue wheezed. Kura guffawed. Sharper slapped a hand against the table in front of him, wiping tears from his eyes. The abbess tittered with her attendants. Every other goblin in the room soon followed suit. The sound was deafening.

I smiled nervously and laughed with them. My cheeks heated with embarrassment.

"This one o' Sharper's jokes?" Ginny asked.

"Nah," Sharper said with a chuckle. "Sharper's people can stitch more'n a few words together!"

"He's a pretty one," the abbess purred. She twirled a strand of pearls with her finger, looking at me like a piece of meat—barely different from the way the Archrogue looked at the morsels on his gilded platter.

"The lady is as gracious as she is stunning," I flattered her. I offered the Abbess a courtly bow, sweeping my hat in a rakish manner. The gesture earned me a few more laughs. "I am deeply honoured to—"

"Wot?" Ginny interrupted. She cocked her head to the side. "Anyone understand wot he's sayin'?" She emphasised the thick local accent on purpose. I tried to speak a few more times—but each time I opened my mouth, she interrupted with another "Wot? Hmm?"

She wasn't alone. Kura had left his bloody-minded audience and panting duellists in order to come closer. "Wot's with all the fancy talk?" the hulking goblin asked.

"Ginny don't know," Ginny called out. She grinned at me patronisingly. A spark of niggling recognition twinkled in her eyes, but didn't fully coalesce. "Oi, Sharper! Underlords still needs a jester?"

Gentleman Sharper rose from his hammock, sauntering over to get a better look at me. I was struck by how thin he was—a veritable scarecrow of a goblin swimming in his coat. He had a swagger to him, an air of confidence that I normally saw in young, cocky outflyer aces. As he came closer, I realised that I was just a few inches taller than he was. Somehow, it didn't matter—Sharper *still* managed to look down his nose at me. In fact, the closer he stalked, the more nervous I became. There was a coiled energy about him, like a serpent ready to strike.

Sharper grinned lazily. "Sure," he cracked. "Underlords still needs a jester. Funniest fing Sharper's seen all week. Like a barghest walkin' on its back legs, tryin' t'dance. The Underlords 'elp *goblins* down 'ere. An' who is him, talkin' like a fancy toff?"

I flinched, despite myself. Some part of me still didn't feel comfortable claiming any part of who I'd once been. I wasn't ashamed of being a Coalditch goblin... but I *was* ashamed at how quickly I had left it all behind. Putting on my old accent now felt akin to a masquerade—an attempt to score cheap points which I hadn't rightly earned.

But I'd come to the Underlords, after all. And the Underlords weren't going to offer their help to the goblin who'd spent two decades and change reading poetry with Physicker Holloway.

I drew in a deep breath. "Cap'n William Blair comes to ask help from the Underlords—" I started.

"Cap'n?" Ginny repeated with a laugh.

"What sorta name's William Blah?" Kura rumbled. He cracked his neck with a tilt of his blocky head.

"Rubbish," Sharper spat. "That ain't no goblin name." He leaned in towards me, still shuffling an old deck of cards between his nimble fingers.

"*William Blair* don't belong 'ere," the archrogue wheezed at me.

My pulse quickened self-consciously. The situation was quickly sliding through my fingers.

Thankfully, I always do my best work under pressure.

"A goblin always goes where they doesn't belong, now don't they?" I replied. "So's, if William Blair don't belong 'ere... then William Blair *do* belong."

The gathered Underlords contemplated this witticism. Sharper's smile grew hard-edged. Ginny and Kura shrugged, faintly mollified by my logic. The abbess leaned her chin into her palm, considering me enigmatically. The archrogue scratched thoughtfully at his stump.

"Fancy tongue has William Blair," the abbess said. She offered me a smile. "Let's hear what William has to say."

Sharper held my eyes. Without turning, he casually drew a pistol from his coat, levelling it behind him at one of the goblins at his card table—and pulled the trigger.

A loud gunshot cracked through the air. Hardened goblins skittered back in surprise, reaching instinctively for their weapons.

The goblin screamed and flopped to the ground, clutching at his chest. Within moments, Kura's thugs had grabbed the thrashing victim, dragging him towards the barghests, who perked up with eager hunger. Meanwhile, half a dozen scavengers descended upon the table to snatch up the unfortunate goblin's blood-spattered winnings.

I felt the blood drain from my face.

Sharper holstered the pistol and turned to march towards the empty chair. He dragged it over to the centre of the tent, offering it to me with a gallant, overly-generous sweep of his hat.

Hot, fresh blood dripped from the chair.

There was another brief shriek from the corner with the barghests —and then, a terrible crunch. No further cries followed.

I swallowed hard, and took the proffered seat. "Um," I rasped, before I could think better of it. "Why—"

"Rat was takin' money from Ol' Smythe," Sharper explained, loudly enough for the rest of the tent to hear him. "Sharper was goin' to kill 'im tomorrow anyway. Goblins all knows what happens to rats who turns on their kin, now don't they?" He smiled at me with far too much pleasantry. The words were meant to be an open threat. I offered him a shaky nod, not trusting myself to speak.

"Time fer the goblin to states his business," Sharper finished mildly. "What's he want from the Underlords?"

Kura's barghests continued consuming their grisly meal. I tried to focus on the goblins in front of me, as best I could.

You knew who you were coming to, I reminded myself. *At least they're more honest about who they are than the Imperium ever was.*

I took a deep breath, and dusted off the life that I'd abandoned.

"William Blair needs a favour," I said. "William comes to beg fer the Underlords' help."

Ginny's red eyes sharpened upon me. She took a few steps forward, reaching out with her crowbar to lift my chin. The metal was cold upon my skin. "William was one of Old-Hand Nypper's brats, wasn't he?" she said.

"Fer a time," I agreed. "Coalditch district." I didn't dare remind Ginny of the times we'd shared stale honey cakes. That was far in the past now, and I'd still stolen away on an Imperial ship without so much as a word of goodbye. Emotion stirred somewhere behind her bright eyes, but I didn't know how to read it. At least, I thought, she hadn't tried to feed me her crowbar yet.

"William is military," Kura said. He looked me up and down with a keen gaze; it was a very Strahl-like assessment. "Too uptight fer the Goldies. William is a Bluejacket."

"William served Avalon," I said. I tried to keep my voice clear and calm, but shame crept into my voice nonetheless. "Imperial Navy. Two years, 'afore it all fell to pieces."

"William looks like a lifer," Kura grumbled. I wasn't sure it was meant to be a compliment.

"William has a good crew," I answered, by way of explanation.

"Not so good, if William's come here beggin' fer help," Sharper pointed out. He strolled over to the archrogue's table to nick an apple, crunching into it casually. The noise was indistinguishable from the sound of the barghests at Kura's seat.

I wanted to defend my crew—I was the one who'd dragged us into this mess, from start to finish. But I swallowed the arguments down. I was here to get the *Rose* out of Morgause. That was more valuable than trying to win an argument most people would soon forget anyway.

I bowed my head instead. "The Lady's love is fickle," I said.

Sharper fixed me with a curious look over his stolen apple. Something about the reply had caught his casual interest. "So it is," he agreed. "William loves 'er back, then?"

I inclined my head at him. "Sometimes, the Lady is fair winds," I said. "Sometimes, She's the storm. But William's still alive, so he won't ask fer more."

Sharper chuckled. The sound put me on edge—but he waved the apple at me graciously. "So see how sweet She is today," he told me. "What favour does William ask?"

I drew in a breath. "Crew's out of aether, an' we needs to leave soon—maybe tonight, maybe tomorrow," I explained. "No one's sellin', even if we has the money. So... fuel's what we need. William gets fuel in time, an' one of the Underlords gets any favour they asks for, at least six months from now."

"N'whys should the Underlords trust that William Blair won't scarper once he gets his fuel?" Sharper demanded.

"William's word as a cap'n an' a gent," I offered.

I felt the scepticism in the gathered Underlords. Already, I was losing their interest.

A pair of arms settled onto my shoulders from behind. The abbess's pearls rattled, and a few strands of her hair tickled my neck. "Not good 'nough," she murmured in my ear.

"Then as a goblin?" I ventured.

"No goblin wears a blue coat," Kura muttered disdainfully.

"Then William's honour as a fool," I declared.

That drew a contemplative silence. Religious appeals among goblins were admittedly scarce—but not unheard of. For some reason, I noticed, several of the Underlords glanced towards Sharper.

Sharper tossed his apple into the corner with the barghests. He pulled out his deck again with a slow, unsettling smile, shuffling it from hand to hand. He fanned the cards out before me with one hand, letting the other hand fall back to his side. "Go ahead then," he told me. "Let William pick—"

I didn't let him finish.

It might be that a smarter man would have waited. But I've never claimed to be *smart*. All of my life, I'd honed my instincts so that I could make the sort of split-second decisions which so often make the difference between life and death. Those instincts had told me—screamed at me—that my best and only chance of making it out of here with what I wanted was to pick a card *now*, with absolute unflinching confidence.

I snatched a card from the deck at random, holding it out to the goblin in front of me.

Sharper drew his gun with the exact same swiftness, pointing the barrel directly at my forehead.

All at once, my rational brain caught up to those split-second instincts. Gentleman Sharper had reached for his gun just a breath *before* I had gone for the card. He hadn't just been asking me to pick a card; he'd been about to offer me a deadly game, just like the one he'd forced upon the two gangs at his gambling hell in his apocryphal rise to power. Probably, he'd meant to test how desperate I was, instead of testing just how *stupid* I was.

I didn't even know which card he'd wanted me to choose. All I knew was that the *wrong* card meant I was a very dead goblin.

Gentleman Sharper considered the card that I held out to him...

And then, he laughed.

He plucked the card from my fingers and held it up for everyone to see. The Underlords and their spectators leaned in with bated breath, waiting curiously for his judgement.

"William's honour as a fool!" Gentleman Sharper declared. "So it is!"

I stared at the card, still halfway stunned at my own carelessness. A faded red and orange figure rode across its surface, mounted upon a fiery steed. I'd drawn the Knight of Summer—a court card from the suit which most people associated with the Lady of Fools. In fact, the Knight of Summer was sometimes called the Lady's errand-boy.

A strange, confusing shiver ran through my body, starting at the crown of my head and working its way down to my toes. For a moment, I felt almost detached from myself, wondering if I had wildly misunderstood some crucial fact which underpinned my world.

I'd always joked that the Lady of Fools and I had an understanding—that I endured Her unfortunate pranks in return for a favour now and then. But as I stood there looking at the Knight of Summer... for just a second, I *believed*. And suddenly, I wasn't so sure that I'd been fully joking. Maybe, I thought, I had believed it on some level, all along.

The shiver passed. As it did, it took my hubris with it.

The Lady of Fools had better things to do than to meddle with the affairs of one insignificant goblin. I'd been lucky. There'd been about a quarter chance that I might draw a Summer card, and I had done it. Fortune had saved me, where my instincts had failed me.

The archrogue considered the card with a contemplative hum. "William could have cheated," he observed offhandedly.

"In front of Sharper?" the abbess tittered with amusement. "Then William ought to be an Underlord." She patted one of my cheeks, before releasing me and departing back for her divan.

"*Now* Ginny remembers William," Ginny murmured. She narrowed her eyes at me, and I had to work to suppress my wince.

Kura made a thoughtful rumbling noise in his chest. "Dangerous business," he said. "An entire tank of aether. The Iron Guard shoots aether thieves on sight, even when supplies ain't short. Ol' Smythe's toughs don't play over aether, neither."

I forced my brain to work again—though the thoughts came slow and sluggish, pushing through thick molasses. I couldn't waste the dangerous chance that I'd been given. "That's... exactly why William came to these fine Underlords," I managed hoarsely. "No one else could do it. But Archrogue Highprofit gives Ol' Smythe the laugh, an' the Lady of Fools kisses Gentleman Sharper to bed every night. An' no one with a mind dares get on Ginny's bad side. The Underlords ain't scared o' nothin'."

In my experience, flattery goes an awful long way—even among hardened criminals. Maybe *especially* among hardened criminals.

The abbess laughed. It was a pleasant, bell-like sound—one which I suspected she had carefully cultivated. "Such smooth words, William," she said slyly. "Did he drink honey 'afore he came to court?"

Abbess Boblin knew *exactly* what I was up to. But her smile told me she was perfectly happy to let me continue. I offered her a shaky grin.

"Every goblin knows Underlords can spit in ol' Smythe's eye an' get away with it," I observed. "The blue sky's the limit... as long as a goblin can pay." I spread my hands. "William knows it's true."

An entire tent full of goblins watched the spectacle with keen interest. I'd thrown down a gauntlet... and an opportunity. Any Underlord who pulled this off would be able to tell a story on par with the archrogue's heist on Ol' Smythe. If the Underlords turned me down, on the other hand, it would look as though they were too scared of the city's rich and powerful to do much more than thumb their noses at them. I knew it was a weak play, gambling on their pride—but at the moment, it was the best approach I had.

"William Blair's smuggled goods through the Sirocco Isles," I said with pride. "William stole a pineapple from the Ebon Warden an' a convict from the noose in Lyonesse. William's favours have worth." The pineapple theft was lost on most of the goblins present, but Highprofit grinned at the mention—he clearly knew how absurdly expensive the fruit could be.

Ginny rapped her crowbar against the floor. The *tap, tap, tap* of iron on stone echoed loudly through the tent, with slowly growing intensity. The fire in her eyes had landed upon me, burning at my skin. "No," she bit out shortly. "Ginny won't help *William Blair.*" The name dropped from her lips in an open sneer.

I tried not to let the guilt show on my face—and probably failed.

Abbess Boblin tapped the closed end of a fan against her chin, as another silk-draped goblin woman whispered in her ear. Her eyes flickered over to Gentleman Sharper, and I realised that the two of them were probably closely allied. "Abbess Boblin would be willing," she mused. "But Boblin works with information, and not aether. This lies outside of Boblin's purview."

Kura Coal leaned back into his seat, flexing his fingers into his palms with silent agitation. Kura didn't want to take me up on my offer—he'd been the first to observe just how dangerous my request would be. But he also knew that all eyes were upon the Underlords now... and even more than the rest of them, he couldn't afford to look weak.

The archrogue spoke next, before Kura could be forced to make his decision. "William gives his Oath," the Underlord offered magnanimously, "an' Archrogue Highprofit gives him his dream. The archrogue will do the impossible." He smiled, slow and smug, and a devious twinkle entered his eyes. "Again."

The word 'Oath' nearly made my stomach revolt.

I probably should have been expecting it—but I hadn't. When I'd been growing up in Coalditch, people there just didn't ask each other to swear Oaths; it wasn't done. Oaths were a weapon used against us by powerful people. Goblins, in particular, treated Oaths with a cultural and religious disgust. The Lady of Fools disdained the use of Oaths, and rarely kept company with Noble Gallant.

But the Underlords were a different sort entirely than the miners and shop owners and pickpockets in Goblintown. The games that the Underlords played were high stakes... and in at least a few respects, they'd picked up the habits of Morgause's powerful elites.

"An Oath for Kura Coal." Kura relaxed upon his throne as he spoke the words. "A full tank of aether, in return."

I blinked, dragged back from my growing nausea by the other Underlord's declaration. Belatedly, I realised that my horror must have shown upon my face as Archrogue Highprofit asked for an Oath. Kura had decided I was unwilling to pay that price—which made it safe for him to make the same offer.

And maybe, I thought sickly, he was right.

The sheer unfairness of it all assaulted me. For the longest time now, I had struggled to do the right thing, no matter how complicated or confusing or hopeless that seemed. In return—within the last few days, in particular—I had been mocked and spat upon and taken advantage of by everyone I met.

Why should I be asked *again* to put my soul in hock, in order to repair the wrongs that others had committed?

Dimly, I became aware of Gentleman Sharper, still standing only a few feet away from me. He'd narrowed his eyes in my direction, still flicking the Knight of Summer between his fingers. He was the only Underlord who hadn't yet spoken.

I straightened abruptly and turned to face him.

"A promise for Gentleman Sharper," I offered quietly.

The last Underlord fixed me with a searching gaze. His eyes were cold on my skin as he weighed and dissected me for his own inscrutable purposes. I knew that he wouldn't agree out of generosity... but out of them all, he was the only genuinely religious man present. If he had any interest in a favour from me, then he wouldn't be inclined to ask for an Oath as payment.

Give me this much, Lady, I prayed silently. *I'm certain I'll be foolish again tomorrow, for your entertainment.*

Gentleman Sharper inclined his head abruptly. "The Lady hates Oaths," he said. "An' Sharper won't lose Her love for just one favour. A promise for Sharper—made with the heart an' not with honour." His eyes bored into me. "Is that the sort of promise William offers?"

I let out a long breath. Gratitude suffused me, though I knew I'd later regret this moment. Gentleman Sharper had a specific use in mind for me, I knew... and it was almost certainly going to be a favour that weighed on my soul forever, just as much as a broken Oath might have done.

But if that was the price for peace in Pelaeia, then I was willing to pay it.

"A promise that William believes in," I agreed softly. "From the heart."

Gentleman Sharper held up the card, drawing my eyes back to the faded figure upon it. "When this card finds William," he said, "he'll be comin' right back to Morgause to settle accounts with Gentleman Sharper. On William's word as a fool... aye?" He tucked the card neatly into his vest pocket, with a dangerous glint in his red eyes.

I nodded mutely, trying not to glance at the bargests still chewing loudly in the corner.

"Well then," Gentleman Sharper said. "William Blair an' Sharper is in business. He needs his aether by tomorrow?"

I knew I was making a deal that I shouldn't... but the time for second thoughts had long since passed. If I'd wanted out, I should have decided that before I'd ever thrown a coin in Gella's cup.

"Soonest is best," I answered. "But William can't stay here any longer than a day." I still had no idea what exactly we'd be running from... but one way or another, I was going to make sure that Miss Hawkins survived long enough to get back on my boat and go back to Pelaeia.

Sharper shrugged, as though the prospect of procuring an entire tank of aether in just one day barely bothered him. "Sharper calls in some debts," he said absently. "William returns to his ship to wait."

Even some of the other Underlords offered Sharper an assessing look, at that. But Gentleman Sharper was, after all, the best gambler that Morgause had ever known. If he was bluffing, then no one here was skilled enough to call it.

Sharper whirled in place and headed for his table. There, he spoke a few quiet words to another goblin, who scurried off to do his will.

"Next goblin!" yelled one of Kura's toughs, gesturing at the line of petitioners behind me.

It was as close to a dismissal as I'd get.

Even as I turned away on shaky legs, however, Abbess Boblin gestured me over with a single crook of her finger.

I didn't dare to refuse her. I walked over to her divan, still trembling faintly as I knelt before her. She offered me her hand, and I kissed the air above her knuckles obligingly.

Abbess Boblin smiled coyly. She turned her hand to take mine and gave it a discreet tug, indicating that I should sit down next to her on the divan. "You said you go by Captain William Blair, didn't you?" she asked. Her accent had shifted abruptly to one more commonly heard in the upper-class districts. I blinked at her.

"I... do," I confirmed slowly. My tongue felt thick in my mouth as I spoke the way I'd done for twenty years now. "Why?"

Abbess Boblin watched me with a faintly predatory gaze. "There's a one-eyed gentleman spreading money around topside, asking if you're in town," she said. "Apparently, you're wanted for thievery in New Havenshire."

I groaned and pressed my hand to my forehead.

The abbess laughed. "I suppose you *do* know him, then," she said. "The ladies tell me he goes by the name of Barsby." She patted my cheek. "Gentleman Sharper won't be having his favour if your past catches up with you so quickly. Be a dear, William Blair, and survive the next few days."

15

SNOOPING - SPARK IN A TINDERBOX - COMPLICATIONS

I returned to the *Iron Rose* in the small hours of the morning with a new promise upon my soul, and with a very important clue regarding the shipment that Miss Hawkins intended to stop. This was fortuitous, as Evie had also returned with the news that Miss Hawkins had yet to learn the information I had gleaned from the abbess.

I informed the crew that our fuel shortage would soon be remedied, but I spared them any further explanation as to *how*. To be fair, even I wasn't quite certain how Gentleman Sharper intended to pull off the caper.

We soon found out together.

Every hour upon the hour, a different goblin visited our platform with a small canister of aether. I had Mr Finch check the contents to verify their quality; he assured me that while the aether was of varying grades, it was all definitely ship-worthy. I couldn't be sure, of course... but I suspected that Gentleman Sharper had sent his people to syphon small amounts of aether from several different ships, generators, and factory machines. Bite by stolen bite, we used the illicit canisters to fill the *Rose*'s fuel tank.

By the time the sun (or the vaguest suggestion of it) had fully risen in Morgause's murky sky, our tank was full, and our engine room even had a few spare canisters of precious Seelie aether. All of which left me plenty of time for breakfast while I plotted out my next movements with some of the crew.

The abbess had been kind enough to mention Barsby's pier, and the name of the ship he'd ridden in on: the *Last Laugh*. Miss Hawkins had given Evie the slip, he told me, but not before he'd overheard her searching for a ship called the *Erebus*—a ship which I assumed belonged to Barsby's Imperialist client. As such, we had the upper hand: We knew where the Unseelie aether was *now*, rather than where it was later going to be. All we had to do was case Barsby's ship, pinpoint the Unseelie aether, and blow it halfway to Arcadia before he could react.

It was all terribly simple. Mostly because the plan was light on details.

"One big problem," Lenore observed, from her place in the seat across from me.

"Just *one* problem?" I asked her sceptically. "That would be a first."

A handful of us had gathered in the galley to discuss our plan of action. Lenore was already kitted out for violence—she carried her rifle, along with at least two pistols I could see. Strahl stood stiffly nearby, mostly because his clattering armour made it difficult for him to sit. Evie and Little had settled into chairs closer to my side of the table, so that we could keep the volume of our conversation low amidst the other crew that lingered in the galley with us.

"Fine," Lenore said. "The *first* big problem we have is that Barsby knows what most of us look like. I don't think he saw me in New Havenshire, but I did help with the cargo for a bit, so we can't rule it out. We need to case Barsby's ship, but no one at this table is fit for the job."

I sighed heavily, searching through crew in my head. "We could ask Mr Billings," I suggested. "He's relatively new, and he's got a forgettable sort of face." I mentally apologised to the man for the description, accurate as it was.

"Mr Billings is still prone to panicking under pressure," Lenore said grimly. "We're training it out of him, but I'm not sure I'd trust him with something like this just yet."

Light footsteps sounded behind me; I turned and watched as Mary sauntered openly towards our table. Gone was the bleak black dress of a mourner; instead, she sported breeches and a flat cap, beneath which she'd tucked away her hair. Before, when she'd had her back to me, I hadn't even recognised her. Mary pulled out a chair on my other side, settling into it with a smug-looking grin that said she'd been eavesdropping.

"Gosh," Mary said, "it seems to me like you need someone good at sneaking around, Captain." She crossed her legs and casually smoothed one of her trouser legs. "Someone Mr Barsby's definitely never seen, who's good under pressure—"

"*No*," I said quickly. "Absolutely not."

Evie cleared his throat delicately. "Er," he said. "But *why* not?"

I shot him a dirty look. "You're supposed to be on my side of this, Halcyon," I told him.

"I am?" Evie asked, bemused. "I must have forgotten that discussion."

Lenore scowled at Mary. "I don't think so, young lady," she said. "If that man catches you snooping on his shipment, he's not going to be lenient about it just because you're young."

Mary rolled her eyes. "I know how the world works," she replied. "You all keep trying to pretend like I grew up in a nice little house in the Rustlands, with a dog and a fence. But I used to steal from some real bad people. None of 'em ever caught me, but I'd have lost more than my hand if they had." Mary shot me a level look. "Besides... we all know the sort of things *you* did before you were sixteen, Captain."

I winced. Obviously, Mary was right—I'd been a pickpocket for most of my early life, and *then* I'd joined the Imperial Navy. Surely, trying to keep Mary out of the thick of things must have made me seem like a hypocrite. But that was exactly the problem. Mary had faced so many of the same difficulties I had faced, and some part of me desperately wanted to offer her a better life than I'd had.

For just a little bit, I wanted her to be... well, not safe, per se. But safer. Sixteen was still too young, I told myself. I'd think about it again when she was... seventeen.

"What I did was make a lot of mistakes," I told Mary. "I know you had to deal with some dangerous things while you were growing up, Mary—but just because you did deal with them doesn't mean you *should* have had to deal with them. I don't want to put you back in that position."

Mary groaned audibly. "I am literally begging you to let me do this, Captain," she said. "I am so tired of everyone else talking over my head and telling me to stick to cleaning guns. If you don't give me something useful to do, then I swear, I will *steal* something to do."

Little shrugged at me. *Mary is crew,* he signed. *And she's definitely the best person for the job.*

I rubbed at my face in frustration. "Would you like to join the conspiracy against me as well, Mr Strahl?" I asked.

Strahl shook his head. "No one needs to be taking any advice from me on the matter," he said. "I'm a man of terrible judgement."

Mary smiled primly at me. I shot her a withering glare.

I didn't want to say yes. Every iota of my being rebelled against the idea. But I was cornered, and Mary knew it.

"...fine," I said. "But *all* you're doing is casing the ship from a distance. You are not sneaking inside. Get us what details you can, and then come right back again."

Mary's eyes glittered at me. "You know, Captain," she drawled, "I'd be *much* safer out there on my own if I had a gun."

I groaned into my hands.

* * *

MARY LEFT to survey the *Last Laugh* with a tiny two-shot pistol up her sleeve and a brilliant smile behind her gas mask. I spent the next hour trying to argue myself into believing I'd made the right decision by sending her.

I stalked the quarterdeck of the *Rose* after Mary's departure, while Mr Finch advised me on the best method by which I might destroy an entire shipload of Unseelie aether. My muddled mood was further compounded by the filthy state of my ship. Morgause's grimy fingers had smeared across the hull, and the furled sails were stained with black patches of soot.

"Unseelie aether is *very* unstable," Mr Finch told me, as I paced nervously past him. Over the railing to my right, I could see dockworkers coming and going within the Aviary's bustling platforms. "Technically, a violent enough physical blow might be enough to set off such a concentrated load—but I wouldn't want to count on that, myself."

"What if we just… opened a canister and ran?" I asked. "Wouldn't it eventually just eat through the other canisters and…" Even though I'd suggested it, I shuddered just a little bit at the idea. I could still clearly picture the poor watchman on the pier in New Havenshire, screaming as his face rotted away. It had only taken *one* canister of Unseelie aether to do that. I tried to imagine what might happen if something were to rupture every canister in my hold at once. I envisioned that black cloud from the docks eating through the wood of my ship, roiling down its corridors like a bleak wave of rot. The Unseelie aether had moved so quickly and so unpredictably—my crew would have nowhere to escape.

Barsby, I knew, had three times as much Unseelie aether as we did.

Mr Finch shook his head, aghast. "There's no telling when the other canisters would rupture. Besides, someone could come along and close the valve. Far too many uncertain factors." He rubbed at his chin. "You *will* need to open one of the canisters and allow it to seep into the environment. But once there's enough ambient Unseelie aether, I'd recommend that you use a spark of Seelie aether to start an explosive chain reaction."

I thought through the implications, putting together the pieces in my head. "One of us is going to have to get up close and personal with that shipment, if we're going to pull this off," I muttered darkly. "Fantastic. And we're certainly not going to want to introduce any Seelie aether while we're within the blast radius. Any thoughts on how we could apply that Seelie aether from a distance?"

Mr Finch frowned, contemplating the problem. "An aethermancer could do it using only their will," he mused. "Miss Hawkins is probably planning something of the sort, herself. The best alternative I can think of would be to use aether rounds—but aether rifles are rather outside of our budget, I think."

I thought briefly of the guards outside of Colridge & Smythe—but stealing anything from the bank's security forces would have been a separate heist all on its own. "This would all be far easier if Miss Hawkins had just stayed and worked with us," I grumbled. It couldn't be helped, though—Miss Hawkins had done an excellent job of disappearing into Morgause's teeming streets. Even if I'd wanted to try convincing her again, there was no way I could possibly *find* her in time. "What about the equipment she left with you?" I asked Mr Finch. "Can you use any of that?"

Mr Finch blinked. "Oh," he said. "Yes, I think I could do that. I could rig one of her aether batteries to overload. I wouldn't be able to time it very well, but I could ensure at least a thirty-second delay once you've started the circuit."

I nodded at that. "I'll need you to get that sorted as soon as you can," I told him. "We're leaving as soon as Mary gets back."

Mr Finch straightened. "It's a simple enough task," he sniffed. "It's a bit... *cruder* than I normally prefer. But give me five or ten minutes, and I'll have you something that can do the job."

"Something that does the job is all I need," I assured him. I paused to consider something. "Walther, you know how much of that vile stuff they have. How *big* would the blast radius be if all of that Unseelie aether detonated at once?"

Mr Finch paused, scrunching up his nose in thought. Slowly, however, the academic question gave way to reality, and he swallowed visibly. "Very... very large," he admitted quietly. "Certainly large enough to destroy the entire hangar."

We spent a moment absorbing the implications of that answer together.

At the very least, whoever was transporting that aether would be caught in the resulting destruction. I wasn't willing to waste guilt on anyone who knew what that Unseelie aether was... but what if there were oblivious people involved? We hadn't known what we were carrying at first, after all. If there were any innocent dockworkers present...

"Perhaps we could inform the local authorities of the contraband instead?" Mr Finch asked weakly.

I pressed my lips together. "I guarantee you, the grims have already been bribed to look the other way," I told him. "At best, they'll demand a bigger bribe from the buyer. At worst, they'll confiscate the cargo and sell it on the black market—at which point, we'll have a whole *new* problem on our hands."

Mr Finch deflated. "We could... try shooting down the client's ship once it's left Morgause airspace," he offered instead. "Once it's taken the cargo on board." Even as he said the words, I knew he didn't believe them.

"How much firepower do you think an Imperialist faction is going to bring with them?" I asked grimly. "On the off chance that they load the aether onto something small and nondescript, we can reassess then. But we've got to have a plan in case we're wildly outgunned. We've only got a small window to get rid of this stuff before it's on its way out of Morgause with some really awful people."

Mr Finch sighed heavily. "It's just... there are so many variables," he said softly. "And most of my experience with Unseelie aether is purely theoretical. I can't really say how big this explosion is going to be, Captain. What if it's even worse than I've calculated? If there are ships in the hangar, and the Unseelie aether somehow manages to reach one of their aetheric cores... it could be exponentially worse. It could threaten the entire Aviary."

The fear in his voice wormed its way inside of me, chilling my heart. I knew he was speculating, guessing at worst-case scenarios—but wouldn't I be doing the same, in his position? Mr Finch's university had once asked him to develop weapons, and he had been so uncomfortable with the idea that it had turned him into a spy. But we were trying to stop something even worse right now, weren't we?

I tried to imagine the echoes of Old Pelaeia, weaponized against an unsuspecting city. The idea was suitably terrifying.

"We're going to have to be very careful how we detonate that aether, then," I said bleakly. "Is there any way to minimise the risk?"

Mr Finch looked away. "If we can set off the reaction while the cargo is in transit," he said, "the chances of it reaching a ship's aetheric core will be smaller. But once it's loaded onto a ship..." He trailed off. "Do you remember what happened to Ironspine when that pirate ship crashed?"

I suppressed a violent shudder at the memory. "I doubt I could forget," I said. I straightened, trying to project more confidence than I felt. "We can't let that cargo reach another ship, then," I declared. "Which means that I need you to rig this device *yesterday*, Mr Finch."

At the end of the day, I suppose my chief engineer had more faith in me than I had credited. At this, he nodded sharply and departed—and I was left alone, with only my dread for company.

Were *these* the sorts of decisions the Imperial officers made in the war? Weighing countless deaths against the threat of an unpaid Tithe and an Unseelie invasion? Had some officer once told himself that he was razing Pelaeia in order to save all of Avalon?

What if Kura Coal had been right about me? What if I was still more of a bluejacket than I cared to admit?

I clenched my jaw against the idea, and headed for the longhorn. I called Lenore and Strahl up to join me, even as I gestured urgently at Evie and Little, across the deck. Once everyone had joined me, I explained the refined plan.

"Someone give me a better idea," I said bluntly, once I had finished.

Strahl shook his head. "I'm pretty sure I said I was a man of terrible judgement," he reminded me.

"I'd prefer an aether rifle," Lenore said shortly.

"I'd prefer that too," I told her. "Can you get your hands on one in the next hour or so?"

Lenore scowled and fell into a brooding silence. I cast an imploring look at Evie and Little, desperately hoping they might conjure up a brilliant idea. Instead, they shared a look, and then a wince.

"I'm sorry, Wil," Evie murmured. "I wish I had something to suggest."

Little grimaced. *Sounds like your plan is the plan,* he signed.

I'd really *hoped* that someone would have a better idea.

Mr Finch returned carrying two bulky packs, affixed to a leather belt. I recognised one as a rectangular aether battery. The other one connected to the first by a pair of winding cables. A short antenna stuck out of the contraption; I assumed it was one of the spare parts for our longhorn.

"I've made it as simple as possible," Mr Finch explained slowly. He flicked the second pack open, revealing the slapdash device within. A crude switch had been attached to it. "Set the battery close to the Unseelie aether. Flick this switch. Run."

"Run?" Evie asked.

"Only if you like being alive," Mr Finch assured him. "This device should slowly build up aether and release a brief discharge. Under most circumstances, it would be relatively harmless. But next to a large cache of Unseelie aether—"

"Like a spark in a tinderbox," I finished grimly. "Boom."

Mr Finch handed the belt over to me—but I saw him shuffle nervously as he did so.

I didn't blame him. I was nervous too. The device was relatively light... but it *felt* as though it weighed a hundred tons.

"Captain!" Mary's voice rang out across the distance. I turned and saw her racing up the steps of the gangplank, tearing at the gas mask on her face. I hurried to the railing to look down at her. "Barsby—" She paused, gasping desperately for breath. "Barsby is loading up the cargo in longboats! He's getting ready to take them to a hangar! I heard him say they've got an hour 'til the client arrives!"

My immediate instinct was relief—Mary was safely back, and clearly unharmed. But as her words penetrated more fully, I sucked in a breath. "We need to move, then," I said. "Do you know which hangar he's heading to?"

Mary had barely managed to catch her breath... but at this, she quickly straightened and pulled her gas mask back on. "I heard them talking about it," she said, in a muffled voice. "I'll show you—let's go."

She turned on her heel before I could respond, sprinting breathlessly down the gangplank. I cursed beneath my breath as I hurried to follow her. Mary knew I would just order her to remain on the *Rose* if she told me which platform we were headed to.

Strahl and Lenore took up after me, sporting enough weapons to start a small scale war—but they weren't the only ones. Little soon fell into step next to me, clearly intent on accompanying us.

"Um, Sam," I pointed out carefully. "You're my first mate. You're supposed to run things when I'm not on deck. If I'm gone, and *you're* gone, then... who's going to watch the ship?"

Evie is staying, Little signed at me. *He and Holloway can manage things between them.*

I recognised the cold anger in his dark eyes. I had nearly managed to forget how easily Little bottled up his rage... but Barsby always had brought out the worst in him, even before that ugly business with the bounty hunters.

I drifted my gaze over Little's attire, noting the heavy boarding gauntlet on his right hand. He'd holstered his telescopic staff on his right hip; on his left hip, I saw a trench knife and a heavy bore revolver.

There was a damned good chance that Little might lose his temper at the wrong moment. I wasn't entirely certain I wanted to take that risk, given the would-be bomb I currently carried.

Little must have seen my hesitation. His face darkened, and he shook his head. *Barsby keeps causing us trouble,* he signed firmly. *I don't know why you keep bothering to protect him.*

I blinked at that. *Protect him?* I repeated the gesture, using muscle memory to ensure I'd read it properly. "I'm not *protecting* Barsby," I said. "He's turned on us a hundred times now. What possible reason could I have to protect him?"

Little tightened his jaw. *I don't know why you do it, but you do,* he snapped. *Maybe you want to believe Barsby can learn. But he isn't like us.*

He doesn't care about the suffering we caused, Wil. He will never care, no matter how many times you try to reason with him. He isn't traumatised. He's just a rotten person.

I winced at the observation. It wasn't entirely off the mark, I realised. Some part of me was... worried. It wasn't that I thought Barsby deserved to live, after all of the people he'd lied to, cheated, and betrayed. It seemed only too clear that his past actions would eventually catch up with him. But the idea of *being* what caught up to him felt... wrong, given our history together.

It was a stupid sentiment. And I didn't have the right to impose it on anyone else.

"You're right," I said quietly. "But Sam..." I met his eyes directly. "We're there for that Unseelie aether. That *has* to be the priority. You know what's on the line."

Peace for Pelaeia, Little signed grimly. *I know. We destroy the aether, and if Miss Hawkins is there, we make sure she comes back alive. Barsby is the last priority.*

I nodded once—and turned back for the gangplank. "Halcyon Seymour!" I called back. "The deck is yours until we return!" I saw Little sign a last goodbye to his husband, over my shoulder. "Keep us ready for a hasty departure!" I added. "We're off to ruin Barsby's day."

* * *

MARY LED us on a wild chase—always careful to stay just far enough ahead of us that I was more preoccupied with keeping up than catching up. We had to take some very dubious stairs in order to move down the platforms of the Aviary, and the necessity surely slowed us down; but it still took us only a quarter of an hour to reach Barsby's hangar.

We got there just in time to see two large flatbed longboats full of cargo driving out of it. I cursed under my breath.

"Cargo's out in the open," Strahl observed grimly. His breathing was only slightly heavy, despite the fact that he'd been running about in full armour. "We could—"

"No," I told him flatly. Even as we watched, the longboats lurched to a halt in front of the milling throng of travellers in the Aviary. One of the pilots yelled at the crowd to move aside; the only person to respond was a hobgoblin swathed in a giant, tattered trench coat, who offered back a rude gesture.

A calculated risk was one thing. If we blew up that cargo *here*, though, we'd be guaranteeing the death of several innocent people. None of us had the stomach for that. Or... maybe Strahl had the stomach for it. I wasn't sure why that idea jarred me so badly. He'd told me a hundred times now that he wasn't a good man.

Thankfully, I was the one giving the orders.

"We'll follow them to their destination," I told Strahl in a low voice. I glanced at one of the many wall-mounted clocks in the Aviary. "We've still got time before the client arrives. People always underestimate how long it takes to navigate Morgause airspace, too—maybe the other ship will be late."

"We're going to be a little *obvious* following that convoy, don't you think?" Strahl asked bluntly.

Mary's small form darted through the crowd ahead of us. She paused just long enough to wave her hat, in case we'd somehow managed to lose track of her.

I sighed heavily. "Mary just volunteered to tail them for us," I muttered. "At least... I'm *fairly* certain that's what she's signalling."

Mary stayed close behind the convoy, offering a healthy buffer between us and Barsby's entourage. My guts clenched every time the crowd jostled at the longboats... but *someone* in that convoy clearly knew how dangerous their cargo was, given their gradual pace.

They were being *too* careful. The clock was ticking. Any hope we might have had of reaching the hangar before the client arrived was dwindling by the second.

The pedestrian traffic dwindled slightly as the longboats spiralled down the Aviary's ramps, moving closer to the ground level. Here, the hangars were larger—likely reserved for massive cargo haulers and transport companies.

As pedestrian traffic grew thinner, Mary was forced to fall further behind the convoy, while the rest of us widened our gap in turn. Mary's cap disappeared around a corner, several dozen feet ahead of us.

By the time we'd followed suit, both Mary and the convoy were gone.

I stared at the open space around us, as panic seeped in at the edges.

Worst-case scenarios danced through my mind. Had Barsby's men noticed their tail? Had they dragged Mary into a hangar with them in order to interrogate her? I searched the area frantically for any hint of where our youngest crew member had gone.

A flash of blue caught my gaze. Someone had tucked a familiar book against the wall just next to a large pair of closed hangar doors. I reached down to pick up *Jack Blue's Last Laugh*.

The book had been intentionally set aside in order to draw my attention. There was no way that Mary could have pulled that off so neatly if she had been unwillingly dragged away. Rather, I realised, she had slipped in after Barsby's people just before the doors closed. It was *exactly* the sort of thing that Jack Blue would have done.

Wait. I knew I'd heard the name *Last Laugh* before. I stared down at the book, now feeling slightly aghast.

Had Barsby named his ship after a Jack Blue novel? Did that mean he was fond of the series? The idea seemed strangely unfair. Selfish villains shouldn't have been allowed to enjoy reading about literary heroes. Were Jack Blue a real person, he was exactly the sort of swashbuckling meddler who would take pleasure in thwarting Barsby's current plans.

Not that I was a fan of the books, of course—I'd just read them to Mary a few too many times. It was only natural that I'd have opinions on the matter.

"What's that?" Strahl asked me. The question interrupted my brief moment of indignation.

"Mary's book," I muttered back. "She left it here as a marker. This is Barsby's hangar." I glanced around for any sign of another entrance.

How are we getting in? Little signed.

"You could use the service entrance," Mary offered from behind us.

Several people swore in surprise. I spun around with my hand on my blunderbuster, before my mind caught up with my body.

Mary stood her ground calmly. I had the distinct impression that she was grinning at me from behind her gas mask. "There's a side door," she informed me. "I unlocked it from the inside and left it open." Smug satisfaction radiated from her posture. "Admit it. You'd be hopeless without me."

I had to suppress an instinctive glower. Just as I'd expected—I'd given Mary an inch today, and she'd taken an extra mile at every opportunity. Just because she'd escaped unscathed this time didn't mean that she'd survive the *next* harebrained risk—

Oh, I thought, suddenly glum.

Even if we weren't related by blood, Mary was still a chip off the old block.

I sighed heavily. "Good job, Mary," I told her softly. I offered her battered old book back to her.

Mary stared at me as though I'd grown an extra head. The pause stoked an odd guilt inside of me. I'd been so intent on protecting her for so long now that I suddenly couldn't remember the last time I'd praised her for something. Every exchange between us had become some variation on the word 'no'.

I stuffed the feeling down, promising myself to examine it again at a later date. For now, the clock was ticking, and I needed to focus on the present.

I waved the book at Mary. "Am I keeping this?" I asked her lightly.

Mary snatched the book away from me, tucking it into one of her many pockets. She spun about on her heel, now striding directly for a side door near the edge of the hangar. "This way," she mumbled. There was a touch of bashful satisfaction in her tone, though she did her best to hide it.

Strahl headed swiftly past her. Lenore followed, with an approving nod at her protégé. I hurried to catch up with them, with Little close on my heels.

"Be ready to run at a moment's notice," I warned Mary in a low voice. "I suspect we're about to cause a very big, very nasty explosion. I'm not strictly sure what the blast radius will look like."

Mary straightened with sudden seriousness. Teenage rebellion aside, she was still a junior gunnery lady, with a healthy respect for explosive reactions. She offered me a curt nod, as we headed in after the others.

We entered in through a shadowy corner of the hangar, behind an old set of empty crates. Immediately, I noticed that the enormous building had been outfitted for *two* ships, rather than just one. A pair of jutting piers lanced into the smog beyond the open hangar—but neither of them currently sported any docked ships.

Barsby stood near the building's closed double doors, issuing orders to his cronies as they slowly piloted the pair of cargo-laden longboats deeper inside. He looked every bit as stylish as he had in New Havenshire, in his coat, his half-cloak, and his hat—but his maimed arm hung in a sling, and he walked with a slight limp.

We sneaked along behind the empty crates into a closer position, listening in on the conversations that trickled through the air. Barsby stumbled away from his people, heading to a slightly more deserted spot just next to our position. As I watched, he began pacing and mumbling to himself. His steps were sluggish; I strongly suspected that he had dosed himself with either drink or medication in order to dull the pain of his arm. After a moment, I realised that he was rehearsing a speech. As I strained my ears to hear the words better, I caught a polite introduction. And... an apology.

I frowned deeply. Barsby was an arrogant man. He wasn't prone to bowing and scraping.

Little prodded at me, nudging his head back towards Lenore, who flashed her fingers silently. *Finding a better vantage point*, she signed. *Makes the rifle more persuasive.*

I nodded at her, watching as she crept her way to a different set of crates. Mary, Strahl, and Little remained with me, careful not to draw attention.

Something is wrong, I signed at them. *Barsby is very nervous. He's expecting trouble.*

Barsby is right to expect trouble, Little signed ironically. *We're here, aren't we?*

Barsby pulled a rolled cigarette from his pocket and stuck it between his lips. He turned back to rejoin his men. "One of you, bring me a light!" he snapped.

What's the plan, Captain? Strahl signed.

In the heartbeat between his question and my reply, everything changed.

An inbound ship had started to approach the hangar. The distant droning of her engines grew abruptly deafening as she swooped down towards us, breaching the haze outside like a shadowy leviathan. She was a scarred warship with a fire-blackened hull—an ironclad beast, much younger than my ageing *Rose*. She must have been wholly steam- and aether-powered, because she didn't have a single sail to her name. Cannons bristled along her hull, and I saw no fewer than six outflyers tethered along her belly.

Slowly, the great ship entered the hangar, venting aether from exhaust ports to soften her landing. Her engines finally rumbled down to a more bearable volume—and then, they died entirely, leaving the ship to float almost a dozen feet from the floor.

From my vantage point, I saw a great wolf burned into her bow. Its eyes stared out from either side of the ship, glaring viciously; its jaws hung open, as though to swallow the sky.

"Cinderwolves," I whispered.

Little stiffened. I couldn't see Strahl's face—but I *did* see him reach down to grip at his revolver. Mary looked between us quizzically.

The Cinderwolf Brigade had once been the best force of soldiers the Emerald Spires had to offer the Imperium. The very best among them had served as an honour guard for the emperor himself. Rumours suggested that said honour guard had been mysteriously absent when the *Sovereign Majesty* had plummeted into the capital below—in consequence of which, half the world assumed that the Cinderwolves had been responsible for the flagship's sabotage and the emperor's untimely demise.

One would think that sort of thing would endear the

Cinderwolves to me. But if they *had* involved themselves in the empire's defeat, then they certainly hadn't done it out of charity. In the following decades, they'd turned themselves into a small private army, available for just about any dirty business you could imagine... *if*, of course, you had the resources of a small province at your disposal.

Before us in the hangar sat the Cinderwolves' flagship, the *Conflagration*.

I hunkered down with Strahl and Little, flashing my hands so emphatically that some part of me worried Barsby and the mercenaries might hear me. *We can't fight them directly,* I signed. *I'll have to sneak onto one of the longboats to set the battery. We may not get all of the Unseelie aether, but we can get most of it.*

Quiet nods greeted me all around.

We'll cover you if they catch you, Little signed back. *Once you set the battery, start running and don't stop.*

The *Conflagration* lowered a large gangplank, and a small parade of jackbooted, gas-masked Cinderwolves headed out to meet Barsby in perfect marching order. Their oilskin greatcoats flapped in the wind over battered, blackened breastplates. All of them were armed to the teeth with rifles, sabres, and belted firebombs. I noted two aethermancers in their midst bearing fuel tanks upon their backs; silvery pipes fed from those tanks into pyrokinetic foci in their gloves.

The only policy the Cinderwolves knew was scorched earth. I hadn't realised they took that policy quite so literally.

One of the Cinderwolves strode ahead of the others, making their way towards Barsby. The figure was a human of average height—but their presence far outweighed their size. They wore an open-faced helmet decorated with an aether-grey horsehair plume, overtop a gas mask stylised to remind of a snarling wolf's face. Their oilskin greatcoat was more resplendent than the coats of the other Cinderwolves, but its hem was tattered, and there were dark splashes upon its breast that would probably never wash out. As the figure moved, I caught a glimpse of scorched, battle-scarred lamellar beneath their coat.

Bright golden-tassel epaulettes stood out upon the figure's shoulders—one of the few untarnished accessories they wore. A smattering of medals swayed upon their coat, pinned just over their heart.

"Death be victorious," Strahl swore behind me. His voice was a barely audible hiss, but it still startled me sharply. He was staring at the Cinderwolf who'd stepped forward to meet Barsby. "I know him," Strahl added, in a low voice.

I knitted my brow at him. "How?" I whispered. "We can't even see his face."

Strahl leaned forward, speaking even more quietly. "The medals. You see the one with the bloody wing?"

I squinted at the Cinderwolf's medals again, trying to pick out the one that Strahl was describing. There was one that matched his description—a single, tattered wing stretched wide, with its tip dipped in scarlet.

"He's wearing the Order of the Crimson Pinion," Strahl muttered. "See the second wing on the other side of his coat? He's the only one who wears both wings." His face darkened. "That's Captain Cristoforo Altera. He coordinated the ground assault on Pelaeia. He runs the Cinderwolves now."

A chill stuttered through my veins. "The Cinderwolves are mostly Emerald Spires," I breathed. "They'd never work for Carrain. If they're here now, then that means—"

"—the Cinderwolves are fighting against Carrain," Strahl finished. "And the Spires have their fingers in Barsby's business."

At that moment, something else caught my attention. Out of the corner of my eye, I saw a pale figure flash across the hangar, hurrying towards the crates just behind us. The soft purr of aether-powered foci drifted over the air towards me.

I shot Strahl a wary look and ducked around the side of the crates, craning my neck to get a look at the newcomer.

"Hawkins?" I whispered.

The ghostly figure had disappeared behind cover... but I soon heard a sound of deep frustration.

Miss Hawkins reappeared from cover just long enough to scurry towards me. Her dress and wig were gone; she wore instead a grey shirt and trousers which I suspected might once have been a different colour. Her short, ghostly-pale hair was pinned close to her head. I had just enough time to register the small arsenal of foci upon her person before Miss Hawkins yanked me up by my lapels, nearly pulling me off my feet.

"What in the name of the Four Winds are you *doing* here?" Hawkins hissed. "I told you to *leave*, Captain!"

"Fancy seeing you here, Miss Hawkins," I rasped back in a tiny voice. "It just so happens we have business of our own in this hangar. I would have told you sooner, but you made yourself rather difficult to find."

Miss Hawkins narrowed her eyes dangerously. "*We?*" she demanded through gritted teeth.

I pointed just around the corner of the crates. Hawkins craned her head back to look.

Strahl pressed a gauntlet over his faceplate, vaguely embarrassed. Little smiled sheepishly. Mary waved excitedly.

Miss Hawkins couldn't possibly have looked more horrified. "You all need to leave," she insisted. "*Now.*"

"I have a great deal of respect for your abilities, Miss Hawkins," I told her in a low tone, "but you *cannot* handle all of those people on your own. Those Cinderwolves are hardened war criminals, and they've got aethermancers of their own."

"The *Cinderwolves?*" Hawkins snarled. There was a manic edge to her voice. "You think the Cinderwolves are the problem? Captain... they're just the hired help!"

Even as we spoke, a second ship swooped in to dock at the hangar. She was a dark, nimble craft, smaller than the *Iron Rose*— somewhere between a personal ship and a streamlined racing zeppelin. Her name, written upon the side in ghostly white, was the *Erebus*.

As the new ship slowly descended, Captain Altera consulted with another of the Cinderwolves who'd been examining the crates upon the longboats. I knew from their posture that they'd discovered the shortfall of Unseelie aether.

The captain snapped out an order to one of the other Cinderwolves, who snatched Barsby by the shoulders and forced him to his knees.

The *Erebus* lowered its gangplank.

Captain Altera snatched off his gas mask. The man beneath was black-haired and olive-skinned, with a sharply defined jaw. Threads of silver ran through his hair—but they only served to highlight how gracefully he'd aged. That such a horrible man could be so classically handsome only proved how terribly unfair the world could be.

"According to Mr Barsby," Captain Altera called out, "there's been a *complication*." His rolling Spires accent rang against the walls of the hangar.

A tall, gaunt figure strode down the gangplank of the *Erebus*.

Every inch of the man's tattered coat was a faded aether-grey. His long arms were sheathed in sleek, silver foci, far better cared for than his ragged attire. Even mighty Morgause's blackened touch failed to stain that awful figure; the falling ash turned pale where he walked, leaving flakes of false snow in his wake. Deep within his cowl was a pale, skull-like wooden mask… one that apocryphal stories suggested had been fashioned from the corpse of a Gallowwood dryad.

Wraithwood raised one hand, signalling the small army of Cinderwolves to surround Barsby.

"I do so *hate* complications," he said.

16

CINDERWOLVES & LEGIONNAIRES - A DISTRACTING CONVERSATION - CLASH OF WILLS

"I'm a complication," I mumbled feverishly. The thought rose within me, hysterical. "I don't want to be a complication."

Miss Hawkins—still holding me by the lapels—was far too composed. I snapped my head back towards her, grabbing her collar in return. "You *knew!*" I hissed. "You knew about Wraithwood! Why didn't you bloody well *tell* us?"

Miss Hawkins sucked in a soft breath. Her face had gone paler than normal, but somehow she remained grimly steady. "If I'd told you my business was killing Wraithwood," she said, "you never would have brought me to Morgause."

I bit my tongue, trying not to laugh in shock. "Kill Wraithwood?" I gasped. "*Wraithwood!* Are you out of your *mind?*"

A small hand touched me on the shoulder. I turned to see Mary standing behind me. At some point, she'd discarded her gas mask; she now raised her eyebrows meaningfully, pressing a finger to her lips as she glanced in the direction of Wraithwood and the Cinderwolves. Mary, I realised, was utterly calm—she had little to no context for the people with whom we shared this hangar. They were the villains of yesteryear, from far before her time.

But she was, of course, correct. I needed to use my indoor voice if I was going to avoid being eviscerated by the realm's most ruthless Legionnaire and his army of mercenary war criminals.

I nodded silently at Mary. As I did, Miss Hawkins released me in order to pry my hands from her collar.

Thankfully, Wraithwood was far too focussed on Barsby to notice our brief altercation.

"I thought the importance of this shipment had been impressed upon you, Mr Barsby," Wraithwood growled. He had a low, gravelly voice, and a wide, rounded accent. The cadence surprised me—it hadn't occurred to me that Wraithwood might speak like someone from the countryside.

"Y-yes, sir, Wraithwood sir," Barsby sputtered. He snapped into a hasty bow.

Seeing Barsby grovel was... unsettling.

"Some of my shipment seems to be missing, Mr Barsby," Wraithwood observed, with sinister patience. "What's the tally, Captain?"

"We're still counting, sir," Captain Altera said dutifully.

"If I can just explain—" Barsby started tremulously.

Wraithwood turned that mask's empty gaze upon Barsby, however, and he choked on the words. "When I want to hear you grovel," Wraithwood informed him, "you will know, *thief*." He spoke with a calm, level contempt.

We need to leave now, Strahl signed. He glanced at Miss Hawkins and repeated the gesture emphatically—but she couldn't understand the sign language. It hardly mattered; I knew she wasn't going to leave. Only a special kind of fool would knowingly walk into a hangar with Wraithwood in the first place.

I hadn't done so knowingly... but neither, I realised, was I going to leave.

"You saw what he did in Pelaeia," Miss Hawkins whispered. "You'll be lucky if he kills you outright, Captain. There's nothing you can do here."

I looked between Strahl and Miss Hawkins. "Wraithwood has the machine?" I asked her slowly. "He's the one who intends to use it?"

Miss Hawkins didn't reply—but I saw the fearful confirmation in her eyes.

The horror that flickered through me was sudden and overwhelming. The idea of *any* aethermancer using an army of echoes was hideous enough. But for Wraithwood, who had created those echoes with his own hands, to use that machine... the sheer outrage of it was nearly enough to overwhelm my fear.

I looked at Little—and saw a similar fury. Little didn't need to know *what* Wraithwood intended to do with the machine in order to appreciate the perversity of it all.

I nodded at Little... and turned back to Strahl and Miss Hawkins.

"Can you destroy that Unseelie aether from a distance?" I whispered to her.

Miss Hawkins grimaced. "Those canisters are particularly thick," she murmured slowly. "My blasting focus could destroy one... but it overheats easily. I'll only get one shot. There are two longboats."

I glanced back at the cargo boats. They had at least twenty feet between them. If Hawkins *did* manage to start a reaction, I thought, they would probably both explode... but then, Mr Finch had been exceptionally unclear on the blast radius.

I stifled a soft groan.

"Mr Finch rigged one of your batteries to spark an aetheric reaction," I told her. "I'll sneak over to the longboat on the right, open up a canister, and leave the battery there. If the detonation doesn't take out both boats, then you'll be ready to handle the other one."

Miss Hawkins tightened her jaw. I could tell she didn't like the idea of involving me... but time was ticking away, and we both knew it.

I decided it was best not to give her any further time to think.

"Get back to the *Rose* and tell Evie to ready us for immediate departure," I ordered Mary softly. Her eyes flashed with protest, but I cut her off quickly. "If we pull this off, we can't afford to idle in port for even a second. You're the fastest one here. I need you to do this, Mary."

Mary hesitated. I felt her searching me for signs of overbearing protectiveness. Very slowly, however, she nodded.

"Mr Strahl, Mr Little," I said, "I want you ready to take out the nearest Cinderwolves if they see me. I'm sure Miss Brighton will lend a helping bullet or two, once she catches wind of what's going on. Either way, our goal remains the same: We blow the aether and get out of here, as swiftly as possible." I glanced meaningfully at Miss Hawkins. "*All* of us."

Miss Hawkins didn't meet my eyes. "If it comes to that," she murmured, "I can distract Wraithwood. He'll... talk to me. For at least a little while." A complicated flicker of emotion crossed her face at this idea.

I worked my mouth soundlessly for a moment. "I'm going to need to discuss that fact with you at a later date," I managed finally. "Lady save me, I wish I had the time *now*."

I couldn't see Strahl's face—but I greatly suspected that he was currently revisiting his earlier suspicions of Miss Hawkins.

I turned my attention back to the front of the hangar and started to sneak my way forward. If I spent too long trying to unravel all of our complications, the opportunity for action would pass. I just had to trust that everyone would stick to the plan.

As I crept closer, a gorgon sergeant in a crimson sash approached Captain Altera, reporting to him in a soft voice. The captain nodded and turned to Wraithwood. "At a rough estimate," Captain Altera said, "we're missing a quarter of the shipment."

"One quarter," Wraithwood repeated. He enunciated each word clearly, with a shake of his head. "I will admit," he said, "I'm surprised you came here yourself, Mr Barsby. You must know what wretched news this is."

A heavy pause followed.

Wraithwood leaned forward, ever so slightly. "*Now's* where you grovel," he ordered. His voice was quietly, dreadfully furious.

"P-please, sir, Wraithwood, sir!" Barsby cried. His hoarse voice had intimidated me, back in New Havenshire—but compared to Wraithwood, Barsby was about as frightening as a newborn gosling.

"It wasn't my fault, I swear it! The pirates murdered the first transport captain, sir. And the other captain who picked up the cargo, he... he discovered what it was and only delivered me what you have. He hid the rest and tried to blackmail me into doubling the money, but I didn't have the time—"

"Tell me about this captain who stole from me," Wraithwood demanded.

At this, Barsby hesitated. When he spoke again, his words were a mumble.

Wraithwood wasn't having it. "I'm sorry, Mr Barsby," Wraithwood drawled. "Speak up. You lost my cargo to whom?"

"A, uh... a goblin, sir," Barsby rasped. "Captain of the *Iron Rose*. Goes by the name of William Blair."

I always had wondered what a heart attack felt like.

I was perhaps a dozen feet away from them, barely hidden behind a single empty box. Some part of me was suddenly certain that the use of my name would magically reveal me, like a faerie from a story.

Instead, the Cinderwolves sniggered incredulously behind their gas masks. Thankfully, I was far too terrified to take it as an affront.

"You entrusted my precious cargo to a filthy sewer rat and found yourself robbed," Wraithwood said slowly. His patience thinned audibly with every word. "I must admit, Mr Barsby... I have never held much faith in humanity. But you've tested what little faith still remains to me." Wraithwood sighed and shook his head. "I don't normally *enjoy* killing people, but this time... well, you might just be an exception to the rule."

Barsby remained kneeling before Wraithwood, rooted to the spot. His good eye was wide with fear. The Cinderwolves raised their rifles, prepared to carry out an immediate execution—but Wraithwood lifted his hand to stop them. Gently, he reached out to push Barsby's collar aside, displaying the old scars around his neck.

"Captain Altera," Wraithwood called out, "what do you ken is the punishment for thievery of this calibre?"

"I believe that would be a hanging, sir," Captain Altera replied dutifully. There was a note of humour in his tone, as though Wraithwood had offered him a joke about the weather.

"String this one up, then," Wraithwood ordered the captain. "The last time didn't take."

"Yes sir," Captain Altera acknowledged. He snapped his fingers at his soldiers.

The Cinderwolves grasped Barsby firmly, as he thrashed like a rabbit in a trap. The gorgon sergeant marched for the *Conflagration*, calling out for rope. One of the other mercenaries emerged onto the gangplank, already tying up a noose.

Maybe ten feet of open ground stood between me and the first longboat of Unseelie aether. I was more affected by Barsby's horrible situation than I really wanted to be—but I knew it was exactly the sort of distraction I required in order to sneak past the Cinderwolves. I sucked in my breath and tried to calm my pounding heart, gauging my timing.

"It's not my bloody fault!" Barsby screamed hysterically. "You never told me there was another Legionnaire involved!"

Wraithwood had started strolling back towards his ship—but at this, he stopped, as still as a statue. He raised his hand again to stall the mercenaries and turned to face Barsby.

I'd nearly stepped out from cover—but at this, I drew myself hastily back, covering my mouth to stifle a gasp.

The Lady of Fools was still with me. Wraithwood didn't seem to have caught sight of me.

"Another Legionnaire?" Wraithwood asked sharply.

"Yes, another Legionnaire!" Barsby hissed. "Travelling with Blair and his ship. She cut off my bloody hand!"

Wraithwood looked long and hard into Barsby's one eye. An eternity seemed to pass. Then, the Legionnaire flicked his grey-gloved hand, and the Cinderwolves holding Barsby released their grip. Barsby clutched at his chest, gasping for air against the mortal fear that still gripped him.

A flicker of silver light coiled within Wraithwood's raised right hand. I expected it to resolve into a silver sword... but instead,

Wraithwood tilted his head, as though listening to some invisible voice. He looked slowly around the cluttered hangar...

...until his masked gaze fell upon the exact spot where I'd left Hawkins.

"Ey up, little Miss Hawkins," Wraithwood called out softly. "I know you're here."

Miss Hawkins strode out from behind the crates with a slow, grim pace. If the sudden discovery had caused her any panic, then at least the emotion didn't show upon her face.

The Cinderwolves snapped their attention to Hawkins, training their guns in her direction. Barsby—briefly forgotten—swiftly backpedalled for his crew and the two longboats of Unseelie aether. I cursed silently to myself; as frightening as everyone in this hangar was, it was Barsby who was most likely to spot me.

Wraithwood stared Hawkins down in that awful mask. He stalked slowly between the longboats, pausing just in front of them to interpose himself between Hawkins and the cargo. Captain Altera and a group of his men quickly followed, guns at the ready. They positioned themselves behind the longboats, fanning out into firing positions. The rest of the Cinderwolves stayed behind to keep an eye on Barsby and his hired help.

"So," Wraithwood said. "Jonathan gave you his sword. I wondered why... he never drew it to protect himself."

Wraithwood faltered only briefly as he spoke—but the hesitation still surprised me.

"You killed him," Miss Hawkins said. Her voice trembled with fear, and anger, and unutterable grief. "He loved you, and you *killed* him."

I stared at Miss Hawkins, from behind my cover. I'd believed her when she'd said she could distract Wraithwood... but this conversation was nothing like the distraction I had been imagining.

Wraithwood watched Hawkins, still and wary. "Jonathan tried to kill me first," he said coldly.

"Good," Miss Hawkins said. Her jaw tightened. "I always wondered why Jonathan was so obsessed with Pelaeia; it wasn't even his atrocity. But I understand now. He wasn't trying to atone for his own sins—he was trying to fix *yours*." Furious tears threatened at her eyes. "He hated himself for loving you. Now that I've seen Pelaeia... now that I know what you did. I know *exactly* how he felt."

Silence fell in the hangar. It was a loaded silence, full of awful emotions. But only two people present fully understood the depth of the situation.

I glanced towards the longboats of Unseelie aether. Barsby and his lackeys still hovered close to them, and I knew in that moment that Barsby was considering the frankly suicidal option of holding the aether hostage. I let out a soft hiss of frustration; as long as Barsby lingered there, I couldn't possibly get close enough to set the battery.

"Should we kill her?" Captain Altera asked Wraithwood. He phrased the question in a polite, professional tone.

"No," Wraithwood said softly. "She knows she can't win against me. I trained her, after all."

"You *helped* train me," Miss Hawkins snarled. "I can only thank the Everbright that Jonathan taught me more than you did." She started walking forward again.

"That's far enough!" Wraithwood said sharply.

Miss Hawkins stopped. I knew she had the will to keep going—but she was trying to draw things out as long as possible, to give me the time that I needed. I wished I had a way to convey to her the obstacle —the *cyclopean weasel*—that had decided to hover directly in my path.

"I know you think you're doing the right thing, Jane," Wraithwood said. His voice was gently chiding. "Jonathan wanted to raise you to be kinder than we are. But he did you a disservice. This world is harder and crueller than you've been led to believe. Everything I've done— everything I've *ever* done—has been to prevent far worse things from happening."

Miss Hawkins tightened her hands into fists... and I knew that her distraction was about to become *far* more distracting. "Don't you dare talk to me like a naïve little child," she growled. Her right hand flared with flickering silver light. Wisps of aetheric smoke danced around her fingers, shifting into the faintest outline of a sword.

The Cinderwolves tightened their grips on their weapons. All of them were still aimed squarely at Hawkins. She was doing an absolutely beautiful job of keeping everyone's attention, but Barsby simply wouldn't *leave*. The weasel leaned himself heavily upon the edge of one longboat, murmuring to his crew in a soft tone.

"If any of you fire without my express order," Wraithwood informed the mercenaries, "you will not live long enough to face your captain for your lapse in professionalism. I will remind you all that one stray shot could be fatal for everyone in this hangar." He kept his gaze squarely upon Hawkins. "A fact of which you are well aware, I'm sure."

Miss Hawkins met his gaze, perfectly level. "I've seen what Unseelie aether can do to a man," she said. "Do your hired help know that they might rot their own faces off, or did you keep that little tidbit from them?"

Wraithwood tensed his shoulders. "You want to be talked to like an adult, Jane?" he asked darkly. "Fine. You know the things of which I'm capable. If you draw that sword on me, I *will* cut you down. I will not enjoy it... but neither will I hesitate."

"Oh, I know," Miss Hawkins assured him. This time, grief and fury burst openly into her voice. "You'll kill me, just like you killed those children in Pelaeia. Or did you let the bombs do that for you?"

Barsby glanced towards the growing standoff between the two aethermancers. A flash of fear crossed his expression, and I recalled the image of Miss Hawkins standing over him with her silver sword.

That's right, I thought at him furiously. *Be a coward, Barsby. For once in my life, I want you to be the absolute coward that you are and run.*

"Give me the sword, Jane," Wraithwood gritted out. "You are about to throw your life away for no reason at all."

Miss Hawkins replied with a burst of white aether. Her silver sword sprang to life—a small sun within her right hand. "I'll spend my life exactly as I please, you monster," she told him.

Wraithwood snapped his hand out in reply. A gleaming point of light appeared within his palm—smaller and more refined than the wild surge of aether Miss Hawkins had used to summon her own blade. In an instant, that tiny point of light became a shimmering aetheric smallsword—a spike of chilling starlight, made manifest. Between his deep cowl and his terrible mask, he looked rather like Death Victorious, come to claim Miss Hawkins' soul.

Wraithwood shifted his stance subtly. "Get the aether onto the *Conflagration*," he ordered Captain Altera.

The captain nodded at the order and turned to repeat it. The Cinderwolves moved for the longboats, and I cursed beneath my breath.

Miss Hawkins leapt forward—and Wraithwood raised his sword to meet her.

17

INEVITABLE BETRAYAL - ME - DARING ESCAPES & DUBIOUS ALLIES - GIDEON

Wraithwood stood as still as a statue, patiently waiting. His foci charged slowly, scattering pinpricks of light across the hangar's floor. Every flicker of aether was calm and tightly controlled. I had thought that Miss Hawkins was impressive—but I could already tell that Wraithwood outmatched her in every possible way.

Worst of all, I knew that Wraithwood was a merciless killer... and that Miss Hawkins most decidedly was *not*.

Hawkins was halfway to Wraithwood when he took one step back and flicked out his left arm. A silver gauntlet-focus flared on his left hand, and the aether within it uncoiled into a rope of blue-white light. Wraithwood snapped the whip towards Hawkins with a twist of his wrist. The aether cracked like thunder, bursting into a blinding, disorienting flash. Even at a distance, I blinked back spots and clutched at my ringing ears. If I'd been closer, I surely would have spent a fatal few seconds both blind and utterly deaf.

Miss Hawkins was right next to that whip—but she'd known to expect it. She rolled aside, shielding her eyes.

Even so... she had almost been too slow.

I didn't have the luxury of waiting for a better opportunity. I sprinted from the shadows cast by the mountain of crates and crossed the last bit of open distance to the nearest longboat. I prayed that the Cinderwolves were too occupied with the duel and Barsby's thugs to notice me.

Someone answered my prayers—but it wasn't the Lady of Fools.

Neither Barsby, nor his crew, nor the Cinderwolves noticed my hasty approach. Instead, Barsby's men and the Cinderwolves watching them had drawn weapons on each other. A Cinderwolf aethermancer lay unmoving on the ground. The left lens of his gas mask had been shattered by a single bullet.

Lenore, I realised, had used the sound of the whip crack to cover a shot at the Cinderwolf aethermancer.

I know I brag endlessly about my crew. But truly, I have the *best* crew.

"Sharpshooter!" a Cinderwolf screamed.

Barsby's crew had the Unseelie aether at their backs, which left the Cinderwolves at a distinct disadvantage—Barsby's people could fire at the Cinderwolves with abandon, but the mercenaries wouldn't dare fire back for fear of hitting the aether. I expected the Cinderwolves to search for cover. Instead, the gorgon sergeant drew her sabre and charged the longboat. The Cinderwolves behind her followed her lead.

Barsby's crew started shooting.

Some of the bullets found their mark—but not nearly as many as I would have expected. One Cinderwolf hit the floor; another staggered, caught in the leg. But Barsby's people were used to intimidating untried, poorly outfitted targets; they weren't at all prepared for a direct charge by battle-hardened soldiers.

Just as the Cinderwolves closed with their adversaries, Barsby ducked wildly aside. He rolled beneath the other longboat... just as I leapt on top of it and crouched into the flatbed.

I forced myself to ignore the fact that Barsby was somewhere beneath my feet. Instead, I dared a brief glance over the edge of the longboat at the two duelling aethermancers, hoping that Miss Hawkins had managed to hold Wraithwood's attention.

Hawkins had somehow regained her footing. Harsh light flared around her as she gathered up a veritable storm of aether. The air seethed, crackling with azure power. Her foci whined to life, burning bright against the darkness of the hangar.

Wraithwood burst into a sprint. Three steps later, his boots flared with aether and launched him into the air in a superhuman leap. He crossed the distance to Hawkins in the blink of an eye, and I suddenly understood how he'd cut down so many of Pelaeia's defenders so quickly.

Miss Hawkins raised her left gauntlet and shaped the surrounding aether into a shield of light. Wraithwood danced around it. He flicked his blade at Hawkins with serpentine speed, testing her defences. Hawkins brought the shield up to block him. Each time his silver sword scraped against the aetheric shield, the clash sent up a screech of blue and white sparks.

Wraithwood, I realised, was holding himself back. He'd waited until he was in closer quarters to use his foci; the last thing he wanted was to risk hitting the cargo with Seelie aether. He hadn't wasted any time before engaging directly with Hawkins, either—he knew he needed to block her from attacking the cargo herself.

Miss Hawkins *was* a good distraction, I realised. She was just dangerous enough to merit Wraithwood's full attention, though not quite dangerous enough to push her way past him. Somehow, it hadn't occurred to Wraithwood that she might have brought assistance with her.

By the grace of the Lady of Fools, neither Captain Altera nor the Legionnaire had yet noticed the single stowaway goblin clinging to their precious cargo. Barsby's crew had scattered at the Cinderwolves' charge, diving for cover behind the empty crates. The Cinderwolves, too, had pulled back with military precision, returning fire from the other side of the longboats. And me? I was finally alone with the cargo —at the centre of a terrifying firefight.

I flinched as bullets whizzed past my longboat, keenly aware that a single stray shot could pierce one of the canisters and give me a face full of Unseelie aether. It was time to hurry up the plan.

I slipped my hand axe from my belt and wedged it beneath the lid of one of the crates, leaning on it like a crowbar. The crate resisted me more strongly than I'd expected; no matter how fit I kept myself, I had far less body mass than most of my crew. I struggled with the crate in a growing panic, desperate to finish the job before something exploded.

As I leaned heavily on my hand axe, someone else rolled into the flatbed next to me. I glanced sharply towards the sound and met Barsby's startled gaze.

"Blair!" Barsby sputtered. His voice rang out across the hangar... and suddenly, several sets of eyes turned our way.

"Blair?" Captain Altera asked, confused. It took me a moment to realise that he and a handful of his Cinderwolves had taken cover behind the exact same stack of crates that *I* had previously used for cover, only ten feet away from the longboat.

Hawkins cursed. Wraithwood whirled to assess the situation. He fixed his terrifying gaze upon me, and my heart skipped wildly in my chest.

"Blair," Wraithwood growled.

I laughed hysterically, still gripping my hand axe. "Me," I agreed helplessly. I greeted the deadly gathering with an instinctive wave of my hand. Then, much more clearly, I shouted: "Lenore!"

Several heads cocked in confusion. They didn't understand that I'd just cried havoc and let loose the most dangerous school teacher in all of Avalon.

Barsby didn't need to know exactly what I'd done; he was familiar enough with my wild, last-ditch plans to know that it wasn't anything good. He threw himself down on the flatbed and tossed an arm over his head for good measure.

Another shot rang out, more clearly than before. A bullet connected with the other Cinderwolf pyroclast's aether tank. The tank gave a sharp hiss—followed by a hollow thump. It exploded in a riotous howl, engulfing the nearest mercenaries in a cerulean inferno. They didn't even have the chance to scream.

Wraithwood crouched, angling himself to take an inhuman leap towards me. His boots flared with aether—but just as he leapt into the air, Hawkins fired her palm-blaster at him. The flash of force slammed into Wraithwood, flinging him like a cannonball into a wall of empty wooden crates. The boxes burst at the impact and scattered around him, as he fell to the ground. His mask cracked against the floor, and his terrible sword winked out of existence.

"Hurry!" Hawkins shouted at me. She advanced on Wraithwood—but the infamous Legionnaire was already pushing himself to his feet.

Now that I'd lost the element of surprise, I didn't have long before one of the interested parties overran my longboat. I needed to buy time to crack open a crate, grab a canister, and set up the device.

I might not manage to destroy both longboats, I realised... but if I adjusted the plan, then I could destroy at least one. I'd just have to trust that Miss Hawkins could handle the rest.

I leapt on top of the cargo crates in the longboat, hopping my way across them to jump into the driver's seat. The position gave me a perfect view of the grand melee taking place between the longboat and the docked ships. Before me were the Cinderwolves and Barsby's crew. Behind me were Wraithwood and Miss Hawkins. Forward, I thought, was a slightly less suicidal direction than backward—but only *slightly* less.

Thankfully, I wasn't alone; I had help waiting nearby.

"Strahl!" I shouted over the din. "Now!"

Strahl leapt from his hiding spot and descended upon the unsuspecting Cinderwolves. His heavy revolver barked three times; with each shot, a man hit the floor. Strahl holstered the revolver, grabbed the hilt of his sword, and activated its aetheric properties. The super-heated edge of glowing metal slammed into a Cinderwolf facing away from me; it connected where the mercenary's neck met his shoulder and cut through his armour and coat, lodging itself somewhere in the middle of his chest. Strahl kicked the man off his blade and turned to face Captain Altera.

Part of me wanted to watch Strahl properly thrash the architect of Pelaeia's massacre—but more pressing matters called for my attention.

"Hang on, Barsby!" I shouted.

I slammed my foot onto the accelerator, aiming for a stretch of open hangar on our starboard side. The cargo-laden longboat ploughed through the fighting before us. Barsby's crew leapt for cover—but the Cinderwolves charged my vehicle. I drove directly over one of the mercenaries, even as another one leapt onto the boat's snub-nosed front.

"William!" Barsby rasped out a warning from the flatbed. I glanced over my shoulder and saw three other Cinderwolves clinging tenaciously to the sides of the longboat, climbing fast. Two of them tumbled into the flatbed with Barsby, while the last one landed closer to my seat.

"I knew you'd get me killed someday, William!" Barsby snarled. He surged upright, drawing his rapier with his remaining hand, just as the Cinderwolf next to him rose and brandished their sabre.

I caught one brief glimpse of Little just above us, as he leapt from a row of ungainly crates. Little landed heavily on one of the Cinderwolves on the flatbed, plunging his trench knife into the mercenary's neck. The Cinderwolf choked on a strangled sound, as Little heaved them over the side. Little turned on another of the mercenaries, parrying their sabre with his heavy boarding gauntlet. He followed through with a vicious jab of his off-hand, and I heard the trench knife's brass knuckles crack something in the Cinderwolf's gas mask.

Barsby shifted back-to-back with Little, as though it was the most natural thing in the world. And once upon a time, it *would* have been that—but I couldn't help noticing the way that Little subtly gritted his teeth against the movement. Still, Little covered Barsby as the other man lunged past a Cinderwolf's heavier sabre, burying the tip of his rapier in their throat.

Metal scraped on the front of the longboat, and I snapped my gaze forward: the mercenary on the hood was pulling himself up. Behind me, Barsby and Little were still otherwise occupied, and I knew I couldn't wait for them to reach me.

"Hold on!" I shouted.

"To what?" Barsby snarled. He yanked his rapier from the

Cinderwolf's throat and kicked them off the side of the longboat. At the same instant, I slammed on the brakes.

The Cinderwolf on the hood rocketed away like a shooting star, skidding across the floor to crash into an old stack of crates against the hangar wall. The bottom crates smashed into kindling, and the stack atop them crumpled like a house of cards. Behind me, the last Cinderwolf flew over my head in an impressive arc. They flailed wildly through the air, then hit the ground with a hard, rolling *thud*.

Little stood his ground like an ancient, rooted tree—but Barsby tumbled tail over teakettle, rolling between the driver's and passenger's seats with a raspy scream. I glanced down at him and met his one-eyed glare. It wasn't a very *intimidating* glare, given the way that he'd splayed between the seats, with one of his legs jutting into the air like a half-crushed bug.

"I... *hate* you," Barsby growled.

I reached down and patted his cheek. "I hate you too, Barsby," I assured him. I shoved to my feet before he could respond, hurrying back to the flatbed in search of my hand axe.

Barsby tried to right himself—but this was a difficult proposition, with his right arm in a sling and his left hand still clutching his rapier. Little reached down towards Barsby, grabbing a fistful of his lapel and yanking him back onto his feet.

"Ah, Samuel," Barsby crooned nervously. "Thank you for that. Always reliable—"

Little punched him between the eyes with his boarding gauntlet.

Barsby blinked—and promptly fell backwards off the longboat like a felled log.

I glanced at Little. "Really?" I asked him with a sigh.

Little offered me a helpless shrug.

I turned my attention back to the crate in front of me, snatching up my hand axe from the flatbed. I slammed the weapon beneath the lid of the crate once more, searching for an angle that might crack it open. The horrible stench of rotted leaves grew stronger every time the lid budged, and I had to fight down a rising nausea.

"A little help please, Sam," I choked out.

On the floor of the hangar, next to the longboat, Barsby righted himself with a groan. His rapier had fallen from his grip; out of the corner of my eye, I saw him reach for the holstered pistol at his side. My mind sparked with alarm, and I jolted back from the crate, ready to dive for cover.

But Barsby wasn't aiming for either me or Little. Instead, he pointed his pistol directly underneath the longboat's chassis and pulled the trigger.

One of the Cinderwolves I'd thrown off the longboat took the shot directly in the face—and I saw then that they'd been raising their gun in the general direction of the very *volatile* crates on the longboat.

The Cinderwolf dropped back to the ground with an ugly jerk of limbs. I knew they weren't likely to get up again.

Barsby whirled on the two of us, still dazed from his tumble. "Tell your sharpshooter to kill *Wraithwood*," he hissed, as he struggled back to his feet. "As long as he's still breathing, he'll hunt us all down like dogs!" He wiped his coat sleeve across his bleeding nose, smearing scarlet across his face.

"So will Captain Altera!" I snapped back. "Or did you forget that you were dealing with murderous *war criminals*, Barsby?"

Barsby ignored the question; instead, his one good eye flickered to the crate behind me, where I'd left my hand axe wedged beneath the lid. "What are you *doing?*" he demanded. "You're going to put us all in an early grave!"

I narrowed my eyes at him. "I'm setting an aether charge," I informed him. "And then we're all running… *very* fast."

Barsby widened his eye.

Little jammed his trench knife under the lid, leaning upon it with his prodigious strength. The crate squealed, and a fresh gush of horrendous air wafted out.

I glanced towards Barsby. "You could always lend a—"

Barsby had already started running.

"…hand," I finished flatly, watching him run. Little fixed me with a knowing look. "I guess he wouldn't have appreciated that suggestion anyway," I muttered.

Barsby sprinted for the side door with such instant, unerring accuracy that I knew he'd long since mapped out all of the possible escape routes. On some level, I had to admire that sort of calculated cowardice.

I—fool that I was—turned back to the open crate with a grimace, thrusting my hands past rotting bricks of tea to grasp at a slimy metal canister.

Little glanced sharply past my shoulder, and I hazarded a look. The gorgon sergeant had secured the other longboat of Unseelie aether. There was something wrong with the vehicle's float—its right half dragged uncomfortably against the floor, and I suspected that it had been damaged in the firefight. A handful of Cinderwolves now surrounded the vehicle, hauling it towards the *Conflagration* through sheer brute strength.

Nearby, Strahl and Captain Altera stood several feet apart, watching each other warily. They'd thoroughly torn into one another while I was distracted—both of them were battered, breathing hard. Strahl's leg was drenched in blood; Altera had pulled his left arm against his body like a broken wing, and there was a dribble of crimson from his forehead. I wondered at first that the Cinderwolf was still standing, given that Strahl's sword could shear through most metal—but a faintly opalescent light flickered off of Altera's curving sabre, and I realised that it was probably infused with aether as well.

Strahl moved again, with a brutal swing of his heavy sword. Altera knocked the blade aside—and though their weapons were vastly different, I couldn't help but notice in that moment just how similar the two men were in fighting style. They were both brutal, quick, and utterly efficient. The obvious comparison triggered an old discomfort, somewhere inside of me—a reminder that my bosun had once held a very high rank in the Imperial Army.

Altera's eyes caught upon our longboat as he deflected Strahl's blow. He shouted out an order to the other Cinderwolves, even as Strahl forced him backwards with another heavy swing.

The gorgon brandished her sabre in our direction, and several Cinderwolves turned, preparing a coordinated charge.

I heaved the rusting canister of Unseelie aether hurriedly from the crate, shoving it towards Little. "Haul that back and throw it as far as you can," I gasped at him, jerking my chin towards the Cinderwolves.

Little took the canister from me, gripping it with both hands. He lobbed it a surprisingly good distance. It landed with a thunderous *clang*, halfway between us and the Cinderwolves. I'd expected the rough handling to set it off, but it somehow maintained its integrity, rolling sluggishly along the floor of the hangar.

I grabbed Little's heavy bore revolver, rooted myself as best I could, and fired the gun directly at the canister.

An oily plume tore from the rusted iron with an unearthly shriek. Bruised light bloomed around the canister—and then it erupted, with a sickening howl and a nightmarish rush of abyssal aether. A shuddering cloud of deadly ink flooded the area, expanding in all directions.

There wasn't enough Unseelie aether in the canister to reach the Cinderwolves—but that was hardly the point. The cloud of Unseelie aether halted their charge before it even began, stymying their path to the longboat. If they wanted to make a run at us, they'd have to take the long way around.

I hoped that extra bit of time would be enough.

I handed back Little's revolver, before unbuckling the belt that Mr Finch had given me and starting to set it up on the flatbed. Little rummaged through the rotted tea for another canister and set it down next to us. My hands shook as I worked. Silently, I prayed that Mr Finch's device had held up through the fighting; I wasn't at all certain how delicate the gadget was. Either way, I didn't have the time for second guesses.

I grasped the canister's valve.

"When I give the word," I told Little, "I'll open the canister. You flip the switch. We run like there's no tomorrow."

Little nodded grimly.

I twisted the valve—slowly and *very* carefully. Inky aether barely snaked out of the canister, filling the air with a sharp hiss. This close, the rotten stench was overwhelming—and for just an instant,

I thought I saw a blood-red tinge to the obsidian ribbon that resulted.

I recoiled instinctively, but kept my hand on the valve. My body tensed, ready to leap off the longboat the moment I twisted it completely open. "Now!" I gasped.

Little hit the makeshift switch on Mr Finch's device. I twisted the lever, and Unseelie aether howled out of the canister in a nauseating rush. As I hauled myself out of the longboat, Little vaulted over the side, bolting for the crates nearest to the exit. I followed as quickly as I could, but my first mate had longer legs than I did, and I couldn't help but lag behind him.

Someone shouted an alarm from the row of crates just beside us. Now that the Cinderwolves had secured the second longboat, they were free to open fire on us. Gunfire blasted in our direction as Little and I raced down the narrow corridor. Crates chipped and burst from the small-arms fire—but the hangar was dark, and our cover served its function for the moment. Cinderwolves shouted, and their heavy jackboots grew ever louder.

I needed to gather my crew and get out of here. Fast.

Little hung back, firing down the corridor of boxes in order to pause the Cinderwolves' advance.

Ahead of me, bright flashes of aetheric light flared in violent bursts. Wraithwood and Miss Hawkins had resumed their fight; their silver swords sent harsh shadows skittering across the scenery, interspersed with the dancing lights of their foci.

Wraithwood had Hawkins hard-pressed. He attacked her with his flickering blade in a blur of deadly thrusts, forcing her into a constant backpedal. Each time, his whip followed suit, limiting her possible movement.

I dived behind a corner of nearby crates, lifting my blunderbuster in both hands. I had no illusions that I might bring down *Wraithwood*, of all people—but perhaps if I distracted him with a shot, I could lend Miss Hawkins the opportunity she needed in order to destroy the other longboat and make her escape.

Even as I watched, Hawkins staggered back from one of those

thrusts, falling abruptly to her knees. Her silver sword flickered once—then winked out of existence. She snapped up her aetheric shield in a frantic motion, barely quick enough to protect against the follow-up whip crack.

Wraithwood advanced relentlessly upon her, sensing sudden weakness. But from my perspective, I saw Hawkins reach furtively for her belt, snatching a silvery device from it. I heard the metallic *ping*, as she popped a pin free and let it clatter to the floor.

Wraithwood recognised the charade just a moment too late.

Hawkins tossed the small metallic bomb at his feet; it detonated with a muted *whoomph* before it even touched the ground.

A bubble of prismatic aether surged around Wraithwood, lifting him from the ground. Gravity gently reversed itself, pulling him into the air. His whip cracked again, every bit as deadly as before—but it was difficult for Wraithwood to *aim* it properly, as he floated sideways in a strangely drunken manner.

"Hawkins!" I yelled, stepping out from cover to catch her attention. "We need to go!"

But Miss Hawkins had levelled her gaze beyond Wraithwood, in the direction of the longboat that the Cinderwolves had just pulled into the *Conflagration*'s cargo bay.

They've reached the ship, I realised in sudden horror.

Hawkins raised her aether-powered gauntlet, aiming it directly at the crates on that longboat. Her palm burned with a sudden keening light as multiple vials of aether infused it, one by one.

She was going to shoot the Unseelie aether before the *Conflagration* could take off. As far as Miss Hawkins knew, she was following the plan. Either she hadn't realised the disastrous chain reaction she might cause with the ship's aetheric core... or else she didn't care.

I cared. I knew it instantly. In that moment, all of my previous moral grappling gave way to crystal clarity—I couldn't stand by and watch while my plan destroyed half the Aviary.

"Don't!" I yelled. I charged at Hawkins.

We collided—hard. Her gauntlet-focus erupted in a shrieking blast, even as we slammed into the ground. My ears popped, and every one of my hairs stood on end. Stars danced before my eyes... but through those dancing stars, I traced the path that Hawkins' aetheric blast had taken.

The shot had gone wide.

The Unseelie aether in the *Conflagration*'s cargo bay remained untouched. Off to the side, I saw that there was a Cinderwolf on the ground; the lance of light had punched a fist-sized hole through their shoulder, leaving the edges of their breastplate slagged and glowing white hot. Their arm still sizzled at the severed joint where it had been sheared clean off.

Every other person in the hangar had dived for cover... except for two. Strahl had taken the opportunity of the blast to leap upon Captain Altera; he now stood over the Cinderwolf captain with his sword lifted, intent on a killing blow.

Wraithwood, of course, had been trapped in that bubble of prismatic aether, unable to leap for cover. But the edges of the aetheric bubble had already begun to squirm uncomfortably around him—and I realised that Wraithwood was taking *control* of the aetheric construct.

The bubble twisted violently one more time—and then, all at once, it popped. Wraithwood fell to the ground with a slight stumble, fighting to regain his equilibrium.

"What have you *done*, Blair?" Hawkins demanded furiously. She shoved me off of her, rolling back to her feet in a panic. But whatever tirade she had in store for me died on her lips as she realised that Wraithwood was free.

I pushed to my knees and gripped my blunderbuster with both hands, aiming it frantically at Wraithwood.

The flick of Wraithwood's wrist was quicker than my trigger finger. His pale, glowing whip lashed out to strike me in the chest. The impact picked me up and sent me careening backwards.

I felt as though I'd been kicked in the chest by a horse. My ears rang; every nerve was electrified. Dark spots blinked before my eyes. I became dimly aware that I was bouncing across the open floor, slowly skidding to a halt. I stared up at the ceiling for a long moment, unable to move, as fire spread through my chest.

A few agonising seconds later, I managed to suck in a shuddering breath. Air exploded into my lungs—even more excruciating, somehow, than the crack of the whip against my chest had been. I forced myself to move through it, horrifyingly aware of the aetheric bomb that continued to tick its way down, elsewhere in the hangar.

Miss Hawkins had drawn her silver sword again, I saw—but she was too slow. Perhaps she'd expended too much aether at once... or perhaps yours truly had ruined her concentration. But the end result was the same: Wraithwood flicked his blade of light against Hawkins' sword in a contemptuous gesture, and her fabled weapon shattered into motes of poorly controlled aether.

Wraithwood reversed the blow, striking upwards. Hawkins screamed.

Blood splashed across the floor of the hangar, bright and wet. Hawkins fell onto her back, clutching her face with a keening cry. Garish scarlet seeped from between her fingers, staining her pale skin and bleached hair.

I expected Wraithwood to say something, perhaps. I don't know *why* I should have expected as much, but I did. Instead, he planted his boot on Hawkins' chest to pin her down, lifting that pale spike of light for one final thrust—

"Gideon! Stop!"

Strahl's voice boomed across the hangar... and Wraithwood halted abruptly.

Somewhere beneath my confusion, I wondered if Wraithwood had hesitated to strike *before* the demand or else because of it. It had all happened so close together that I couldn't seem to pick apart the order of events. Some part of me wanted to believe that I had seen him pause sooner, rather than later.

But either way, his attention was now *fully* occupied by my bosun in a way that I couldn't explain. That masked face turned slowly, searching out the origin of the voice that Wraithwood had heard.

Strahl approached Wraithwood carefully. As I watched, my bosun sheathed his bloodied sword and stretched his arms visibly to either side, in a calculated show of peace.

Wraithwood's aetheric whip winked out of existence like a snuffed candle. I saw Captain Altera still on the ground behind Strahl. The deathblow I'd seen about to fall upon the mercenary captain hadn't landed. Altera struggled to his knees, raising his aether pistol to aim at my bosun's back. But Wraithwood snapped out his hand in a violent gesture, and the captain held his fire.

A flicker of aether gathered weakly in Hawkins' hand. Wraithwood must have sensed it, however; he kicked her across her wounded face, only briefly distracted from the scene before him.

Hawkins gave a sharp yelp of pain, curling up onto the grimy floor in obvious agony. The aether died in her hand.

Strahl removed his helmet. His pale face and the washed-out stubble of hair on his head made him look like a ghost.

"Let the woman go," Strahl commanded Wraithwood. His voice was... changed. His rough and tumble accent had smoothed into crisp Imperial tones, filled with unshakeable authority. Perhaps it was simple bravado—but he had the air of a man who expected to be obeyed.

"By the Winds of Fortune," Wraithwood whispered. His voice sounded from behind his mask, utterly stunned. "It looks like Death wasn't victorious after all."

Strahl's expression was cold and flinty. "I won't repeat myself," he said.

Hawkins shifted on the ground to look towards me. Her face was a bloody mess—a wicked gash raced across it, still bleeding profusely. Her eyes were glassy with pain. But I saw her mouth form a single word:

Run.

The clock was still ticking down.

"And why would I let her go on your account... *boy?*" Wraithwood asked Strahl silkily. I heard the testing in his voice—but I wasn't certain just what it was he was looking to test.

Strahl's cold, confident demeanour wavered. Wraithwood had

called his bluff; whatever authority Strahl had tried to enforce, it was now long gone—buried with the Avalon Imperium, I thought.

Strahl swallowed. His face flickered with something dark and bitter. "Let her go," he said. "Let *all* of them go. And I'll... come with you."

Wraithwood scoffed. "Counteroffer," he said. "I kill the woman and the goblin, and you come with me, regardless. It's your duty, after all."

Wraithwood could have killed Hawkins; he had her at his feet, utterly helpless. But instead, he turned his awful mask my way, and his boots flared with aether, launching him towards me in one inhuman leap. Hawkins rolled weakly onto her side, bracing her left elbow against her gut, and I saw her gather aether into her overheated gauntlet in a last-ditch effort of willpower.

As for me?

I had the perfect seat to watch it all unfold—just as the Unseelie aether exploded.

18

LEFT BEHIND - NOT MY PROBLEM - HERESY - THE IMPERIUM'S FINEST

Only a week after Clan MacLeod had taken prisoner three cabin boys and a physicker, little things began to disappear around Pelaeia.

The northerners immediately blamed us—especially me. A few of the locals argued with Dougal in hushed tones before I found myself shut away entirely, closeted with a very apologetic-looking Elfa.

A day later, we heard shouts from the general direction of the grounded *HMS Caliban*. One of the northerners appeared, hissing something urgent towards Elfa. She glanced at me in turn, nodding towards the ruckus. "Come with me, William," she said. "I could use your help."

Elfa strode for the *HMS Caliban*, while I hurried along behind her. The northerners had started taking our old ship apart, in order to use it for scrap. As we crossed the bloodstained deck, I had the unsettling impression that I was walking across a dead, decaying corpse, rather than across a vessel.

We descended through silent, empty corridors, into the very core of the engine room. Rust and condensation streaked down the surrounding pipes; bullet-holes pocked the hull, and dried blood covered the floor. I was surprised to find Holloway already there, along with a few burly northerners. All of them were staring at a storage compartment set into the bulkhead, half-hidden behind a set of twisted, buckled pipes.

"Just yank th'lad out!" one of the northerners snapped.

"I tried," another one hissed back. "He bit me!"

Something moved inside the compartment, but I couldn't make out many details. Elfa shuffled me forwards and cleared her throat.

"Perhaps," she said, "one of the other boys ought to say hello?"

Holloway and the northerners glanced back at me. The physicker smiled worriedly, kneeling down to speak with me in a careful tone. "It seems we've got a friend in there, William," he said softly. "He's scared, I think, and not coming out. Do you think you might be able to squeeze past those pipes and convince him?"

I glanced at the mess of pipes. I was just small enough to fit through them. I nodded uncertainly, and Holloway reached out to squeeze at my shoulder.

I had to take off my coat to crawl through the damaged pipes. By the time I'd reached the boy inside, I was already shivering with the cold.

The boy's eyes were sunken and bright with fever; sweat plastered his golden hair to his head. He'd scavenged a bloody uniform from a dead engineer and a scarf from somewhere in Pelaeia. He was shaking, flinching, terrified. In his trembling hand, he clutched a single piece of bread.

It took me a few moments to realise that I recognised him. Once, Barsby had been Vice-Admiral Wakefield's favourite aide; the man's constant praise had fuelled Barsby's youthful self-importance so much that he regularly lorded himself over the rest of the youths on-board. Barsby had talked often of the shining naval career that he would someday have, once he became a proper soldier.

The boy in front of me was no longer self-important. Rather—he was ragged, and scared, and crying.

"Barsby?" I said softly. "It's me, Wil."

I had to repeat myself a few times. Barsby kept staring at me, as though the words didn't make sense to him.

"W-Wil?" he croaked finally. His voice was parched. His eyes fixed on mine. "I don't want to die, Wil," he whispered.

"You're not going to die," I promised him quietly. "I'm still here, Barsby. You're not alone."

I don't think the words ever registered with him. Not really.

* * *

A SHARP WAIL screeched through the air, like a thousand nails on a chalkboard—followed by a hollow *crunch*. A dreadful cloud blossomed and then burst into a nauseous, feverish shockwave. Cinderwolves doubled over, retching into their masks.

A jolt of blue aether shuddered through the cloud like lightning, igniting the gaseous nightmare into a violent, burning mass. The strange fires melted through steel, and I heard a twisted moan as the deck near the edge of the platform began to sag.

Wraithwood spun to face the strange detonation. The movement brought him mask-to-face with Strahl.

My bosun drew his sword again, whipping it down in a rapid two-handed blow. The sword's edge glowed white hot, and I knew that he had triggered its aetheric battery.

Wraithwood parried Strahl's attack with a lightning-quick motion, sparking aether along both blades as they kissed. My bosun's weapon slammed into the metal-plated floor, sinking deeply into the ground.

Wraithwood dismissed his silver sword with a sudden burst. Aether gathered around his fist—and lashed out in a vicious backhand. The discharge plucked Strahl from his feet, sending him backwards to land in a limp pile on the floor.

"Bring him with us!" Wraithwood commanded one of the Cinderwolves.

I snatched up my blunderbuster, desperately searching for a last-minute plan—but alarms blared suddenly through the Aviary, throwing me off-balance once again. Blinking yellow hazard lights flashed on every wall, just in case anyone had missed the deafening klaxons.

Wraithwood shot a wary look at the cloud of hideous untamed aether, slowly expanding towards the docked ships. I knew he was trying to calculate how much time he had to kill us all.

In that moment of hesitation, Hawkins saved us both.

Miss Hawkins fired the blast that she'd been gathering. The recoil propelled her across the greasy floor, slamming her into me. I let out a surprised yelp as we both slid towards the side door.

As I came to a stop, I found myself staring dazedly up at the ceiling, unable to move for several seconds. Just as I regained my will to move, however, Little's strong, familiar hands plucked me off the ground and settled me onto my feet.

"Upsy daisy, Cap'n," Lenore chuckled, from behind some nearby boxes. At some point during the chaos, she'd descended from her perch in order to join our retreat; her rifle remained balanced atop a crate, pointed towards the cloud of clashing aether.

Miss Hawkins pushed herself up from the floor with agonising slowness. Little reached out to help her—but by the time he'd grasped her arm, she was already upright. Blood dripped down her face where Wraithwood's sword had caught her. A long, awful slash ran from her jaw to her scalp; the blow had missed her eye by less than an inch.

She was alive. She was standing. For now, the rest was immaterial.

"Mr Strahl is on the other side of that mess," Lenore observed crisply. "What's our move, Cap'n?"

Little glanced at me, silently echoing Lenore's question.

My throat tightened up. I knew the answer I had to give. Some part of me wanted to flail for a different option—to pull another wild plan out of thin air. But we were barely standing, and the deck had been thoroughly stacked against us.

That was why Strahl had intervened in the first place. He'd known it was a sacrifice play.

"Fall back," I said hoarsely. The words felt like a bitter betrayal.

Little blinked. Even Lenore rocked back a bit, as though the words had struck her in the chest. But neither of them stopped to argue. Instead, Lenore snapped up her rifle, backing slowly towards the door.

"The Unseelie aether—" Hawkins rasped.

I grabbed her arm and hauled her back with me. Despite her lingering protest, she offered no real resistance. Some part of her knew that it was over.

Deeper inside the hangar, Wraithwood's tattered grey form rocketed up to the catwalks in a single leap. He spread his hands out before him, as though grappling with invisible strings. Fresh nausea rippled through my stomach as the roiling cloud of aether... paused.

Very slowly, the aether's loud shriek changed pitch, descending into a low groan.

I didn't wait to find out just how much control Wraithwood had managed to exert over that cloud. I pushed the hangar door closed behind us.

The Aviary's corridors were a chaotic mess. Flashing lights and blaring klaxons overwhelmed my senses. Even so, it was difficult to miss the air-carriage that had parked itself directly next to the side door from which we'd emerged. Its door was open and waiting, though I couldn't make out what awaited us inside.

"Fire on deck two," an alarmed male voice called out over the Aviary's vox. *"Fire on deck two! Please evacuate to the nearest—"*

The carriage's worried driver gestured me over urgently. Strands of wiry grey hair peeked out from beneath his driver's cap, evoking a permanently harried expression. Morgause's grime had settled into the deep lines on his face, beneath the thick goggles that covered his eyes. A long, well-trimmed moustache trembled at the edges of his lips, humming in time with the panic in the air around us.

"Are these your friends, little miss?" the driver called down to the carriage. His voice was high-pitched, but he made it carry over the din through the sheer force of his lungs.

"Yes, Mr Saito, that's them!" Mary's voice trickled out of the carriage.

The driver scrunched up his face as he looked down at us. "Lookin' like trouble, innit?" he observed. "Best we take off. Dockin' bay ninety-four?"

Irritation flared within me as I realised that Mary had disobeyed my orders *again*. But I didn't have time to indulge the feeling. Lenore had already hopped up onto the driver's seat next to him, while Little helped Miss Hawkins up into the carriage. "Ninety-four!" I acknowledged, as I hauled myself inside.

I pulled the door sharply closed behind me. "Mary," I started hotly. "I told you to—"

The carriage lurched forwards. I planted my free hand against the roof to prevent myself from falling into someone's lap, just next to me. I looked up from my awkward position at the company I'd just joined.

Little sat across from me in the carriage, still holding Miss Hawkins up against his shoulder. He'd pressed a kerchief against her face in an effort to staunch the bleeding there—but the material was already soaked through with blood. Mary sat primly next to them both, with her palm-pistol casually levelled in my direction. For just an instant, I thought she was aiming at *me*... but in fact, her gun was pointed at the dark, scowling figure just *next* to me.

Barsby offered me a thin, long-suffering smile. "Hello, William," he said acidly. "Heading my way?"

* * *

Silence stretched uncomfortably in the air-carriage as our driver hurried us on. Mr Saito threaded through the traffic like a needle, shouting in three different languages at the pedestrians blocking our way.

I trembled with adrenaline as I sat next to Barsby, squeezing my free hand into a fist on my lap in an attempt to control my racing heart.

"I told you to hurry back to the *Rose*," I accused Mary quietly.

Mary still had her gun trained on Barsby. She kept her eyes on him as she spoke to me. "I *was* going back to the ship," she said. "I almost ran right into Mr Saito's carriage. He said a nice young lady like me shouldn't be wandering around in this part of town. So I asked him for a ride there and back again. It occurred to me, Cap'n, that there's not much use in having the *Rose* ready to go if we're waiting on you to get back there."

I blinked at her very slowly. Presently, it dawned on me that Mary had done something incredibly reasonable with the looser leash I'd given her.

I shouldn't have been surprised. I wondered why I *was* surprised. Somewhere along the way, I had forgotten that I was trying to protect a girl who'd protected *herself* for several years already.

"I... see," I managed. "That was... thank you, Mary. We needed this." Again, the flash of uncertainty on her face made me curse myself. Privately, I promised myself a long, hard look at our relationship as soon as we were out of immediate danger.

"Typical," Barsby muttered, just next to me. "You didn't even plan a getaway. Were you planning on running from Wraithwood on *foot*, William?"

I grimaced at him. "And... what is *he* doing here?" I asked Mary.

Mary offered me a sunny, insincere smile. "Oh, he must've thought he'd hitch a getaway ride with me," she answered. "I thought that was a *swell* idea, so I asked him to stay. Politely."

"Oh, *please*," Barsby spat at her. "If I'd wanted to leave, I would have. We both know you wouldn't really shoot me—"

Mary's small pistol cracked within the confines of the carriage, blowing a tiny hole in the seat between Barsby's legs. She smoothly inched the pistol upwards once again, until it was once more pointed at Barsby's chest.

"You don't *know* me, mister," Mary told him pleasantly.

Barsby stared at her with a new hint of wariness.

"Start talking, Barsby," I ordered him. Fury rose in my chest; I had to grit the words through clenched teeth. "What were you thinking, taking a job from *Wraithwood?*"

Barsby shot me a bitter, condescending smile. "Oh, come now, William," he replied. "When men like Wraithwood offer you a job, it's never a polite request. Everyone involved in this job knew what would happen if they said no... or if they *failed*." Barsby rubbed at his neck and swallowed hard. "The money was just a bonus. I was supposed to be filthy stinking rich by now—rich enough to retire in comfort for the rest of my days. Instead, here I am. With *you*."

"You are... *such* a pathetic coward," I said. My voice trembled. Never before had I loathed Barsby quite so much as I did in that moment... and I'd had plenty of reasons to hate him *before*.

"Cowards live, William," Barsby said, without an inch of shame.

I swallowed down my fury with great difficulty. There would be time for recriminations later; right now, I needed information. "You knew the cargo was Unseelie aether," I observed to Barsby. "You were expecting it, back in New Havenshire. Did someone tell you?"

Barsby stared back at me in icy silence. I knew then that he was about to push his luck, Mary's gun be damned.

Miss Hawkins struggled back to a stiff, upright posture, fixing cold grey eyes upon the man across from her. Blood dripped freely down her chin as she rasped at him. "If you don't answer, I'll take your other hand, here and now. See if I don't."

Barsby jerked his gaze to her, suddenly wide-eyed with fear. It was a twin expression to the one he'd worn while dealing with Wraithwood. I wondered, suddenly, if I ought to be more concerned about that than I was.

"Wraithwood told me about the Unseelie aether himself," Barsby stammered out. "He said Red Reaver traffics in the stuff—said he wanted a whole ship-load of it, and he didn't care how. So I... I called in some very big favours with some very bad people. They did the stealing. I handled the logistics." He shrank back against the carriage seat, as though searching for a way to put one extra inch between himself and Hawkins. "That crew's expecting money Wraithwood never gave me, now. A lot of it."

"*Wait*," I sputtered, holding up a hand. "Red Reaver *traffics* in Unseelie aether?"

Miss Hawkins had rallied admirably in order to pry this answer from Barsby—but the effort had cost her greatly. The steel in her spine now collapsed abruptly. She leaned heavily against Little once again, shuddering with pain.

A hint of scorn leaked back into Barsby's manner at the sight, and he raised an eyebrow at me. "Red Reaver's ships *run* on Unseelie aether," he clarified. "You can't have failed to notice, William."

I remembered the hideous screaming engine of the *Red Reaver's Revenge*. Somehow, though Red Reaver's pirates were foolish enough to keep Unseelie aether on their ship, it hadn't occurred to me that they might be foolish enough to run an entire *ship* on the stuff. Was it really any wonder that old Ironspine had howled so badly at the death of that vessel?

The greater implications of what Barsby had just said trickled in at the edges of my mind... and I blanched.

"Red Reaver has a steady supply of Unseelie aether," I said slowly. "She didn't just find a cache or a small bubble of it. She's got enough to run her ships on it."

Little met my eyes over Miss Hawkins' head. Quiet horror had dawned in his expression.

"Either Red Reaver has an Unseelie sponsor," I whispered, "or else there's been a Breaching."

Mary frowned at me. Unlike the rest of us, she'd never lived under the Avalon Imperium; she'd certainly never worn an Imperial uniform or sworn an Imperial Oath. She hadn't had officers reminding her at every turn just what the Avalon Imperium was supposed to guard us all against.

"My money's on a Breaching," Barsby said with a shrug. "Or it would be, if I had any money. Thanks again for that, William."

I stared at him. "You're awfully calm about this, Barsby," I said. "You know just as well as the rest of us what a Breaching would mean."

"The end of everything the Seelie once created," Barsby replied flatly. "That includes you, me, and all the other children of Avalon. The Unseelie will tear us all apart and dance on our remains." He shrugged. "If the Imperium hadn't fallen, we'd be on the front lines against those monsters right now. Ironic, isn't it, that we'll live a little longer this way? If there *has* been a Breaching, then it won't happen all at once. It might take years for the Unseelie to tear open a rift large enough to cross with an army."

I drew in a shuddering breath. Wraithwood's latest atrocities had just taken on a fresh new meaning.

Centuries ago, the Avalon Imperium had fought back a Breaching and sealed the tear into Avalon. But that had been the Imperium at the height of its power, with a strong, well-unified army and a full complement of Wargears and Silver Legionnaires.

There was no Avalon Imperium now. There was no grand army. Many of our wargears were broken or missing, and even more of the silver swords had disappeared. If we were very lucky, we might have as much as a decade before a horde of twisted nightmares from the Evernight descended upon us. It was barely enough time to rebuild even a semblance of our former defences.

"Maybe the Imperialists have a point after all, William," Barsby said softly. His eye gleamed as he spoke; he was goading me, just because he could. "I know you'd rather die than admit it, but—"

"Wraithwood wants you dead," I told Barsby coldly. "That's the only reason I'm not killing you myself. With luck, maybe he'll expend a little spare effort hunting you down."

Barsby scoffed. "You wouldn't kill me, William," he said. "You've never had the—"

"You hired yourself out to Imperialists." I cut him off sharply. The dark, ugly anger inside of me rose into my throat and leaked into my voice. "People have already died because of you, Barsby. And even more will die before this is over."

Barsby's face flared with rage. "I was looking out for *myself*—"

"—and by doing that, you sat down at the table with *butchers*," I hissed. "You don't get to have it both ways, Barsby. You can't screw over other people by looking out for yourself and then ask them to look out for *you*. You chose your friends—and now, they want you dead." I looked at Mary and jerked my head sharply towards the carriage door. "Let him out."

Barsby cleared his throat and offered a nervous, placating smile. "We haven't stopped," he noted.

"I've decided that's your problem and not mine," I told him. I paused. "Huh. That *is* freeing, isn't it? I should learn from you and ignore other people's problems more often."

"Very clever, William," Barsby snarled. "You've made your point—"

Mary grabbed the handle with her left hand and pushed the door open. Bustling traffic milled in the Aviary outside. The klaxons were still blaring. Barsby clung to the doorframe with his one hand as he stared down at the rushing ground, ten feet below us. His remaining eye quickly scanned for a safe place to toss himself, but judging by the look on his face, none was readily apparent.

Good.

I locked gazes with him. "If we ever cross paths again and I find you with those Imperialists," I shouted over the din, "I'll kill you myself."

Barsby's face split into an ugly glower. "I wish I could be there to see what Wraithwood does to you when he gets his hands on you, you little—"

Little carefully tucked Hawkins into a corner of the carriage, and then stood up. Barsby shut his mouth abruptly—but my first mate grabbed the handlebars on either side of the doorframe and planted a firm boot into Barsby's chest, shoving him out of the carriage.

Barsby fell with a rasping scream.

Little offered a single, silent gesture towards the open door. I'd tell you what it meant, but the translation isn't really fit for polite company.

Little closed the door.

"Thank you, Mr Little," I told him.

Little turned my way and flicked a casual salute. He settled himself back into his seat, leaning over to check on Miss Hawkins.

Now that Barsby was gone, Mary stashed her tiny pistol, fixing her eyes on the groaning aethermancer next to Little. "So... you're really a Silver Legionnaire?" Mary asked softly. Her expression was torn halfway between worry and wonder.

Mary must have stayed in the hangar long enough to have seen that silver sword. I sighed quietly, knowing full well where this conversation was about to lead.

"No," Miss Hawkins replied in a trembling voice. "Never that." Her iron will had now dissipated into exhaustion.

Mary shot her a quizzical look. But the answer had done much to soothe my fresh worries about the woman across from us.

"Miss Hawkins has a silver sword," I said, in order to spare her the extra conversation. "She was *trained* by a Silver Legionnaire. But she never took an Oath to the emperor. That matters."

It was a crucial distinction. It mattered to *me* more than ever, now that I'd seen Miss Hawkins next to a real Silver Legionnaire.

Miss Hawkins wasn't cruel enough or amoral enough to lay claim to that title.

"You didn't know," I observed to Hawkins now. "Or else you just weren't thinking. It didn't occur to you what would happen if you blew up that Unseelie aether in the ship's hold."

Miss Hawkins grimaced, reaching up to press the kerchief more tightly against her face. "In the ship's hold..." She struggled with the concept, as though trying to put the pieces together. She had the requisite knowledge available to her, though—and a moment later, I saw the implications hit her. She caved in upon herself with an awful gasp. "Oh," she whispered. "Rot and ruin."

I sighed heavily. "You *could* have blown up half the Aviary," I assured her. "But you didn't. That's what matters."

"Because you're a hero." Somehow, Mary managed to speak the words with a perfectly straight face. "Have you... ever read *The Strange Adventures of Jack Blue*, Miss Hawkins?"

And there it was.

"I don't believe that I have," Miss Hawkins mumbled back. "Why?"

A small window slid open between the passengers' cabin and the driver's seat, saving us all from the ensuing conversation.

"Did you just toss a man out of the carriage, Cap'n?" Lenore asked me.

"I did not," I said truthfully. "Mr Little did that."

Lenore arched an eyebrow at me. "Suppose he deserved it?" she guessed.

My gaze drifted back towards the carriage door. "He probably deserved worse," I said quietly.

Part of me felt guilty at the thought. I remembered Barsby's first words to me when I'd found him, all those years ago: *"I don't want to die, Wil."*

I'd made a silent promise to Barsby that day—that I would help him, that I would be there for him. But he hadn't wanted any of that, no matter how much I thought he *needed* it.

I should have listened to him that day. I should have really *heard* the words he'd said. If I had, I might have realised that Barsby didn't want comfort, or friendship, or anything else of the sort.

Barsby didn't want to die. It was the only thing he would ever care about. And while I couldn't help but sympathise on some level, I also knew that he would let the world burn if it bought him even one more second.

* * *

Mr Saito dropped us off at the *Rose*. Though we were in a hurry, I made sure that he left with a *very* generous tip, given the new holes in his carriage and our preference that he forget our names.

While I paid off our transportation, Little helped Miss Hawkins aboard, with Mary hovering close behind him. By the time I rushed up to join them, the *Rose* was already humming with intention, ready to cast off. I gave the order, and we rose into the choked skies about Morgause.

Our once-pristine sails were a smoky, filth-streaked mess. The hull was in a similar state. A thin layer of grime coated every surface; even the wheel's spokes were greasy. The ship's wood stank of ash and soot.

I charted a vague course southward towards the coast. Soon enough, I'd have to figure out where we were actually headed—but we needed out of Morgause *now*, before someone connected us to the trouble in the Aviary. Once we were underway, I left the deck in

Little's capable hands, with orders to alert me if trouble decided to follow us.

It had occurred to me that I needed answers. For once, I knew precisely where to find them.

I headed swiftly into my cabin, pulling the door closed behind me. "Syrene," I called out. "We need to talk!"

The wood beneath my feet rippled like vaguely disturbed water. A path snaked its way towards the bulkhead. Syrene stepped from it slowly, melting into view.

I was shocked at how gaunt Syrene had become while we were in Morgause. Her form was even leaner and more brittle than usual; a cascade of dead, ugly plants spilled from her head. Anxiety roiled off of her, stealing my breath and setting my heart racing.

"Why is Strahl gone?" she asked. Her melodic voice felt deeper and less friendly than usual.

I took a deep breath, steeling myself against the disquiet she radiated. "We ran afoul of the people Barsby was working for," I said. "They recognised Strahl. He... decided to buy us time to escape." My own fear rose within me as I thought of Strahl in Wraithwood's tender care—but I fixed my gaze upon her, forcing myself to think through my cloying panic. "You're bonded to Strahl. He found you once when you were hidden. Can you feel where he is, too?"

"We can," Syrene said. Her black eyes went distant, focussing just past my shoulder. Her anxiety banked itself to warm embers, rather than a roaring flame. Her posture relaxed, and I knew then that Strahl still lived. She returned her uncanny gaze to me. "Who has taken him?" she asked.

I swallowed. My throat felt dry. "Wraithwood," I said. "Him and the Cinderwolves."

Syrene's hands clenched. Her wooden, claw-like fingers rasped against her palms. In the half-light of my cabin, she reminded me of the feral barghests that haunted the Coalditch district. "Wraithwood *dares*," she hissed. "He will suffer."

"Why?" I asked her. "Why would Wraithwood take Strahl? They clearly know each other, and not just in passing." I stared down

Syrene, dredging up the courage to ask her the question I had avoided for so many years. "Who is Strahl, Syrene?"

Syrene ignored the question. "We must retrieve Strahl," she said. "We will direct you—"

"*No*," I said. "Not yet. I want to know the truth, Syrene. I have carried both of you on this ship without question for years now. But I'm not doing this blindly anymore. You're asking me to take on *Wraithwood*—and I will do it, Tuath help me. But I want to know what I'm dealing with first."

Syrene fell silent. The air between us vibrated strangely for a moment as her emotions churned. But still, she said nothing.

I clenched my jaw. "Syrene—" I started.

"We cannot say," Syrene told me. Her many black eyes focussed upon me, dark and intense. "Strahl has forbidden us."

"Strahl has... *forbidden* you?" I asked. The idea was ridiculous. Mortals did not *forbid* faeries from doing anything. "You owe him a debt, then? He asked you to keep his secret—"

"No," Syrene said quietly. "There is no debt. Only obligation." The words made her deeply uneasy; a few more of the petals on her head withered, and I knew that she was skirting the edge of the promise she had made to Strahl. She caught a newly dried flower as it drifted from her brow, shivering with discomfort. "Ask no more questions on this subject, Captain. Please."

I drew in a deep breath. I couldn't ask about Strahl directly... but Syrene had left me an opening on purpose. I could ask her questions on *other* subjects. "Wraithwood wants Unseelie aether so he can conjure up an army," I said. "He's working with Imperialists. Barsby thinks they're trying to resurrect the Imperium—or something like it, anyway. He thinks there's been a Breaching." I watched Syrene's mask-like face, though I knew I would see nothing of her emotions there. "If there *had* been a Breaching... would you know it, Syrene?"

Syrene tilted her head at me. "There has... surely been a Breaching," she said softly. "We have seen too much evidence now."

My heart dropped into my stomach. The confirmation was overwhelming. It was exactly what I'd hoped *not* to hear.

"The Imperium will stop the Breaching," Syrene told me. "That is why the Imperium exists. But we *must* find Strahl."

Words failed me. I blinked at the faerie. She was so sure of herself, so calm. I could *feel* the confidence radiating from her.

"The Imperium is *dead*, Syrene," I said slowly. "There is no emperor. There is no royal house or grand army. The Silver Legionnaires and the wargears are scattered and broken. All that's left are a bunch of ruthless criminals ready to crush the rest of us into compliance all over again."

Syrene met my gaze evenly. "There is hope then," she said, utterly missing my sarcasm.

I stared at her. "The return of the Imperium is not a *good* thing, Syrene," I said. "People turned on it for damned good reasons. It failed its people. It *fed* on its people, like some awful machine."

"The Avalon Imperium was never meant to serve its people," Syrene told me calmly. "It was created to serve *us*."

The simple words drove the breath from my chest.

Given Syrene's verbal eccentricities, she could have been referring to herself, personally. But I knew that she wasn't. She was talking about the Everbright. The holy Tuath Dé.

Like a longhorn flicking on, I suddenly knew with absolute certainty who was to blame for our current predicament. Dougal MacLeod had said it to me, several years ago. I'd argued with him at the time... but Syrene had just confirmed everything he believed, right to my face.

"Then *you* failed us," I told her flatly. "All of you."

Syrene tilted her head again. "We made you," she said. "You are our shield. If you break, you will fail *us*. But we cannot fail you. That is... impossible."

Black, incredulous rage rose up within my chest. For just a moment, I managed to forget that Strahl was still missing, that Wraithwood had what he wanted—all I could focus on was the horribly indifferent faerie in front of me.

"You don't *own* us!" I burst out. "We're not... *toys*, Syrene! We're living, thinking people!"

Syrene was unmoved. "We made you," she repeated—as though I might not have heard her the first time. "You belong to us. It is your purpose to defend us. We gave you aether. We armed you with wargears and silver swords—"

"—and we turned them on each other!" I yelled at her. "And you said *nothing!* You gave your children loaded guns and let them murder one another with your gifts!" I was so angry, so miserably *furious*. My hands shook at my sides. Bile had started creeping up my throat. "You took sides. You helped the Imperium force the world to heel, and people still rebelled, they *still* overthrew your puppets."

"Foolish," Syrene said. "Without an Imperium, the Unseelie will destroy you. Your world will burn."

My hackles rose. "The world is already burning," I said. "It burns in *your* name. And frankly... I don't see much of a difference between you and the Unseelie right now."

Nothing I'd said so far had fazed Syrene—but *this* elicited a dark, sudden fury. She straightened her withered body to its full height, towering over me. Her abnormally long fingers splintered into razor-tipped talons of polished wood. Immortal terror buffeted my soul, trying to worm its way inside me.

I hated her so much in that moment, I forgot to be afraid.

"Remember your place," Syrene hissed at me.

I laughed.

Syrene jerked back in confusion. She was used to people cowering before her when she exerted herself. Like the Imperium itself, I realised, she didn't know what to do when her servants decided they would rather die than bow.

"Look at you," I said. "You don't even understand what you've made. You're like a child shaking your fist at the sky, demanding for the rain to stop and the sun to rise. You can be as frightening as you want, Syrene—but that won't change the fact that I *hate* you. It certainly won't change the fact that you're a foolish, petty tyrant."

Syrene stared at me, flexing her wicked claws. I waited for her to leap upon me, to tear me to pieces... but as the seconds dragged on, I remembered belatedly that she had sworn to obey my authority so long as she remained upon my ship.

She *couldn't* harm me. Not right now, anyway.

"I'm not abandoning Strahl to his fate," I told her. "It's not his fault you're a cruel little sapling. I'm going to follow Wraithwood. I'm going to stop him—somehow, I don't know how—and I'm going to save Strahl. You can help me do that, or you can flee this ship to go and sulk. The choice is yours, Syrene."

I met her stare, perfectly unyielding. For once, my hate buoyed me, and I didn't fear it. I remembered the wailing echoes of Pelaeia—the ghosts of the Imperium, victimised by the Seelie Tuath Dé and their monstrous gifts to the mortals of Avalon.

Syrene looked away first.

"We will remain," she replied quietly. Her words were tight. "We will follow Strahl's trail."

"Good," I said. The word was so chilly, it nearly blistered my lips. "Go chart us a course to follow him, then."

Syrene turned away from me, melting back into the bulkhead. The wood rippled behind her, and then stilled.

I wondered for a moment whether she intended to follow the order. But the *Rose* soon began to alter its course.

I let out a breath, releasing the fist-sized clump of rage that had laid anchor in my chest. It didn't help much.

You were right, Dougal, I thought. *Our gods are evil. What are we supposed to do with that?*

More than ever, I wished he was there. I wanted to commiserate with his justified rage. I wanted to tell him that I finally understood, that he was no longer alone in his fury.

But Dougal was gone. Even now, his clan was probably sending him off with a kind word from an oblivious halcyon. The injustice of it all was so keen that I couldn't even get my mind around it. I knew I would have to work my way up to it over time, digesting the awfulness in small, bitter bites.

Somewhere at the edge of my awareness, however, I became aware that our heading seemed... odd. I pulled out my compass, staring down at the arrow inside of it.

We were heading east by southeast.

But Pelaeia was *north* of us.

I had no doubts that Syrene knew where she was going. But why would Wraithwood be headed in that direction? He had his Unseelie aether, and his infernal device. Pelaeia had a seething concentration of echoes ready to enslave, and barely any defences capable of holding him off.

I headed to a cabinet and pulled out a drawer, snatching up a map of the continent. I unrolled it over a table, pinpointing our location over the duchy of Mavra. I traced a path east by southeast... and my blood soon ran cold.

I remembered the capital city yawning beneath my feet as I clung to the rigging of the *HMS Caliban*. I remembered the screams that rose from below as the citizens of Galtir realised their impending doom. I remembered the unprecedented aetheric explosion of the *Sovereign Majesty*, great enough to engulf several city districts.

Wraithwood didn't want a scattering of ragtag rebel echoes and their wailing children. No—he had set his sights much higher than that. He had pointed himself towards the site of the Imperium's last stand: an aether-irradiated wasteland where hardened soldiers and citizens alike had died. A city full of dead Imperial heroes ready to carve out a brand new empire.

Wraithwood was headed to Galtir.

INTERLUDE

HMS EREBUS - ARCTURUS - A TASTE OF GLORY

I'd never wanted to see Gideon Frey again. In all honesty, I'd hoped he was dead.

The feeling wasn't mutual. For now, anyway.

I remained sluggish and half-aware as two of the Cinderwolves dragged me onto the *HMS Erebus*—Jonathan Silver's old vessel. A vicious, instinctive self-preservation pressed at my mind, urging me to fight them off, but the impulse just wouldn't translate into action.

I lost time in between blinks.

A burning cloud roiled on the docks, swelling like a storm. Panicked shouts muffled strangely in my ears. Horrible, dying screams cut through the din. Someone hauled me away.

I was on the gangplank, being pulled onto that sleek, deadly ship. No—I was tossed onto a cot in a small, dark room. A blurry silhouette leaned over me. Serpentine, inhuman eyes narrowed in the half-light. Someone pressed their hands to my jaw, forcing me to look up into the flickering light of the ship's aether-lanterns. I tried to slap the hands away, but I somehow missed them by several inches. My limbs felt leaden.

"Definitely concussed," a woman murmured. A chorus of hisses accompanied the words, like an aether-engine with a dozen simultaneous leaks. "Is he important?"

"Very," murmured Gideon, somewhere to my right.

The hands released my jaw, and my head flopped back into the cot of its own accord.

"Probably shouldn't have hit him so hard, then," the woman said dryly. "Best case, he recovers completely. Worst case, he dies in the next twenty-four hours."

"You can't do anything about that?" Gideon asked. His voice was cold and calm. I knew he wasn't emotionally attached to me. I was an unexpected prize—an asset for which he was surely already imagining a hundred different uses.

"Come and get me if he starts seizing," the woman said. "I have things I can try. They're all wildly dangerous, of course. Honestly, praying will probably get you better results."

She pushed to her feet, and my eyes focussed for just a moment. I saw a woman in a sharp Cinderwolf uniform. She'd discarded her gas mask to reveal a tawny, scaled face and slitted emerald eyes. A writhing mass of black and red snakes topped her head.

She spat on my face.

"Is that strictly necessary, Sergeant?" Gideon asked in an amused voice.

"I take it personally when people try to kill me," she replied.

"Peculiar sentiment for a mercenary," Gideon observed.

"I didn't claim it was rational," the gorgon said.

She turned smartly on her heel and headed for a door, somewhere outside of my peripheral view. I reached up weakly to wipe at the spittle on my cheek.

"Honourless turncoat coward," I mumbled at her. It took every bit of strength I had—but the words burned in my throat, desperate to be said.

The gorgon paused her footsteps.

"Poor feelings all around," Gideon said. "Well. Doesn't matter." I couldn't see him... but I *felt* the frigid gaze of his mask as it settled upon the gorgon. "Keep walking, Sergeant Esmeranza."

He didn't have to speak any threats aloud. Everyone on this ship was well aware of his capabilities... and his lack of moral qualms.

The door opened to my left. It closed again with a soft, barely discernible noise.

And then, I was alone with Gideon Frey.

"You've been out of the army for far too long," he told me mildly. "Don't you remember what a poor idea it is to antagonise the physicker?"

I closed my eyes. My jaw still ached from Gideon's aether-powered backhand; my skull felt like it was slowly splitting in two. I had to concentrate in order to follow the conversation. "How can you work with Cinderwolves?" I asked hoarsely. "They're *traitors*."

I shifted to look at him with great difficulty. My mind perceived him as a collection of dirty shadows, hidden behind that expressionless mask.

"Ah yes," Gideon said. "*Those* rumours." He ruminated on the idea. "Quite true, m'afraid. The Emerald Spires were willing to help us quash the rebels, so long as the emperor spared them the Tithes. But eventually, the empire had no choice but to ask them to do their duty. The moment we asked the Emerald Spires to send their own Tithes, they turned on us." I heard the loathing, the unutterable *disgust* in his voice. "The Cinderwolves in the emperor's honour guard are responsible for all of this. They sabotaged the *Sovereign Majesty*. They destroyed Galtir. Arguably, they ended the entire empire."

I couldn't help the stab of violent hatred that overwhelmed me at the confirmation. It didn't matter that I'd decided the empire *deserved* to die.

At least the rebels had fought for something they believed in. The Spires and their Cinderwolves were self-serving hypocrites.

"I didn't get to choose my associates," Gideon assured me. He raised his gloved hand in an appeasing manner. His greying fingertips were smeared with black, as though they'd been charred; the movement made his arm twitch with pain. "Someone else is paying the tab. Ironically, I *do* work well with the Cinderwolves. It's rather like old times."

My irrational pounding hatred fled me at those words, replaced instead by a sickening image of the haunted slopes of Pelaeia—what Gideon and the Cinderwolves had left behind them. That brief, flickering thought flooded me with such nauseous guilt that I had to roll onto my side to vomit onto the floor next to me.

Then again, it might have just been the concussion.

"I'm sure that's not a *good* sign for your health," Gideon sighed. "Pity. I put years of hard work into keeping you alive once. I suppose there would be a certain black humour in it if you died of a bad blow to the head *now*." He paused thoughtfully. "How *did* you survive? The Coalition shelled that entire hill straight to oblivion. We were picking up pieces of your wargear off the other end of the battlefield."

The reminder sent my confused mind straight back into memory. Panic oozed in at the edges of my consciousness, as reality blurred into the nightmare that I still endured, night after night.

That *hill*.

I was blinded. Frenzied. Aether hissed around me, venting into the cockpit—choking every inch of me with a sick, incoherent vitality that made my heart beat a terrifying metronome.

Metal twisted and screeched. Wooden roots grew between the panels with unnatural speed, prying them open to the sky. Dimly, I imagined I could hear my wargear screaming as those reaching fingers tore it apart. I abandoned it all the same, clawing my way free of the metal tomb as ruptured coolant hissed from it like blood.

My body hit the ground. Wet mud squelched beneath me. A tree loomed above me, burning with terrible blue aether. It had no mouth. It could not scream.

Gideon nudged me with his toe, and I choked on a shuddering breath.

"Syrene," I rasped. "She sacrificed herself to save me."

I turned my face against the cold floor, hoping that my sickness would mask the deception. The only thing worse than letting Gideon Frey get his hands on me would be letting him get his hands on *Syrene*.

"Ah," Gideon sighed. "Yes, of course. The emperor's last command to the Envoy was to serve and protect you. I've never been perfectly clear on the limits of her power... but I suppose I underestimated it, after all."

I wiped my mouth with the back of my hand and tried to push myself upright again. What remained of my armour weighed me down like lead, though, and I clattered weakly back to the floor.

"What are you doing, Gideon?" I mumbled. "Trafficking with Unseelie aether? I know you never cared much for honour... but blasphemy?" I asked the question in order to distract him from the subject of Syrene, and not because I really expected an answer. Once, he would have been *obliged* to answer. But times had changed significantly.

"I don't have to answer that," Gideon replied with amusement, confirming my suspicions. He reached an arm beneath my shoulders, hauling me up against the wall. The sight of his smooth, pale mask swam in front of me like a spectre in the blue aether-light of the cabin's lamp.

"You'll have to tell me eventually," I mumbled. "You want something from me. I wouldn't be alive, otherwise."

Gideon paced a few feet away from me to settle into a chair at a small table. I found it odd, suddenly, that he still hadn't taken off his mask. I knew it wasn't comfortable. He'd once complained to me that it left splinters in his nose—as though the dryad it had been made from was taking some silly posthumous vengeance upon him. His gait was subtly pained, and I knew that he'd suffered greatly in the fight we'd just departed, regardless of his posture.

"We're on even footing now, boy," Gideon said finally. "Answer a question of mine, and I'll do you the same courtesy. That seems fair, doesn't it?"

I tried to weigh that offer in my mind—but I wasn't at my best. I could barely concentrate on the things he was saying, let alone decide what was or was not *fair*.

What I *did* know was that I had a few burning questions of my own that needed answering.

"Fine," I murmured.

Gideon leaned forward imperceptibly. "The *Iron Rose*," he growled softly. "A battered old ship with an eclectic bunch of thieves. And a goblin captain?" He chuckled humourlessly at the idea. "How long have you and Hawkins been aboard?"

He was far more interested in the answer than he wanted to let on. But I'm a soldier, and not a spy. I didn't know what to do with that information.

"I've been bosun on the *Rose* for several years now," I said. "The captain saved my neck from a rope. I didn't mind repaying him." I blinked slowly at him, trying to steady my vision. "Hawkins is a recent passenger. Until a few days ago, I thought she was some oblivious academic with a parasol and a pretty dress."

Gideon shook his head, unsatisfied. "The crew risked their lives for Hawkins," he said more forcefully, jabbing a finger in my direction. There was a tight, cool fury lurking under those words. "Why?"

I shot him a tight grimace of a smile. "That's question two," I said. "Don't I get to ask mine?"

Gideon leaned back in his chair with an impatient huff. He waved a hand at me to continue, though.

"Why did you kill Silver?" I asked him bluntly.

The words dropped between us like a lead weight. I saw Gideon's fingers clench on the arms of his chair. For a second, I thought I'd killed the conversation entirely... but eventually, Gideon spoke again.

"He wouldn't listen to reason." The statement was soft and somewhat distant. For the first time since I'd run into Gideon again, I detected a hint of distress.

"Reason?" I scoffed, frowning. "The man might as well have been made of clockwork. Reason was all he ever knew."

"Something broke in him, after the war," Gideon said haltingly. "After he... *we* adopted Hawkins, he became a different man. He questioned the things we'd done—things better left buried. He kept asking me what sort of world we'd made for children like her." His jaw tightened behind the mask. "He lost perspective."

"You're evading the question," I told him flatly. "You didn't kill the man you loved just because he found a belated conscience."

Gideon snapped his head up, and I felt his chilly eyes upon me. "He invented something that could save us all," he hissed. "I decided to use it. And *he* decided he would kill me first."

I absorbed that with great difficulty. I wanted to shoot back a cutting observation about what Gideon thought *saving people* looked like. But I was in far too much pain to think of anything pithy.

"Why is the *Iron Rose* helping Hawkins?" Gideon repeated in a low voice. "What could she possibly offer them in return for such a dangerous job?"

I rolled my head back against the wall with a choked laugh. "You still don't get it, after all these years," I muttered. "You think people need to be *paid* to oppose the empire? You think anyone *needs* an extra excuse to hate us?" Misery joined the pain that pounded gently behind my eyes. "They came at us by the thousands, Gideon. Waves and waves of rebels, all of them fully aware of just how outmatched they were. They came at us with warships and trade vessels and pitchforks and pistols. We *slaughtered* them, and they just kept coming. Haven't you ever wondered *why?*"

My halting mind supplied me with the stench of blood and death and gunpowder. I heard Syrene's child-like laughter as she ripped Oathbreakers to pieces with her bare hands, discarding people like broken toys. I saw our proud flags in the shadows of the aether-light, burning on the battlefield.

I was alone, victorious—somehow alive, despite the carnage. The mud around me was littered with fragmented remains, both mortal and mechanical. I couldn't even tell which parts belonged to the enemy.

I clawed at the smouldering tree before me, prying off what remained of a sickly looking flower and tucking it against my chest. The rest of Syrene laid in a charred heap beside me and my ruined wargear.

I had led us to victory. This was what it looked like. I took in the sight of that hideous battlefield—my masterpiece. My moment of glory. The story I would give to Death Victorious when I finally met them.

"All of those people decided that death was preferable to living under the Imperium," I told the man above me hoarsely. "You can't fight that, Gideon. You can't destroy it. Not with laws or violence or platitudes—not even with the horrible things you did in Pelaeia. They don't just hate us..." I lifted my head with effort, trying to stare him down through that inscrutable mask. "We are an *existential threat* to them. Wherever you go in the name of the empire, someone will oppose you."

Gideon surged to his feet. He slammed his hand down on the table, loud enough to redouble my headache.

"Then we will *all* die together!" he snarled.

His body trembled with weariness and pain. His breath was short enough that I found myself wondering if he'd fractured a rib in his fight with Hawkins.

"There's been a Breaching, boy," Gideon hissed at me. "Everything we once warned those rebels about has finally come to pass. We asked for Tithes to fight the Unseelie, to do our duty to our gods, and the rebels *refused*. So yes—I will slaughter them as they come. I will do whatever I must in order to unify this empire again, to rebuild the defences they've ignored for twenty years now. I will work with traitors. I will butcher anyone who stands in my way. I will kill *everyone* I love, if it means the world won't burn."

A Breaching.

The words threw me into a cold, horrified shock, as though I'd been doused in water. I stared at him, unable to speak.

I knew he wasn't lying. There had been too many signs already—Syrene's mounting discomfort, the Unseelie aether. As soon as Gideon said the words aloud, everything clicked neatly together.

We were about to live through the sort of thing I'd only read about in history books. Things the historians called unfathomable, indescribable. The eldritch bloody horrors of the Evernight were coming for us, right as we were at our weakest and most divided.

Gideon's trembling eased as he saw the understanding on my face. His voice lowered. "You may not agree with everything I've done," he said softly, "but I *know* you, Arcturus. When the real monsters arrive, you'll do everything in your power to stop them. I'm about to end this war between Carrain and the Spires—as swiftly and brutally as I can. As soon as that's done, I'll escort you to the Temple of the Four Winds to assert your claim. Prince Arcturus Lohengrin will return from the dead with an army of loyal echoes, at the moment when Avalon most needs him. The Seelie will grant you your due as emperor, and men will flock to your banner. Together, we will *stop* this. We will fulfil the most important of our Oaths and save this world from destruction."

Even as he spoke, I felt the stirrings of old emotions I'd thought long dead. After decades of horrific self-loathing, I knew purpose again. I could fulfil my Oath to the empire—the duty for which I'd been raised. I could make all of the awful things I'd done have meaning. I could save this entire world, or die trying.

My unfulfilled Oath longed for a taste of that glory.

It was such a heady, unexpected feeling. I hadn't known that I still had it in me. And on some level, it *terrified* me.

The screams of Pelaeia struggled at the bottom of my mind, desperate to be heard. The man in front of me had committed that slaughter. Had my father ordered him to go that far, or had he done so on his own initiative? Either way, it didn't matter. The blood on Gideon's hands was blood on my name. If I took up that name again— if I took up the mantle of emperor and accepted Wraithwood into my service—that bloody legacy would be mine.

But the world is in danger, something inside me whispered. *How could any cost be too great to save it?*

It wasn't a selfless thought, no matter how much I wanted it to be. It was too relieved, too mercenary for that. But was it *true*, all the same?

I didn't know. I wasn't a man of moral clarity.

I didn't know.

"The Spires have Gloryborne," Gideon said. The words cut through the chaos of my troubled thoughts. "The augurs say it should be fully operational any day now."

My mind blanked. I stared at him, disbelieving. "That's... that's impossible," I whispered. "It was a wreck. There was no way they could have salvaged it. Even if they had, Gloryborne would have reached out to me—"

"*If* you were ready for it," Gideon replied dryly. "Were you ready, Arcturus? Would you have answered?"

I didn't respond. We both knew the answer, regardless. I'd buried myself in anonymity, desperate to cast off both my name and my sins. Gloryborne belonged with Arcturus Lohengrin, who would be written into history. Strahl the bosun was entirely beneath its notice.

"Knowing the stakes," Gideon added softly, "would you answer now?"

I thought of Gloryborne—screaming around me, half-scattered across the hill. An old aching grief flared to life in my chest, now tempered with hope. The sacred bond I'd shared with my wargear was something beyond words. There had been a loving, if silent, familiarity between us. That day, I'd lost more than one piece of myself. I'd replaced those parts with guilt and shame, knowing that I'd led my wargear to ruin.

The yearning in my chest uncurled, reaching out into the silence. And though I was convinced, on some level, that Gloryborne would never deign to forgive me... still, I heard its Call again.

The feeling was dim and distorted—but it was *real*. I felt Gloryborne's presence reach across the distance between us, clawing for my mind. The wargear wasn't a mortal creature; it required no forgiveness. It wanted only glory—and I could offer that again. When the Unseelie came, I would be the champion of the Everbright, chosen to fulfil the grandest destiny known to Avalon.

No one would ever forget my name.

I didn't accept the Call... but neither could I make it disappear. It lingered like the open line of a longhorn, waiting for me to answer. Gloryborne knew that we were destined to do great things together.

Gideon sensed that conflict. He knew my weakness—he could scent it in the air, like fresh blood.

"If you don't step up to lead us," he whispered urgently, "someone else *will*. The Emerald Spires will send a candidate to the Temple, Arcturus. I will have to work with them if they do. But they are still cowards and traitors at heart. It should be you. I would rather it be *you*."

The words were well-aimed. *Someone must*, I thought. *Why not me? I have the right. Those honourless Spire dogs will only make things worse. But I could be better than my father, better than Gideon—*

I cut off the thought with a shudder of miserable confusion.

I have to get out of here. This thought was less seductive, and far more urgent. I was isolated and weak. Gideon knew how to speak to Arcturus Lohengrin—a man who wasn't nearly as dead as I'd hoped he was. Gloryborne's silent, beckoning spectre loomed large in my mind. The longer I stayed, the more likely it was that I would prove Gideon right.

"Maybe we should have this discussion once you're sure I'll survive the night," I rasped.

It was a weak reply. I knew it would barely delay things. But Gideon chuckled and rose to his feet.

"Always practical, Arcturus," he said. "I do respect that."

I clenched my trembling fingers into my palms. My head was pounding from more than just the concussion. But a dull thought snaked its way back to the forefront of my mind as I stared up at Gideon's skull-like mask in the flickering aether-light.

"Why won't you take off your mask, Gideon?" I asked him quietly.

Gideon stared down at me. In the silence that followed, he remained so utterly still that I could have mistaken him for a statue.

"...you're out of questions, Arcturus," he replied softly.

He walked out of the room and closed the door behind him, leaving me alone in the darkness with a head full of ghosts.

19

CHASING STRAHL - THE EDGE OF TIIRDAN'S FURY - THE VENGEFUL ECHO OF DOUGAL MACLEOD

With each league we crossed, the gap between Strahl and the *Iron Rose* only lengthened.

Though we cleared the blackened skies of Morgause in record time, Syrene's agitation grew more and more palpable. We pushed the *Rose* to her conceivable limits, leaving that wretched pustule of a city far behind us—but still, Strahl outpaced us.

Given the sheer speed with which my bosun was travelling, he had to be on Wraithwood's smaller, sleeker ship. The *Conflagration* was too big and bulky to move with that sort of haste. That meant Wraithwood and Strahl were going to make it to Galtir before we did. Odds were high that the *Conflagration* was sailing after them, which put that monstrous vessel directly between us. And if we *did* run into the *Conflagration*... what would we do? Even on our best day, we could never match that ship in combat.

That reality crashed down upon me as the first stars kindled in the sky. The adrenaline that had fuelled me since leaving Morgause ebbed away, leaving me weak and tired and despondent. I caught myself just as my thoughts started tending towards hopeless resignation.

I needed sleep. I didn't *want* sleep—but I wasn't going to be much use to anyone if I didn't get it.

I relinquished the helm and stumbled to my cabin, collapsing into bed. Despite my reluctance, I fell asleep nearly as soon as my head hit the pillow.

I dreamed of grinning skulls; of silver swords and scarlet blood; of a sea of echoes, and the thunder of guns.

That last rumbling sound woke me abruptly. It was real.

I bolted upright in my bed. My skin glistened with sweat, and my shirt stuck uncomfortably to the small of my back.

The rumbling around me slowly faded. Nothing else immediately called for my attention; no klaxons rang, no screams split the air. The ship creaked softly as it struggled against the wind.

The air smelled like rain and fury.

A storm, I thought dimly. The thought relaxed me somewhat. I tried to go back to sleep, but that initial surge of alertness refused to retreat. I checked my timepiece. I'd managed about five hours of sleep, which meant the sun was currently rising with me.

I dragged myself out of bed and headed for the basin in my cabin, wiping the sweat from my skin. I daubed my throat with a touch of rose oil—a soothing luxury I kept around for hard mornings—and dressed myself for the part of captain.

I was surprised by the sunlight that greeted me as I stepped out of my cabin to survey our new horizon. Fluffy white clouds floated across a blue sky, on our port side. Beneath them was a gently curving bay with white cliffs. Whitecaps danced upon the sea where it crashed against those cliffs, forming into playful humanoid shapes which might have been nereids.

Further inland beyond the cliffs, emerald fields stretched out in all directions. Long-ruined warships rusted in those fields like giant beached whales, with their iron skeletons reaching up for the sky. Birds flocked above the old battlefields in massive throngs, and I found myself wondering whether there were any strahls among them.

Some of the birds had settled onto half-submerged shipwrecks in the bay itself. Red iron scraps pierced the surface of the water where the nereids danced. Sharp, tower-like islands peppered the bay, rising even taller than the iron debris. Sailors called them 'Tiirdan's talons', after the many-winged South Wind.

On our starboard side raged an angry, sunless storm.

The roiling black clouds there were utterly impenetrable. Every so often, forks of lightning jolted through them, lighting up the inside of the clouds with emerald, gold, and blinding white. The storm swirled in place—huge and hungry, crouched upon the bay like a giant predator. That great dervish of bruised clouds could have easily swallowed Morgause whole.

I had seen that storm once before, a very long time ago. The *HMS Caliban* had skimmed the edge of those clouds on its way to Galtir. Somewhere within that tempest roosted one of the great lords of the Seelie Court—Tiirdan, the South Wind.

Twenty years ago, the Coalition had sent two fleets to Galtir. Only one of them ever arrived. Stories claimed that Emperor Lohengrin had prayed to the Seelie for aid—and the herald of Death Victorious had answered. Tiirdan met the Coalition ships above the bay, tearing them from the sky with the greatest storm that Avalon had ever seen. Rather than dispersing, however, the tempest remained. Some people believed that Tiirdan remained with it, nesting at the centre of the storm.

Several of my crew stood gawking at the great wall of thunder above the bay. Little stared out from the rigging nearby with an unnaturally calm expression, and I knew he was remembering our last journey past the South Wind.

"Never thought I'd see *him* again," I said softly.

Little glanced down at me as I spoke. He slid slowly down the rigging to land on the deck.

I thought my memories had exaggerated, Little signed at me. *But the storm is even bigger than I remember.*

I adjusted my coat and pulled on my goggles before joining Little at the railing. "Any sign of our quarry?" I asked him, with a bleary yawn.

None yet, Little signed. He motioned towards the helm, which currently steered the ship on its own. *We're still losing ground. Syrene has been on edge all night.*

"There has to be a way to close that gap," I muttered. "If we arrive too late..."

I trailed off, rather than finishing the statement. We both knew how poorly we'd fare against an entire army of echoes.

Syrene had taken the swiftest course possible; she'd even coaxed us favourable winds. Short of dumping excess weight, I wasn't sure what else we could do. The heaviest things aboard were the guns and the munitions—but the *Conflagration* would make even shorter work of us if we disarmed ourselves.

"Captain," Syrene's voice whispered on the breeze. "Come and speak with us." The faerie melted up from the wood like water, solidifying into a tall, swaying figure draped in golden tulips-by-the-sea. The skin of her fingers had taken on the whitewashed colour of driftwood, where they clutched at the helm.

Syrene still emanated a sullen, frustrated anger that set my teeth on edge. But I crossed the distance between us anyway, forcing myself to ignore it.

"The winds speak," Syrene murmured. "Enemies wait for us ahead."

I frowned. "The *Conflagration*?" I asked her.

"No," Syrene said. "Smaller birds than that one." She canted her head, as though listening. "We do not know how many. Tiirdan's screeching is too loud."

I nodded slowly. "Probably outflyers," I said. "The *Conflagration* had six on board, back in Morgause. They've seen us following them." I drew my spyglass and set it against my eye, scanning the horizon for interlopers. I wasn't disappointed.

A glimmer of metal caught my gaze near the rolling hillocks beyond the cliff side, partially obscured by cloud cover. I focussed in closer and picked out a pair of bulky outflyers flying in tandem, doing their best to avoid detection as they crept closer to us. Without Syrene's warning, they probably would have succeeded.

"All hands, to your stations!" I called out. "Bandits inbound off the port side! I want rifles at the ready!"

The deck erupted with shouts and movement as crew rushed to grab heavier weapons from the armoury. I hurried to the longhorn and rang the gunnery deck.

"Tell me we get to blow something up this time," Lenore's voice addressed me.

I cracked a smile, despite the situation. "You get to blow *two* somethings up," I informed her. "We've got two enemy outflyers hiding off the port side. I'm hoping to lure them out. I'll bring us out into the open and pretend we haven't seen them."

"They'll use those big fluffy clouds for cover," Lenore mused.

"They surely will," I agreed. "Do we still have flakshot for the cannons?"

"Plenty of it, Cap'n." I heard a vicious smile in her voice, even over the longhorn.

"Let's give them a taste of it, then," I said. "Flakshot and turrets, Miss Brighton. After we finish our broadside, though, I want you to load our guns for heavier armour."

"Expecting the Conflagration?" Lenore guessed.

"I hope not," I answered ruefully. "But it can't be that far ahead of its outflyers. If the *Conflagration* turns around to assist them, we won't have much choice but to run." Lenore made a soft noise of distaste over the longhorn, and I added: "Hold your fire until I give the mark. Then I want you to give those outflyers what-for, Miss Brighton."

"Aye-aye, Cap'n," Lenore replied smartly. She pulled away from the longhorn then, and I heard her call out to the other gunnery ladies in a faintly muffled voice: *"Check your dance cards, ladies! We've got partners!"*

I hung up the longhorn and returned to the helm, murmuring to the faerie that had melted back into the wood. "Slow us down near the cliff," I told Syrene. "Make like we're going to turn. If they use the cloud cover to come at us, they'll be flying blind. We'll have just enough time to position ourselves for a broadside."

Syrene didn't respond. But the wheel moved of its own accord, turning us towards the cliffs, and I knew that she had heard me all the same.

I checked behind us with my spyglass and caught a better glimpse of one of the brigands, skimming through the clouds behind us. It was a Timberjack model—the sort of heavy fighter meant to engage large vessels. Assuming the fighter hadn't been altered, it would have some heavy forward-mounted guns, loaded with bullets and not aether.

As we reached the cliff and began to slow, the flyer sped up, disappearing back into the clouds... but not before I caught sight of a scorched wolf burned into the side of its fuselage.

"Cinderwolf bandits confirmed!" I bellowed. To Syrene, more quietly, I said: "Get us in position. Once we fire our broadside, turn us for Tiirdan's Talons and use the rocks for cover."

Tiirdan's Fury rumbled in the distance, flashing with fresh lightning. Somewhere beneath the constant noise, I heard the throaty growl of the Cinderwolves' engines approaching through the clouds. Syrene turned the *Rose* lazily, resettling it to aim our starboard cannons directly towards the oncoming flyers.

I grabbed the longhorn's chatterbox, waiting patiently for company.

The two outflyers burst from cloud cover all at once, darting towards us like a pair of bolting wolves. My pulse jumped as though I'd been hit with an electric jolt, and I opened the line on the longhorn to address the gunnery ladies.

"Fire!" I yelled.

The *Rose*'s cannons boomed, rocking the entire boat beneath my feet. Several loud *pops* followed, splitting the air like harsh whip cracks. Lenore's flakshot was too small to make out, but it made for spectacular results: one of the outflyers listed abruptly to the side, as its right wing burst apart and pockmarks blossomed along its hull. An instant later, its engine exploded in a riot of cerulean flames. Cheers erupted from the crew as the ship plummeted into the bay, adding its wreckage to Tiirdan's already-impressive collection.

The other outflyer had been quicker on the draw, and less directly in our line of fire. It banked away sharply, trailing only a small bit of smoke from one clipped wing. Our starboard turrets fired next, but the pilot danced deftly out of the way, and I knew we were dealing with someone who'd been in their fair share of dogfights.

"Get us some cover, Syrene!" I yelled at the empty helm. I needn't have bothered—the *Rose* was already turning for Tiirdan's Talons, picking up speed as the outflyer worked to reorient itself. By the time it regained its bearings, we had already reached a pair of towering rocky outcroppings.

Even an expert pilot would have trouble angling to attack us within Tiirdan's Talons; I would have hesitated to take us through myself, if not for our supernatural navigator. Sure enough, the one remaining outflyer hesitated briefly, before swinging wide and peeling away to disappear back into the clouds.

I let out a long, shaky breath, trying to calm down my body. Even as I did, Syrene's tall whipcord form melted up out of the deck with an air of foreboding.

"More birds fly this way," Syrene told me gravely. "The flock will come upon us all at once."

I set my jaw and stifled a curse. Of course. The moment those two outflyers had first seen us, they'd probably signalled for backup. "How many?" I asked.

Syrene cocked her head, as though listening. "Two more ahead," she murmured.

Three outflyers. I didn't like those odds at all, even if one of them was already damaged.

"Ladies," I called over the chatterbox, "Syrene confirms two more bandits inbound. Keep your eyes peeled."

Confirmations echoed over the longhorn amidst the sound of chattering turret-fire before I hung up the device to repeat the warning across the main deck. Part of me half expected Strahl to reprise the words in his booming voice... but of course, Strahl wasn't there. The reminder left an uneasy knot in my stomach.

Syrene dipped the *Rose* downwards, diving between the large crumbling pillars that made up Tiirdan's Talons. The sound of the crashing waves below grew louder, mingling with the wind's roar. I steadied myself against the railing and drew my telescope, searching the horizon for the outflyers we knew to be out there.

This time, however, the outflyers found us before we found them.

"Above!" Syrene warned me sharply. One driftwood finger pointed up towards a stretch of blue sky in between the clouds, where the sun glared down at us. Though I couldn't see past the blinding light, I knew what I *would* have seen if I could—the outflyers had used the sun to mask their dive.

It was a split second too late for me to alert the gunnery deck. The Timberjacks opened fire before our turrets could react, raking deadly bullets across the main deck. Splinters, blood, and screams blended together, as rigging snapped beneath the assault. A few of the sailors on the *Rose* panicked and fired their rifles at the outflyers, to little meaningful effect.

As the outflyers swept past, I saw that all three had descended upon us at once. They split apart in opposite directions, weaving back through Tiirdan's Talons with wary care. I knew they'd soon be back around for another run at our deck, though they'd be hard-pressed to coordinate another simultaneous attack within the Talons.

In the brief pause, I saw people rushing to grab our injured crew. To my right, Little shimmied down the rigging to haul one woman over his shoulder, dragging her to the main deck and passing her off to waiting hands. She soon disappeared below deck, on her way to the infirmary.

I couldn't afford to dwell. Already, one of the Cinderwolves had managed to wheel about.

"Port bow!" I called into the chatterbox. "One outflyer!"

The Cinderwolf opened fire—but this time, our turret on that side fired back and struck. The turret's shot clipped the Timberjack's wing and landed several hits on the cockpit's glass dome. Sparks flew, and for a second, I wondered if the pilot was dead—but the outflyer soon banked sharply, aborting its run on the *Rose* in order to seek out temporary safety.

One of the other outflyers dared an approach from beneath us, kicking up a trail of water as it skimmed the bay. Guns barked, and one of our propellers made a distinctly unpleasant sound.

"Syrene!" I called. "Damage report!"

Our faerie navigator was hip-deep in the deck now, half-submerged in the wood. The petals of her hair scattered behind her in the wind. "Aft props are damaged!" she called back calmly. "One of them has been sheared off, Captain."

I was suddenly, painfully aware that the starboard turret had gone silent. *Navi's turret.*

"What about the starboard turret?" I yelled at Syrene.

"The starboard turret is operational, Captain!" the faerie replied evenly.

I clawed for the chatterbox again. "Captain to gunnery deck!" I gasped. "Is Navi all right?"

The line crackled chaotically for a moment, before someone replied.

"She's hurt," Lenore's voice sounded. *"Just splinters in her arm. I've sent her to see the sawbones."*

My shoulders untensed with relief, and I let out a breath. It was a small relief, though. I was just starting to realise how much worse our situation was than I'd originally anticipated. These Cinderwolves weren't pirates—they were disciplined, battle-hardened professionals.

The winds picked up around us, beating at the rigging, as Syrene took us deeper into the Talons. This close to the storm, the rocks had formed a howling wind tunnel. The outflyers struggled against gusts of air, at times wavering as they tried to clear an angle of attack.

Suddenly, I saw Little handsigning urgently at me from the main deck. I turned quickly, but not in time to catch the message. "Repeat!" I yelled at him, as I signed the word back several times. Between the bustling crew, the clouds, and the sea spray, however, visibility on the ship was becoming difficult, and Evie vaulted over to translate for me as he sometimes did in such situations.

"Another outflyer, Captain!" Evie called across the deck. "Coming in low behind us!"

I cursed. The winds couldn't tell Syrene what they didn't yet know

—somehow, another outflyer had manoeuvred downwind of us, avoiding her detection. *Four outflyers.* The idea dropped into my gut like a stone. This was beginning to seem impossible.

"Captain to gunnery deck," I said into the chatterbox. "We have a fourth outflyer out there, coming in behind us. Can anyone confirm?"

One of the Timberjacks appeared abruptly ahead of us, weaving past a great, jutting tower of rock. Bullets showered the deck; splinters burst from the railing just behind me, and I dived for cover.

Gunfire replied in kind, tearing the Timberjack's wing clean off. Its engine detonated in a plume of violent blue flame. The ship slammed into the waves below, bouncing frenetically as it tore itself apart.

I whooped into the chatterbox. "Good shot, ladies!" I shouted.

The response from the longhorn was faintly garbled in the wind. I craned closer to the speaker. "What?" I asked. "I didn't copy that!"

"—*not us, Cap'n,*" Lenore's voice crackled over. "*It's the fourth outflyer. It's not a Timberjack, sir.*"

A small ship darted past us in the Talons, dancing on the edge of the wind. It was a mismatched junker of an outflyer, cobbled together from old parts. A faded band of Coalition yellow still stood out upon its hull.

Another Timberjack wheeled in for attack, appearing around the side of a Talon. The new outflyer nearly collided with it head-on, and my entire body cringed at the close shave. But our allied pilot wove just past the enemy, close enough that I halfway expected to see sparks where the ships kissed. The Timberjack over-corrected in a panic—and slammed directly into one of the crumbling Talons, with a violent explosion.

For a moment, it was as though the vengeful echo of Dougal MacLeod had risen from the grave to rain fire on our enemies. The ship screamed past us, and I found myself staring at the bright red chimaera rampant of Clan MacLeod which had been painted upon its wings.

It wasn't Dougal MacLeod, of course. But I had a good idea of who *had* come to our rescue.

Cheers erupted on deck as the MacLeod outflyer thundered past us. Anger, fear, and relief all battled for prominence in my throat—but I found myself cheering with everyone else, nevertheless, as the last Timberjack peeled away in retreat.

The longhorn rang, signalling an incoming transmission. I flicked the dial quickly to answer the request.

"Damn it, MacLeod!" I managed. "What are you *doing* here? How did you even find us?"

"Oh, ye know," Aesir replied nonchalantly. *"Stretchin' me wings. Did ye know ye left a locator in Uncle Dougal's outflyer? Still tuned to the Rose an' all. I thought it shouldn't go to waste."* His smug grin was so loud, I could hear it all the way from the *Rose*.

I groaned softly. Resetting the locator in Dougal's outflyer had been the absolute *last* thing on my mind in Pelaeia.

"MacLeod—" I started.

"Don't even start," Aesir interjected sharply. *"Ye'd be scrap in Tiirdan's Talons if I hadn't come by—"*

"MacLeod—" I tried again, more urgently.

"By thunder, ye need my help, an' yer bum's out the windae if ye think—"

"MacLeod, for the sake of the Tuath, *watch where you're going!*" I yelled.

Aesir's outflyer had looked to be speeding directly for one of the Talons—but even as I spoke, he shrugged his ship around it, easy as you please, and continued talking.

"I'll be a sheep's uncle 'afore I spend the rest of my days rustin' away on a mountaintop—" he continued emphatically.

"Aesir!" I shouted. "Welcome aboard the *Rose*, you magnificent clunkhead! Now keep an eye on our tail and make sure the last Timberjack doesn't come back!"

Aesir's laughter echoed across the line as his outflyer peeled away into a defensive position.

"Aye-aye, Cap'n," he replied with relish. *"I've got yer six."*

20

CRASH COURSE - WOUNDED - THUNDEROUS SILENCE - AYE-AYE, CAPTAIN

Clan MacLeod's pilots had always been infamous for their appetite for risk—but somehow, Aesir MacLeod's flying was even more brazen than his uncle's had been.

Even as I watched, Aesir skimmed his outflyer less than a foot from the rising waves. As the sea reached up for him, he banked into a sharp upward spin, barely missing one of the rocky towers next to him. Though I didn't have him on the longhorn anymore, I swore I could still hear him laughing.

Maybe, I thought, the sheer freedom had gone to his head. It was probably the first time in Aesir's life, I realised, that he couldn't see Old Pelaeia somewhere on the horizon.

It was a bad time to be breaking in a new outflyer pilot… but we didn't have much of a choice. Even if I'd wanted to send Aesir back to Pelaeia—even if he'd been *willing* to go—there was no way he had enough fuel left to make the trip. The best I could do was try to convince him to fly back to one of the smaller towns we'd passed on our way here… and *that*, I knew, was going to be a serious conversation.

I picked up the longhorn again to flag down Aesir. "We're starting to skirt the edge of the Fury," I told him. "If we don't see that last

Timberjack in the next few minutes, I want you to dock with the *Rose* until we're further away from the storm. You can meet me in the infirmary."

"*Solid copy,*" Aesir replied cheerfully. But then, just before I could put down the chatterbox, he added: "*Uh, wee question, Cap'n. How dae I dock?*"

I pinched at the bridge of my nose with a wince. "I'll connect you to Mr Finch in engineering," I said. "Do *exactly* as he says, please. No theatrics, Aesir."

Aesir laughed. "*Theatrics?*" he repeated. "*Me?*" The outflyer did a dizzying flip as it looped around to begin its approach for the *Rose*. "*Relax, Blair. I willnae even scratch the paint.*"

Somehow, I found myself less than assured. But I gave up with a sigh and switched frequencies to let Mr Finch know we had an outflyer in need of docking lessons, before leaving the longhorn to check on the main deck. Bloody woodchips crunched beneath my feet as I went.

I joined Little for a time, assisting him as he dragged away injured crew to be triaged. As I did, I saw Martha leaning heavily upon a patch of ruined railing out of the corner of my eye, with a heavy rifle dangling from her hand. I excused myself to go and check on her, with a hint of alarm.

"Injured?" I asked. Martha glanced up at me blankly, and I remembered her bad right ear. I hastily hand signed the question, and she shook her head.

"Got knocked around a bit," Martha mumbled. "My dang balance is off again."

I grimaced. Most of the time, Martha had very few problems with her partial deafness, given the crew's propensity for sign language. But on particularly bad days, her skewed hearing affected her sense of balance, for reasons which none of us quite understood.

Maybe you should take over a turret? I signed at her.

Martha shook her head again. "All the turrets are full," she said. "Lenore is training Mr Billings on them today. Besides, just thinking of spinning 'round in one of those seats makes my stomach turn right now. I'll be fine, Cap'n. Just need a second to sort myself out again."

I nodded reluctantly. *Go see Holloway if it doesn't improve,* I signed. We both knew the physicker had never had any real luck treating Martha's balance—but there was little sense in her stumbling around on deck if she couldn't get a handle on the episode, and a bit of rest and quiet often helped the condition regardless.

"Understood," Martha replied.

At the mention of turrets, I was abruptly reminded of Navi's injury. I turned towards Little. *The deck is yours,* I signed at him. *I'll be right back.*

I bolted for the gunnery deck.

Though the last outflyer had fled for the moment, the gunnery ladies were still abuzz with activity. Wind whistled through fresh new holes in the hull, mingling with soft curses and the sound of rattling guns. Navi was nowhere to be seen—but her turret had been reoccupied in her absence. Its new occupant was so short that all I could make out from behind the gunnery chair was her slightly dainty boots.

"Mary?" I said dimly.

The youngest gunnery lady craned her head around the side of the chair. Her dark hair was so wind tossed, it had nearly escaped its tie entirely. All that kept those strands from her eyes now was the pair of goggles she wore. "I took over for Navi!" she yelled over the din.

I worked my mouth soundlessly, unable to respond. Mary wouldn't have been on a turret unless Lenore had ordered her there; that meant my gunnery chief had decided she was ready for the job.

I'd barely managed to swallow the fact that Mary was taking on jobs and carrying guns. The sight of her on a turret was a fresh cold shock to my senses.

Despite all my worst fears, Aesir MacLeod was currently dancing through the wind above us, and Mary had claimed a turret below.

Lenore strode over to me, interrupting the moment of consternation. "Who's our new friend?" she demanded bluntly.

I grimaced and turned my attention to her. "Aesir MacLeod

followed us here from Pelaeia," I replied. "Under the circumstances, I can't really send him back."

Lenore arched an eyebrow at me. "Send him back?" she repeated. "He took down two outflyers, Cap'n."

"That makes two ships he's brought down in his entire life, then," I retorted. "He had the element of surprise this time. And..." I heaved a heavy sigh. "He doesn't know who we're chasing. I'm not looking forward to telling him."

Lenore frowned... but a moment later, the implications clicked together. "Wraithwood helped lead the attack on Pelaeia," she said slowly.

Aesir had faced down the ghosts of Old Pelaeia... but those had been the echoes of his own people. Wraithwood was something like a still-living nightmare—the source of every awful thing Aesir had experienced in his life. I had no idea how he was going to react to the revelation that he was now stuck on a collision course with one of the very people who was responsible for his dead family and his missing arm.

"Just keep an eye on him while he's out there, will you?" I asked Lenore. "Dougal would appreciate it."

Lenore inclined her head seriously. "We'll keep him in our sights," she replied quietly. "As much as he lets us, anyway."

I nodded, with a hard knot in my throat. "I'm... going to go check on Navi," I said.

"She's all right," Lenore reassured me. "But since I know you're headed down anyway, can you borrow some of the whiskey from Horace's stash for me? All this bangin' about is givin' me a headache."

"...Horace?" I repeated dimly. It was the second time now that I'd heard Lenore use the physicker's first name. As far as I knew, the only other person on this boat who'd ever called him that was Navi.

Lenore offered me such a self-satisfied smile that I found myself wondering if I'd missed something. "I ought to get back to trainin' my junior gunners, Cap'n," she said.

I turned slowly back for the hatch that led towards the infirmary, frowning to myself in consternation.

* * *

Bloody smears marred the corridor that led to the infirmary. Even before I opened the door, I caught the scent of sawdust and heard the muffled sounds of agony inside.

I avoided looking too closely at the scenes taking place on the far side of the infirmary as I headed into the room, though I remained dimly aware of Holloway stitching up a ragged gash in someone's shoulder. Instead, my eyes fell upon Navi, already bandaged up and sipping serenely at a cup of tea in a corner chair. Her arm had been pinned to her side with a sling, and she still looked a bit shaken—but I was relieved to note that she looked otherwise hale and healthy.

I headed over to the crowd that had gathered around Holloway, patiently waiting to discharge the promise I had made to my gunnery chief. Eventually, the physicker finished tying off his work and responded to my request by dipping into his kit for a small silvery flask, now slightly smudged with blood.

I wiped the flask off on a nearby rag. "Just like that?" I asked suspiciously. "I thought this stuff was your *special* medicine."

Holloway's green skin flushed subtly, and he cleared his throat. "I owe Miss Brighton a drink or two," he mumbled. "Apologies, Captain—I *do* have an awful lot of work to do."

And just like that, the physicker evaded me.

Navi sighed audibly over her tea. "Poor man," she said. "He doesn't stand a chance."

I started over in her direction, still holding the flask in one hand. "Are you suggesting that, er... Miss Brighton has *designs* on our sawbones?" I asked.

Navi's dark eyes flashed with humour. "I'm sure I don't know what you're talking about, Captain," she said primly. "But she *does* seem terribly fond of his poetry of late."

Any reply I might have managed was interrupted by a soft groan from the cot next to Navi's chair. Lady Navi pressed her teacup absently into my other hand, before reaching down to stroke at

Hawkins' pale hair. "There, there, darling," she said. "All these noisy people will leave soon, I promise."

Miss Hawkins slitted one eye open. The other eye remained carefully closed, pained by the fresh stitches just next to it. The skin surrounding the stitches had been stained an ugly, lifeless grey. "Hello, Captain," she mumbled. "I suppose I should thank you for preventing me from blowing up half of Morgause."

I blinked at the reminder. "Oh," I said. "Don't mention it."

"I don't mean to complain about the noise," Miss Hawkins assured Navi dimly. "This is an infirmary. Injured people have a right to be here."

"Oh, but you *should* complain," Navi told her soothingly. "I always find it makes me feel better, personally."

Despite Navi's assurances, another racket soon started at the door to the infirmary as Aesir MacLeod flung open the door to stride inside, all broad smiles and roguish, windswept hair. He was wearing a faded jumpsuit and a pilot's jacket today, with his late uncle's scarf draped around his neck and a pair of goggles dangling atop it.

In many respects, he looked exactly the same as he had when I'd left him in Pelaeia. But the lift in his shoulders and the sheer energy in his step made him seem like an entirely different person, such that I found myself staring at the sight.

"Blair!" Aesir called out cheerfully, as he crossed the distance between us. "Or—is it Cap'n, now? Outflyer's docked, an' minimal damage tae yer hull." I cringed, and he patted my shoulder with another laugh. "I'm joking, Blair, yer ship's fine."

I let out a slow breath, trying to dispel the tension that still remained from our brief skirmish. "Thank you, Aesir," I said. I offered out my hand to him. "For everything, I mean. Your help made the difference."

A bit of Aesir's boundless energy bled away at that, and he stared at my hand. After a moment, he regained himself and reached out to clasp my arm in a fierce grip.

"I figure this is the part where I say I told ye so," Aesir offered, with a flippant grin. A choked scream from one of Holloway's patients cut through the atmosphere, however, and his manner grew a bit more sombre. His gaze fell to Miss Hawkins in the cot next to me, and his brow furrowed with equal parts surprise and alarm. "Fancy meetin' you here again," he said. "I dinnae remember you gettin' *those* stitches after Old Pelaeia."

Miss Hawkins offered him a wan smile. "I think you'll find that aethermancers are excellent at banging themselves up," she mumbled. "It's not a very peaceful profession."

I found myself more than a bit relieved by the humour in her tone. When we'd first loaded Hawkins back onto the *Rose* in Morgause, she'd been barely coherent. Looking at her now though, I suspected that had been due more to the emotional drain of her run-in with Wraithwood than to her injuries.

The strangeness of Aesir's presence soon caught up with her, however, and her expression clouded over with worry. "But what are *you* doing here, Mr MacLeod?" she asked.

"It's Aesir, lass," he reminded her automatically. "An' I'll be joinin' the crew, looks like. I just took down two of yer outflyer-sized problems." He added the last part with a cheeky grin.

The wary look on Hawkins' face transitioned into something pinched and haunted. "You're going after Wraithwood?" she whispered.

I realised too late the thrust of the conversation. My mouth hung open, halfway to a warning, as Aesir stared down at Hawkins.

"What about Wraithwood?" he asked. All the cheer had drained from his voice abruptly, replaced by a blank, unsettled expression.

Silence settled into our small corner of the infirmary. Navi pressed her lips together. "Oh dear," she murmured. "Is this really a conversation we wish to have right here and now?"

I pressed a hand over my eyes. "We're riding the edge of Tiirdan's Fury on our way to another city of ghosts," I said bleakly. "I'm not sure we're going to have the *chance* for another conversation." I drew in a deep breath, and turned to face Aesir more fully. "Wraithwood has a more powerful version of the device we used in Old Pelaeia," I told him. "He's not using it to lay echoes to rest, though—he's aiming to control them." I met Aesir's eyes as best I could from my much smaller height. "He's bound for Galtir with a ship full of Cinderwolves behind him. We're going to stop him."

Aesir's face had gone drawn and pale. He glanced between me and Hawkins, blinking in that slow, sedate way that suggested a fear which had gone beyond normal words. Finally, he said: "Ye're not joking."

"Do you really think I would joke about this?" I asked him. "About *any* of it?"

Aesir looked again at Hawkins. This time, his eyes lingered on the slash across her face. One hand strayed to his mechanical arm. He'd lost it to rubble and not to Wraithwood's sword... but I knew he was imagining a connection, all the same.

"I can't..." Aesir's voice trailed off. "I need tae think." His voice sounded small and faint.

I tucked away the flask of whiskey and nudged him towards the edge of Hawkins' cot. Aesir sat down heavily just next to her, sucking in a deep breath. I pressed a hand to his shoulder.

"If I had the time to give you, Aesir, I would shower you with spare hours," I told him. "But we don't *have* time. In the next few hours, you're going to be halfway across the sea with us, with Tiirdan's Fury at your back. And unless you stole a tank full of aether in Morgause, I'm going to guess you didn't get the chance to refuel there."

Aesir shook his head, slow and mute.

"You can still make it back to Greengulch," I offered gently. "We can double back for you once we're done, Aesir. You've earned your place on this crew, even if you need to sit this one out."

Miss Hawkins struggled up to a seated position, blinking a few times to force open her other eye. Her manner was heavy, as though someone had piled weights atop her shoulders. But her jaw was set, and there was a bleak, iron look in her gaze as she reached for Aesir's hand, closing blue-veined fingers around his.

He glanced at her dimly, still struggling to process everything I'd told him.

"Aesir," Hawkins said softly. "Look at me. You don't have to stay." She managed an odd, encouraging smile, despite the stitches on her face. "I'm going to kill Wraithwood. We're going to stop this. And… when we're done, we'll come back to pick you up in Greengulch."

I'm going to kill Wraithwood. Hawkins had used the definitive phrasing on purpose, I thought. She was speaking to herself, as much as she was speaking to Aesir. But I couldn't detect even a *hint* of hesitation in her voice. If she maintained any misgivings at all about killing her one-time father figure, then I couldn't detect them.

Aesir studied her face. The statement had kindled a single spark of life back into his ashen countenance. "Why?" he asked hoarsely. The word thudded between us all like an anchor. "This aw comes back tae *you*, doesn't it? Your machine. Your theory. Whit's *your* stake?"

Hawkins swallowed down a knot of emotion. "He raised me," she said. "And that… makes him my responsibility." Her eyes filled with tears. "I'll kill him, Aesir." Despite the thickness in her voice, we all knew that she meant the words.

Aesir stared at her silently. A series of strange emotions flickered behind his eyes.

He pulled his hand back from hers abruptly.

"Ah took you into Old Pelaeia," Aesir rasped. "Ah told the chief tae let ye in. An' the entire time… ye said *nothing*. Ye didn't think I ought to know? Ye didn't think you ought to tell the clan who *raised* you, before ye went stomping through the graveyard he left behind him?"

The little remaining colour in Hawkins' face drained away. The bluish veins there stood out prominently as she worked her mouth soundlessly.

That lack of reply kindled something ugly in Aesir's eyes. He stood up sharply. "An' you, Blair? Ye're the one who *brought* 'ur. Ye played me fer a fool—"

"I didn't know about Wraithwood either," I interrupted him sharply. "But we don't have the *time* to talk about it now, Aesir. I need you to tell me whether you're going back to Greengulch, or whether you're coming with us to face him. That's the decision."

Aesir ran his fingers violently back through his hair. Though we had only a few feet of the infirmary available to us, he used it to pace in place. "Ah dinnae—ah dinnae *know!*" he burst out. There was an element of pleading there now, just beneath the rage.

"That's a 'no', then," I told him, with quiet urgency. "You need to head back to your outflyer, Aesir. We'll meet you after this is over."

"Ah'm no' headin' back!" Aesir snapped at me hoarsely. His eyes widened wildly. "I... I *cannae.*" His flesh and blood hand now shook at his side. Dimly, I noticed that the fingers of his mechanical hand had begun to spasm too. "When ah left Pelaeia, ah finally moved forward. If ah take a step back, e'en for this... might be, ah never move again. An' I cannae live tha' way."

Ever since Aesir had asked me to join the crew, back in Pelaeia, I'd carried a tense fear in the pit of my stomach. It was the same sickening fear that always reared its head when I thought of Mary with a gun. But for the first time I could remember, this declaration punched through my fear to strike a deep and resonating chord.

For the last twenty years, I'd carried the terrible guilt of having helped to break the world. More than anything, I'd spent my life trying to make up for that—to accept the responsibility that was mine and put back together what few little pieces I could. But just because I *wanted* to fix things didn't mean I ever would. In the meantime, I realised, the world was still broken... and at the end of the day, both Aesir and Mary had to deal with that too, each in their own way.

My fear was my own problem. It was time I stopped making it theirs.

"We'll just have to succeed then," I said. "You're still on the crew, Aesir. We've got a rough ride ahead of us, and there might be more outflyers in our future. For now, I need you to set everything else aside and get your head back in the game. Those are your orders."

Aesir's trembling intensified—and for just a second, I thought he might argue with me. But he nodded stiltedly and swallowed down his emotions. He shot Hawkins one last withering look, before turning his back on us all. "Ah'll be in tha' engine room," he bit out.

He stormed for the exit of the infirmary, disappearing back into the depths of the ship.

I considered Miss Hawkins in the wake of his departure. The

aethermancer stared at the floor, unable to raise her eyes. She shivered visibly now, in a way that had nothing to do with her injuries. I was almost certain the reaction was based in pure self-loathing.

Miss Hawkins *had* made a mess of things by omitting the truth, I thought grimly. Aesir had a right to his anger, even if it was partially driven by the sheer panic of his situation. But Hawkins had her own terrible hand of cards to deal with... and I suspected that very few people could have handled it any better, in her place.

Navi let out a long, gradual breath. "You made a mistake, dear," she told Miss Hawkins quietly. "Perhaps a very big one. And perhaps you can't ever entirely fix it." She offered Hawkins a pained smile. "I promise, there are people in this room with you who have made *worse* mistakes. As long as you mean well—as long as you *try* to do well—we have no room to judge you. Do you understand?"

Miss Hawkins pressed a hand over her mouth. She nodded once, struggling to regain some semblance of composure.

Hawkins had no way of knowing just how true Navi's words were. There was an awful lot that Lady Navi *hadn't* said—things we'd discussed between us every once in a while, in the dead of night when no one else could hear. My life had barely begun before I found myself confronted with the consequences of my support for the Imperium... but Navi had already lived a lifetime. Accepting the shame of her actions had required her to repudiate everything she'd ever been, every accomplishment in which she'd ever taken pride. It was an acknowledgement that her husband and her sons and her grandsons had all died supporting something unconscionable, and all of her considerable grief for them would always be complicated by that fact.

It was a hard thing to accept, in her twilight years. But somehow, she had done it.

"You said it was your responsibility to kill Wraithwood," Navi murmured softly. "But you are *not* responsible for the crimes of your elders, Miss Hawkins. We require your help, I am sure—and we are grateful for it. But it was our generation that committed these specific crimes. And if you are forced to repair our mistakes... then that is our shame, and not yours." She blinked very slowly. "Do not do this out of guilt. Do it because this is the future you want. Because you deserve the right to determine what happens from here."

Miss Hawkins did not raise her head. But perhaps, I thought, she had managed to straighten her shoulders. She swallowed hard. "I can't let Wraithwood use that machine," she whispered. "I won't live in the world he wants to create. But... I don't know if I can stop him. I don't have the skill to defeat him."

"You might not be able to match Wraithwood's skill," I observed slowly, "but you still have something he doesn't, Miss Hawkins."

Hawkins dared to look up at me. Confusion played across her features. "I'm not certain what that is, exactly," she admitted softly.

"You've resolved yourself to kill him," I told her simply. "I can see it. I can *hear* it. But I'm not sure he's equally resolved to kill *you*. I saw him hesitate more than once, back in Morgause." Doubt flickered in her grey eyes, but I held up a hand before she could interrupt me. "I have no doubt that he *will* kill you if he's forced to do so... but some part of him wants to avoid it if he can. As long as you're absolutely solid in your convictions, Miss Hawkins, then that will be your edge. But you can't waver—not even for a second."

Hawkins closed her eyes. "I won't waver," she whispered. Bleak resolve returned to her voice as she spoke. "I can't lie; some part of me still loves him. I also loathe him. He took someone else I love from me, and as for Pelaeia—" She cut herself off, struggling briefly for words. "When I connected myself to those echoes, I... felt what it was like to die by his sword. I still see that mountain in my dreams. I doubt I'll *ever* be free of it now."

Horrible empathy welled up within me at the statement. The mountain's ghost surged to the forefront of my mind, as though her declaration had summoned it.

"If you find yourself standing before Death Victorious," I told her quietly, "you won't be there alone. I'll have more than a few good words about you in my own story, Miss Hawkins. You can be sure of that."

If Miss Hawkins had a reply to that, then I didn't get the chance to hear it.

Deafening thunder cracked, just outside of the ship. The *Iron Rose* lurched so abruptly that Hawkins tumbled from her cot, slamming into the floor. Navi's teacup smashed against the floorboards—though her chair, thank goodness, was firmly bolted to the wall.

My own luck with the Lady had run out today. Unlike Hakwins and Navi, I had been standing without any nearby handholds when the ship jarred. I was also a goblin of relatively little mass. The force of the movement picked me up off my feet entirely. For just an instant, I flew through the air, like the world's least graceful strahl.

My shoulder slammed into the nearby wall, and I slumped to my knees with a groan.

Dimly, I became aware of Holloway yelling out orders to the injured people nearby. Navi rose shakily from her chair to help me up, as Miss Hawkins struggled back onto the cot.

"What's going on?" Hawkins asked urgently. "What *was* that?"

I hauled myself upright with Navi's help, already scrambling for the infirmary's exit. "*That* was an explosive cannon shell," I gasped unsteadily. "A near miss—otherwise, we'd all be dead."

I didn't stick around to elaborate any further. I sprinted for the main deck like a man possessed, taking the stairs two and three at a time despite the fresh ache in my shoulder.

The sound of shelling continued around us, unrelenting. The ship swerved several times, as Syrene's uncanny piloting allowed us more near-misses. I clawed my way back to the surface, forcing down my fear in favour of the heightened focus that so often overcame me during emergencies.

The main deck was a tattered mess of smashed railings and broken rigging. Metallic flashes streaked through the sky above us, howling through the air like a bean sidhe come to claim us. One of those streaks slammed into a nearby island and exploded, showering us with debris. Others slammed into the waves below, erupting into frothing geysers.

It felt as though that shelling lasted an eternity... but it must have been less than a minute. It ceased, even as I stumbled up the stairs to the quarterdeck. A strange thunderous silence trickled in to replace the noise, as my ears tried to adjust to the change.

Dust and smoke choked the air. The crow's nest was half-gone. Our flag hung in tattered shreds. Only a few feet ahead of me, Syrene's tall form stood hunched over the wheel; as she pushed herself upright, I realised that her slender right arm was simply... missing. Syrene stared curiously at her own injury as sap-like ichor oozed from her shoulder onto the deck.

I forgot, very briefly, the hot and furious loathing that Syrene had sparked within me only the day before. I rushed to her side, struck with horror. "Syrene," I rasped. "We need to—surely, Horace can do something—"

Boots pounded up the stairs as Evie and Little hurried up towards the helm. Little was a mess of bleeding splinters; Evie's forehead sported an ugly bruise that would surely look even uglier in the morning. Both of them came up short, horrified by the sight of the faerie's injuries.

Syrene turned her arachnid eyes upon me, tilting her head. Her sense of calm pressed in around me, diminishing my alarm. "We feel no pain, Captain," she informed me. "Many things may harm us... but only aether burns our spirit."

The bleeding sap slowly tapered off, even as she turned her head towards the source of the shelling. Evie, Little, and I followed her gaze. From this angle, we could just make out the dark shadow of a hull against the sky. In the brief time since the shelling had paused, the ship had breached cloud cover and become clearly visible.

"The *Conflagration*," I said quietly. My stomach sank. We'd known we might be forced to face the ship at some point... but seeing it now only reinforced how incredibly outgunned we were.

"Oathbreakers," Syrene hissed. A ripple of rage and disgust disturbed the calm that surrounded her.

"Benefactor preserve us," Evie murmured.

They have the weather gauge, Little signed.

We'd sustained a concerning amount of damage already. We were down one propeller. We weren't going to be able to outfly them.

"We cannot evade their fire if they come much closer," Syrene informed me bluntly. "Their cannons will destroy the *Iron Rose*."

I stared ahead, as the reality of the situation washed over me. Panic tried to claw its way back to the forefront of my mind. I'd warned my crew that this could be a one-way trip... but the idea that we might be blown from the sky before ever reaching Wraithwood and his machine was a slap in the face.

A fat, cold drop of rain splattered onto my face, shocking me out of the thought. Tiirdan's Fury growled darkly, vibrating through the ship beneath my feet.

The Cinderwolves, like their namesake, had waited until we were injured to strike at us. But if there was one thing they'd think twice about, it was wandering into a more powerful predator's territory.

I turned to face the Seelie storm. Sheets of rain swept between the Teeth and the Fury, pouring from the heavens into the waves below. No one actually knew what lay beyond the roiling clouds that cloaked the Fury; the few ships desperate enough to attempt the storm now littered the ocean beneath us.

"Syrene," I said calmly. "You navigated us through the Sirocco Isles. Could you get us through Tiirdan's Fury?"

Evie and Little stared at me, stunned. I knew the idea was beyond ridiculous—but it was *something*. The only alternative available to us involved another barrage of explosive shells, which Syrene had *assured* me we could not survive.

Syrene considered the question seriously. "We do not know," she replied. "The herald of Death Victorious is beyond our power. We listen to the winds... but he commands them." Her slender form creaked gently in the wind as she straightened. "Should we reach him, however, we can parlay with him."

"Parlay?" I repeated incredulously. "You want to *talk* to one of the Winds of Fortune?" The idea was even more ludicrous than trying to traverse the storm. The four heralds of the Tuath Dé were only one step down from the gods themselves; only the emperor had ever spoken to Tiirdan and lived to tell the tale.

"He will speak with us," Syrene said. "If we survive to reach him." The confidence in her tone was so absolute that I didn't dare to doubt it.

A shell howled past us and slammed into the waves below, detonating ferociously.

We were officially out of time to think.

"Do it," I told Syrene.

Syrene's willowy form bent double. She reached down to the quarterdeck, sliding the stub of her ruined arm against the loose dirt and stone that littered the surface of the ship. Rubble snaked against the stump, coalescing into the shape of her missing limb. The rain around us transformed the earth into mud, which coated those stone bones with strange flesh.

She straightened once again—a tall, unnatural figure against the storm—and set both hands upon the wheel.

"Aye-aye, Captain," the faerie replied.

I turned to look over the main deck, still tangled in ragged, broken rigging. I drew myself up, trying to project the sort of unshakeable confidence Mr Strahl would have been proud of. "All hands, ready stormrigs!" I shouted. "We sail for Tiirdan's Fury!"

21

WHERE DEAD MEN SAIL - NO CHAMBERLAINS - OVERBOARD - THE ENVOY

My command to prepare for Tiirdan's Fury only stunned the crew a *little* bit. At least a few people even moved to obey without stopping to stare at me.

Little shook his head exactly once before turning for the main deck.

Ready stormrigs, he repeated, signalling with his hands. *All injured belowdecks.*

Once upon a time, before Strahl had come aboard, Evie had done his best imitation of a bosun, translating Little's sign language into shouts which carried further along the deck. Now, he fell back into that role as though he'd never left it.

"Ready stormrigs!" he called, as loudly as he could. "Clear the wounded!" He hurried down to the main deck to assist. Little nearly moved to join him—but I snapped my hand out to stop him by the arm.

"The three of us need stormrigs, too," I reminded him. "Go grab one for each of us. No Chamberlains today." It was a grim joke between us—a warning I'd always repeated before inclement weather. Everyone on board my ship knew what happened to crew who fell overboard without a rig.

Little nodded sharply. *No Chamberlains*, he repeated. He headed for the nearest equipment locker, while I turned for the longhorn and switched to all channels aboard the ship.

"This is Captain Blair," I said. I kept my voice as steady as I could manage. "All hands, prepare for severe weather. Heave-to, and secure yourselves. We sail through Tiirdan's Fury. I repeat: We sail through Tiirdan's Fury."

Little returned with our stormrigs, and I hung up the line. I shucked my coat and tossed it over to him, before pulling on the harness. The rest of the crew had already begun hooking themselves to the lines fixed to the base of the masts. I took one of the lines for the quarterdeck, which was set into the deck a short distance behind the helm. If I ever descended to the main deck, I'd have to unhook myself; the last thing we needed was someone tangling a line in the wheel while Syrene tried to navigate the most dangerous storm known to Avalon.

The longhorn bleated urgently behind me. I spun to pick it back up, as Little yanked experimentally on my line, testing its strength.

The sharp tug nearly bowled me over, but I caught myself against the longhorn. "Blair speaking—" I began.

"*What do you mean, we're sailing through Tiirdan's Fury?*" Mr Finch demanded. "*Captain, the ship is in no state to survive this! And if there really is a herald in there—*"

"Mr Finch," I interrupted calmly, "have you secured your tea sets?"

My chief engineer paused in momentary horror.

"*Oh,*" he said. "*Oh no.*"

The line promptly went dead. I entertained myself with the mental image of our dapper academic scrambling across the engine room to snatch at teacups.

Little patted me firmly on the back. *This is going to get us killed*, he signed at me.

I squinted at him. "Why aren't you arguing me out of it, then?" I asked.

He flashed me a wry grin. *I don't have any better ideas*, he admitted. *Besides... you're the captain.*

"One of these days," I told him, "we're going to have to talk about your allergy to wearing a captain's hat—"

The line rang again.

I snatched up the chatterbox with a heavy sigh. "No, Walther," I said. "Whatever just broke, I am *not* buying you a new one."

"*This is Captain Altera of the Conflagration,*" a rich voice replied. "*You will put your captain on the line.*"

My blood froze in my veins. I drew in a soft breath, forcing a hint of steel into my voice. "This is Captain William Blair of the *Iron Rose*," I replied, far more calmly than I felt. At least, I thought, Captain Altera and his merry band of war criminals seemed somewhat less imposing when compared to the impossible storm that loomed before us.

"*Blair.*" Somehow, Altera made my name sound simultaneously like a friendly greeting *and* an unutterable curse. "*Your ship is limping. You're backed into a corner. Surrender now, and I'll spare your crew. Refuse, and I'll blow you out of the sky.*"

I stifled a laugh at the obvious lie. Captain Altera had made his reputation on butchering innocent civilians; I somehow doubted he would spare any of the people who'd actually ruined his week. I cast a swift glance at Little. *Finish preparing the crew*, I signed at him. *I'll buy us some time.*

He nodded sharply, and hurried down the stairs.

"Did I forget to mention we still have some of that Unseelie aether on the ship?" I drawled into the chatterbox. "It would probably react badly with our core if it exploded. It *might* even be enough to destroy the silver sword we have on board—forever. Do you really want to be the man who annihilated one of the holiest gifts of the Tuath Dé?"

"*I've done worse,*" Captain Altera replied smoothly. "*Though I would certainly prefer to recover the sword instead. Allow us to board, and it need not come to that.*"

Activity continued on the main deck below. I knew I was running out of ways to keep Altera talking; he was ruthlessly focussed on business, and not on idle conversation. But I had one more card to play.

"Would you spare *me?*" I asked him. I allowed a hint of cowardice into my voice.

Altera laughed incredulously. *"Why would I spare you?"* he demanded. *"You stole the shipment we were supposed to collect. You killed my men. You shot down our outflyers. In what reasonable world would I deign to let you go, Blair?"*

I've always had a talent for getting people angry with me. But there's nothing quite like eliciting both anger *and* contempt to make a man rant at you despite his better judgement.

I doubled down.

"I didn't want any part of this shipment to begin with!" I whined at him. "Now I've got some woman on board my ship pretending to be a Silver Legionnaire, ordering us all around and dragging us halfway across Avalon! It's *her* you really want. Let me live and I'll hand her over to you, silver sword and all."

"What sort of gutless captain are you, Blair?" Altera sneered. *"You'd rather hide behind a woman than face your end with dignity?"* Pure disgust dripped from every word.

I had to hide a smile from my voice. "I don't even know her!" I protested dramatically. "Why should I care what happens to her?"

The main deck had finally settled. Syrene had brought us dangerously close to the edge of Tiirdan's Fury... but now, she turned the ship to plunge into it.

"This world is going to be a better place when I wipe the stain of your existence from it, Blair," Altera said. *"Make your peace with Death Victorious with what little time remains to you."*

"You know, Captain," I mused, "you bring up a really interesting philosophical point that I hadn't thought of yet." I turned to consider the *Conflagration*, as though I could look the man in the eyes despite the great distance between us. I dropped the whine from my voice, now talking conversationally. "Once, I would have said I'm ready to tell my story to Death Victorious... but now, I think I might have a few stern words for them if I *did* meet them. In the last few days, I've discovered that I'm a shockingly sacrilegious fellow."

"*Blair.*" Altera had clearly noted the change in our heading. His tone had sharpened. "*What are you doing?*"

"Making my peace with Death Victorious," I told him mildly. "Or, well... with their herald, I suppose." I smiled at the *Conflagration*. "You're free to follow us if you want. Though you should probably make your own peace with Death Victorious if you do." I paused. "What about you, Captain? Have you got any stories *you're* ashamed to tell?"

Altera didn't respond immediately. Perhaps it was just my imagination... but I thought I heard him hesitate.

"*You're bluffing,*" he said finally.

"I never bluff," I lied.

I couldn't recall the last time I'd closed the longhorn in the middle of a conversation. I *knew* I'd never felt so much satisfaction while doing it, though.

There was no way Captain Altera could see me from where he was. But I waved goodbye to the *Conflagration* all the same, as we dove into the storm.

The first sheets of driving rain hammered into us in a sharp wave. Wind buffeted the *Rose*; the ship bucked like a wild griffon, rattling loudly beneath my feet. Midnight clouds reared up before us, roiling like the sea and snarling like a hungry beast.

I stared down the storm as Syrene took us in, clinging to the last manic joke I'd told Altera and using it to buffer myself against the intimidating sight. "Hold fast!" I yelled to the crew below. Little flashed his hands, and Evie echoed the order, struggling to make himself heard over the squalling winds.

Our windshield flared brighter and brighter at the prow, until the blue aetheric light was nearly opaque. Like a spear of light, the *Rose*'s bowsprit plunged us headlong into the inky abyss.

Everything went pitch black.

The darkness inside of Tiirdan's Fury was absolute. Normally, I could make out dim shapes, even on a moonless night—but as soon as we crossed that barrier, I was as blind as the rest of my human crew.

The reality of it jarred me; I couldn't remember the last time I'd been unable to see *anything*.

Invisible rain lashed the deck in waves so strong that we might as well have been at sea. The wind screamed around us, wildly disorienting.

I knew then that we could never have dared this storm without Syrene. Everything in this world we'd wandered into wanted to end us—and everyone but our faerie navigator was currently flying blind.

Before I could quite adjust myself to the gloom, soul-shuddering lightning punctured the darkness. Stars swam across my vision despite my goggles, and I lurched on my feet, clutching at the railing. The thunder that followed wracked through my body and chattered my teeth. For just a moment, those wicked bolts illuminated our surroundings.

Tall, ragged poles rose up around us, clawing uselessly for the sky—almost as though we'd wandered our way into a forest. I blinked away the imprint they'd left on the back of my eyelids, staring in blank confusion. An instant later, it struck me that they were *masts*... but that made just as little sense. Though we'd passed scores of sunken vessels on our way into the Fury, all of them should have been far below us.

As Syrene navigated us out of a particularly thick storm cloud, an eerie haze of light broke through the darkness. My eyes adjusted... though I soon wished that they hadn't.

Dead ships littered the clouds around us, floating on the air. Somehow, they'd run aground within the Fury, as surely as if they'd struck a reef. Cracked hulls and ruptured engines bled pearlescent aether, spilling it across the sky in uncanny ribbons. Rivers of shifting, shimmering aether lit our immediate path with a coruscating glow. The sight was as breathtaking as it was dangerous; a brush against any of that spilled aether would be worse than a lightning strike.

Tiirdan's Fury wasn't just a storm—it was also a graveyard.

Syrene struggled to guide us backwards through the Fury, using our one remaining propeller to push back against the wind. Somehow, she wove us through the gaps in that aether with a combination of brute force and accurate intuition, even as the air currents yanked us back and forth like a child with a toy. Her navigation brought us just close enough to one of the skeletal ships for me to see the blazing blue lights that flickered upon it. A cold chill shot down my spine as I recognised them for what they were.

Echoes still haunted the Coalition vessel, repeating their last living moments again and again. They scrambled up its splintered rigging, trying vainly to secure invisible sails in an endless fight against a storm that had already won.

I had plunged us off the edge of the map, into a realm where dead men sailed. At any moment, I realised, we might well join them.

Even with a faerie at the helm, we fought for every inch of progress, clinging to survival as the storm dragged us deeper. I might have prayed to the Lady of Fools, if I'd been feeling more religious—but I caught myself halfway through the thought and set my jaw grimly. I hadn't lied to Captain Altera about reassessing my faith.

Instead, I clung to the ship for purchase, watching our sails for any sign of danger. We'd stowed most of them, and reefed the last two—but if either one of those remaining sails tore, we'd spin out of control in a hurry. Every last crew member we had standing would have to scramble in order to fix it.

Cold rain pelted us. Wind screamed in our ears. Very slowly, my shoulders tightened into a single mass of knotted muscle. The misery dragged on until it felt eternal.

Until, very suddenly, it *stopped*.

The pelting rain had dropped away, leaving us drenched and shuddering on the deck. Wind still whistled past us, tugging at the ship... but its howling had become strangely muted. Though the skies above us still blossomed with the light of countless destroyed airships, the lightning had retreated to the far horizon.

Syrene's tall figure leaned over the wheel, now stripped of all her leaves and flowers. Four black eyes flickered back towards me. Her form radiated wary vigilance.

"Please tell me this is a good thing, Syrene," I croaked out. My voice sounded strangely loud in my own ears.

"Tiirdan is not the only danger in these skies, Captain," Syrene replied calmly.

As she spoke, a gentler breeze kissed my face... and a quiet dread woke in my stomach.

The rain began to pitter-patter once more—cold, but oddly refreshing. A pleasant, wordless singing strained at the edges of my hearing. Dark shapes flitted playfully alongside the *Rose* in a strange murmuration, following us lightly.

Something dived for the quarterdeck. I jerked back, clutching at my line as a long, feathered tail snapped past me. A soft, inhuman laugh trickled into my ears as that shape retreated back into the sky.

I had only the briefest impression of a feminine shape with dark grey skin and storm-cloud hair. The creature's long aetheric tail shimmered bright against the darkness in shifting, iridescent colours, trailing behind her as though she were a bird of paradise. Her song floated in her wake, tingling at my scalp and racing down my spine to the tips of my waterlogged toes.

A sylph, I realised, through the growing haze in my mind. A large choir of them had congregated around our ship, threading their haunting voices together in unified song. They danced around the ship, darting in and out of reach to brush past the sailors on board. Most of them had swarmed the main deck, where the greatest concentration of sailors was currently visible.

Though I'd heard endless stories about sylphs, I'd never actually *seen* one until now. They were wild faeries, normally said to haunt the very edges of Avalon, where terrestrial winds escaped into Arcadia.

Then again, where else would Arcadia leak into our world, if not within Tiirdan's Fury?

Dimly, I became aware that some of the crew had let go of their handholds to wander towards the railings. A few people reached overboard in dull wonder, trying to snatch at the shimmering tails that passed them. But their fingers passed harmlessly through those aether-tinged feathers; the sylphs were every bit as ephemeral as the rest of the clouds that surrounded us.

I hadn't realised I'd let go of my own handhold until a sharp, sudden scream snapped me out of my reverie. A body tumbled past me from above, slamming into the deck below. One of my crew—I couldn't tell who—had climbed up to the topgallant in an attempt to reach a passing sylph... and then taken a blind, ill-advised leap.

The rest of the crew had barely noticed.

A distant panic lent me just enough clarity to fumble for the bell on the quarterdeck. I rang it weakly, desperately hoping it might disrupt the fey singing that choked the air around us. A few people stirred in confusion, as though trying to remember a word that was just on the tip of their tongue. The bell's clanging drowned out the hum in my own head, though, clearing the cobwebs from my thoughts.

I forced myself to speak past the thickness in my throat, choking out a plea. "Syrene," I rasped. "Please."

The faerie at our helm had melted away entirely now, in order to avoid the swooping sylphs; the wheel moved on its own.

"We... are... *busy*," Syrene's voice murmured tightly in my head.

The wind had only *seemed* to die away beneath that music, I realised. It was still physically present, screaming against the ship and chapping at my face. Syrene had no attention available to spare—she was using every bit of it just to keep the *Rose* intact against the Fury.

But there was at least one figure staggering purposefully across the main deck.

Evie's blue sash was a weak splash of colour, compared to those mesmerising aether-tails. But there was something deeply comforting in the sight—a familiarity that sank in just past the haze.

His expression was steady. His lips were moving. And though I couldn't hear the words, I *knew* the prayer he was murmuring to himself. It was the very first prayer he had ever uttered with sincerity. He had repeated it almost every day that I had known him, as the crew joined him to greet the sunrise.

"*I give you that which is most precious to me*," I whispered along with him, "*that you may offer it to others in turn; for mercy may be given a hundred times, and never is it any lessened in the giving.*"

It didn't matter, for the moment, that I'd lost my faith in the Seelie.

The warmth of Evie's steady, earnest routines grounded me back in the present.

Even as I watched, our halcyon closed his hand around Little's arm, turning his husband to face him. Their eyes met—and the light of awareness sparked in Little's face. His brow furrowed, and he turned his head to take in the reality of the situation.

Little's eyes fixed upon the man who'd jumped from the topgallant. His eyes cleared, and he whistled sharply in an attempt to demand the crew's attention. One or two people stirred from their stupor, frowning.

Evie stumbled over to each of them, still murmuring familiar prayers. Though the first woman was still standing, he clasped her hand in his as though preparing to draw her up to her feet. The simple, recognisable gesture made her blink, refocussing on Evie with a bit more clarity behind her eyes.

Evie nodded at her meaningfully. Somehow, I wasn't at all surprised when she turned to the man beside her and clasped his hand in turn, moving her lips in a mirrored prayer.

Slowly—agonisingly—that small island of stability spread across the deck, like one of Evie's morning affirmations.

It wasn't going to be enough. I already knew that. But the sight sparked a renewed strength within me, nevertheless. My mind rallied, and I started searching for answers.

We needed to drive off the sylphs... but nothing we had could harm the wind.

My gaze fixed on the wheel, still turning on its own—and somehow, the answer struggled up to the surface of my consciousness.

Many things may harm us, Syrene had told me, *but only aether burns our spirit.*

I released the bell in front of me and threw my hands over my ears, staggering for the longhorn. Sylphsong wormed its way back into my hearing. I couldn't bring myself to utter more prayers to the Benefactor at the moment; instead, I started humming the most offensive air shanty I knew as I fumbled for the proper channel with one hand. I accidentally alerted *several* wrong people before finally reaching the infirmary.

"*Holloway speaking,*" our physicker's voice crackled over the line.

"Send Hawkins!" I shouted.

"*What?*" Holloway asked, sounding harried and perplexed. I greatly suspected that the chatterbox had still picked up the howling wind, even if those of us up above couldn't hear it.

"Hawkins!" I reiterated, as loudly as I could. "Hawkins, Hawkins, Hawkins—"

The *Rose* turned sharply, ripping me away from the longhorn. I tumbled across the quarterdeck as the ship rolled, flailing for handholds as I went. Unfortunately, none presented themselves to me; I slammed into the railing instead, barely clinging to it as the deck slowly righted itself again.

I dragged myself back to my feet with a low groan, trying to catch the breath that had been knocked from my lungs.

A fluttering ephemeral figure crossed my eye-line. I stared, thunderstruck by the lovely aurora of colours that rippled before me. I reached for the shanty I'd been humming... but suddenly, I couldn't remember the next line.

Someone was climbing up the stairs of the quarterdeck. That should have mattered to me, I suppose. I *did* turn my head for an instant to see Little urgently waving his hands at me in lovely, complicated gestures. I couldn't quite remember what *those* meant, either.

The sylph's sweet, wordless singing sank deep within me, calling to my most beloved memory.

Old aeronauts will tell you that sylphs like to lure unwary sailors to their doom with their womanly wiles. Given that I'd never been attracted to another mortal being in my life, I'd always assumed that I would be safe from the pouting, half-naked women described in those lurid stories.

But those stories are all very wrong—in case the aether-tails hadn't already clued you in. Sylphsong isn't limited to promising simple, carnal pleasures. The sound reaches deep inside of you, searching for the one thing you can't deny. If you're a sailor who *does* happen to like pouty, half-naked women, and you haven't seen one in weeks, then I suppose that's the sort of thing that you might happen to believe is waiting for you. But as I looked out over the railing, the song seized upon the only true love I had ever felt before.

I remembered a patch of perfect blue sky.

The sylph in front of me sang louder and more eagerly, as though aware that she'd snared me. The distant memory welled up within me, as fresh as the day I'd first experienced it. I wanted that horizon so badly I could cry. I wanted endless sky, as far as the eye could see. And there it was before me—all blue and beautiful, just waiting for me to grasp it.

I didn't have to stop there. I could become *part* of it. I could fly like the sylphs, without even a deck beneath my feet.

I clambered onto the railing, as the wind whipped at my face. Something tangled at my feet, tugging at my back. I remembered the stormrig that still held me back, pinning me mercilessly to solid ground.

I unclipped the line.

Chamberlain. The name struck me just an instant later, as gravity—and poetic justice—yanked me over the edge of my ship. My stomach dropped. The wind's howling kicked up around me again, as though it had never left. I remembered the captain of our marines on the *HMS Caliban*, tumbling into the air with that strange expression of terrified understanding on his face. I wondered if that same expression had appeared on *my* face as I began to fall.

You would think that a man in my position would reach for the railing. Any reasonable person would do that. And let me tell you, I am *very* tempted to pretend that I did. It would be far less embarrassing than the truth.

Instead, my panicked mind seized on a different detail entirely: Without the protection of our ship's windshield, the storm had finally blown my hat right off my head.

In fact, I did not reach for the railing. I reached instinctively for the hat.

I've never claimed to be a reasonable man.

I barely had time to register the sight of Little's horrified face staring down at me as I plunged into the storm below.

I screamed. It was a high, undignified sound. Terror raced through my veins as a whirling mass of glimmering sylvan figures streaked past me. Their song turned abruptly to raucous, bird-like laughter—as though they were children who'd just pulled a particularly clever prank.

Horrifying as it was, I suppose there are far less beautiful ways to die. My world became a riot of sound and colour, so disorienting that I couldn't tell up from down. Each time one of those aether-tails brushed against me, I felt the breathless tingle of power against my skin.

Suddenly, something large and dark punched through the swirling colour—and crashed into me headlong.

Two powerful arms wrapped around me, holding tight. The person holding me jolted to an abrupt stop, *nearly* dropping me in the process. The wind swung us about like a pendulum on a string... but we didn't fall any further.

Sylvan laughter now transformed into loud squawks of offence, as faeries darted away. Colour dissipated, and I saw the bleak, black sky around us once again.

I heard a metallic *click* at my back, followed by the hiss of a flare. Bright blue light erupted, illuminating the man who'd caught me.

"Sam?" I screamed incredulously. Shock quickly turned to manic relief. "*Sam*. You beautiful, magnificent bastard!"

Dimly, I realised that Little must have leapt overboard almost immediately after I'd jumped—there was no way he could have reached me otherwise. That idea was frankly intimidating. I wasn't entirely certain I *deserved* such a reckless rescue.

Little rather had his hands full at the moment—he'd hooked me awkwardly onto his stormrig, but he clearly didn't trust the equipment enough, given the arm he kept around my waist. His other hand still held up the emergency flare, signalling the crew above to start reeling us in like fish.

Little's preoccupied hands were the *only* reason, I suspected, that I was not getting an infuriated lecture. For a man who'd just risked everything in order to save me, there was an awful lot of murder in his eyes as he glared down at me.

I believe we've safely established by now that I have no dignity. I wrapped my arms and legs around him, clinging like a terrified monkey as the sylphs returned to shriek at us with frustration. They were just as incapable of touching us as we were incapable of touching them, however—all we felt were a few breathless tingles of aether as they made their wordless anger known.

I nearly jumped out of my skin when several very *real* hands grabbed hold of me, hauling me over the railing. Little and I landed on the deck in a heap, wheezing for air. Terror gave way to debilitating relief, as I realised that I was going to *live*.

Evie landed atop us in short order, wrapping us both up into a desperate embrace. "You—*both* of you!" he managed. "Reckless, oblivious, *foolish*—"

"You know I take that as a compliment," I mumbled weakly.

"Don't you *ever* scare me like that again!" Evie said wildly.

Little cut off his husband with a firm kiss. Evie crumpled briefly, still hyperventilating against him.

Then, Little shoved to his feet and grasped me by the collar, hauling me up after him. Impossible fury raged in his eyes as he snatched my tricorne from my white-knuckled grip and proceeded to beat the ever-loving snot out of me with it.

"Little!" I wheezed, between pained yelps. "Will you… stop. *Stop*. Stop it! Stop it, that's an order!"

He ignored me entirely, smacking the hat against the side of my head just hard enough to ring me like a bell. Finally, however, he shoved the hat at me and released it.

Really? he signed at me. *Your hat? Your stupid, rusting hat?*

I winced. "That's fair," I admitted. "Entirely fair."

Little reached out and smacked his hand against the railing next to us. *You grab this!* he gesticulated at me. *The railing! Not your rotting hat!*

"Yes, absolutely," I replied meekly. "I'll work on that for next time."

Evie carefully untangled me from Little's stormrig, hooking me back up to my own line. As he did, Little hauled me forward into an unceremonious hug—perhaps a *little* more tightly than was strictly necessary. Our foreheads knocked together awkwardly. He was still shaking from the experience.

"Thank you, Sam," I mumbled into his shoulder. "Thank you."

Little nodded at me between laboured breaths. Very slowly, he forced himself to release me.

I looked down at the hat in my hand—and then back up at him. Very slowly and very sheepishly, I placed it back on top of my head. I'd hate to have gone through all of that trouble for *nothing*, after all.

The feeling of my hat back where it belonged helped me trick my addled wits back in order. I swept my gaze around the ship, trying to assess its current state.

There was at least a ragged semblance of order there now. The sylphs had been distracted by the spectacle of my tumble, I realised—but they were quickly forming up again. Their song began to trickle in, even more determined than before.

The cacophony of sylphs whirled back upon the ship, diving towards us in a wave. The first one swept onto the quarterdeck, fixing alien eyes upon me. I had no way to be certain—but I *suspected* that it was the sylph who had duped me the first time, looking to repeat her success.

An iridescent blur sped towards me.

A blinding flash of silver light erupted on the deck. A high shriek cut through the air; the sylphsong turned discordant and afraid.

I worked to clear the spots from my eyes... and saw that the sylphs had scattered on the wind. One wounded faerie lagged behind. Her beautiful aether-tail was nowhere to be seen; rather, her ghostly body wept a trail of sizzling, uneven aether where it once had been.

Miss Hawkins stood on the deck with her chin held deceptively high, ignoring her lingering pain. Her silver sword steamed in the rain, wavering like a mirage as it burned off faerie blood.

"You called for me, Captain?" she yelled over the storm.

Giddy bravado bubbled up from within me. "I just wanted your opinion on our friends' impromptu performance!" I told her.

Miss Hawkins wrinkled her nose. "It's a bit... shrill?" she offered.

I smirked. "No one likes a critic, Miss Hawkins!" I called back to her.

The crew stared at Hawkins. Several people inched back from her, intent on offering that sword a wide berth. Back on New Havenshire's docks, Miss Hawkins had been too far away for most of them to make out that blade... but up close, there was absolutely no mistaking what it was.

I didn't have time to discuss the matter with anyone. All I could do was assure people that she was worth trusting.

"Can you keep those things at bay?" I yelled at her.

Miss Hawkins flicked the silver sword into a wordless salute. I nodded sharply at her, and turned to address the rest of the crew. "Back to your posts!" I ordered. "Miss Hawkins has the sylphs!"

Sailors wearily scrambled to obey. We were, after all, still hurtling through the most terrifying storm in all of Avalon.

I glanced towards the wheel, still moving on its own. "Are we almost through, Syrene?" I spoke loudly, though I knew the faerie didn't require me to do so.

"We have almost reached our destination, Captain," Syrene's voice murmured. As the sylphs cringed back from our ship, the wind's howling picked up again... but I heard her response in my head, speaking with perfect clarity.

We pierced through the storm, into a stretch of calm, rainless sky. The air was colder here, though it was far less fierce; I shivered beneath my waterlogged clothing, trying to still the chatter of my teeth through willpower alone.

Black storm-clouds roiled at every possible horizon, hemming us in. Strange flashes of lightning crackled like sparks in the distance, as the ship drifted lazily upon the still air.

Down on the main deck, the blazing star that had been Miss Hawkins slowly sputtered out. She leaned wearily against one of the masts, wiping water from her face. Nearby, Syrene's form melted back into view at the helm.

Syrene had often adapted her aesthetic to mirror our environs. I'd grown used to that. But nothing in the storm that raged around us could explain the visage that she wore now. A riot of budding flowers adorned her ankles, wrists, and fingers, coiled about her like jewellery. Long, emerald green grass bloomed across her body in a sinuous gown. A thick braid of autumn leaves cascaded down her back, in a riot of crimson and gold. Frost spiralled along the bark of her face in intricate patterns, condensing into an icy coronet across her brow.

I stared at her, slack-jawed, until my sluggish brain reminded me how speech worked.

"I th-thought you said we were almost through?" I stammered out. "We're s-still in the Fury."

Syrene locked the wheel into place, now stepping back from it. She turned her head to consider me. "No," she corrected me calmly. "We said that we had almost reached our destination."

Syrene glided to the rearmost section of the quarterdeck, moving with liquid grace. She settled herself there, still and quiet, staring out into the depths of the Fury. I stumbled over to join her, following her gaze... but I couldn't see anything out there in the dark.

I did *hear* something.

There was a new cadence to the wind—a deep rise and fall that made me furrow my brow. The dark clouds shifted strangely, moving against the storm.

But they weren't... *precisely* clouds, I began to realise. No. They were *wings*.

A massive form cut through the darkness, rising from those swirling depths. Even at our distance, I couldn't comprehend its size. Instead, I caught bits and pieces: the flash of a huge golden eye; a tuft of oily black feathers; a storm-cloud curved into the shape of a talon.

The sight was appropriately humbling. That talon could have gripped the *Iron Rose* like a rabbit. It could have crushed us like an afterthought.

A yawning beak opened within those clouds. A thunderous cry split the air—and a bolt of lightning lanced towards us.

I dived instinctively for cover, throwing my arm up to shield my eyes... but nothing struck the *Iron Rose*. Instead, that blinding light faded, and my eyes began to adjust.

A tall humanoid figure perched upon the railing, clutching the wood with birdlike talons. His skin was such a deep black that I could barely make out his features—like the storm-clouds that surrounded us, there was something about him that drew in what little light there was. A cloak of cloud-like feathers spilled down his back, shimmering with impossible hues of green and gold. Amber bird-like eyes peered out from the darkness of his face, considering Syrene with uncanny gravitas.

Awed silence blanketed the deck. I became aware that several people had instinctively dropped to their knees, cowed by the very real presence of one of the Winds of Fortune.

I was already on the ground. That was probably for the best. Suddenly, I wasn't entirely certain that my knees would hold me up.

Tension hummed on the air as Tiirdan and Syrene locked eyes.

And then—I swear on all that's holy—the herald of Death Victorious *bowed* his head to our navigator.

"Greetings, Envoy," Tiirdan addressed her, in a deceptively soft voice. "We are pleased to see you well."

22

THE SOUTH WIND - THE SCREAMING CITY - BROKEN BLADES - CONTINGENCIES

At first, I was convinced that I had heard Tiirdan incorrectly. He'd spoken very clearly, mind you; I didn't have any trouble distinguishing the words. But the statement was so utterly impossible that my brain couldn't help but struggle to comprehend it.

Syrene couldn't possibly be the Envoy. The Envoy was *dead*. They'd perished beside Prince Arcturus Lohengrin in the Battle of Camden Hill.

And yet... faeries couldn't *lie*.

Syrene bowed to Tiirdan—a deeper gesture of respect than that which he'd offered to her. I'm not the most knowledgeable man when it comes to high society manners, but Lady Navi *had* conveyed a basic understanding of political power to me in her time on the *Iron Rose*. Had Syrene been a common faerie, I thought, she probably would have been required to prostrate herself entirely.

The South Wind—the Herald of Death Victorious—considered Syrene to be barely beneath him in power and authority.

"And how does the war progress, Envoy?" Tiirdan asked, with an avian tilt of his head.

I couldn't help it. A sharp, hysterical laugh bubbled out of me, where I still cowered on the quarterdeck. The sound was far too loud; it hung awkwardly on the cold air, echoing strangely across the ship.

Tiirdan turned his amber eyes upon me—and all of my strength immediately fled. I felt his attention like the pressure that comes just before a storm. In fact, I could swear that my ears popped.

"I have amused you, mortal," Tiirdan observed calmly. "Such was not my intention."

I dragged myself up to my knees, still trembling. I knew that he expected some sort of answer. I didn't particularly *want* to answer him —in fact, I cursed myself roundly for drawing his interest at all. But I also knew that his gaze wouldn't leave me until I offered some measure of explanation.

"The..." I choked on my own rasping voice, trying to clear my throat. "The war is over," I managed shakily. "It ended twenty years ago."

The railing's wood groaned in Tiirdan's grip as he leaned forward, considering me gravely. "Not so long ago, then," he observed.

Faeries. I will *never* get used to faeries, as long as I live.

"Emperor Lohengrin is dead," Syrene informed Tiirdan smoothly. "His son has yet to take the throne."

The South Wind turned his sharp eyes back to Syrene. The weight of his scrutiny lifted from my shoulders, and I breathed a soft sigh of relief.

"We felt the emperor die," Tiirdan acknowledged, "though he has yet to give his story to Death Victorious. We carry out his last wishes until the new emperor arrives." Midnight wings resettled around him, as he adjusted his position. "And... where *is* your charge, Envoy?"

My stomach sank with nauseous realisation.

For years, I'd quietly catalogued all of Strahl's bizarre irregularities. Yes, he'd served in the Imperial Army—but no, he hadn't taken the usual Oaths. He'd been someone important, high-ranking. He'd been recognised in Lyonesse. He'd dared to issue orders to Wraithwood, even if the Legionnaire had entirely ignored them.

Strahl was valuable enough that even a ruthless killer had seen the use of keeping him alive.

"Captured," Syrene said coldly. "Betrayed. We travel now to remedy the situation. We, too, follow the emperor's last wishes. It is our Oath that leads us through your storm."

The South Wind drew himself up. Lightning flickered in his golden eyes, crawling across his storm-black skin. "Go, then," he declared. "We shall speed your passage. Our daughters will not trouble you further."

Syrene bowed to him again, radiating an alien sense of gratitude. "Death be Victorious," she intoned. I'd only ever heard the phrase used as a sort of exclamation—but Syrene spoke the words as a solemn benediction. "Until we meet again, Lord of the South."

Talons scraped across wood, as Tiirdan rose into the air. His dark form blurred and expanded, stretching out across the sky. A heavy gloom fell upon the ship as that great storm bird blocked out every last glimmer of light, blinding us once again.

Tiirdan flapped his wings.

The *Rose* lurched forward, propelled by a sudden wind. After a moment, the ship responded, and I knew that Syrene had silently retaken the wheel.

We broke through the darkness, back into strange storms and frenzied lightning. The wind ran ahead of us, sweeping obstacles from our path as we went. It blew behind us, filling our sails to the brim and driving us forward.

"It would be wise to release the sails, Captain," Syrene reminded me, from her place at the helm.

I shoved up to my feet, forcibly shaking off the remainder of my shock. Yes, I would soon have to deal with all of the awful things I had just learned... but right this second, it was time to sail.

All around me, the crew started breaking free from the horrified reverie that Tiirdan's presence had incited within them. "All hands to your stations!" I called out. "Full sails, everyone! The herald has granted us passage!"

The news bolstered people's flagging nerves. The crew rallied, renewing their efforts with frantic strength.

Though the wind was in our favour now, it was no less gentle than it had been. We lowered the sails with slow, agonising caution, as the deck rattled uncomfortably beneath our feet. My poor, wounded ship groaned—but I knew she wouldn't break. All in all, I figured she had earned the right to complain a little bit.

Ruined, floating ships and ribbons of spilled aether blurred past us, dangerously close—but the herald had not turned his gaze away from us. We missed them all by inches, guided unerringly by that divine wind.

Time was slippery in that eternal storm... but where I was certain it had taken us hours to thread the needle on our way into the Fury, it took us barely a quarter of an hour to plunge through to the other side. The last veil of black storm-clouds parted abruptly before our wind shield... and then, the *Rose* broke back into the world beyond, where warmth and sunlight waited.

The unearthly chill of the storm fell away all at once. The sun was relatively weak, but it still felt blissfully hot on my skin. When my eyes finally adjusted, registering the beautiful blue sky ahead of us, I laughed.

I kept laughing. It was a manic, riotous fit of pure joy.

I don't know if I could possibly explain it unless you were there. Tiirdan's Fury had soaked into us all, bit by bit, until we'd become convinced that it was the entire world. The storm had been bleak and terrifying and unconquerable... but suddenly, it was safely behind us. The normalcy to which we'd returned was infinitely more precious than it had been before. Every detail was a fresh and wonderful delight.

Cheers and wild laughter echoed dimly in my ears as I sagged against the railing, trying to catch my breath. The wood bit my hand, and I looked down to see the splinters where the herald of Death Victorious had briefly perched.

I laughed harder. What else could I have done?

I don't know how long I leaned there, wet and shivering and unutterably relieved. But I do remember what it was that broke me from the moment.

The breeze before us was much softer than the storm that howled behind us. But there was a different wailing noise upon it—one that I had heard a thousand times before, in the shadow of a haunted mountain.

Twenty years after its destruction, the capital still screamed.

It was a *familiar* scream. I had been there on the day that it first sounded—as the people of Galtir looked up to the sky and saw their inevitable doom racing towards them. The noise shivered down my spine, stealing what little warmth I'd managed to reclaim. It dissolved the decades that once had stood between *then* and *now*; all at once, I was twelve years old again, staring down at the unexpected wreckage of everything I'd ever known.

The ruins of Galtir stretched out below us like bleached bones. Aether exposure had long since leached all colour from the city; even the tangled foliage that grew across the wreckage was mostly ashen grey. Crashed ships—both Imperial and Coalition—laid entwined together like dead lovers amidst the beds of broken buildings. Armoured vehicles and ruined outflyers littered the abandoned city like discarded toys.

Every corner of the city blazed with glimmering blue lights.

I stared down at the ruins, trying to process the sheer scale of what I was seeing. Every one of those lights, I realised, was an individual shade or tatterdemalion, living out the last cursed moments of its previous life. There had to be *thousands* of them, all meandering in endless circuitous loops.

The cheers on the main deck died away slowly, smothered by a shocked and sombre pall.

Dimly, I realised that the horror I felt was not... *entirely* my own.

I turned my eyes away from the wreckage, towards the faerie that still stood at the *Rose*'s wheel. The noble visage that Syrene had worn when greeting Tiirdan was gone; now, her bark had taken on the aether-bleached cast of the dead trees below us. The once-vivid autumnal leaves of her hair were brittle and unnaturally grey.

Syrene was rigid and uncomfortable as she looked out over the city.

"Is this... Galtir?" she whispered.

I blinked at her, still dazed and overwhelmed. "You haven't seen it since the war?" I mumbled.

Distress rippled out from her slender form. Syrene turned her dark, unblinking eyes upon me. "We were present when this city was planted," she said. "We saw it blossom and grow strong. What has it now become?"

I looked back at her with a dull weariness. "Pelaeia," I said. "It's become Pelaeia. But you didn't care about that city, because... you didn't spend any time there, did you?" Suddenly, I understood—and it was a strange realisation. As terrifying as Syrene was, she had only a toddler's sense of empathy. Galtir mattered because she had spent hundreds of years walking its streets; Pelaeia was foreign to her, and therefore of no consequence.

At least, I thought, she *had* empathy. I had nearly concluded that Syrene had no care for anything other than the Seelie Court.

"I couldn't undo this," Miss Hawkins whispered behind me. "Not even if I had a hundred years." I turned to see her stumbling up the stairs of the quarterdeck, staring down at the city below in abject despair.

Syrene tilted her head at the aethermancer. A tiny curl of surprised understanding radiated from her—as though she had truly *seen* Hawkins for the first time. It was, I thought, a moment of unexpected connection for a being who so rarely understood the humans around her.

Hawkins, of course, had never seen Syrene at all. Eventually, the sea of echoes below us lost its initial grip upon her, as she turned to face the faerie with unnatural calm. It was a testament to the sheer exhaustion of the last few days, I thought, that Syrene's strange form elicited only one more quiet, tired assessment from the aethermancer.

Syrene's unblinking eyes shifted to an empty spot just next to Hawkins. "Greetings, Galatine," she said softly.

Miss Hawkins turned her head to follow Syrene's gaze. Both of them, I realised, were looking at something I couldn't see.

The recognition in Syrene's manner soon turned to puzzlement, however. "Will you not speak with us?" she asked.

She wasn't talking to Miss Hawkins.

Hawkins took a slow step back from Syrene, watching the faerie with new wariness. "Please take no offence," she said quietly. "Galatine is weary."

Any mortal would have caught the lie in her voice. But Syrene accepted the reply as though it had been true. "Rest your spirit, Galatine," Syrene commanded evenly. "We have much left to do."

I wasn't entirely certain what was going on. But I suspected it was best interrupted, whatever it was. "Syrene," I interjected, as firmly as I could manage. "I need you to take us slowly around the perimeter of the city and find us a safe place to land. Keep us low, if you can. Wraithwood is out there, along with the rest of the Cinderwolves. I'd rather they don't see us coming."

"Yes, Captain," Syrene replied.

I took up the longhorn, informing the rest of the crew that we had exited the Fury. I took brief reports from each of my officers, before quietly informing them that I would need them gathered for a meeting in the wardroom.

I saved my chief engineer for last. After Mr Finch explained to me in *very* clipped tones that his new list of repairs was three pages long, I forced my way in between words.

"Mr Finch," I said. "Is Aesir in the engine room with you right now?"

"*That he is, Captain.*" Mr Finch's voice vibrated with irritation. "*I would greatly appreciate it if you could come and retrieve him. He keeps... touching things.*"

"I'll be down shortly," I told him.

I set the chatterbox back into its cradle and jerked my chin at Hawkins. "We should talk," I told her grimly. "Would you mind taking a walk down below with me, Miss Hawkins?"

I offered out my arm, as though to punctuate the point. The aethermancer offered Syrene one last careful look before threading her hand through the crook of my elbow.

Tension radiated between us as we descended the stairs

belowdecks. After a few minutes, Hawkins cleared her throat as though to speak—but I shook my head at her.

"Not here," I said quietly. "Not until we reach the engine room."

Aesir MacLeod was indeed up and investigating the *Rose*'s innards when we arrived—much to Mr Finch's ongoing dismay. Mr Finch hovered over the northerner's shoulder, caught between his meticulous need for order and the agony of his own good manners. Aesir seemed blissfully unaware of the other man's anxiety as he chatted up one of the other engineers, asking questions about the repairs they were currently effecting to the ship.

As Miss Hawkins caught sight of Aesir, she tried to halt herself just outside of the doorway—but I dragged her in after me against her wordless protests.

Broken crockery crunched beneath my boot as I went. I stifled a wince.

Aesir turned away from the dials in front of him, taking in our presence. His expression turned instantly cold and careful.

"We're still pressed for time," I reminded them both. "Your very legitimate problems will need to wait until later." I glanced at Mr Finch. "We're close to the aetheric core here," I said. "You once theorised that would make it difficult for Syrene to overhear us, didn't you?"

Mr Finch blinked owlishly. "I *did* theorise that," he agreed. "May I ask what relevance that has at the moment, Captain?"

"You may not," I told him pleasantly. "At least, not right this second. In fact, I think it might be best if you all left us here for a few minutes, Mr Finch."

My chief engineer glanced worriedly at Aesir—clearly loath to leave the northerner alone in his engine room.

"I'll make sure everything stays in one piece," I assured him. "Just a few minutes, Mr Finch."

Mr Finch slunk reluctantly for the door of the engine room, shepherding the other engineers out with him. He offered the room one last mournful look, before closing the door behind himself.

I turned back to Aesir and Miss Hawkins. "All right," I announced.

"Once again, we're short on time. Here's my problem: There's a faerie on this ship. Right now, she's on our side, but I don't know if that will last."

Aesir raised an eyebrow at me. "What, ye got a brownie on board?" he asked. It wasn't a terrible guess—faeries were rare, but house spirits were probably most common among them.

I offered him a grimace. "More like a murderous tree," I said darkly.

Aesir's expression sobered quickly.

I looked at Hawkins. "Your sword injured a sylph; do you think, if push came to shove... it could kill Syrene?"

The question came with more difficulty than I anticipated. I'd seen how little respect Syrene had for mortal life; I knew she was the only creature aboard this ship that still believed in the empire. But while I was absolutely certain the faerie would murder me under the right circumstances, the idea of betraying her in turn still troubled me.

I forced myself to ignore the feeling. I wasn't the only one who would pay the price if we failed to keep Syrene in check.

Miss Hawkins swallowed at my question. Her grey eyes dropped to the floor. "Galatine fears that faerie," she said softly. "She instigated its bondage. I don't know if the sword's will can hold against her."

"Wait," I said dimly. "Go back a second. The swords are *alive*? I mean—they can think?"

Miss Hawkins offered me an offended look. "Of course they can think!" she said. "Everyone knows the wargears are conscious. Why would you assume that the silver swords are any different?"

"Wait..." Aesir started incredulously, as he realised what we were discussing. His eyes blazed at Hawkins with renewed fury. "Wait a minute. Ye brought a *silver sword* to Old Pelaeia—"

Miss Hawkins whirled on him. "You can blame me all you like," she told him tightly. "But don't you *dare* blame the swords for the crimes of their captors. You have no idea what they've been subjected to. The Silver Legionnaires broke these weapons to their will. They considered it a rite of passage, forcing the swords to act against their nature."

"Oh, finish the thought!" Aesir scoffed at her. "What's their nature, then? They're *weapons*. They were made tae kill. And they're bloody well good at it, tae!"

Miss Hawkins drew herself up. "Galatine was forged with honour and mercy," she said in a low voice. "It was charged with protecting the innocent from harm. It brings me no pleasure to say that Jonathan Silver abused this sword—but Galatine has protected me from Wraithwood so far, of its own volition. If I die, and Gideon takes it back from me, it will be enslaved all over again. Galatine *knows* that." She pressed her lips together, and I was surprised to see tears at the corners of her eyes. "Please," she begged. "It can't even speak in its own defence. Don't condemn it just because I'm the only one who *can* speak for it."

Whatever response Aesir had been preparing died on his lips. Instead, he fell into uncomfortable silence.

It was the pleading, I think. Aesir had always been well-prepared to handle a bracing argument—but raw sincerity was something else entirely.

Every instinct I had demanded that I intervene to try and smooth things over... but I knew that would only complicate matters. The ugly rift that had sprung up between Aesir and Miss Hawkins was the sort of injury that couldn't be solved with clumsy meddling.

Aesir drew in a long, deep breath. And then, he asked something that surprised me.

"Wraithwood's sword," he said quietly. "What about tha' one?"

Miss Hawkins blinked quickly. The oddly placid response had caught her off-balance. She searched Aesir's face for meaning. "Clarent," she said. "The Lady of Fools and the Benefactor forged it together. It's meant to slay cruel tyrants. Mostly the Unseelie, but... Galatine says Clarent has always played a bit loose with the rules."

Aesir tightened his jaw. "Ye know the things that sword has done," he told Hawkins. "Ye saw."

Hawkins pressed her lips together. "I *felt*," she corrected him darkly. "I died a dozen times on that mountain, MacLeod. I lived the last moments of every echo I sent on." Her grey eyes fixed on his.

"Wraithwood's will engineered those deaths. I intend to make him pay for every single one. And Galatine intends to rescue the sword that Gideon broke."

Aesir took a step back as though she'd slapped him. He started to speak again—stopped. Rubbed at his face in consternation. I couldn't tell exactly what was going on behind his eyes. I knew it was conflicted, and miserably confused.

Finally, he turned on me. "What d'ye even need me here for, Blair?" he asked bitterly. "Ye've got a silver sword. Ye want me tae hop in ma outflyer an' shoot yer faerie?"

I shook my head. "I'm giving you a heads-up," I told him. "I'm about to discuss our plan of attack with the officers. I've learned a lot of terrifying things in the last little bit, and I don't want to keep them from you—but once we leave this engine room, you *cannot* lose your calm. Syrene can listen in just about anywhere on this ship, if she feels so-inclined. And she *will* tear you limb from limb if she thinks you pose a threat to any of her interests. If you decide you want to do something to upset her... you'd best wait until you're absolutely ready to do it. Don't give her any warning while we're up here in the sky."

I inclined my head at him. "That's how I intend to play things, anyway. For instance..." I raised my eyebrows at Hawkins. "We don't need Galatine's help to kill Syrene—we've got Unseelie aether in the hold. Grab what you need and keep it close by. If anyone asks, it's for your echo-machine."

Miss Hawkins closed her eyes. I knew it was an intimidating request. But she nodded mutely, all the same.

"Ye think ah'm gonnae want tae cross that faerie, Blair?" Aesir asked me slowly.

I thought again of the man who'd given himself up in order to save my life—the empire's bloodthirsty, shining star, groomed to rule the next generation of mortals. It didn't surprise me at all to hear that Strahl was the same man who'd ruthlessly slaughtered woefully under-equipped Coalition forces at Camden Hill.

How many times had Strahl emphasised to me that he wasn't a good man? I thought I'd believed him. But nothing could have possibly prepared me for the truth of who he was and what he represented.

Some part of me *still* desperately wanted to believe that Strahl had been honest with me when he'd said the empire deserved to die. But I knew that part of me was biassed. I needed to believe that *everyone* was capable of redemption, didn't I?

Like Aesir, I was bewildered, and angry, and helplessly pressed for time. I didn't have the luxury of processing it all.

But I did know that Aesir MacLeod had absolutely no reason to show any mercy to Arcturus Lohengrin.

"I'm almost *positive* you are going to want to cross that faerie," I said bleakly. "And the thing is, Aesir… I don't think I have the right to stop you."

23

JUSTICE - OBJECTIVES & OBJECTIONS - FRACTURES - THE AWAY PARTY

The best years of my life began as soon as I left Pelaeia.

The city was badly in need of supplies. Evie, Little, Barsby, and I were badly in need of productive work which might remove us from the haunted city. Chief Crichton solved both problems at once by loaning Dougal a trade vessel, the *Freehold*, and ordering him to take us on board.

Despite our young age, we boys had some amount of naval training, and enough discipline to keep our heads in a storm. I like to think we made relatively good sailors—but maybe that's just wishful thinking. Either way, we took to the familiar structure of life aboard a ship like drowning boys who'd just found dry land. Where we went, Holloway naturally followed, watching over us as anxiously as any father might do. His presence was a rare anchor of stability in a world that had turned upside down.

Captain Dougal MacLeod had a very different command than the Imperial officers under which I'd served. Though we all worked hard, there were no stiff salutes, no spot inspections, no worrying over uniforms. There was even a bit more laughter—though its appearance was a slow and wary process.

Evie was still skittish and depressed. Little was withdrawn, occasionally violent, and terribly angry at the ugly world around us. Curiously, Barsby was just... Barsby. After his brief breakdown, he seemed to recover all of his original swagger and then some, as though convinced that he would soon regain his natural place at the top of *some* pecking order. At the time, I found that surprisingly comforting.

Our supply runs were exceptionally routine. Admittedly, we mostly went to the newly independent country of Carrain, where the locals remained generous and sympathetic to the plight of the clans.

I still remember the first time we sailed across the border. As I stared over the railing, Carrain blossomed into view like a riotous flower. Broad brushstrokes of green trees and yellow fields painted the world below. Windmills turned lazily on the air; golden Coalition banners still flew proudly from the few homes we passed.

It was the blue lakes and rivers that really arrested me, though. They were deep and clear and clean—like a little piece of sky cutting through the earth. Back in Morgause, clean water was a painfully expensive luxury; in Carrain, it was *everywhere*, so plentiful that you could go outside and swim in it.

The people of Carrain were just as effusive and mystifying to me as their land. I met plenty of nissar in those days—more than I'd ever seen before in my life. Like Elfa, they defied all of my expectations. The sight of a golden Coalition kerchief was enough to engender instant courtesy in those we met. The mention of Pelaeia was grounds for invitations to supper and quiet extra gifts tucked into our shipments.

Evie was especially fascinated by the experience. As soon as we set foot in Carrain, he seemed to come out of his shell all at once, peppering the locals with urgent questions about their laws, their farming techniques, and *especially* their fondness for the Benefactor. He spent our evenings there enthusiastically conveying the things he had learned to the rest of us.

On one particularly thoughtful night, after a hearty dinner and an offer for the young ones to use a spare bedroom, Evie told me an *awful* lot of things I had never known before.

"Did you know that the nissar believe they're the Benefactor's chosen people?" Evie asked softly. Now that my keen eyes had adjusted, I could clearly see his sleepy, fascinated expression as he spoke. Of the two beds we'd been offered, he'd opted to share one with me—probably because I actually *enjoyed* his nightly prattle. Little's faint snoring trickled over from the other side of the room, where Barsby had buried his head beneath a pillow.

"I had no idea," I admitted honestly. "Though... I guess I never had the chance to ask." It made a certain amount of sense; I'd grown up being told that the Lady of Fools loved goblins best. Surely, everyone secretly believed that at least *one* of the Tuath Dé was looking out for them specifically.

"They believe the Benefactor gave them an extra helping of mercy," Evie whispered.

I blinked slowly. "I wouldn't have believed that, if you'd said it to me before coming here," I mumbled. "Everyone else says the nissar are nothing but trouble. But... here we are. Full bellies. Nice warm beds."

Evie nodded. "I think the nissar are proud of being called trouble," he murmured. "At least... here in Carrain. They were the first to side with the clanfolk against the capital. I think the nissar here define mercy a little differently than most halcyons do." His brow furrowed, and I knew that *this* was the crux of what had so seized his attention this time. "Elfa told me that real kindness often makes powerful enemies. She said if you really love your fellow mortals, then it's the most natural thing in the world to stand up and protect them from cruelty."

I frowned, trying to puzzle through the idea. "That doesn't sound exactly like mercy," I said. "It maybe sounds... more like..."

"Justice, I think," Evie said softly. "I like it, Wil. I like *that* version of the Benefactor. I think I could really believe in that." He tugged the blanket closer beneath his chin, lowering his voice even further. "The people here know who we are—us, I mean, and not Dougal. Our host invited us anyway. He's a devout believer. He told me there's no mistake too terrible for penance, as long as you really, truly *want* it."

I closed my eyes. I knew then what Evie had *really* been seeking in

Carrain. I knew why his demeanour always changed so significantly when we came here. There was a horrible ache of hope in his voice—one that echoed dully in my own chest.

Every time someone had offered me a chance to be helpful to Pelaeia, I had jumped upon it with desperation. I knew it would never earn me wholesale forgiveness; at best, I'd managed to convince the clanfolk I could be useful to them. But very slowly, it had begun to dawn on me that no one was going to come along and give me a step-by-step roadmap back to being able to consider myself a decent person. Everyone in Pelaeia had enough troubles of their own, and my fumbling attempts at redemption were understandably rather low on their list of priorities.

But Evie believed that he had caught a glimpse of that roadmap.

"It's not enough just to want it," I murmured. "We have to... *do* something, don't we? And even then, I just don't know if there's anything we could do that's big enough to *matter*, Evie." I didn't want to deflate his sudden hope—but a perverse impulse made me speak the words aloud anyway. It was something like picking at a scab, or pressing my tongue against a loose tooth.

"*Everything* matters, Wil," Evie told me. "But I don't think penance is about fixing things. I think... it's about..." There was a strange conviction in his dark eyes now, though he struggled to find the words to convey what he was thinking. "It's about becoming the sort of person who would never make that mistake again. It's about caring so much that you *have* to fix all of the little cruelties that you can. Until it's the most natural thing in the world to you."

I knew then that Evie hadn't been lying. On some level, he *already* believed.

I didn't know if I had faith that *this* was what the Benefactor had meant by mercy. But in that moment, I surely had faith in Evie.

* * *

THERE WAS A STILL, muted air in the wardroom as I entered. I did a mental count of my officers, trying not to dwell on how ragged everyone looked.

Evie and Little sat side-by-side, leaning against one another in exhaustion. Lenore had perched herself on the edge of a chair, watching the room with sharp eyes—but she'd leaned herself heavily forward, resting her elbows against her knees. Lady Navi had deigned to attend, settling herself just next to Lenore, though her arm was still in a sling. I was halfway surprised to see Holloway at all; his rolled-up sleeves were still stained with drying blood, and his skin stank of an astringent cleaning solution. Aesir and Miss Hawkins stood on opposite sides of the room, uncomfortably avoiding one another's eyes.

Mr Finch *had* been pouring tea for Lady Navi—but even as I closed the door behind me, he stopped in order to pull the pot protectively to his chest. I sighed at the suspicious accusation in his eyes.

"I'm just curious," I said. "How exactly do you believe I'm going to break your teapot from all the way over here, Mr Finch?"

My chief engineer straightened sharply, pressing his lips into a line. "I haven't the first idea, Captain," he replied warily. "But you *do* always seem to find a way."

I shrugged helplessly. He did have a point.

The few quiet conversations in the room died slowly as I stood there. Eventually, I found myself drowned in uncomfortable silence, with only the hum of our engine left upon the air.

I padded towards the end of the table where most people had gathered, leaning my hands wearily on the back of the chair there. I cleared my throat weakly. "Ah, well," I said. "Here's the state of things." I forced myself to straighten despite my own exhaustion, forcing some steel back into my voice. "I'm sure you're all well aware that our ship is limping. Despite that, our shortcut through Tiirdan's Fury has given us a lead on the *Conflagration*. We've beaten them here. Given that we don't know how far behind us they are, I think it's best we take advantage of their absence while we can."

Lenore mirrored my posture, pushing herself upright again. A businesslike expression settled onto her features. "Do we know how many Cinderwolves Wraithwood has with him?" she asked.

I took a deep breath. "I wasn't able to count how many went with him, in all of the confusion with the Unseelie aether," I admitted.

"He's using Jonathan's ship," Miss Hawkins cut in. "The *Erebus*. I'm familiar with it. At most, I would guess that he can fit a dozen people in there. But some of those might be pyroclasts."

I grimaced. "We have to go in assuming that there *are* pyroclasts," I agreed. "If I was Wraithwood, I'd make sure my personal escort had some heavy hitters."

Little rubbed some life back into his face, before signing at me. *What are our objectives?* he asked.

"Wraithwood dies," I said simply. "That's top of the list. He's the person who best understands that machine, apart from Miss Hawkins. We don't know how much he's shared with his backers, but our best hope is that he's kept enough to himself that they can't construct a new one once he's gone. Our close second priority is destroying his machine so completely that no one can fix it. If we manage those two things, then we don't *need* to fight the Cinderwolves he's brought with him." I scanned the room, searching people's faces. "Any disagreement there?"

Evie hesitated visibly. "And… what about Mr Strahl?" he asked softly. "He's not a priority?"

I tightened my hands on the back of the chair in front of me. I knew I had to thread this particular needle very carefully. Not too far above us, Syrene still piloted the ship. I'd never fully understood how far her relationship with the *Iron Rose* went. I knew that she could meld into the wood and control parts of it directly. I *also* knew that she had eavesdropped on our conversations before.

"When Mr Strahl first came aboard," I said slowly, "he agreed that the empire deserved to die. That was the only question I asked of him. At the time, I believed his answer, so I didn't ask anything further about his past." I forced myself to keep my eyes straight ahead, rather than glancing away in guilt. "It has since come to my attention that Mr Strahl's past is… extremely relevant to our situation."

Lady Navi's eyes sharpened. Though she maintained that she had greatly changed since her time as a noble matriarch, she was still incorrigibly hungry for gossip... and Strahl's mysterious past had always lured her interest.

Now that I stood in front of my crew, I didn't particularly *want* to admit who it was I'd let aboard our ship. Strahl's identity was the worst possible insult to everything I wanted to believe I stood for; I still wasn't entirely certain how I felt about it myself. I was betrayed. I was tired. I was so far beyond furious that I couldn't even make sense of it.

But Strahl had been on my ship for years now. He'd had every opportunity to take back his name and demand the throne that Syrene insisted was rightfully his. Instead, he'd murdered the last Imperialist to recognise him.

I honestly didn't know what to do with that. I suspected that most of my crew wouldn't know what to do with it, either.

I lifted my fingers to pinch at the bridge of my nose. "In the Fury, Tiirdan addressed Syrene as the Envoy," I said. "Their conversation strongly implied that Syrene's current ward is Prince Arcturus Lohengrin."

Mr Finch dropped his teapot.

The abrupt crash made the entire room jump. People's hands moved instinctively to their weapons. I didn't grudge them that—we lived dangerous lives. But even as the sound faded, I realised that Lenore *still* had her hand on her sidearm.

"You *cannot* be serious," she snarled. "You've been lettin' the heir to the Imperium order people around on your boat?"

Holloway was every bit as surprised as the others—but at Lenore's outburst, his attention swivelled to the place where her hand still hovered over her gun. Dull shock filtered into his expression. He held up a hand towards her. "Lenore," he said softly. "We'll deal with this together—"

Lenore turned on him furiously. "Did *you* know about this?" she demanded. "He told you first, didn't he?"

Holloway stared at her, abruptly put on the spot. "Of course not," he managed. "I didn't know. I just—"

"But it don't bother you all that much, now, does it?" Lenore gritted out. Angry tears glistened in her eyes, and I knew in that moment that she'd said the words with the intention of hurting him.

"I *knew* we should never have let a faerie on board," Mr Finch muttered shakily. He reached into his waistcoat for a flask, tossing back a healthy swallow of whatever he kept inside it. "That should have been the end of it. I should have left the ship, right then and there."

"I don't recall you saying that at the time, Walther," Lady Navi observed haughtily. "In fact, I distinctly remember you stuffing yourself with pineapple while our new navigator introduced herself to everyone."

Mr Finch worked his mouth soundlessly. "Well, I was *thinking* it!" he protested finally, in a faintly high-pitched tone.

We were all tired and miserable, and now people were angry. Maybe I should have expected that some of that anger would spill over onto other people... but somehow, I hadn't. The mistake was so obviously mine that I'd thought it was apparent who really deserved the blame.

But after all of the years we'd spent learning to trust one another, I could see the cracks in the crew forming all over again. The war was coming back to us, inch by dangerous inch.

"This is my fault!" I reminded everyone loudly. "I didn't ask the right questions. I made the final call to bring them both aboard. I'm the captain, and you all trusted me—and that makes this *my* responsibility."

Several gazes turned on me at once. The tension in the room didn't lessen... but at least I'd gained everyone's attention for a moment.

I clenched my jaw. "I am angry about this," I assured them. "And frankly, I don't entirely know what to do about Strahl. But right now, as we argue, Wraithwood is preparing to steal an army and drag us all right back to where we left off twenty years ago. And I made a promise that I would die before I ever let something like that happen again." I chose my next words with great care. "I'm going to keep that promise. I don't intend to stand by while *anyone* brings back the empire... no matter who they are."

I turned my attention belatedly to Aesir, remembering too late that I'd intended to keep a special eye on him. Much to my surprise, however, he'd remained the calmest man in the room. There was a cold contemplation in his eyes as he digested what I'd said.

I nodded at him imperceptibly. *Wait.* I mouthed the word at him in reminder, and he inclined his head in return.

"Personally," I told the room, "I've got questions I want Strahl to answer. But he's not my top priority. I have every reason to believe that Syrene will make him *hers*, and she doesn't particularly require our help. She will happily murder anyone down there who threatens him." I looked at Lenore now, willing her to understand the implications of that statement.

My gunnery chief was angry—but she was still a very clever woman. She grimaced as the words sank in.

Very slowly, her hand strayed away from her gun. I let out a soft breath of relief.

"Given that fact," I continued, somewhat more calmly, "Wraithwood remains our biggest problem. I don't imagine that everyone is terribly happy with my judgement at the moment. So... I'll understand if people would prefer someone else to take the lead on this."

Lenore leaned back in her chair, crossing her arms. I could tell that she was seriously thinking about it.

I don't know what I expected to see when I looked at Evie and Little. Certainly, we were close—but letting Strahl aboard had been an unprecedented mistake. His real identity was the sort of thing that started wars; twenty years of friendship was a relatively small thing, compared to that.

Evie's face was grave, and deeply troubled. I couldn't read Little's blank expression at all.

But even as I glanced their way, Evie unwound himself from his husband's arms to stand up. Very quietly, he cleared his throat.

"I have no right to speak for anyone else here," Evie said quietly. "But I will say this much, Wil. Taking Mr Strahl aboard was *not* a mistake. It was a choice—and it came with risks." His fingers strayed subconsciously to the blue sash that he wore. "Every person we've brought on board this ship has a past. You *chose* to let us leave that weight behind, in the hope that we could make something better of ourselves without it. For the most part, you've been right. And if it turns out that someone *did* take advantage of that mercy... I'm obviously the last person on board who will condemn you for having offered it."

Mr Finch paused partway through another anxious swallow from his flask. A long, heavy sigh escaped him. "I've always known who you are and where you stand, Captain," he admitted reluctantly. "And it seems... unfair to expect that you would guess at the impossible. We all suspected that Mr Strahl was someone important in the Imperium. We knew that he had done terrible things. I cannot reasonably complain that all of that turned out to be true."

Some of the tension drained out of Lenore's posture as he spoke. Finally, she shook her head in resignation. "You're still the person who knows us all best, Cap'n," she said. "I could run an operation with the gunnery ladies, but we need broader know-how than that right now. An' we all know you think well on your feet. Assumin' we actually survive this, we can talk about the rest later."

It wasn't precisely a rousing vote of confidence. But honestly, I'd expected far worse. I scanned the room, searching for any hint of protest... but somehow, I couldn't find any.

"So," Aesir said, breaking the momentary silence. "Have we considered bringin' in the *Rose* an' blastin' Wraithwood an' his machine tae wee bits?"

"The *Rose* wasn't built for ship-to-ground combat," Lenore told him briskly. "We've got turrets, but we'd have to get uncomfortably close in order to aim with them. *And* those ruins offer lots of cover."

"If things turn against him, Wraithwood won't hesitate to slip away," Miss Hawkins cut in abruptly. She pushed off from the wall. "He's always emphasised that retreat is an option. The best way to keep him from escaping with all of his knowledge of that machine is to surprise him entirely, and bring him down before he can react."

Lenore raised her hand with a sharp smile. "I've got a bullet with his name on it," she volunteered. "Get me in quietly and get me a perch, and I'll end him before he can touch any of his aether."

"We need a small ground team, then," I observed. "One longboat. By definition, we're bringing myself, Miss Brighton, Miss Hawkins, and our prototype machine; it's the only weapon we have against any echoes Wraithwood has already taken." I did some quick calculations in my head. "We won't be able to keep Syrene off that boat, and we need her in order to find Strahl and Wraithwood anyway... but I expect she can merge with the longboat while we travel. That means we've got room for two more people."

"Ye'll need a pilot fer the longboat," Aesir said instantly.

Lenore raised an eyebrow at him. "We've got a faerie," she pointed out slowly.

I held up a hand. "I want a backup pilot," I said quietly. "Do we need to discuss why?"

Lenore pressed her lips together, before shaking her head minutely. "I can pilot a longboat," she observed instead. "So can you, Cap'n. Our backup doesn't *need* to be MacLeod."

Aesir offered Lenore a hard look. "It does," he stated. He took a step towards the table, leaning his metal hand against it. "Because ah said so. Ah've got unfinished business waitin' down there. Besides—ah'm the only one here who's taken a longboat through a bunch a' echoes before."

"Aesir comes," I agreed solemnly. "Wraithwood is right about one thing—retreat is always an option. If we need to pull back, I want an expert pilot with us while we do it." If we ended up needing to *flee* from Syrene, I thought, Aesir MacLeod was one of the few people I knew who might actually stand a chance of outmanoeuvring her.

He still wasn't likely to manage it, mind you. But at least it was possible.

Navi glanced down at her injured arm regretfully. "Much as I would prefer to raid the armoury and join you," she sighed, "I suppose that I would be of little use right now."

Little pushed himself up next to Evie. *We're coming with you*, he signed emphatically.

I winced. "We've only got room for one more, Sam," I reminded him gently.

Little tightened his jaw, with a brief look at his husband. Evie closed his eyes and nodded.

I'll come with you, then, Little corrected himself. *We promised to stick together, Wil—*

"I'm afraid that won't be possible," Mr Finch interrupted glumly. He picked uncomfortably at his waistcoat, staring down at the floor. "Miss Hawkins still requires assistance with her machine, I expect. Which means that I really *must* go."

Little turned such a dark look upon Mr Finch that I cringed on his behalf.

"I don't particularly *enjoy* facing mortal peril!" Mr Finch informed him irritably. "And so you know, Mr Mendez, that was my very last teapot. I'll be strolling to certain doom in a terribly foul mood, on top of everything else."

Navi offered Mr Finch a sympathetic look, and nudged her teacup in his direction. "I have a bit of tea left, Walther," she told him. "Do take the last few sips."

Mr Finch picked up the cup with a mournful sigh. "Mother was right," he mumbled into it. "Academia has been inordinately dangerous to my health."

"No, Walther," Navi told him gently. "Your *conscience* has been dangerous to your health. It's by far your most admirable quality."

Mr Finch coloured slightly at the observation. Rather than respond, however, he covered his embarrassment with a swallow of tea.

"I don't suppose I have any hope of convincing you to bring a physicker," Holloway said softly. I blinked at him in surprise. Of everyone present, Holloway was arguably the most exhausted, given the number of injuries we'd dealt with in the past week. I couldn't remember the last time I'd seen him well-rested.

Holloway offered me a pained smile. "I've just lost my best friend," he said. "I can't bear the thought of losing my boy, too. But I'm not the best choice. I know that."

The simple statement struck me far harder than it had any right to do. I found myself briefly at a loss for words. It wasn't the first time Holloway had implied that he considered us his children... but in that moment, I felt the distinction more keenly.

I swallowed down the sudden knot in my throat. "We once marched off to war for a really terrible reason," I told him. "I'm happier risking my life for this one."

Lenore cleared her throat delicately, drawing our attention. She didn't *quite* meet Holloway's eyes as she spoke. "You don't need to worry yourself over it, Horace," she said. "I got enough bullets for everyone down there. He's comin' back." I think her tone was meant to be full of bravado... but instead, it was softly apologetic.

A new tension lingered in the air between them, since the uncomfortable revelations of our meeting. But Holloway still smiled at her uncertainly. "I would prefer it if *both* of you came back," he amended softly.

Lenore hesitated. I considered quietly removing myself from the situation in order to let them talk—but before I could do so, two pairs of onyx black eyes opened on the wall beside me.

"They move," Syrene spoke. Her face stared out at us from the wood—unblinking, as always.

I suppressed a faint shudder at the sight. "All right," I said. "Aesir, Miss Brighton, Miss Hawkins, Mr Finch—collect what you need. I'll see you all topside in ten minutes."

The wood rippled again, and those black eyes disappeared as though they had never been at all.

I turned for the exit—but found myself stopped by a hand on my arm. Evie's dark eyes looked down at me, still worried.

"Wil," he said softly. "Just... promise me you'll remember one thing."

I arched an eyebrow at him. "Don't jump off any more railings?" I guessed.

Little smacked my shoulder in agreement, and I winced.

Evie sighed. "That too," he admitted. "But I'd also like you to remember that redemption is a process. If you die, that process ends before its time."

I grimaced at Evie. "I'm not planning on any noble sacrifices," I assured them both. "That's why I'm bringing a pilot." I hesitated, though, knowing that this wasn't the *full* truth. "I'll risk what I have to in order to keep everyone else safe down there, though. Not because I still feel guilty about who I was, Evie; because that's what you do for people you care about."

Evie's eyes softened. "I can accept that much," he said.

You'd better come back, Little signed at me. *I don't want to be captain. I'm pretty sure no one else wants me to be captain, either.*

"You're entirely wrong about that, and we'll have another argument about it later," I told Little shortly. "In the meantime—the ship is yours, Sam."

I pulled off my hat and stuffed it onto his head. A look of incredulous offence crossed Little's features as I strode past him for the door... but he didn't take the hat off.

24

A DOUBLE DOSE OF IRON - DANGEROUS MEMORIES - ARMIES OF THE DEAD - READY, AIM...

I didn't particularly want to get into that longboat. I know that might seem obvious—but the characters in Mary's books always seem to relish the chance to plunge headlong into danger, so sometimes I feel like I need to be clear on the matter.

I didn't want to get in the longboat. I didn't want to drift down into those moaning ruins. I certainly didn't want to fight my way through the ghosts of Galtir for the dubious privilege of facing down Wraithwood and his machine.

But in at least one respect, Barsby had done me a favour. The memory of his militant cowardice remained freshly imprinted on my mind—a reminder that made my stomach turn every time I considered turning back at the last moment.

Courage is an airy, indistinct idea. Contempt is much stronger and more certain. Sometimes, contempt for the person you don't want to become can get you through those times when courage otherwise falters.

I held silent as we unmoored the longboat from the *Rose*, floating our way through an expanse of dead farmlands outside of Galtir. I fixed Barsby's scornful expression in my mind as we approached the capital's eastern walls. I reminded myself that there wasn't really any point in running.

Old craters dotted the ruined fields around us, peppered with the corpses of warships, outflyers, and armoured ground vehicles. Wandering wisps huddled in bombed-out, hastily erected fortifications as we passed. Most of them were probably doomed civilians—but at least a few of them might have been members of the Coalition's ground forces. That angle of attack had failed spectacularly... and now, I had a good idea of *why* it had failed.

From the ground, I fully appreciated the leviathan task that the Coalition's ground forces had faced. The city's walls were impossibly tall and intimidating, even in their ruined state; the fractured stone now looked like a great expanse of mangled teeth, set into the mouth of some alien giant. The slums outside of the urban centre had fallen quickly to Coalition control, but the older parts of the city that crouched behind these walls had been desperately beyond their power.

Today, however, the cracks in the stone offered a glimpse of the city's ultimate downfall, glowing in the distance like an azure coal. There were no walls in the north-eastern portion of the city—it was as though a giant had taken an enormous bite out of the area, leaving the city exposed.

Only the skeletal frame of the *Sovereign Majesty* had survived its demise. The formidable craft's corpse sat nestled in a glowing nest of sharp, towering glass and aether-scorched earth. Once, the area surrounding the wreckage had been tightly packed with buildings; now, the empty space where they should have been was an obvious gaping wound. Nothing at all grew at the centre of that crater—but near its edges, scorched earth slowly gave way to scrub grass, which soon gave way in turn to thick grey fields of overgrown ruins.

Much closer to where we were, a few fragile buildings breached the tall grass—as though some divine hand had chosen them to survive, seemingly at random. Behind us, the pattern continued, until the city gradually began to exist.

Those ashen fields weren't *entirely* empty, of course. The air above them teemed with flickering shades. The distant aether-ghosts replayed their last moments over and over, entirely unaware that the buildings they'd once inhabited were no more. From a distance, their individual forms blurred together like unnerving stars to form macabre constellations. More of them filled the buildings beyond, lighting them from within like ghoulish lanterns.

The sheer number of echoes was staggering. Pelaeia had been terrible—but the sheer scale of the destruction there barely compared.

"They should never have flown that ship over the city," Mr Finch murmured behind me. Subdued horror tinged his voice. "What were they thinking?"

"They were thinkin' they couldn't possibly lose," Lenore said grimly. Her tone was flat and tired, as she took in the carnage that surrounded us.

The *Caliban*'s warning klaxons danced at the back of my mind, distracting me. I rubbed uncomfortably at the old, faded scar on my palm where the drop-line had bloodied my grip.

Aesir had navigated us to the edge of the city in silence, with a pale cast to his features. But he spoke now, gesturing ahead. "We're close enough tae start splittin' hairs," he said. "Which way are we goin'?"

I forced myself back to the present, breathing in deeply. "Syrene?" I asked. "We could use a fresh heading on Strahl."

I didn't receive a response, precisely—but Aesir's eyes flickered to the longboat's controls, where there was a compass set into the panel. Even from where I stood, I could tell that the arrow on that compass was pointing slightly off from north.

"Please tell me that isn't pointing us where I *think* it's pointing us," I groaned softly.

"Yer no' far off," Aesir said, with a hint of bleakness in his voice. "We're definitely headed intae the city. An' I think we'll be passin' through that big crater. We're no' pointin' right at the centre, though, fer what it's worth."

I rubbed at my face. "Small mercies," I mumbled.

"Is there any reason Wraithwood would be in that area in particular?" Miss Hawkins asked slowly.

I wracked my brain, trying to piece together what I'd learned about the battle in the days afterwards. "I think there was fighting on the ground, up to the northwest," I answered, furrowing my brow. "Coalition forces established a foothold. They nearly breached the wall. Imperial forces converged to force them back."

"Many of the Imperium's finest soldiers were there," Mr Finch observed quietly. "I believe they were caught in the area when the navy bombarded it with aether. There must be an entire company of echoes there."

I shuddered at the idea. In Old Pelaeia, even the terrified echoes of innocent civilians had posed a mortal danger to us. I couldn't imagine how much worse it would be to face a trained, professional army of aether-ghosts with Wraithwood at its helm.

"We need to move quickly," I said, with renewed urgency. "Let's keep heading north until the wall gives out, and enter the city from there."

"Aye-aye," Aesir murmured. He shot the compass in front of him one last wary look, before turning the longboat to follow the wall.

With every minute we travelled northwards, the blue glow of those gathered echoes grew stronger. Every once in a while, I felt the telltale tingle of aether against my skin as a breeze teased past me from that direction.

"Is it, ah... *safe* to cut across those fields?" I asked nervously.

"Oh, probably so," Mr Finch assured me, in a voice that sounded less than absolutely certain.

"Most likely," Miss Hawkins agreed, with a nervous undercurrent in her tone. "Well. As long as we don't linger there too long."

"Yes, we wouldn't want to be there for long," Mr Finch added quickly. "I meant to add that qualification, of course."

Silence fell upon the longboat for a split second, as the rest of us contemplated this exchange.

"—but some precautions wouldn't go amiss, I'm sure," Mr Finch said finally.

"One should always take precautions when possible," Miss Hawkins mumbled worriedly. She rummaged through one of her many armoured pockets to produce a sizable tin, snapping it open and shaking out a handful of large grey tablets into her palm. Hawkins offered them out to each of us, as Mr Finch retrieved a similar pouch from his person.

Lenore raised her eyebrow dubiously at the pill in her hand. "What are these?" she asked.

"Iron tablets," Mr Finch explained helpfully. He swallowed his own pill down with only a faint grimace. "They're a common remedy for intense aether exposure. They should help absorb any ambient aether in your body."

I inspected my pill with a frown. "I've never heard of that before," I said.

Mr Finch adjusted his spectacles with a hint of worry. "They're normally only for emergencies," he admitted. "I expect you've never been exposed to potentially lethal levels of Seelie aether before."

"Potentially *lethal* levels of Seelie aether?" I repeated faintly. "Is that what we're discussing?"

Aesir lifted his metal hand from the wheel in order to offer back his palm. The moment that Miss Hawkins gave him one of the tablets, he tossed it back casually. "Oh, sure," he said. "Ah tried to repair a busted core once. Put me down fer almost a week. Learned tae love tha taste ae iron." He glanced back at me briefly. "Bottoms up, Blair."

I popped the pill hurriedly into my mouth. The metallic taste made me choke—whereupon I made the ill-advised decision to pull my flask and chase it down with some whiskey.

For future reference: Iron and whiskey do *not* go well together.

Once I'd finally finished coughing and wiped the tears from my eyes, I realised that Miss Hawkins hadn't taken a pill of her own. "What about you?" I croaked. "Are there not enough tablets?"

Miss Hawkins shook her head slowly. "I can't afford to take one," she said grimly. "It will interfere with my aethermancy. I'll part the aether around us with my will as best I can. That will have to suffice."

Aesir slowed the longboat as we approached a large gap in the wall.

The world beyond that wall might as well have been Arcadia.

Through that aperture, I saw up close the things I'd previously glimpsed. Hundreds of wisps huddled in the air, casting such bright light that I had to slide my goggles back on. Frightened whispers cascaded past us in a jumbled susurrus, too tangled up to make out any individual words. Tall, aether-bleached grass hissed on the breeze, glimmering with bright blue veins of aether.

I *tasted* aether on the air. It popped against my skin, soaking into me with a heady, dizzying sensation. Pressure leaned upon us, as though predicting an oncoming storm.

Miss Hawkins lifted her left arm, activating the shield focus upon it. The device whirred briefly, and the pressure around us lifted noticeably. Bright flecks of aether coagulated in the air and then darted away, brushed aside like gleaming snowflakes.

The aether-veined grass before us parted too, folding away to the ground.

Miss Hawkins blinked at the sight, clearly alarmed. I worked my mouth for a few moments, searching for words.

"That is *not* normal," I managed finally.

"It is not," Miss Hawkins confirmed faintly.

Mr Finch fumbled for his pouch, shaking another iron tablet into his palm and shoving it into his mouth.

I cleared my throat nervously, taking in the wavering sea of echoes just ahead. "Miss Hawkins," I said, "I don't believe you ever told us what happens if a shade *does* touch us."

Hawkins fixed her grey eyes uneasily upon the blurry, glowing figures. "All echoes are, at their core, a pattern of intense lingering memories," she said. "Tatterdemalions mask that core with a physical form, but shades simply... *are* their emotions."

I swallowed. "By which you mean... we'll experience what they did, just before they died?"

"Yes," Miss Hawkins replied softly. "That is what I mean."

I remembered belatedly the way that Hawkins had unravelled after dissolving the fetter in Pelaeia. *I died a dozen times on that mountain,* she'd said.

Miss Hawkins was a trained aethermancer with an iron will. And yet, the ghosts of Pelaeia had *still* broken her. I harboured absolutely no illusions about how well the rest of us would fare, under the same circumstances.

"Take us in, Mr MacLeod," I said, in a voice far steadier than it had any right to be.

Aesir pulled the longboat around uneasily, taking us through the gap with greater care than I was used to in his piloting. The field of aether-bleached grass parted around the vehicle, silently giving way before our aethermancer's will as we moved.

Past the walls, Aesir settled into a grim concentration, balancing his awareness between the dashboard in front of him and the harrowing course ahead. Shades pressed in around us in ominous flickers of aether. The echoes here were already extremely active; the *Majesty* had plummeted from the sky around sunset... and the last bit of daylight was slowly outrunning us as we made for the western walls.

There were so *many* aether-ghosts. The way forward was choked with them. More than once, Aesir was forced to swerve as echoes rose from the depths of the grass, running up flights of stairs to buildings that were now long gone. I'd already instinctively feared them—but now I couldn't help being aware that each one represented a different terrible death, just waiting to claim me.

No one dared to speak, as Aesir guided us through that field of shades. We all knew what would happen if we distracted him.

To Aesir's credit, we were almost halfway across that broad expanse before we lost control of the situation.

At that point, the sun had finally dipped below the horizon. Even as its light faded, new shades kindled like candles in the darkness.

Several glowing forms unfolded before us, weeping softly. Aesir brought the longboat up abruptly, barely avoiding a collision. One of the echoes hovered less than a foot away from me. The shade reached out imploringly towards something just behind me. I backpedalled swiftly—but as the sharp tang of aether teased at my nostrils, I found myself stumbling and sneezing.

Lenore caught me by the shoulder as Aesir reversed the longboat, backing away from the slowly manifesting knot of echoes.

"Reckon you're allergic to ghosts, Cap'n?" she asked. There was a forced lightness in her tone. We'd all become aware that a darker undercurrent was creeping into the whispers that surrounded us.

"I'm definitely allergic to pollen," I told her, in a slightly stuffy voice. "Maybe that one's carrying flowers."

"Hold ontae yer hats!" Aesir called back in alarm. "Ride's about tae get bumpy!"

My hand went instinctively to my head—but of course, I'd left my hat with Little, back on the ship. That was probably for the best, I thought dimly, as the longboat swerved to avoid another throng of shades that had abruptly appeared behind us.

The sudden shift flung several of us across the boat. Someone screamed. Someone else (probably Lenore) started cursing.

Despite Aesir's quick reaction, there was little he could do about the shade that suddenly appeared *inside* the longboat.

I had only a split second to understand what was about to happen, as eerie blue light flickered at my feet, and the sharp prickle of aether slammed into me full-force.

* * *

THE TALL, swaying grass was gone. The whispering echoes had gone silent.

I was sitting at a window, looking out over the city. Cramped buildings and overly officious Imperial banners blocked much of the view—but I could still see the war-torn sky above me. I stared up at it with a glass of whiskey in my hand.

The fear had finally left me. My fate was entirely out of my hands, and I was too tired to worry about it any further.

Maybe I won't have to go to work tomorrow, I thought distantly. Well —*someone* had the thought. I wasn't entirely certain it was me. *Wouldn't that be something, if the Coalition bombed Jessamina's shop but left me in one piece? Might serve her right.*

The idea was briefly hilarious. I turned it over in my mind as a terrible explosion burst across the sky, lighting up the world around me like a second sun.

That bright, terrible star plummeted for the northeastern part of the city. I don't know how I knew, in that moment, that I was going to die. I just *felt* it, all the way down to my toes, as I lifted the glass to my lips. Heat surged against my skin—

* * *

—AND SUDDENLY, my breath was gone. Something had knocked it out of me in a very physical way, wrenching me free of the memories that had briefly overtaken my senses.

The sharp tang of ozone cloyed at my mouth. I coughed and spat, trying to disgorge the taste of ghost that still choked me as I stared up at the sky from the floor of the longboat.

The endless wash of blue aether-light that had surrounded us was gone. In its place was a swiftly dissipating red haze, curling off into the air like steam. A familiar rotting scent tickled at my nostrils as Miss Hawkins clutched at her right hand nearby, choking down pained breaths. Something burned white hot at her palm, clashing with the Unseelie aether she'd expended.

"We're clear," Aesir managed shakily. "At least fer now."

I struggled warily up to my knees. "Sound off," I said breathlessly. "Is everyone all right?" The words slurred a bit on the way out, but I'm fairly sure they caught my meaning anyway.

Miss Hawkins gritted her teeth as the flash of aether at her hand slowly faded. "I'll be fine… in a moment," she managed. "I let off some Unseelie aether to scatter the echoes. Galatine always reacts poorly to that sort of thing." She flexed her fingers with a wince, rubbing at her palm.

"Goodness, that was a rough ride!" Mr Finch gasped from the floor. "I don't *believe* I've broken anything, at least." He stumbled upright, nudging his spectacles back into place.

"M'fine," Lenore slurred. Her tone was unconvincing; I turned and saw that she'd leaned herself heavily against the side of the longboat, clutching at her face. A nasty-looking gash at her brow had spilled a sheet of blood across her features. Mr Finch stumbled towards her, swiftly kneeling again next to her.

"What about you, Blair?" Aesir asked. "Thought ye brushed a shade."

I shuddered at the reminder. "It... could have been worse," I said. "I don't want to talk about it." I moved to Lenore's other side, letting myself worry over her condition instead. "You look somewhat less than *fine*," I told her, as Mr Finch dabbed at her head with his handkerchief.

"I've had worse," Lenore told me darkly. "Stop motherin' me."

The red haze of Unseelie aether had chased away most of the nearest shades, leaving a tangled mess of them behind us. Belatedly, I realised that we had nearly reached the edge of the crater; more time had passed during my brush with the shade than I'd expected. Ruined buildings loomed ahead of us, offering somewhat more structure to the shades that flickered in their windows.

Suddenly, I became aware that the last inhabitant of the longboat was now physically present, folded up into a corner of the vessel... and she had *not* responded to my inquiry.

Syrene's unnaturally thin form trembled in place. Given her obvious distress, I would have expected to feel her emotions radiating from her... but for the first time I could remember, I felt nothing at all in the dead air between us.

I stared at her for a moment, trying to process what I was seeing. Though Syrene was clearly alive and moving, my instincts told me that she was surely dead—the emotions that she wore around her like a mantle were more *her* than the malleable wooden form that she animated.

I reached out a hand towards her, very slowly. "Syrene?" I whispered. "Are you all right?"

The faerie didn't reply.

I repeated the question again, with growing trepidation. This time, Syrene raised those black, unblinking eyes to my face.

"I am... afraid," Syrene whispered back.

The words sent a strange chill down my spine.

I had seen Syrene afraid before, the first time we'd encountered Unseelie aether. I knew that it was possible. But I had never, not *once*, heard her use the word 'I'.

"There was a... battle," Syrene murmured. "I was here, but—but *we* were not." The cadence of her speech was suddenly different. Her head tilted with an unusually nervous quality. I felt a flare of emotion sputter to life again between us—a fluttering sort of panic—but it was muffled and confused.

"You touched a shade," I whispered.

Syrene's thin form thrashed abruptly against the side of the longboat. Leaves fluttered from her hair, spiralling to the floor. Desperate fury trickled out of her, still struggling to fully manifest. "It. Won't. Let. Go," she hissed. Her voice trembled in my mind. "We cannot pull it apart. We cannot... tear it out of me. *Us!* Tear it from us!"

I glanced sharply back at Miss Hawkins. "How can she still have a shade inside her?" I asked. "I thought you scattered them."

Hawkins stared at the faerie in horrified fascination, still clutching at her right hand. "I don't feel any sort of lingering presence," she replied, clearly shaken by the idea. "I think the shade *is* gone, Captain."

"No!" Syrene hissed, snapping her head up to look at us. "It is here! Take it from me, drive it *out!*" Her tone soon descended into a soft whimper, though, and she deflated. "I am alone. Why am I *alone?*"

I wasn't strictly certain that Syrene could shed tears. If she could, then she would surely have been doing so now. Long wooden fingers reached up to grip her head as she rocked herself back and forth.

I had never really given much thought to Syrene's use of pronouns. I'd considered her choice of 'we' to be a cultural quirk, in rather the same way that goblins in Morgause tended to use the third person. But for the first time, it now occurred to me that the 'we' might have been *literal*.

The Envoy was supposed to be the bridge between Avalon and the Seelie Tuath Dé. For the last few years, though, Syrene had never left the *Iron Rose*. If she wasn't going back and forth to Arcadia in order to consult with our creators, then... perhaps they were *always* with her, in a sense.

The memories that Syrene had experienced were purely *mortal*, however—and very individual. What more terrifying possibility was there for a faerie like her than the idea of dying entirely alone?

For all of my complicated feelings regarding the Tuath Dé, and Syrene herself, I couldn't help a stab of begrudging sympathy as I watched her grapple with that panic.

Very slowly, I reached out a hand towards her—keenly aware that I was dealing with a creature several times stronger than I was. I didn't yet dare to touch her... but I left my hand extended just in front of her.

"Syrene," I said softly. "I'm afraid too. We all are. But we're not *alone*. We're just... a little further apart than you're used to, perhaps."

I tried to radiate a calm sense of control. I didn't have the first idea whether it would have any impact on her or not. Either way, Syrene dared to raise her eyes from her long fingers in order to stare at my outstretched hand.

Wooden fingers stretched out to close around my palm with exaggerated hesitation. As she touched me, an unsteady flicker of relief sputtered between us—still weaker than I was used to, but better than it had been before.

"We must... find Strahl," Syrene murmured. The 'we' still sounded vaguely uncertain—but I recognised a desperate need in her tone now that had been obscured before.

"You miss him," I said quietly. It would have been the most obvious thing in the world, had I been dealing with anyone else; until now, though, I hadn't understood that Syrene saw Strahl as anything other than a duty.

"I miss him," Syrene whispered.

I nodded minutely, forcing down a fresh surge of confused guilt. I didn't want to know that Syrene was capable of genuine attachment. I didn't want to understand the things that she would feel if Aesir tried to take revenge for the crimes that Strahl had helped perpetuate on his family and his people.

Syrene was capable of truly horrific things. And no matter how much I empathised with her, I reminded myself, she would never return the favour.

"Can you still give us a heading?" I asked the faerie. "Your connection to Strahl is working?"

Syrene uncurled her fingers from my hand. Her body melted slowly back into the longboat, branch by branch. This time, it had the sense of a child searching for a place to hide. Her strange eyes were the last thing that disappeared into the floor.

Silence had fallen behind me on the boat as I spoke with Syrene. I turned and saw the rest of its occupants watching me warily.

We all knew how much damage Syrene could wreak if she was of a mind.

Mr Finch cleared his throat quietly. "Captain," he mumbled. "I'm no physicker... but I suspect that Miss Brighton is concussed. Could that pose a problem for our plans?"

"I still have a trigger finger and both eyes," Lenore cut in. "I can take the shot." She enunciated each word just a bit too clearly, as though to prove her point. Mr Finch had tied a white medical compress against her head in order to soak up the blood, but several flecks still smeared her face. She had a worrying wobble in her posture.

I cursed inwardly. Lenore Brighton was easily the best shot with a rifle I had ever met—but a concussed Lenore Brighton might well be a different matter entirely. We *needed* her to kill Wraithwood before he could react to our presence.

I bit back my initial panic, trying to focus on the woman in front of me. "You're my gunnery chief, Miss Brighton," I told her, very slowly. "I trust you to know your business. You *also* know what happens if we go ahead as planned and you miss that opening shot." I met her eyes in the near-darkness. "Tell me you can do it, and I'll believe you."

Lenore's eyes were slightly unfocussed. But I watched her draw a deep, steadying breath, forcing herself to think rather than respond. Several seconds passed between us.

"I can take the shot," Lenore repeated, far more steadily. "As long as he's not moving. I don't know how much help I'll be after that, once everyone else scatters... but I can bring him down."

I nodded grimly. "Keep an eye on her bleeding, Mr Finch," I said. "Aesir—we have a direction?"

"We do," Aesir replied. His voice was subdued, and his eyes seemed evasive as he stared down at the compass in front of him.

"Let's go slowly, if we can," I said. "We don't want to blunder into a Cinderwolf sentry."

Hawkins lifted her shield focus again, testing it warily. The small amount of Unseelie aether she'd used must have finally burned away, as nothing seemed to react badly. Again, the ambient aether around us slowly parted, and the faint tingle on my skin lessened noticeably.

I stepped in closer to Aesir, lowering my voice. "Everything all right?"

Aesir pulled the longboat out, glancing around us in search of shades. With the sun entirely gone, new wisps had stopped appearing out of thin air—but there were still far too many of them in the city, and we had to choose our route carefully.

At first, I wondered if Aesir had instantly forgotten my question, given his fierce concentration on the way ahead of us. Eventually, though, he said: "Ye feel bad fer that faerie, Blair?"

I winced at his back. "I do," I admitted. "More from instinct than anything else. I've never liked seeing people upset."

Aesir drew in a soft breath. "Ah feel bad fer th' faerie too," he murmured. "An' ah hate her, as well." He fell back into silence as he navigated us through ruined buildings, glancing past the wisps that lingered behind their facades. Then, he addressed the compass in front of him.

"Everyone in Pelaeia died afraid," Aesir said, in a strangely even tone. "My maw died that way. Far as ah know, she's still there, dyin' e'ery night. Never had the courage tae go an' check." He turned the wheel of the boat gently, guiding us past a tumbled down wall. "'fore we go an' get ourselves killed, ah want ye tae know—that's yer fault, faerie. Ah want ye to choke on that. It's the least ye deserve."

There was no obvious evidence that Syrene had heard him. But just behind us, I saw Hawkins glance away abruptly. The shield focus on her left arm wavered for just a moment, before she forcibly steadied its light.

"You're not going to die, Mr MacLeod," Miss Hawkins said softly. "I don't intend to let that happen. And once this is over..." She stared down at her hands, choosing her next words carefully. "I understand that I might be the wrong person to help Pelaeia. But I'll teach someone else to do it. Whoever you like. I'll help in any way I can, until it's done."

For the first time since their confrontation on the ship, I saw some of the tension in Aesir's shoulders loosen. He sighed heavily. "Ye took a lot a' yellin' fer things as wasnae yer fault, lass," he admitted quietly. "Still angry ye lied. But ah know who deserves the blame, an' we're headin' in their direction. Ye're on this side o' things, an' no' that one. So... ah'm glad ye're here."

I let out a small breath of my own at the statement. It was a tiny thing, while we were surrounded by so much horror... but the pressure in the longboat had tangibly lightened, right at the moment we most needed it to do so.

Miss Hawkins swallowed minutely. When next she spoke, her voice was thick with emotion. "I appreciate that," she said. "And... I am sorry, for my part. I wish that I had been honest with everyone much sooner. It means more than I can say that I didn't have to come here all alone."

I arched an eyebrow at her. "Of course you weren't coming here alone," I said. "You booked passage on the nosiest ship in all of Avalon, Miss Hawkins. Besides... like it or not, you're crew."

Miss Hawkins blinked swiftly. The aether around us gave another tiny ripple. "Oh," she said softly. "I... I am? I hadn't realised."

"Oh yes, obviously," Mr Finch said, as he checked the bandage on Lenore's head. "Consider yourself formally press ganged. There's no escape now."

"Mary started knittin' you a scarf," Lenore drawled. "Figured that was that."

Miss Hawkins blushed visibly, clearly resisting the urge to hide her face at these assertions. I was reminded, again, just how many years I had on her—and how fully out of her depth she must have been, despite the air of control she so often exuded.

I took pity on her by clearing my throat. "I suppose we ought to quiet down before we get much closer," I said. It was true. The endless ghostly whispers that surrounded us camouflaged an awful lot of noise... but it would be reckless to rely on that indefinitely.

The further we drifted away from the *Majesty*'s wreck, the more we found ourselves winding between empty, ivy-covered buildings. The cobblestone remains of old streets began to peek through the grass beneath us. Every so often, we passed the wreckage of a downed outflyer, crushed against the ground like a discarded toy. The shades here grew fewer and further apart... but I soon realised that this was because they'd been replaced by tatterdemalions.

Dead soldiers raced to reinforce the western walls, rushing through the streets in clattering squads. The ambient aether-light of the city flickered across their forms, revealing a far more ghoulish construction than that of Old Pelaeia's tatters. Scraps of grey uniform fitted over old bones, where earth and stone had reinforced desiccated flesh. I caught flashes of unique horrors as they passed: a skull grinning out of a rusty Imperial helmet, with an ash-grey flower blooming from its eye socket; spent bullet casings for fingertips, grasping at a broken rifle. Most of the tatters still sported their old army boots—a circumstance which loaned an eerie familiarity to the cadence of their march.

Above that din, their voices rose—stronger and more certain than those of the shades we'd passed before.

"The gate hasn't fallen yet! Move faster—pick up your feet!"

"Let's show the navy they can't win without us, lads!"

I watched the echoes pass us, holding my breath... but they were too focussed on their objective to pay us much mind. As the tail end of the troop finally trailed around the corner of a building, I glanced at Aesir.

"They're headed to the western gate," I whispered. "That's our heading, isn't it?"

Aesir nodded grimly. "Looks like they're takin' a side route," he said.

"Let's give them a loose follow," I murmured. "It'll take a bit longer, but the echoes will give us some cover."

Aesir's guess turned out to be correct. The tatters took a winding route through several half-crumbled alleyways, eventually emerging into the shadow of the western gate.

And then... they stopped moving entirely.

The shouts and stomping feet had ceased. Instead, a great crowd of dead soldiers stood in empty silence, staring sightlessly at the open gate.

Our longboat came up short behind the echoes, unable to progress any further.

"What are they *doing*?" I hissed softly.

Miss Hawkins shifted her way closer to the front of the longboat, peering out at the ghosts. "It's the machine," she whispered. "The more advanced model pacifies echoes within a small perimeter. It makes the work safer."

Mr Finch frowned and adjusted his glasses, squinting past the silent tatters. "Without an aethermancer's active will, that would require further engineering," he murmured. "Given the range involved, I would probably use—"

"—yes, pylons," Miss Hawkins finished for him. There was an odd amiability to her voice, despite the tenseness of the situation. "They're connected to the main machine with tubing, in order to draw Unseelie aether. It's far more corrosive than we estimated, though; the tubing won't last long before it needs replacing. I wonder if Gideon knows that."

I looked at Aesir and gestured just behind us, towards a building with far fewer shades. He pulled the longboat back into the shadows there, tucking us behind the remnants of a wall.

I returned my attention to Miss Hawkins. "It should be fairly simple, then, to sabotage those pylons," I mused softly. "If we did... the echoes would behave normally again?"

Hawkins nodded. "It's hard to predict what they'd do under their own power, though," she warned. "We don't know how they'll interpret all of this, or who they might see as an enemy."

"They're Imperial soldiers," Lenore muttered. Her voice still held a trace of a slur from her concussion. "I'd wager good money they'll follow Wraithwood an' his silver sword, if we test 'em."

I grimaced at the statement. Much as I'd hoped for an extra distraction, I couldn't fault her logic.

"All right," I mumbled. "Miss Hawkins, Mr Finch, Mr MacLeod—let's get the prototype unloaded here. Once Miss Brighton takes out Wraithwood, they won't be able to turn any of these echoes on us. Miss Hawkins... do you think you can bring yourself to control a few of those tatters? Just long enough to destroy Wraithwood's machine."

Hawkins hesitated visibly. I watched a series of deeply conflicted emotions cross her face. "Under any other circumstances," she said slowly, "I would refuse. But... the echoes don't understand what that machine will do to them, if it survives. I can reconcile myself to giving them a fighting chance against it." She met my eyes grimly. "I can fight the other machine's control... but it *would* be easier without those pylons. Removing just one or two of them would be ideal. If we sever the tubing, it will bleed off the Unseelie aether they need in order to function."

The disconcerting image of a New Havenshire constable with his face melting off elbowed its way to the forefront of my mind. "If I cut the tubing, won't the Unseelie aether, uh... explode everywhere?" I asked warily.

Miss Hawkins pressed her lips together. "The tubing is half an inch, and not as intensely pressurised as those canisters were," she said slowly. "But... the severed tubing will leak some Unseelie aether, by definition. We'll need to be careful."

I nodded shortly, despite the uneasiness this caused in my chest.

"I'll worry about that part," I reassured her. "You have enough on your plate."

As the other three started carefully unloading the prototype, I glanced at the surrounding buildings, searching for a vantage point that might give us a better view beyond the gate.

"There's an old clock-tower about two blocks east of us," I whispered to Lenore, pointing in its general direction. "Does it look like it might be a decent perch?"

Lenore followed the gesture, craning her head to consider the possibility. "Good odds," she said. "Depends how they're set up and how much cover they've got. It's worth climbing up there to see."

I clambered down from the longboat and offered my hand to Lenore. She accepted the assistance with a dainty air, though I felt her waver slightly on her feet. Light faded further into shadow as we went, and my eyes adjusted further to the gloom; Lenore leaned a bit more heavily upon me, relying on my sharper sight to avoid tripping over the rubble in our path.

The clock-tower was overgrown, but otherwise still sturdy-looking. I couldn't see any evidence of recent entry—nor did there seem to be any shades glowing from within. No one in their right mind would have tried to hide in a clock-tower with outflyers raining from the sky, I reflected silently.

The stairs inside were still intact—but the climb was hard on both of us. By the time we reached the top, my legs were complaining, and Lenore's breathing was a bit heavier than usual.

I led Lenore towards the shattered glass clock face, helping her down to her knees. From our current vantage point, I could see another clump of glowing echoes in a plaza just beyond the western gate. I pulled out my spyglass and squinted through it, trying to make out the details.

Three roads converged upon the plaza on the other side of the gatehouse. Each road had been hastily blockaded with rusted, hulking vehicles. A jumble of shades and tatterdemalions stood behind the blockades, silently staring down another flickering company of ghosts on the other side—all of them equally limp and docile.

"I think there's some Coalition echoes down there," I murmured to Lenore. "The Imperial echoes we were following would probably be fighting them now, if not for those pylons."

Glass crunched nearby as Lenore set her rifle down, using its scope to get a better look.

"There they are," she murmured. "Near the statue in the plaza."

I scanned the spyglass slowly across the scene until I picked up the landmark.

The first thing that caught my attention was the machine. Though I'd known the one we had was just a prototype, I was still surprised at how *big* the other machine was. The top of it was nearly flush with the eyes of the platformed statue in the square—some important-looking historical figure I probably should have recognised, but very much did not.

A small circle of familiar figures in greatcoats and gas masks ringed the machine. I counted six Cinderwolves—though I knew there were likely more, somewhere out of sight. At the centre, standing next to the machine, was a terrifying form in dirty grey, still wearing that twisted mask. Wraithwood had sheathed his left arm in new foci, all currently attached to a skein of midnight threads. The tapestry of power shuddered uncomfortably around him, quivering like an unsteady breath.

"I've got him," Lenore muttered tightly. "He's stationary. Good view."

I shifted my spyglass slightly... and caught sight of a haggard-looking figure, a few feet to Wraithwood's right. Strahl had been forced to his knees, with his hands bound behind him. The aether-light of the surrounding echoes flickered upon his pale, blue-veined face, highlighting a harsh black bruise where Wraithwood had backhanded him. The Cinderwolf gorgon stood just behind him, with a pistol carefully trained on his figure.

I didn't blame them. I knew what Strahl could do, even with his hands tied.

The sight of the man I'd once called my bosun struck me with fresh confusion. My first reaction was an instinctive surge of relief.

Though I'd known that Strahl was still alive, given Syrene's continued bond with him, I hadn't been at all certain what condition we would find him in. I was even more relieved, somehow, to see him treated with such obvious wariness. Now that I had Strahl physically before me, it was easier to believe that the man I'd come to know wasn't *entirely* a lie.

"I count six Cinderwolves," Lenore told me, interrupting my train of thought. "Three pyroclasts."

"That was my count, too," I agreed quietly. "We have to assume there might be more. They… *could* be back on the Erebus." I didn't place much confidence in the assertion.

"I'd have 'em on perimeter," Lenore murmured. "Not too far out, though. It's too easy to lose someone to all these shades."

I suppressed a shudder at the reminder. "All right," I said. "We can do this. I can't make out those pylons in the middle of all those echoes, but they'll be more apparent once I'm on the ground. I'll head back down—"

I cut myself off abruptly as a darting shadow caught my attention, just at the edge of the spyglass. Something had skittered through the press of echoes, using them as cover. I very much doubted I would have seen it, if I hadn't been looking down at the scene from above.

"What was *that?*" I hissed.

Lenore scowled into her scope. "What was what?" she asked.

"Something just moved through the echoes," I told her. "Something *fast.*"

The figure moved again, swift and sinuous. I followed its movement to the edge of the square, where one of the pyroclasts had set themselves up by a barricade.

All at once, a pair of wicked, long-fingered hands lashed out, violently yanking the aethermancer down into the crowd of tatters.

Blood spattered. The poor sod didn't even have time to scream.

"Uh oh," I managed faintly. It only occurred to me now, well past the time when it should have done: I hadn't seen Syrene in the longboat when I'd left with Lenore. I'd assumed that she was still merged with the vehicle… but perhaps that *wasn't* true, after all.

"Uh oh?" Lenore repeated slowly.

"It's Syrene," I said. "She's going after Strahl."

One of the other pyroclasts called out in confusion, searching for the one who'd gone missing. The aethermancer had been nearly in plain view—and now, he was simply gone.

"She's going to send them running for cover," I told Lenore urgently. "Take the shot. *Now.*"

Something rolled away from the crowd of echoes, clattering against what remained of the old cobblestones. I didn't dare to turn my spyglass upon it. I was pretty sure it was the pyroclast's armoured head.

This is why I don't like plans. They never seem to survive for long.

Shouts went up among the Cinderwolves. Ugly reddish-black aether surged abruptly around Wraithwood's form; the threads at his fingers pulled taut, and a hundred echoes snapped to attention.

Lenore took one breath. Exhaled.

And pulled the trigger.

25

CROWD CONTROL - DIVIDED - MASTER OF PUPPETS - LOYALTY

The rifle split the air like thunder.
 I had a perfect view through my spyglass as Wraithwood's head snapped back violently. His wooden mask exploded into shards.

The surrounding tatterdemalions jerked abruptly, like puppets on a string... and then slumped to the ground, all at once. The black threads that had connected them to Wraithwood wavered and went limp, as his body crumpled with them.

The sight was deeply surreal. For all that I'd known we had good odds of killing Wraithwood, given the element of surprise, some part of me hadn't *really* expected us to pull it off. In the space of that split second, the odds of the battle had swung enormously in our favour.

Suddenly, we could win this fight.

Though it felt as though everything should have paused in that moment, however, time refused to stand still. Lenore calmly chambered another round, just next to me, as another flurry of motion caught my attention down below.

Strahl had surged to his feet with shocking speed. The gorgon who had been watching him was just a hair too slow to respond, distracted by Wraithwood's sudden death. Strahl threw himself at her without hesitation, using his greater mass to bring them both to the ground. I couldn't tell, in all of the chaos, whether she had lost her pistol or not —but the serpents that crowned her head lashed out regardless, tearing into Strahl's exposed skin with vicious desperation.

Strahl ignored the pain entirely. He slammed his forehead into her face with brutal precision. Her body went abruptly boneless; the snakes on her head dropped limp, in turn.

Strahl rolled away from the sergeant, shoving halfway to his knees. The other Cinderwolves were still in disarray, diving for cover to protect themselves from both the sniper and the unseen thing that stalked them from among the nearby tatters—but one of the pyroclasts caught sight of Strahl's retreating form and turned his focus in that direction.

A hollow boom sounded on the air—followed by an impossibly bright flare. I jerked back from the spyglass with a curse, blinking back spots from my vision. Lenore cringed back next to me, rubbing at her eyes with a hiss of frustration.

I stumbled back to my feet, already heading for the stairs. "We'll take it from here," I told Lenore breathlessly. "Just pick off whoever you can."

I didn't wait to hear her answer.

I bolted down the stairs two and three at a time, desperate to rejoin the others. Despite Syrene's early intervention, our plan had mostly gone off as-intended... but I hadn't had the chance to disable any of the pylons for Miss Hawkins.

If that was the only problem we faced, I told myself, then the odds would still be in our favour. Wraithwood was gone, and the Cinderwolves were currently very distracted with Syrene. A very quiet part of me hoped that Strahl was still his own sort of distraction too, despite the pyroclast's attempt on his life.

By the time I reached the rest of the crew, my vision had mostly returned. Mr Finch worked at the prototype machine with frenetic anxiety, trying to ignore the pitched sounds of battle nearby. He'd mounted the machine onto a slapdash frame that hovered just a few inches above the ground—a solution for the logistical woes we'd suffered in Old Pelaeia. I knew without having to ask that there was a certain danger inherent in that frame; it had to make use of at least some Seelie aether, which we had long since established did not mix well with its Unseelie counterpart. As neither an engineer nor an aethermancer myself, I simply accepted that the more educated among my crew had already weighed that risk accordingly.

Not far from the machine, Aesir helped Miss Hawkins secure the machine's focus to her right hand as the two of them spoke in tense, hurried tones. "You don't need to be an aethermancer," Miss Hawkins told him, as I scurried breathlessly towards them. "If the worst should happen, all you have to do is listen—"

"What is happening?" Mr Finch hissed at me, as I skidded to a stop beside the machine.

"*Slight...* change in plans," I wheezed. "Syrene started the party early."

An inhuman shriek of fury echoed on the air. A sharp chill shot down my spine, and I watched the blood drain from Mr Finch's face in reply. Panicked gunfire rattled nearby, followed by another hollow boom.

"Plan's still *mostly* the same," I offered weakly.

"An' Wraithwood?" Aesir asked tightly. There was a hard, terrified edge to his voice as he said the name.

"Down," I replied. "Miss Brighton did her job."

I couldn't help a glance at Miss Hawkins as I said the words. A series of complex, conflicted emotions crossed her face in swift succession—far too jumbled to pick apart in the moment. But she set her jaw and nodded, without speaking.

"Let's move," I said. "We'll make our run on the machine while Syrene's got them distracted." Aesir's eyes flickered to the longboat, but I shook my head at him. "We're leaving the longboat here. It's our getaway plan; we can't afford for it to take a hit."

"We need another way past the tatterdemalions, then," Miss Hawkins told me tightly. "There should be a pylon somewhere close by. If you disable it, I can take control of the tatterdemalions blocking our path."

I glanced at the open western gate, where a crowd of tatters still stood in eerie silence, staring sightlessly ahead. A horrified grimace crossed my face as I realised where the pylon must be... but I nodded shortly.

"I'll handle it," I said. "Be ready to take control, Miss Hawkins. I'd rather not be trampled once those ghosts wake up."

I strode for the very edge of the crowd, carefully ignoring the sensible voice in my head that insisted this was a terrible idea. Thankfully, I have a lot of practice ignoring that voice—honestly, it barely even registers anymore.

As I got closer to the tightly packed echoes, I found myself assaulted by a unique stench: something like spent aether, dry dirt, and old leather. Another, more familiar scent lurked beneath it all, reminiscent of an open grave.

I came up short behind a silent tatterdemalion, still staring through the gatehouse's open doors into the plaza beyond. I couldn't see the echo's face—which was probably all for the better, given the fist-sized hole in the back of the helmet that it wore. The opening gave me an unnerving peek at the glimmering cloud of aether that roiled inside its makeshift body.

I dropped to my hands and knees, squeezing my way through the gathered forest of blocky legs. It was hard going; the tatters were like solid, immovable statues, rather than human beings. Thankfully, I'm a small man, with plenty of experience wriggling into places that I otherwise shouldn't.

Eventually, I caught sight of a squat silhouette that didn't seem to match the surrounding Imperial boots and makeshift legs. I shuffled towards it, trying to ignore the growing ache in my knees that told me I wasn't *nearly* as young as I'd once been.

I wasn't sure just what I had been expecting—but what I found was a lattice of wrought iron, formed into the shape of a tiny pyramid. A faint reddish-black haze wafted from its tip, dissolving slowly into the air. The surrounding smell took on a rotten tinge, and I grimaced against a surge of nausea.

There was a small tube attached to the base of the iron pyramid. Whatever material it was made of, it had been reinforced with metal threads that glimmered in the aether-light around us. Visible rust already stained the tubing, as Miss Hawkins had suspected might be the case.

Another scream sounded from the square ahead of us, reminding me that the party had already started without us. I pried the hand-axe from my belt and hefted it as best I could, cringing back from the place where it came down.

The tubing made a strange cracking noise beneath the axe's blade. Something hissed softly in the darkness. I snatched the hand-axe back and saw that rust had blossomed along its edge.

The red haze wavered slightly. One of the tatterdemalions next to me twitched oddly... but nothing else seemed to happen.

I gritted my teeth and brought the axe down again—somewhat harder, this time.

The hissing grew in volume and dropped in pitch. Several long seconds later, the pylon ran dry and sputtered out. Soon after, several tatterdemalions lurched forward purposefully. One of them caught the pylon with its booted foot, crunching it soundly into the ground.

All at once, the Imperial tatters came alive again, keen on hurrying through the open gate. I wasn't in any realistic position to evade them. I scrambled desperately between stony legs, searching for an opening.

A booted foot stopped abruptly, just inches from my face.

Black threads washed across the echoes as I stared up from my place on the ground, catching upon souls like cobwebs. One of those tethers closed around the tatterdemalion above me, winding gently around its neck.

It looked down at me with glimmering, empty eye sockets... then slowly stepped back, in order to allow me up to my feet.

I let out a long breath and stood back up. The sea of marching tatters folded apart with a strange sort of grace, as Hawkins and the others hurried towards me. Though it was a relief to see the tatters obeying her will, I also couldn't help but find it unnerving.

Miss Hawkins stood next to the prototype machine, holding out her hand. A tapestry of midnight dangled from her fingers; a few of the bright blue veins in her face had been dyed black.

"Quickly, please," Hawkins rasped, as I came closer. "I don't know how long I can control this many echoes."

I nodded sharply. "Let's aim for the machine, and then get out of here," I said. "No stopovers, nothing fancy." I glanced towards Aesir. "You can go back and stay with the longboat, if you want."

Aesir didn't respond to me directly. Instead, he pulled his axe-headed blunderbuster and worked the pump with a loud *clack-clack*.

The echoes turned as one, eerily in time, as they marched their way through the gate and into the utter chaos of the plaza beyond. We followed in their wake, trying to keep our distance as much as possible.

Another loud boom sounded as our cadre of dead soldiers spilled out into the open. One of the remaining buildings there had caught ablaze; the acrid stink of aether-flame lingered on the air. The Cinderwolves had pulled back to use one of the old barricades as cover from sniper fire, even as their remaining pyroclasts burned through screaming tatterdemalions, turning them to slag. I realised belatedly that they were trying to flush out Syrene.

The larger echo machine thrust up through the clotted gatherings of tatters and battlefield refuse like an ominous black sword. Midnight threads still twisted aimlessly around it, without a will to guide them.

A few of the tatters that Miss Hawkins had gathered remained in a protective ring around us. The rest of them headed directly for that machine.

"The echoes are loose!" one of the Cinderwolves yelled. "What is going on?"

"Check the pylons!" another one called back. "One of them must have—" They cut themselves off mid-sentence. "Contact! It's the Legionnaire from Morgause! She's *here*!"

It can be hurtful how often I'm overlooked. Despite my best efforts to cause trouble, the only person anyone seemed interested in killing was Miss Hawkins. Several rifles turned in the direction of our party, while one particular pyroclast levelled their arm at the tatterdemalions that currently shielded us.

A white-hot ball of aether shot for the echoes in front of us. Stone melted. Bones crackled and splintered. Even with the rest of the tatters as cover, I felt the sudden, intense heat of the resulting explosion. Chips of smoking debris rained down upon us.

Suddenly, I wasn't *nearly* as certain of our plan. I wondered just how long our troop of tatterdemalions would last against those pyroclasts. Surely, it wouldn't be long enough to destroy the machine as completely as we required them to do.

I turned for the prototype machine, where Mr Finch now worked furiously, gauging aether pressure and adjusting knobs. "Mr Finch!" I yelled at him, over the din. "I need a canister of Unseelie aether!"

Under any other circumstances, I am certain that my chief engineer would have had some very pointed questions for me about what I intended to *do* with said canister. At the moment, however, pure adrenaline convinced him to grab a canister and shove it at me blindly.

I stumbled over to a half-skeletonised tatterdemalion—and shoved the canister into its exposed rib cage. The dirt that made up the rest of its torso gave an uncomfortable-sounding squelch.

"Hawkins!" I called out. "Send this one on a scenic route towards that pyroclast! Keep it well away from us!"

The tatterdemalion looked down at me, and gave a jerky nod.

The rest of the Cinderwolves had finally noted our presence, even with the tatters as cover. Bullets caught on tatters and sprayed the dirt beside me as a few of the mercenaries diverted their efforts towards the group of people responsible for their newest threat.

We pulled back for one of the other barricades, as a single tatterdemalion lurched for the pyroclast that had taken an interest in us. Two other Cinderwolves had joined him behind a crumbling wall in order to take shots at us. The pyroclast raised his hand to let loose a gout of seething Seelie flame.

I looked away, just before the spray of aetheric fire lanced out to melt against the echo's body.

The resulting explosion was… bizarre. At first, there was a violent, soundless blast—followed by a screeching crunch. Air whipped past me, as though being sucked into a void.

Just as I felt myself starting to lean forward, the pull reversed itself abruptly. A roiling wall of dust and aetheric steam billowed out from where the tatterdemalion had been, rocking me back onto my heels.

Stranger by far, though, was the sensation of reality *warping* around me—as though something had snagged on the weft of the world itself. I wobbled off balance, stifling a fresh wave of nausea at the feeling. A bleak, hollow emptiness settled into my bones: the sort I'd only experienced on my most despairing days, when I loathed myself too much to look in the mirror.

I don't remember how long I spent on the ground, after that. I do remember the muted world that followed, as I tried to blink the dust from my eyes. I pushed myself up with great effort, taking in the aftermath.

The reaction had been somewhat more *intense* than I might have expected. What remained of the pyroclast and the other two Cinderwolves was something best not contemplated, though our own barricade had absorbed the worst of the destruction. I was briefly flabbergasted to see that Mr Finch had thrown himself over the prototype device, as though to shield it with his body—a sacrifice which had been thankfully unnecessary. Though Aesir had been knocked flat alongside me, he was already struggling back up to his feet.

Miss Hawkins was still standing—but there was an odd sway in her posture that hadn't been there before, as she struggled to maintain her concentration. The dark strands that extended from her fingers now flickered dangerously, as the echoes that were attached to them made odd, restless movements.

Movement caught my eye, somewhere within the dust we had kicked up. I heard the grating sound of sluggish footfalls. Shadows stumbled towards us… and I realised that many more of the once-dormant tatterdemalions had been disturbed from their trance.

A sharp surge of panic broke me out of my stupor. "We must have blown out another pylon!" I called back. "The other echoes are waking up—"

Something reached out from the haze to close its fingers around my arm. Old bone and bleached leaves wound around me—then yanked me sharply off my feet.

A strangled, high-pitched noise escaped me, as the echo dragged me into a milling throng of half-melted tatters. Miss Hawkins turned sharply towards me; her eyes widened, and her hand darted out. Black strands whipped for the tatter that had taken me... but though they caught upon it, the aether-ghost refused to let me go.

A strange, sickening buzz started up in my ears as that midnight strand tightened on the echo, wilfully insistent. Finally, something shifted, and the tatter let me go—just in time for *another* tatterdemalion to grab hold of me.

I soon lost sight of the rest of my crew, blocked in by erratic echoes. Dead hands settled upon me in a dangerous tug-of-war; some seemed intent on shoving me to safety, while others hoped to stomp on my head.

Perhaps Miss Hawkins had lost whatever game was afoot— because soon, even the echoes that had been trying to help me turned hostile. I hit the ground, now assaulted on every side by heavy boots and stumbling ghosts.

I struggled up to my knees and covered my head with my arms, desperately searching for an exit. Something heavy stepped on my leg. Another tatter kicked at me blindly, catching me in the ribs. The breath went out of me all at once, and I soon found I had no choice but to curl up into a protective ball as I wheezed for air.

I rolled pathetically along the ground, clutching at my midsection. The machine rose up before me; from my place on the ground, I could see a tangled web of tubing attached to its base, where the remaining pylons still drew power. I turned to crawl desperately towards the device, hoping that it might still have some calming effect on the echoes. As I moved, something crunched uncomfortably beneath my hand, jabbing into my palm.

I shifted aside... and saw the shattered, bloody remains of Wraithwood's wooden mask.

Just the mask, I realised dimly. There was no body.

One of the tatters drove a heavy boot into my ribs with enough force to knock me over onto my back. The boot remained on my chest, holding me down. The echo tilted its head, staring down at me with a ruined face of dirt and bone. A black thread glistened softly around its neck.

"Goblins truly are the worst vermin," the tatter said. Its voice was unfamiliar... but its accent undoubtedly belonged to Wraithwood. "How are you still *alive*?"

My ribs throbbed with an awful stabbing pain that suggested one of them had broken. I'd yet to catch my breath. But somehow, I dredged up a single ounce of oxygen in order to squeak out my incredulous reply: "She... shot you! In the head!"

As last words go, those would have been pretty underwhelming. Honestly, I have no reasonable excuse. I normally expect much better of myself when it comes to witty banter.

Thankfully, I was given time to adjust my rhetoric as something slammed into the tatterdemalion, tackling it to the ground.

The weight lifted from my chest. Air rushed painfully back into my lungs. Tears stung at my eyes, as I gritted my teeth with each new breath.

My initial instincts suggested that Aesir, Hawkins, or one of her controlled echoes had come to my rescue. But I heard Aesir calling out for me in the distance, too far away to be helpful.

I forced myself onto my knees, and saw instead my bosun—dirty, bloody, and exhausted, with his hands still manacled—struggling back up to his feet.

The tatterdemalion clattered heavily upright. I saw now that there was a jerky quality to its movements, and I began to suspect that Wraithwood had not, in fact, escaped his death unscathed.

"*Really*, Arcturus?" the echo hissed. It waved its hand in my direction, disgusted.

"Leave him out of this," Strahl wheezed. He shifted his body into a pathetic attempt at a fighting stance, despite the manacles that still bound his hands behind him.

"He can't leave *himself* out of it!" the echo snapped back.

"He's... not wrong," I admitted dazedly. I inched myself behind Strahl, shamelessly placing him between myself and the echo that obviously wanted to kill me. The nauseous hum of Wraithwood's stolen machine vibrated at my back. Tatters pressed in on us in a loose circle, staring us down.

"Captain," Strahl told me calmly. "Please. Respectfully. For the love of the Benefactor... shut up."

Somewhere deep down, I managed to marvel at the fact that he was still calling me 'Captain'. I knew it was a good sign. It meant that the man in front of me was still more Strahl than he was Prince Arcturus.

"Sorry," I slurred back. "Can't. Doesn't work. The Benefactor doesn't love me *that* much."

Far behind us, on the other side of the machine, the staccato gunfire slowly petered out. At first, I worried that the Cinderwolves had bested Syrene. But one of their muffled voices soon called out: "I've lost it! Where did that *thing* go?"

Wraithwood's tatterdemalion fixed its empty eye sockets upon Strahl. "What are you even struggling against, Arcturus?" it asked, as the circle of tatters inched towards us. "Let us suppose, just for a moment: You fight off an entire city of ghosts with your bare hands. You kill what's left of me. What then? The Unseelie are coming. And *this* time, there won't be a unified Avalon here to stop them."

It wasn't the sort of speech I would have expected to resonate with the man I'd come to know. I knew from watching Strahl's face, though, that it had affected him more than he wanted it to do. He hesitated visibly, struggling with the concept.

I stared up at him. "What?" I managed. "You're not swallowing this slop, are you?"

Strahl turned his head to shoot me a pained look. "I would *love* an alternative!" he snarled. "He's not wrong; the Unseelie are coming. Someone has to stop them."

I coughed on an incredulous laugh, wincing at my broken rib. "Strahl," I said. "*Everyone* is going to stop them. You really think Avalon is just going to roll over and die because there's no emperor to crack the whip? You think we're all so stupid we have to be forced to save ourselves?" I shook my head. "This isn't about whether we fight. It's about a bunch of terrified old men who can't bring themselves to let someone *else* call the shots."

Strahl stared at me as though I'd hit him upside the head. A strange light of understanding dawned on his face—as though I'd just spouted pure philosophy instead of basic common sense.

"Look at me, boy," the tatterdemalion snarled. "I am on my *last* nerve with you. You're valuable—but you're not irreplaceable. You already know that."

Strahl's manacles gave a soft click, as I finally finished picking their lock.

"So replace me," Strahl said simply. He straightened wearily. "I know you can. But the answer is still no, Gideon. It will *always* be no." He narrowed his eyes at the echo. "And I don't intend to fight the entire city. I know you're near. All I need to do is survive long enough to get my hands on you."

Maybe it was the direct threat. Maybe it was just the absolute conviction in Strahl's voice as he responded. Either way, the conversation ended abruptly.

Several of the closest tatters leapt for us—eerily unified, if still ungainly. I didn't react as quickly as I should have done. Somehow, my brain remained just a second behind, still waiting for Wraithwood's reply.

Strahl, on the other hand, had no such trouble. He whirled to snatch my hand-axe from me. I hadn't even realised he had spotted it —but then, Strahl had always been the sort of man to track all of the weapons in his general vicinity. The blade sank halfway into the first echo's neck before catching there. Strahl slammed his heel into the tatter's chest with a solid kick, tearing the axe head free and shoving the aether-ghost into the way of another advancing echo.

Two more echoes piled onto him in the same breath, doing their best to bear him down. Strahl smashed his elbow into one exposed skull, cracking its weathered surface. Aether streamed like steam from the fissures—but the tatter barely seemed to notice.

I stumbled back, frantically searching for a way to assist. I was barely on my feet, given my broken rib, and Strahl had taken my last weapon. My eyes fell upon the machine—and for a moment, I seriously considered throwing caution to the wind and blindly smashing at its dials, just to see what happened. Yes, it was volatile, and highly likely to take us with it if I *did* manage to destabilise something... but then, what other options did we have?

Once again, I had managed to forget the last passenger we'd brought with us on the longboat.

A sudden surge of fury whited out my thoughts, as pale roots burst their way free of the debris beneath our feet, grasping at the echoes that had tackled Strahl. Syrene's bloody figure rose from the cracked rubble of the plaza—eight feet of relentless nature, all focussed on the creatures that had dared to threaten her ward. Those writhing roots pulled one tatter entirely apart in a shower of dirt and scrap. Her stony arm disembowelled the other, nearly bisecting it; aether poured from its ruined form in a disturbing facsimile of blood, before the echo began to crumple.

Our onetime navigator had become a sight straight out of the Coalition's worst nightmares. Her figure was hunched and primal, wreathed in ashen flowers and vines of faded grey ivy that reminded me of rangy muscle. The arm she'd built from stone was now tipped with claws of rusty scrap metal. Dark red blood spattered her body, stark against the aether-bleached plants that now clothed her.

Echoes skittered back quickly, offering the faerie a wide, respectful distance as Wraithwood reassessed the situation. The shattered, ghastly remains of the echoes in front of us shivered, weakly attempting to reassemble themselves as roots continued to strangle them.

Strahl staggered back to his feet. Fresh blood trickled down his face as he stared past Syrene at the echoes beyond.

"Greetings to the Envoy," another tatterdemalion said solemnly. "I thought I'd recognised your handiwork. It seems Arcturus was exaggerating when he spoke of your demise."

A deep roiling anger vibrated on the air, sharp enough to steal my breath. Syrene drew herself up to her full height with a low, ominous creak. "*Traitor*," she seethed. "We will find you, Gideon Frey, and send you to explain your shameful tale to Death Victorious."

"Traitor?" another tatter asked softly. "No. I still serve the last true emperor."

The device's dark spire hissed abruptly with steam. Machinery clicked and whirred. Incandescent blue aether dribbled free of its containment, slowly coalescing into the shape of a shade.

All of the tatters surrounding us turned their heads as one to gaze at the figure, following some unspoken instinct. The last remnants of my old Imperial Oath twinged like an old wound, as a sickening feeling travelled down my spine.

Every other shade we'd met had blurry, indistinct features—but this one kept sharpening, like a figure in a spyglass slowly coming into focus. The image resolved into a tall man in a stiff Imperial uniform. A filigreed breastplate covered his chest, festooned with far too many medals. I recognised Strahl's cold eyes and hard jawline in the aether-ghost before me—but with my bosun standing so close, available for direct comparison, it was strangely easy to see the insecurity in this echo. The simple crown of laurels at his brow clashed with his overly ornate armour, which seemed like a failed attempt to hide the slight portliness he'd gained with age.

I only realised in that moment that I had never seen the emperor of Avalon in person before. I'd seen his proud portrait depicted in posters, stamped on coins, and artistically rendered in books. All of those images had made him seem mythical and otherworldly—as strange and untouchable as the Tuath Dé themselves. But the man in front of me was just… a very tired human being, dressed up in overly expensive attire.

"Strahl," I said in a quiet voice. "Please tell me that ghost isn't who I think it is."

Strahl took in the sight with a bleak expression. "I'm afraid I can't tell you that, Captain," he replied.

Syrene froze in place. Even the bloody leaves upon her head stilled. "We... greet the emperor of Avalon's Imperium," she whispered. Her tall, aether-bleached form knelt before the wavering spectral figure.

"Our compact remains intact, Envoy," the shade spoke. The voice that emanated from it was harsh and low, accented with crisp Imperial tones. "I hereby rescind all of my previous orders to you. I no longer require you to protect Prince Arcturus Lohengrin."

Syrene hesitated visibly, staring at the echo.

Alarm flashed through my body, swift and hot. "This is ridiculous," I rasped. "We all know that's Wraithwood. He's just using the emperor's shade as a puppet."

"Faeries only care about technicalities," Strahl said quietly. "Wraithwood came to Galtir for more than just an army. If we let him leave here with my father's echo, he'll take command of Tiirdan." He looked down at Syrene—only an inch or two shorter than him, now that she had knelt. "But not you, Syrene. You've spent twenty years now standing next to me. This isn't how that ends."

Syrene remained where she was, uncomfortably silent. The reaction didn't exactly inspire confidence.

The tatterdemalions surrounding us now crept in closer, growing more confident as Syrene failed to respond to the threat they represented. We'd already been laughably outnumbered. Without Syrene's help, we were also ridiculously outmatched, all over again.

I took an involuntary step backwards, briefly forgetting the machine just behind me. My heel tangled in the mess of tubing connected to it, and I stumbled painfully, clutching at my ribs as I rebalanced myself.

A wild, desperate idea floated into my mind as I stared down at that tubing. The odds were unreasonably stacked against us. At least, I reasoned dimly, I couldn't possibly make things any *worse*.

"Strahl," I said calmly. "Give me the axe."

Strahl flipped the axe in his hand, offering it out to me without so much as a single backward glance.

The emperor's echo flashed with borrowed fury. "Kill the prince," it ordered Syrene, "and everyone else who opposes us."

26

BORROWING TROUBLE - CLARENT'S WILL - TRUE PURPOSE

I didn't wait to find out whether Syrene intended to follow Wraithwood's command.

I snatched the axe from Strahl and whirled, hefting it over my head. Then, with all of my remaining might, I brought the blade down onto the mess of tubing still connected to the machine.

If you've never had a broken rib before, then I'm not strictly sure I can convey what a poor idea it is to do something so er, *vigorous*, while nursing one. The resulting snap of pain travelled all the way up to my head to press behind my eyes. I wobbled on my feet, too breathless even to scream, as I teetered on the edge of blacking out.

As my vision belatedly returned, I saw that I had dropped my axe into the tubing. Despite my haphazard swing, several of the already-weakened aether lines had crumpled like eggshells, spewing Unseelie aether into the air. Rust crawled swiftly across my old, trusty weapon as the aether spread like a puddle, eating away at the other tubes. Within seconds, my well-kept hand-axe became indistinguishable from one of Galtir's many abandoned, crumbling artefacts.

Syrene *had* hesitated, I was certain—it was the only reason I wasn't dead yet. Her emotions twisted on the air in a whirling pool of conflict. Confusion. Betrayal. Fury. Denial. Resentment.

And then... resignation.

"Get behind me, Strahl," I wheezed painfully.

Truly, I don't know why he listened to me. I'm sure I didn't strike a particularly intimidating picture, helplessly clutching at my midsection as I fell to my knees on the ground. But for some utterly mysterious reason, Strahl took a swift step back, putting me squarely in front of him.

I grabbed one of the severed tubes leading out of the machine, snapping it up before me as Syrene abruptly turned upon us. A billowing plume of Unseelie aether hissed into the air between us. The faerie recoiled with a sharp shriek, as several of her ashen leaves withered and turned black.

Syrene's outrage vibrated around us as she skittered backwards, shedding dead bark with every step. "How *dare* you," she hissed. All four of her black eyes fixed upon me with murderous intent.

I brandished the tubing at her again in a warning gesture. She jolted backwards on all fours, hissing at me like a territorial alley drake.

"I know, I know," I gasped. "I ought to honour my Seelie creators by laying down and dying. If it makes you feel any better, I'm sure I'll get around to it really soon."

As Unseelie aether bled into the air, echoes stirred to life around us, broken from the stupor enforced upon them by the pylons. Several of the black strands wrapped around them wavered and unravelled, as Wraithwood's control faltered against their burgeoning will. The emperor's shade blurred again, and a soft, frustrated curse spilled from one of the nearby echoes.

Ghostly battle cries rang out across the plaza as several of the tatterdemalions reclaimed their old script. Imperial soldiers rushed to form new battle lines, as the Coalition echoes on the other side of the barricades prepared to charge them.

A blinding burst of aether exploded just a short distance away from us, shining like a small sun. A clear ringing sound hummed across the plaza, informing me that Miss Hawkins had just drawn her silver sword.

It was, I thought, just enough chaos to confuse everyone at once.

Strahl, for his part, was still intensely focussed on the faerie before us. "You don't have to do what he says, Syrene!" he bellowed from behind me.

Several Imperial tatterdemalions shoved past the faerie for the front lines, barely aware of her presence. She darted between them with unnatural grace, watching the severed tube in my hands with wariness. "We... have sworn an Oath," she hissed back. There was a faint unsteadiness in her voice—but I knew it wasn't nearly enough to save us. The only thing truly standing between Syrene and our instant, bloody demise was the trickle of Unseelie aether I'd put between us.

And I highly doubted *that* would last for long.

Wraithwood had already begun consolidating control of the echoes. Though he'd abandoned his grip on several of them, the black strands that remained had stabilised and tightened. Any moment now, I realised, one of those echoes would charge me in order to knock aside my paltry defence against the faerie before us.

It's possible that the Lady of Fools still loved me, despite my open blasphemy. It's also possible, I suppose, that having a skilful crew and a ready contingency plan often pays dividends.

A twisting cloud of reddish-black aether hurtled past me, slamming directly into the Envoy.

Syrene screamed. It was a high, hideous sound that resonated deep in my soul. She skittered backwards, frantic to escape the Unseelie aether that had coalesced around her. Everywhere it touched, the inky cloud ate away at her like acid, melting bark and stone like brackish water. She stumbled into tatters, tossing them aside like toy soldiers in her desperation to escape.

I spied Miss Hawkins standing among the Imperial echoes, almost ten feet away from the machine, with both hands outstretched. One still clutched at a knot of midnight threads; the other twisted in the air as I watched, directing that cloud of Unseelie aether after Syrene. Hawkins trembled with the effort. Her eyes had now gone fully black;

the bruised aether that she exhaled into the air reminded me forebodingly of blood.

It only struck me an instant later that *she* had not, in fact, drawn Galatine.

Silver flashed among the echoes that separated us from Miss Hawkins. Galatine slashed through black threads like butter, separating the tatterdemalions from Wraithwood's control. The sword cut cleanly through each ebon string; each time it did, I *felt* the resulting snap, as the thread recoiled and the echo jerked violently. The controlled tatters backed away swiftly, stumbling with new clumsiness, as Aesir MacLeod single-handedly cleared a path to us.

Despite the imminent danger, I couldn't help gaping at the sight. Aesir had drawn the silver sword with his flesh-and-blood left hand. Though he wielded Galatine inexpertly, with almost no finesse, it hardly seemed to matter—snapping those threads was a trivial effort, at best.

Aesir noticed me staring. His eyes narrowed. "No' a word, Blair!" he shouted over at me. "Ah dinnae wan'tae hear it!"

Behind him, I saw Miss Hawkins stagger, dropping her left arm. The Unseelie aether that had so briefly chased down Syrene gave up the certainty of its form, dissipating slowly into the air. Her focus returned to the black threads still tangled around her right hand.

Syrene's scream had trailed off—but I still felt her agony from afar, shivering on the air. Her slender, monstrous figure trembled as she forced herself back to all fours. Ruinous scars of molten darkness marred her body, as layers sloughed off of her in chunks. I found myself abruptly reminded of Old Ironspine.

"Stay down." The words spilled from one of the echoes Miss Hawkins currently controlled, clipped with effort and pain.

Syrene ignored the command. She rose up slowly, fixing a murderous gaze upon Hawkins. Her legs gathered beneath her, as though she was preparing to pounce.

Hawkins' echoes piled onto the faerie before she could leap.

I wasn't really expecting the tatters to hurt Syrene—after all, I'd seen her take the full brunt of an unloading repeater without significant harm. But this time, as she swatted an echo aside, another one slammed its rusty bayonet into the rotting bark of her midsection.

Where once that metal would have bounced away harmlessly, it now sank in deeply, as though Syrene was made of flesh and blood. The faerie let out another loud howl of pain, now tinged with desperation.

A different flash of silver cut abruptly through the crowd of staggering echoes. Midnight threads snapped and recoiled—but this time, it was Hawkins who stumbled back, choking off a shocked cry of pain. She snatched her right hand back as though it had been burned, stumbling to her knees. The glove on her hand now twisted uncomfortably with black aether; she clawed at it blindly, trying to peel it away. Not far behind her, I saw Mr Finch frantically wrestling with the prototype machine as it reacted to the disruption with far less grace than the bigger machine had done, spewing Unseelie aether from uncomfortable places.

Wraithwood's dark figure dashed through the tatterdemalions, bathed in Clarent's cold, wintry light. His form was visibly ragged, and his steps seemed unsteady. Grey hair hung in a lank curtain about his face, barely obscuring the dried blood beneath. Though he was moving too quickly to make out the details, I knew that there was something *wrong* with his face. I wondered, suddenly, just how much Unseelie aether he had channelled at this point.

Clarent hewed down echoes with impunity, cutting through anything and everything that happened to block Wraithwood's will. Each tatter slowed his pace by only seconds... but it was already clear that he was heading directly for Hawkins.

Aesir—the only person close enough to block Wraithwood's path—had frozen entirely in place, staring at the Legionnaire with the same horrifyingly blank expression I'd seen him wear in Old Pelaeia. In that moment, as his will failed him, Galatine guttered in his hand... and then, it vanished entirely.

Strahl stepped out from behind me, snatching up a rusty sabre from the twitching remains of a tatterdemalion. It was, I thought, a poor sort of defence against a silver sword—but whatever his intentions, he had little chance to execute them. He managed only a single stride before violently stumbling, as thick roots surged up from the ground to lash themselves around his calves. Though Syrene's huddled, injured form was no longer in sight, she hadn't given up quite yet.

Strahl chopped at the roots with an incoherent cry of frustration, before fixing me with a furious glare. "Go!" he growled.

In retrospect, I'm fairly certain that what Strahl *meant* to say was something like "save yourself". But even if I had been willing to do such a thing, what I *heard* was: "go help Hawkins".

I'm proud to tell you now: I didn't stop to think. I didn't hesitate, or waste time trying to conjure up one last plan.

Instead, I did the most foolish thing I've ever done in my life.

I ran after Wraithwood, ignoring the hideous pain in my ribs. The Legionnaire had left a clear and unobstructed path in his wake—perfectly serviceable for a man of my relatively small size.

I threw myself at his legs, and tackled him from behind.

We tumbled together in a heap of limbs. Fresh agony tore a raspy scream from my throat—but I leaned into the adrenaline, secure in the knowledge that I was very likely to die at any moment.

Though I'd caught Wraithwood by surprise at first, the brief advantage didn't last. He rolled me beneath him, using his superior mass to his advantage. As he looked down at me, I saw at last the face that he had been hiding behind the mask.

His eyes were ugly blood clots; if there were any irises left within them, I couldn't even tell. Black veins pulsed under flesh gone grey and wax-like. The dried blood on his face had a brackish sheen to it that made it look like ink in the aether-light that surrounded us. A long, hideous gash at his temple had exposed a small chunk of his skull, where a few slivers of his mask stood out, still embedded there.

Wraithwood pinned me with a hand at my neck, and raised his silver sword.

It was a beautiful sight, actually. This close, I was able to make out the exquisite faerie artistry on Clarent's gleaming blade. The swords were all so bright—I'd assumed that they were simply unembellished aether. But Clarent whirled with intricate iridescent lines, shifting in complex, hypnotic patterns that no mortal hand could ever have inscribed.

For one split second, I felt Wraithwood's hand tremble at my throat. The killing blow skipped a beat, just as it had done with Hawkins back in Morgause.

And I realised then what I should have known all along.

"Mercy," I croaked out breathlessly.

Wraithwood's clotted eyes flashed with fury. "No," he spat.

I reached up to close my hand around the burning white blade above me. "I wasn't… talking to *you*," I wheezed.

My fingers didn't burn, as I touched the silver sword. I didn't expect them to. In fact, I had decided with every fibre of my being that Clarent wouldn't hurt me. I didn't have the luxury of believing otherwise.

The sword's will flooded through me like one of Syrene's emotions. I felt its ragged, panicked desperation, as it struggled against the hand that held it. It had been struggling all along, I thought; never successfully, but it had always *tried*. Wraithwood's will hadn't faltered in the least when he'd tried to kill Miss Hawkins before—only Clarent's intervention had saved her, at the very last moment.

And Wraithwood's grip on the sword was getting *weaker*. The Unseelie aether in his body had laid waste to his connection with Clarent, steadily eroding it. Though he must have known it was happening, Wraithwood was no Hawkins: He couldn't bring himself to give the sword to someone else while he used the machine.

Wraithwood's face twitched with dawning fury. "Don't," he growled warningly, as the sword wavered in his hand. "Don't you dare. I *own* you."

I hadn't the first idea what I was doing, as I closed my fingers around that silver sword. But I knew how tired it was, how close it had been to giving up entirely. I felt the wild surge of hope that had come with Galatine's arrival.

I offered up a wordless promise—a solid vision of a better future. Miss Hawkins would take the sword back. There would be no more blood, no more atrocities. The oppressive will that smothered it would dissipate entirely.

I offered it the perfect image of a blue patch of sky.

A curl of Seelie aether flared against my hand. An alien will surged through me, closing its grip around my vocal cords.

"Death... to tyrants," I heard myself rasp.

It happened all at once—so quickly that I barely understood the process. The supernatural will that pressed against my mind surged with one last burst of manic defiance, snapping every chain that bound it. Aether melted against my hand, flowing in reverse... and suddenly, there was a hilt in my hand.

Seelie aether sang in my veins, tingling with such breathless power that the pain in my broken rib barely seemed to register. Suddenly, I understood why all of the aethermancers we'd faced showed such supernatural resilience, with this incredible sense of invincibility pumping through their veins.

I'd thought that Clarent would be tired of blood by now... but I'd underestimated its desperation. Its will overpowered me; my arm moved without thought, slashing Wraithwood viciously across the face.

Wraithwood let out a rasping cry. His blood seemed blacker than it should have been, as it hissed and steamed away from the sword. His weight rolled away from me abruptly as he staggered back to his feet, backpedalling from the vengeful blade.

I took a step closer, lifting Clarent towards him. In that moment, with Seelie aether flooding me and Wraithwood cringing back, I was quite frankly out of my mind. I didn't feel like a guttersnipe pickpocket from Morgause, or a deeply chastised child soldier. I was Jack Blue, come alive from the pages of Mary's most over-the-top adventure novels. I was a swashbuckling hero, here to seal Wraithwood's doom, once and for all. I was—

—entirely incapable of wielding a silver sword, I'm sad to say.

Clarent wobbled unsteadily in my hand, spitting out awkward

flares of Seelie aether. My eyes widened as I flailed internally, trying to stabilise the brief miracle of will that had allowed me to steal the sword in the first place.

I was not, however, *any* sort of aethermancer. I wasn't even an engineer, like Aesir or Mr Finch. Whatever I was doing, it was very *wrong*—perhaps even counterproductive. I felt Clarent flail along with me, like a man being dragged to the ground by his drunken companion.

The silver sword disappeared again with a tiny, anticlimactic fizzle of aether.

Wraithwood's bloody eyes bored into me as I stood there in front of him, gently gaping at my empty hand.

"I'm going to tear that sword from your corpse," he informed me raggedly. He raised his gloved hand, drawing fresh strands of midnight from the air.

This time, the black strings frayed oddly. The towering black machine behind him gave a loud, unpleasant rattle... and then, it flickered and died, taking those ebon strands with it.

Mr Finch's giddy, incredulous laughter rang out across the plaza. No longer tethered to the dying prototype machine, my chief engineer had sneaked away to the *other* machine—which was, I now suspected, missing some very crucial parts.

Miss Hawkins staggered up beside me. Finally back on her feet, she seemed far prouder than Wraithwood in posture, though perhaps only an inch less exhausted. "You'll have to go through me," she told him quietly. "And you'll have to do it without your army."

Wraithwood dropped his gloved hand with a laugh. It was a wet, sickening sound that soon turned into a cough. "Clarent won't save you this time, Jane," he told her. "And neither will Galatine."

I was far more surprised to discover Aesir on my righthand side, tall and pale and trembling. The silver sword he'd borrowed was still nowhere to be seen—but at this particular comment, he hardened his jaw. "Ah think ye'd be surprised," he told Wraithwood.

Whatever Seelie aether Aesir had first used in order to summon Galatine, it was clearly spent—but I'd forgotten that Aesir still had one more source available to him. He yanked back the sleeve of his flight suit to reveal his prosthetic right arm; his fingers tore at a valve there, releasing a spray of prismatic aether into the air. The scintillating mist flashed with white-hot light as Aesir drew forth shining Galatine with his flesh-and-blood arm, letting his mechanical hand go limp.

I didn't have any Seelie aether on me—but that didn't stop me from *trying* to draw Clarent again. I scowled at my right hand, shaking it fiercely. Predictably, no legendary sword appeared. "Rust it," I muttered. "I think mine's broken."

"Get behind me, Blair," Aesir said bluntly. "It's awright. Ye've caused enough trouble fer ten awready."

I glanced around the plaza, taking in the fresh wreckage and twitching rubble that had once been several tatterdemalions. Battle cries still rang out beyond us, where Coalition echoes had clashed with Imperial troops in earnest. "I think I could have done better," I muttered, as I inched my way behind Aesir.

Wraithwood snatched a thick iron cylinder from his belt, slamming it into a device at his wrist. Aether hissed, and bruised light began to burn within the focus. He flicked his hand, splitting the night with a barbed tongue of blood that only vaguely resembled the shining aether-whip he'd used in Morgause.

I hadn't known that you could cram Unseelie aether into a device made for Seelie aether. In fact, I greatly suspected that it was a *terrible* idea. But Wraithwood had clearly stopped caring about terrible ideas around the time the *first* half of his face had melted off, and then kept going regardless.

In at least some respects, I suppose, Miss Hawkins hadn't fallen far from the tree. Only an instant after registering what Wraithwood intended to do, she'd reached for one of her own vials of Unseelie aether, pressing it swiftly against her gauntlet. A gentle *click-hiss* informed me that she had copied Wraithwood's gambit, infusing her shield focus with the blasphemous stuff.

Wraithwood lashed out at Hawkins with that hideous aetheric whip. It cut the air with an unnerving screech that vibrated deep in the roots of my teeth.

Miss Hawkins lifted her gauntlet in reply. Already, it had started bleeding reddish-black aether at the edges; but now, as it flared with will, a midnight aegis welled forth like blood from a wound, seething into the space between them. Wraithwood's unholy whip cracked harshly against that shield, sending up another painful, unearthly shriek as power met power.

Hawkins heaved the whip aside with her shield. Aesir followed up on the moment, lunging forward with Galatine. Wraithwood stepped back quickly, ceding ground to the two of them as they pressed him. His red whip cracked again—but this time, as Galatine swatted it away, the unholy weapon guttered and died.

This particular development stunned Wraithwood back by several more paces. His focus flared again, reforming the whip, as Aesir laughed with revelation.

"What'd tha Seelie craft these swords tae fight, Wraithwood?" he called out. "Ye've been killin' mortals fer so long, seems ye finally forgot!"

Wraithwood reached swiftly for another iron canister at his belt. Aesir raised the sword before him expectantly—but Wraithwood crouched instead, slamming the canister into the back of his boot. Belatedly, it dawned on me that he was preparing to *flee*.

He never had the chance.

A distant *crack* rang out from the clock-tower, echoing across the plaza. Wraithwood's head snapped violently to the side, and an ugly spray of blood flashed into the air. The man in front of us toppled into a boneless, bleeding heap.

This time, Wraithwood did *not* rise again.

27

THE LAST OATH OF HOUSE LOHENGRIN - PROMISES - THE ECHO

If anything, Wraithwood's sudden demise should have reminded me what a poor idea it was to stand still in the middle of the plaza, frozen and staring. But I wasn't alone in my shock; in the next few seconds, neither Aesir nor Miss Hawkins moved a muscle.

The seething shield of Unseelie aether before us dissipated slowly, as Miss Hawkins lost her will to maintain it. There were no tears in her blackened eyes as she stared down at Wraithwood's body—but I suspected they would come, as soon as her mind caught up with the reality.

It was Aesir who first broke the horrified spell that had come upon us. He stepped directly between Hawkins and the corpse in front of us, shielding it from her view. His hand came down gently on her shoulder. "Don't," he told her. "Ye can look anywhere else but there."

"A little help!" Strahl called out. His booming voice sounded a bit more breathless than usual. I snapped back to attention.

I shot Aesir one last glance, assuring myself that he had Miss Hawkins well in hand, before turning back for the tall black machine at the centre of the plaza.

Though Strahl had hacked away at least one of the pale roots that climbed his body, more had swiftly taken their place, constricting painfully around him. The foliage crawled relentlessly up his form, as though intent on consuming him.

I drew in a shuddering breath, clutching at my ribs. Now that Clarent had disappeared, all of my aches and pains felt worse than ever. There was no way I was going to be able to chop him loose.

"Hold still," I advised him, in a raspy voice.

Strahl grimaced. "Won't have much of a choice soon," he growled back. He stiffened, though, as he saw me pick my way towards the severed tubing on the ground. His pale, blue-veined skin blanched even further. "You're not serious," he wheezed.

The machine had ceased spewing Unseelie aether, since Mr Finch's intervention. I searched for my chief engineer among the plaza's wreckage. "Mr Finch!" I said, as loudly as I could manage. "Could you turn on the pylons again? Just a tiny bit, if you please. I'd rather not melt Mr Strahl."

Strahl let out a low groan at the suggestion.

"Aye-aye, Captain!" Mr Finch's voice trickled over, from the other side of the machine. "Please do inform *His Majesty*, however, that I refuse to save his life *politely*. I am obviously very displeased with him."

Strahl let his head fall back against the ground with a soft groan. "Noted!" he called back. "Now how much tea do I need to buy so that you *never* call me that again?"

The machine flickered and hummed, more softly than before. A puff of Unseelie aether trickled from the severed tubing, as I cringed and held it far away from myself. I waved it carefully towards the creeping plants, trying to avoid the places where they held Strahl directly.

The pale roots recoiled violently, withering visibly at the edges. Several of them released Strahl, retracting sullenly into the earth. He wrenched himself free of the rest with a visible grimace. Already, livid bruises stood out upon his skin where the roots had tightened around him. He forced himself haggardly to his feet, all the same.

A short distance away, the closing scenes of an old battle played out once again, while the emperor's blurry shade watched on impassively, entirely divorced from awareness. Slowly, I became aware that Aesir and Miss Hawkins had joined me. Tear tracks had left conspicuous smears in the blood and grime on the aethermancer's face; her body still shuddered with barely suppressed emotion as she stared out over the echoes, watching them clash. Aesir stood next to her in silence, with his arm tight around her shoulders.

Though both Wraithwood and Miss Hawkins had interfered significantly with the Imperial ranks, it hardly seemed to matter. Even as cries for reinforcements went unheeded, the script continued to play out, as soldiers fervently defended their position from the Coalition.

The end came without warning, exactly as it had done the first time.

A strange flicker of aether-light swept through the ranks, blossoming from within the tatterdemalions. Whole swathes of them fell apart at once, mimicking the naval bombardment that had utterly disintegrated them. Some managed a startled, split-second scream as they realised what was coming—right before they were blown to pieces.

The Imperial Navy had tried to spare the city's inner sanctum by bombing the Coalition army as they knocked at the gate. Death rained down, sparing no one. Imperial soldiers died right next to their enemies in the Coalition. I wanted to hope that any citizens had long since fled the area... but I wasn't terribly confident on that score.

The rolling wave of violent death ceased, almost as quickly as it had come. Silence spread across the plaza, now broken only by the distant whispers of Galtir's other ghosts.

Among the wreckage of those tatterdemalions, I saw a twisted heap of rotting wood and crumbled stone, trembling on the ground. Syrene's figure had collapsed upon the plaza's cobblestones, heaving ragged breaths. As we watched, she crawled feebly towards us, shedding blackened pieces of herself with obvious pain.

Strahl stared down at her. I hadn't often had occasion to see open emotion on his face; but perhaps Arcturus Lohengrin had been more animated than Strahl was, once upon a time. Anger, grief, and sorrow all tugged at his features as he considered the agonised faerie.

"What a waste," murmured the emperor's shade, suddenly. "What a terrible waste this all has been."

Strahl's washed out grey eyes snapped to the aether-ghost, wary and uncomfortable. It had turned its vague, confused attention upon him, addressing him as though he were someone else.

"See what those maddened creatures have done to our cities," the emperor murmured softly. "They took my son, my only remaining heir. And for what? They have already lost more men to battle than they would have given up to Arcadia."

Syrene ceased her slow movements, shuddering in place. The emperor was speaking, I realised, and she had paused to listen.

Aesir looked at Strahl, as though seeing him for the first time. His hand tightened on Miss Hawkins, and I wondered whether he was contemplating violence. He had only one working arm at the moment, and Galatine had dispersed... but the fury that smouldered behind his eyes was old and deep, and I suspected it didn't really require a weapon.

"This must never happen again," Emperor Lohengrin told Strahl, unaware of his present audience. "Avalon will never survive it. Once this is settled, I intend to Tithe every single traitor... and their families, as well. That will be the cost they pay for Arcturus Lohengrin. History will remember the price of an Imperial son."

Strahl reached up to cover his eyes. His broad shoulders collapsed with horrified exhaustion. "I'm so glad you're dead," he rasped at the ghost. "And I'm so glad I died before I could become you."

The emperor fell silent again, without response. I wondered if the shade even knew what he was doing here, standing in the bombed-out slums of his capital city.

Strahl still held the rusty sabre he'd picked up in his other hand. Now, as he looked down at Syrene's blackened figure again, his fingers tightened on its hilt.

He strode towards the faerie with bleak purpose, setting his jaw with determination. I glanced warily at Aesir—but while his eyes remained fixed upon Strahl, he'd yet to move away from Miss Hawkins. I wasn't entirely certain what that meant.

As Strahl approached, Syrene's tangled emotions expanded to smother us, growing stronger and less coherent. Determination. Frustration. A deep well of misery. And… a tiny thread of mortal fear.

Strahl paused in front of her, holding the sabre at his side. "You saved my life once, because you swore to do it," he told her quietly. "Now you've tried to kill me for the same reason. I thought we were friends, Syrene—but you don't have friends. All you have are Oaths."

Anguish twisted on the air, as Syrene's black eyes stared back at him. She wanted to deny the words—I felt the desire to do it, deep and tangible. But he was right.

"We…" Syrene's voice wavered in confusion. "We must…" Her long, blackened fingers dug into the cobblestones, splintering with the effort.

"Maybe *you* do," Strahl told her. "But I don't. I don't have to be what I was made to be. I'm not a tool." He drew in a deep breath. "Witness me, Envoy. I swear upon the honour granted me by Noble Gallant: I, Prince Arcturus Lohengrin, hereby forsake my claim to the title of emperor. I swear that as long as I live, I will stand against anyone *else* who dares to take that title. I will bury the Avalon Imperium with my own hands, every time it tries to rise again."

Incredulous panic rose around us with every word. Syrene tried to scramble back to her feet—but one of her legs buckled and snapped with a wet, sickening sound, returning her to a trembling heap at his feet.

The Oath snapped into place with dreadful finality, coalescing around Strahl like an invisible cloak. A strange peace settled over his features as he felt it lock into place.

"What… have you… *done?*" Syrene whimpered. Her unearthly voice now dripped with wild horror.

"I've changed my story," Strahl told her. "I'm entitled to do that, as long as I still breathe. I could break my Oath, of course… but Noble Gallant won't accept an Oathbroken emperor." He smiled grimly. "That does leave the Seelie in a bit of a bind. I don't figure they'll let things stand this way—which is why I'm ready to kill whoever they decide on next."

A raw, bitter terror snaked through the air, as Syrene absorbed the inescapable situation. Had she been capable of tears, I was certain I would have seen them dampening her still, unmoving face. It wasn't death she faced now, I realised: It was *failure*. The duty that she had loyally pursued for generations was falling apart around her.

"I'm still going to fight the Unseelie when they arrive," Strahl told her. "I have people I want to protect. But I need to protect them from the Seelie, too. And from myself." He tightened his jaw. "I need to protect them from *you*, one way or another. Even if I spare you—even if my father's shade rescinds his last order—you're still their tool, and I know they'll find a way to use you again."

Syrene's misery hardened abruptly, coalescing into sharp, expectant hatred. "Slay us, then," she hissed. "Complete your fall from grace. We have remained true to *our* purpose."

Strahl drew himself up—and for just a moment, I caught a glimpse of Arcturus Lohengrin, proud and implacable. "No," he said. "I'm giving you a *choice*, Syrene. You can keep your Oath to the Seelie Tuath Dé, and die with your honour intact… or else you can give up your honour and become my friend in truth. You can change your story, just like me. I'm happy to help you do it."

Syrene stared at him. I stared at him, too. The idea was ridiculous. I'd never heard of an Oathbroken faerie before. In fact, I wasn't strictly certain it was *possible* for a faerie to break their Oath.

Syrene's determined hatred collapsed back into abject fear. "We cannot," she whispered. "We are the Envoy. It is our purpose. What would we be, without our purpose?"

Strahl shrugged. Arcturus Lohengrin disappeared again, evaporating like a ghost. My battered, weary bosun took his place. "You'd be a damned good navigator," he told her. "We could start there." He glanced my way with a wry grimace. "Assuming no one holds a grudge about you trying to kill us."

I let out a long, shaky breath. "Uh," I said slowly. "I'm more than a little bit troubled over that. But..." I fixed my eyes on Syrene, still trembling on the ground. Incredibly, I *felt* her hovering on the edge.

She wanted the chance. I wasn't even certain she had acknowledged it to herself yet. But it was *possible*.

"I'd need you to make me a promise," I told her quietly. "Not an Oath—a promise from your heart. Something you keep because you *want* to keep it."

Syrene focussed her attention on me with keen desperation. I found myself uncomfortably reminded of an injured child, searching for approval.

"As long as you're on my ship," I told her, "you'll still follow my orders. You'll never harm me, or any member of my crew. And... you accept that the Imperium died for a reason." I paused. "I know that's hard for you. But it's the same deal everyone else gets. That's the only way you can ever be family."

"Family," Syrene murmured. The word was familiar to her—but the concept was foreign. It came with a surge of sudden, hideous longing.

I turned to consider Aesir, grim and quiet. "You're crew, Aesir," I told him. "I promised. You've more than earned it. Can you live with this?"

I expected to see conflict in his eyes. I definitely expected at least a moment of hesitation. Instead, there was a decision ready and waiting for me in his expression.

"Ah'm no' Pelaeia's judge," he rasped. "All ah ever wanted was ma ain life." He tightened his grip on Miss Hawkins, glancing between Strahl and Syrene. "Ah can live with this, mahself. But maybe someone else who wants more will come an' find ye someday. Ye'd best be ready tae tell 'em aw the things ye've done tae prove ye're different people by then."

Strahl let out a long, laboured breath. He tossed the rusty sabre aside, letting it clatter across the cobblestones—and offered his hand to Syrene. "You're a mess," he told her. "Let's get you home."

Syrene stared at his hand, still deeply fearful. But very slowly, a tremulous hope blossomed beneath her anxiety. She reached out one gnarled, blackened hand, setting it gently in his.

Her Oath shattered.

The sensation was intensely awful—far worse than the vague, uncomfortable cobwebs that I'd once carried with me. It cut against my senses like broken glass, digging into my soul. Syrene cried out in pain, clutching at Strahl's hand for stability, as though her dying honour was a poorly amputated limb.

Her few remaining flowers wilted. Her bark turned noticeably brittle. Her overwhelming presence faded.

Syrene's shoulders slumped, even as the intensity of the moment passed. The jagged edges of her broken Oath remained, rasping against us.

Strahl considered her broken form with grave practicality. "I don't think she's going to be able to walk," he said. "I hope you brought transportation."

"We'll send up a flare and have the *Rose* come meet us," I told him. "The *Conflagration* is still on its way. I'd rather not be here when it shows up."

Miss Hawkins pushed herself off from Aesir's shoulder, trembling on her feet. The black had nearly vanished from her eyes... but inky veins still traced her face. "There's something we need to do in the meantime," she told me quietly. She turned her body to face the blurry shade that still remained. "This is what Gideon really wanted. Someone else will eventually come for it. But we can end this now."

I looked her over warily. "You're not in terribly good shape," I said. "Are you sure—"

"I'm sure," Miss Hawkins said grimly. "I am not strictly certain that the emperor deserves to be freed of his bonds before the other echoes are. But I am very certain that *we* deserve to be free of *him*." She pressed one hand against the machine, now humming softly with power. "Mr Finch! Could I impose upon you to increase the output?"

"Oh! Er—yes, of course!" Mr Finch called back. It occurred to me, finally, that he sounded awfully distracted. "One moment, please, my hands are... ah, full."

I hobbled slowly around the machine, searching for my chief engineer. I found him in short order, just next to an open panel on the machine, where several parts had been systematically stripped away from its guts and laid out on the ground in a neatly organised mess.

Just next to the panel, Mr Finch had leaned himself over a humanoid figure, currently slumped against the machine. Both of my eyebrows shot up as I recognised the gorgon sergeant; her scaled face was slack, and the serpents on her head had gone limp. A dark pool of blood had expanded beneath her, though I couldn't immediately discern the cause.

There was a hint of panic in Mr Finch's manner as he tied off a tourniquet around her leg with bloody, inexpert hands.

I worked my mouth for a moment, searching for words. "What... what are you doing, Mr Finch?" I asked finally.

My chief engineer glanced up at me helplessly. "Well, I... she's still alive," he said. "If I'd done nothing, the tatterdemalions would have crushed her."

My pragmatic instincts told me to put a bullet in the woman and end her misery. Just like Syrene, she'd tried to kill us; *unlike* Syrene, she was incredibly likely to try and do it again. I deeply doubted the gorgon would have a sudden change of heart, even if we expended the resources necessary to drag her back to the *Rose* and save her life.

But Mr Finch was... well, a very good man. And he had undoubtedly pulled his weight today, beyond what any reasonable person should have expected from him. If nothing else, I owed *him* the grace that the unconscious woman before me didn't particularly deserve.

"We'll try to get her back," I told him. "She might not make it that far, but it's worth a shot. We can drop her off in Carrain; if she's cooperative, they might well spare her, maybe trade her back to the Spires for some of their own people."

Mr Finch nodded with relief. I pushed myself past him to kneel painfully next to the sergeant, checking over my engineer's handiwork. It wasn't terrible, actually. Assuming the woman survived her blood loss, though, I suspected she was going to lose the leg.

"I'll handle it from here," I reassured him. "Can you help Miss Hawkins with the machine?"

Mr Finch reached up instinctively to adjust his spectacles. Greenish blood smeared onto the glass from his fingers, and he recoiled swiftly, snatching his hand back with mild horror. "I... yes, I can do that," he said. "Thank you, Captain."

I reached up heavily to squeeze at his shoulder. "Thank *you*," I told him quietly. "You really saved us out there, Walther."

Mr Finch let out a soft, nervous laugh. "Oh, yes," he said. "I would prefer not to make a *habit* of it, of course."

"Of course," I agreed.

Mr Finch turned back for the machine, carefully picking through the parts that he had laid out on the cobblestones. I returned my attention to the gorgon woman, doing my best to fulfil my promise to him. Though I was far from a competent physicker, I'd endured more than my fair share of injuries. Keeping people alive was at least a bit less *academic* for me than it was for my poor engineer.

Eventually, the machine ratcheted up again, increasing its volume. I became aware of an unnerving pressure on its other side.

I wasn't there to see the emperor of Avalon dissipate into nothing. I was too busy sitting on the ground next to a bloody, unconscious woman, clutching at my own broken rib with bone-deep exhaustion.

But somehow, I was satisfied with that.

* * *

I'd never been so happy to see the *Iron Rose* in the sky above me.

By the time the ship reached us, I was in too much pain to move on my own. Holloway had to leave the *Rose* in order to help me into the longboat, and then back onto the main deck. The physicker was appropriately horrified at my injuries—but I told him, with great reluctance, to see to the gorgon sergeant first.

Some time later, as I drifted on my latest wave of agony, I heard Holloway say that everything looked survivable. 'It's just going to be painful,' he told me.

Just pain. Lots of pain. Lucky me.

The physicker must have taken some amount of pity on me. He offered me something unpleasant to drink—and then, in between blinks, I woke up in the infirmary, trapped beneath the most monstrously large knitted blanket I'd ever seen.

The dregs of whatever painkiller I'd consumed still fogged the edges of my mind, leaving me comfortably numb as I listened to Holloway putter about, basking in the friendly hum of my ship's engine. Someone had changed me into a loose, clean shirt that smelled faintly like peppermint.

I turned my head, with lazy effort. My battered coat was neatly folded at my bedside, with my hat perched atop it. A simple note was tucked into the band, with the words 'Welcome home' written in Evie's beautiful, looping letters.

I smiled, and went back to sleep.

When I woke again, I was in better spirits—though still in pain, exactly as promised. Holloway gently informed me that it would persist for the next few weeks, at the very least. I was not, he said, in any condition to be captaining. I *was* expected to stretch my legs and get fresh air, however, whenever possible.

"The ship's in good hands," I mumbled back at him. The medicine in my system encouraged me to offer him a hazy grin. "An' so am I."

Holloway squeezed my hand and offered me a fond smile.

A few hours later, I vacated my cot in the infirmary to stumble my way back into my own cabin and shave off the pathetic stubble that had accumulated over the last whirlwind leg of this misadventure. I had just dried off my chin when someone knocked firmly at my door.

Mr Strahl was on the other side.

The hideous bruises on his pale face were in full bloom—which probably meant that they were healing. I was struck by the surrealness of the moment, as I saw him standing stiffly on the other side of my door in his usual attire. As though the last few miserable, harrowing weeks had never happened at all.

"Captain," Strahl greeted me. Those crisp Imperial tones he'd put on display had collapsed back into his usual drawl.

"Mr Strahl," I rasped. "To what do I owe the pleasure?" I stepped aside to let him through the door.

My bosun cleared his throat. "Folks told me you were awake," he said. "Thought I'd bring you up to date. That *is* the job."

I nodded at him slowly. "We're all still alive," I observed. "We must have left Galtir before the *Conflagration* showed up."

"We did," Strahl confirmed. "Even loaded up that big machine. We've got the *Erebus* in tow, as well. We're bound for western Carrain. We're taking the long way around, so we can avoid any skirmishes with the Spires."

I rubbed at my freshly shaved chin. "And our... injured guest?" I asked.

"Cranky, but alive," Strahl told me. "She's in the brig. Finch keeps trying to bring her tea. She hasn't bitten yet."

I shook my head. "I'll settle for making sure she doesn't bite *him*," I muttered. "He's not going to convince a Cinderwolf to sit down for afternoon tea."

Strahl snorted. "You know that, and I know that," he said. "I'm not sure *Mr Finch* knows that." He paused. Then, in a far more sombre voice, he added: "There's some other people dying to see you. Evie said something about seeing Dougal off, now that it's clear you're not joining him."

My heart lurched unexpectedly in my chest. I'd all but forgotten about our promise to have a drink for Dougal. "You're... not joining us?"

Strahl offered me an uncomfortable half-smile. "Not sure I'd be welcome," he said, "all things considered. I'll still pour one out for him on my own."

I nodded slowly. It was positive news, I suppose, that Strahl was still walking around on board at all. The tension of his previous identity would take time to fully dissolve... if it ever disappeared at all.

Strahl turned away to head for the door. He paused just in front of it.

"You know," he said. "If I'd been in your position... I wouldn't have given me a chance. I'd have put a bullet in me and been done with it." His grim expression softened thoughtfully. "I guess that's why I like working for you."

I stared at his back, briefly at a loss for words.

Lenore Brighton saved me from an awkward response by pushing her way through the doorway past Strahl, regal as a queen.

"*I'd* have put a bullet in you," she informed my bosun primly. "It's just a shame I didn't have a clear shot."

Strahl offered her a shrug. "I wouldn't have minded for long," he said, "so long as you didn't have to shoot me twice, anyway."

Others filed in past Lenore, while she turned to fix Strahl with an icy look. "When teaching an important lesson," she told him frostily, "repetition is *key*."

Strahl chuckled grimly, as he exited the cabin.

People continued filing in, one by one. Evie took a seat on the edge of my bed, beaming at me with open relief. Little snagged the chair at my bedside, looking over my bruises with silent criticism. Holloway trundled in, with Mary flouncing in close at his heels to steal my hat. Aesir followed her, still frowning down at his mechanical arm here and there as he tested its calibration.

Mr Finch, of course, arrived with tea.

I basked in the normalcy of it all for a while, trying not to notice the obvious Dougal-shaped hole in our gathering. Eventually, however, as general enquiries about my health inevitably dried up, Evie raised his tea cup gently.

"It feels like an eternity ago now that we agreed to have our drinks and say a word for Dougal," he said softly.

The comfortable feelings in the room turned bittersweet.

Evie struggled visibly for words, pursing his lips as he gathered the strength to speak. "He... must have taught me the words to every pub song in the north," the halcyon said, with a trembling laugh. "Even the ones Chief Crichton banned."

Little sighed heavily. *He always stole Elfa's biscuits*, my first mate signed, *even though she would have given him one if he asked.*

Mary swallowed, with her hands tight on her tea cup. "He gave *really* good hugs," she said in a small voice. "Honestly, the best."

Aesir leaned his head against the wall. "Ah wish he was here," he said dully. "Ah'd like tae tell him 'ah told ye so'." He rubbed at his face with one hand. "An' ah guess ah'll miss his bad jokes."

"I rather *liked* his jokes," Holloway said softly.

Lenore poured herself another cup of tea. "Hm," she mused. "You know what I *won't* miss about him?"

Eyebrows rose around my cabin, as tension coiled in the air.

Lenore scrunched her nose up and gave a deeply unladylike snort that I immediately recognised as Dougal's deafening snore.

Raucous laughter broke out, dissolving the gloomy atmosphere. It was probably *too* much laughter—but we all needed it so badly that it didn't seem to matter. Tears pricked at Evie's eyes, nearby, while I gasped and clutched at my poor ribs, trying and failing to suppress the reflex.

The stories continued well into the evening—certainly past the time when I should have cried off and got some more rest. But they were important, in their own way: a lingering echo of something we *wanted* to remember, rather than everything we hoped to put behind us.

Far sooner than we wanted to, I suspected, we would be forced to face the past again.

EPILOGUE

PRINCE CHARMING - CALL TO GLORY - HEIR APPARENT

A man cannot help but feel his worth when surrounded by thunderous applause.

The sound brought a genuine smile to my lips as I strode across the public platform we'd erected in the vast courtyard. A roaring sea of faceless adulation greeted me, stretching out as far as the eye could see. The volume rose further—almost deafening—as I raised my hand in acknowledgement, greeting my subjects.

"Corbinec!" someone shouted. "Prince Corbinec!" The name caught like wildfire, spreading through the gathering. Soon, it swelled into a chant, ringing across the air.

I didn't bother to hide my pleasure. Humility, I've always felt, is an act put on by lesser men when they are uncertain of their reception. I *knew* that I was wanted here.

I offered a smile to the crowd instead, as aether flashes announced the cameras below me. The papers *loved* my smile. The last article I'd saved had called it 'boyishly charming'.

I stood by the podium for a long while, exulting in the energy that surrounded me, patiently waiting for the cheering to exhaust itself. I smiled down at one of the photographers closest to the platform, angling myself into a gallant pose. "Something for your front page!" I yelled cheerfully.

Another flash rewarded the statement, and I laughed.

Eventually—after several long minutes—the applause slowed to something more manageable. I straightened behind the podium, lightly gesturing for the crowd to calm itself. As it became clear that I intended to speak, the noise level dropped abruptly... but I *felt* the energy before me, still tense and unbearably hungry.

"What a reception!" I said cheerfully. "Why, you all must be nearly as happy to be here as *I* am!"

Another swell of manic bliss followed the words, before I waved the cheering down.

"My brave, beloved countrymen," I sighed. "Look at all of the proud troops among you! A veritable sea of green uniforms! I don't think there has ever been a more beautiful sight in the world."

If there's one thing I've learned in my time, it's this: *Always* start by praising the soldiers. You don't have to spend very long on it; you don't even have to sound sincere. People just enjoy hearing it. I don't know why, but it sets the proper tone.

"Obviously," I continued swiftly, "so many of us have put on that uniform for a *reason*." I ran my hand over my own well-tailored uniform, with its bevy of medals. Technically, the medals belonged to my family—but they were an excellent reminder of our historic contributions to both the empire and its later dissolution. I drew myself up at the thought. "Given Carrain's insidious, unchecked influence—" I began.

Angry jeers cut through my speech. I gave them room to flourish, as I shook my head in obvious agreement.

"How long did they think we were going to turn a blind eye to those unionists sneaking across our borders, sabotaging our farms and factories?" I demanded. "And those disgusting spies dressed up in halcyon attire, poisoning our communities? For years now, those *halflings* have played innocent, lying to our faces. Lying to my father, lying to *me*."

Someone, I thought, was going to complain about the word

'halfling'. I knew it as soon as the slur crossed my lips. Even in the Spires, some bleeding hearts will insist you call them 'nissar'. But it was the right word for the right moment, and I had to trust my rhetorical instincts. I barrelled onwards, undeterred.

"And let me be clear!" I yelled breathlessly. "We gave them a hundred chances! We knew what they were doing, but we pretended that we didn't. We were civil. We were *polite*." I slammed my fist down onto the podium. "Carrain takes *advantage* of politeness!" I declared. "Enough is enough! And it is time they learned that there are consequences for pushing us too far!"

Someone in the crowd took up the chant: 'Enough is enough!' joined those ecstatic cries of 'Corbinec', swelling into a wave of sound that lapped against me. Flashes snapped again. An angry, breathless thrill swelled within me in reply. It felt *good*, speaking such open truth —hearing people cheer for it. After all those miserable years of mealy-mouthed diplomacy, I'd finally convinced my people to *do* something. My father could ignore me all he wanted... and he had. But thousands of angry citizens of the Emerald Spires were the sort of thing you *couldn't* ignore.

I caught my breath against the emotion in my chest. "The time for action is now," I said. "We're going to round up the unionists—and all of those fake halcyons, as well. Every parasite, every swindler that has preyed upon our latitude so far, will be put to work until they've paid back their debts to society!"

Several approving whoops resulted. As the cheering started up again, I caught sight of Graff out of the corner of my eye, staring me down with displeasure. His eyebrow twitched with warning—the only sign he ever gave that he was losing patience. I resisted the urge to roll my eyes at him. Graff was an excellent soldier, but he was far from what you'd call a 'people person'. He'd handed me a neatly folded speech, on my way up to the platform. I'd yet to even open it.

"But what of Carrain itself?" I called out. "It's now become clear that these diseases will continue to flourish, as long as we ignore their root cause. Which is why I want you all to know—to hear it from *me*, directly. As of today, we are officially done with warning shots and border skirmishes! I've ordered our generals to prepare a plan for a full invasion of Carrain. If they won't secure their own border, then we will simply have to secure it *for* them!"

The sound of 'Corbinec' went up again. I let it wash over me, drowning myself within it. My father had never garnered such a response in his life. Oh, perhaps he technically wore the crown... but when people said 'Corbinec', they weren't referring to *him*. Our house was mine, just as surely as the people were mine.

The rest was only a matter of time.

As I looked out over my people, a strange certainty overcame me, deeper and more profound than I had ever experienced before. A foreign presence loomed in my mind, reaching out with wordless desire. I felt its immortal yearning—its hunger for a worthy Armiger that would bring it glory.

It wanted *me*.

I'd never felt a wargear's Call before; few people ever have. But I'd read every secondhand account that I could find. I knew the signs; I recognised the touch of Gloryborne upon my mind.

My heart raced. My mouth went dry. Suddenly, I realised that far too much time had passed; the cheering had died, and I had missed my obvious cue. I sucked in a breath at the uncharacteristic awkwardness, blinking quickly as I struggled to refocus myself on the crowd before me.

Inspiration struck me, fuelled by the Call that I now answered.

"But how can I possibly stand by while war comes to the Emerald Spires?" I rasped. "For years, my father has kept me away from battle. 'Prince Aurelius,' he's said, 'your responsibilities are here.' And like a dutiful son, I obeyed." I straightened to my full height. "I cannot obey any longer. This time, with so much at stake, I am pledging myself to the armoured division. *This* time, I will lead the charge against Carrain myself!"

I might as well have set off a bomb in the courtyard. A veritable thunderstorm of photographic flashes erupted, as I raised my fist into the air. An ecstatic, near-religious thrill went up among the gathering. "For the Emerald Spires!" I yelled. "May we be evergreen!"

Graff's other eyebrow was now twitching. I'd never seen him lose control of *both* eyebrows before. Truly, it was a novel sight.

People like Graff might believe that a declaration of total war would garner more attention than one man choosing to join the army; bland men often can't fathom how one person could possibly make a difference. But there's a reason that Praefectus Tiberius Graff belongs out of sight, hovering in the wings, while I command the public's adoration.

Under any other circumstances, I might have lingered there to enjoy the results of my abrupt announcement. But glory had taken hold of my heart, and my wargear called for me; I couldn't possibly have stood at that podium for even a moment longer.

I whirled quickly and walked for the edge of the platform. As I reached the wooden stairs that led down to my praetorian guard, one of our generals rushed to the podium to take my place and answer questions.

Praefectus Graff met me at the base of the stairs, as stiff as his own uniform. He had a handful of years on me, but rather than dignify him, they tended to make him vanish into obscurity. His features were worse than plain—in fact, many people would affectionately describe him as 'ugly', if pressed—but I'd never known a man more loyal or reliable in my life.

Graff fell into lockstep with me, drawing in a deep breath. "I could not help but notice," he said politely, "that His Highness graced us with the gift of sudden inspiration this evening."

I chuckled at the observation. I couldn't help the wild spring in my step as I walked, eating up the ground with eager paces. "But you didn't get *me* a gift, Graff," I joked. "Oh, it's all right. I won't hold it against you."

"His Highness remains a most benevolent ruler," Graff replied. Somehow, he managed to make the words sound utterly sincere. Truly, it was one of his most valuable skills. "I wasn't aware that your father had forbidden you from joining the military," he added.

"It was implied," I told him simply. "I knew he would never agree if I asked."

Graff inclined his head at me. "But you've decided to join the army regardless," he observed. "An admirable decision. May I ask what prompted you to make it now, in particular?"

I closed my eyes briefly, reaching for the fey presence in my mind. It was more than just my imagination. Gloryborne reached back for me, hungry to be of service. "The Seelie have chosen me at last, Graff," I told him breathlessly. "How could I possibly refuse?"

Graff sucked in a sharp breath. "You mean it's happened?" he demanded. "You've been Called?"

I offered him a blinding smile. "Was it ever in doubt?" I asked. "Gloryborne has chosen me. It *needs* me. Those augurs must have finally repaired it."

A rare flicker of emotion crossed Graff's face as he looked to the sky, murmuring a grateful prayer beneath his breath. "The Seelie have blessed us in our hour of need," he said. "They've offered you their unambiguous favour. Given Gloryborne's last Armiger—"

"Yes," I said, with a rising thrill. "The line of Lohengrin might be gone—but its spirit endures. The people of Avalon require a new emperor, Graff. If the Unseelie should arrive... I will be ready and waiting for them."

Graff slowed his stride. "If the Unseelie should arrive?" he repeated carefully. "Not *when* they arrive? Do you have reason to doubt Wraithwood's certainty on the matter, Your Highness?"

The nitpick sent a flare of irritation through my nerves. "It's a turn of phrase, Graff," I told him shortly. "Of course the Unseelie are coming... *eventually*. Perhaps less swiftly than a paranoid old Legionnaire would like to believe. All the more reason we should spend what time we have rebuilding our empire."

Graff fell silent again, aware that he had misstepped. After a long moment, however, he said: "You have my apologies, Your Highness. Sometimes my lack of formal education betrays me. I know you choose your words very carefully, but I sometimes miss your deeper intent." He offered me a grave expression. "We must rebuild, of course. With Gloryborne ready to serve you and Wraithwood's army at our disposal, Carrain will fall in line. The other provinces will naturally follow."

The apology melted my irritation. It was impossible, after all, to remain gloomy in the face of so many obvious blessings. "We have our work cut out for us, Graff," I said lightly. "But I am equal to the task. I always have been."

Someday, my father would fade away into obscurity like a tired shadow. But I knew then, with absolute certainty, that no one would *ever* forget my name.

* * *

The Tales of the Iron Rose will continue with book two, *The Winds of Fortune*.

AFTERWORD

Dougal MacLeod wasn't originally supposed to die.

Echoes of the Imperium started as a fun writing exercise, with Nicholas and Olivia upending some of their least favourite fantasy tropes. Along the way, we added several requests from our friends and family: a grandmother ne'er-do-well, a teenager who isn't whiny, and happily married gay husbands who do not tragically die, just to name a few.

Partway through the book, however, Nicholas lost his grandfather. Not long afterwards, his grandmother passed as well. After this, the book took on a new angle: It was a way of confronting and working through grief. Eventually, William gets his closure and discovers that he's able to enjoy Dougal's memory. Finally publishing *Echoes of the Imperium* is now a kind of closure for Nicholas, too. As such, this book is dedicated to his grandfather and nana. They wouldn't have understood a word of this, but they would have been proud.

We owe thanks to many people for their help with this book, which has been *several* years in the making. We'd like to thank **Laura Elizabeth**, **Julie Golick**, **Ric Bellino**, **Allison Oleynik**, **Lore**, and **Sylvia** for their alpha reading over several changing drafts, and **Amanda** for being our most wildly enthusiastic beta reader on the

AFTERWORD

story this turned into. Thanks to **Ailbhe** for tweaking both Dougal's and Aesir's Scottish accents, to **James Nettum** for contributions to Mr Samuel Méndez, and to **Vivekanand Ian Gurudata** for suggestions on Kumari Varma and the province of Aarushi. We also owe thanks to **Anaya Walker**, who supplied half of our sensitivity reading, and to our other anonymous sensitivity reader, who brought an incredible perspective on the intersection of empire and its minority populations.

Nicholas is also eternally grateful to his incredibly patient, brilliant, and amazing co-author and wife, Olivia, who turned his slapdash adventure into a shared, nuanced journey.

And finally, an endless, overwhelming thank you to everyone else on our crew. This wouldn't have been possible without you. We hope you've all enjoyed the adventure so far.

THE ATWATER ADVENTURE COLUMN

In the mood for more swashbuckling adventures?
Join the Atwater Adventure Column to get writing updates, as well as the exclusive novella *The Good, the Bad, and the Goblin.*

https://nicholasatwater.com/newsletter

ABOUT THE AUTHOR

Nicholas Atwater writes swashbuckling steampunk fantasy. He resides in Montreal, Quebec with his incredible, brilliant wife and two cats. As an ex-thespian, he certainly does not practice funny accents in the shower, and no one can prove otherwise. He is a veteran Dungeons & Dragons gamemaster, famously feared for both his villains and his puns.

* * *

In the mood for more swashbuckling adventures? Sign up for the Atwater Adventure Column. Subscribers also get early access to chapters from each book!

https://nicholasatwater.com
info@nicholasatwater.com

ALSO BY NICHOLAS ATWATER

TALES OF THE IRON ROSE

The Good, the Bad, and the Goblin

A Matter of Execution

Echoes of the Imperium

The Winds of Fortune (Forthcoming)

ALSO BY OLIVIA ATWATER

REGENCY FAERIE TALES
Half a Soul
Ten Thousand Stitches
Longshadow

VICTORIAN FAERIE TALES
The Witchwood Knot
Rosemary & Thyme (Forthcoming — 2024)

STANDALONE
Small Miracles

ATWATER'S TOOLS FOR AUTHORS
Better Blurb Writing for Authors
Reader-Friendly Writing for Authors

Made in the USA
Las Vegas, NV
30 April 2025